the Oath

Janie Holloway

For Bobbie Jo
with Many Thanks!
Janie Holloway
4-9-09

PublishAmerica
Baltimore

ISBN: 1-4137-7167-X
PUBLISHED BY PUBLISHAMERICA, LLLP
www.publishamerica.com
Baltimore

Printed in the United States of America

Dedication

To my husband Terry, and our sons Jake and Nate, for believing in me and for their support, also, to a beautiful young woman, my daughter Jasmine, for her insight and helpful criticism during The Oath's creation.

Acknowledgments

Thanks to my friends and former co-workers at Women's Crisis Services of Poteau, Oklahoma for encouraging me in this endeavor. You truly are special ladies.

And a special thanks to all songwriters for their great lyrics and to the talented artists who performed them. I can't imagine my life without music.

Chapter 1

April 24, Saturday

The unseen apparition, hovering in the corner, woefully watched the scene unfold below her. The overhead fixture and lamps buzzed and flickered strobe-like upon the couple nestled in the king-size bed. There was nothing she could do about the lights. She knew it frightened the man and the woman, especially the woman, but there was no way she could tell them that she drew from the electric's energy. Her own energy having been seriously depleted over the years from trying to make contact was draining fast and time was running out for her. If only the woman would stop being so afraid and pay attention to the clues.

She shivered, floating higher up into the corner as the other menacing presence entered the bedroom. She could always tell when he entered a room. So could the living. The cold oozed from his evil existence as chilling as the frosty air wafting out of a deepfreeze when the door is opened.

She must stay hidden, mustn't let him know she is here.

She cautiously slid backward into the wall, leaving just enough of herself to watch as the cold tentacles which passed for his fingers opened the dresser drawers with the unmistakable scraping sound of wood against wood. She knew the man and the woman could hear it. How could they not? The Other wanted them to. He was very good at frightening people. But the girl knew that this was also a part of his ritual search for something she hoped he would never find.

Fear sunk into her ethereal soul as the woman flung back the rose-colored comforter and began yelling. She knew what was coming next: The harried packing. The girl had witnessed this many times before.

Please, you mustn't go, the girl pleaded with the woman soundlessly, uselessly. Of course, the woman paid her no heed. The woman could not or would not hear her. No one could. The girl's panic rose as she helplessly watched the woman march to the huge closet, throw open the doors, grope the top shelf, and then spin around flinging her suitcase on the floor. She was leaving. Just like so many others before her had left, fleeing in terror in the middle of the night. If only she could communicate with her. Beg her to stay. Beg for her help. If only...

"I can't stay another night, Bill. I have to get out of here." The girl watched as the woman, dressed only in a white cotton nightgown, snatched clothes pell-mell from the hangers and threw them across the room. Some landed in the opened suitcase but most of them scattered across the room.

Please don't go, the girl silently begged once more.

The blond man sat up in the bed. "Melissa, honey. I know it's a little weird, but nothing dangerous has happened so far."

Yes. Yes, whispered the girl. *Talk her out of leaving. You mustn't go.*

She watched as the woman called Melissa, stomped to the dresser, her short, curly red hair bobbing with each footfall. Her hands came out of the drawer filled with silky panties and bras.

For one comical moment, the girl wondered how a woman with such large hips could wear those tiny lacy things. She then mentally shook herself, gazing below, as Melissa held them up in the air, shaking them in anger. "You want to help me pack? Is that it?"

The girl shivered within herself. Was Melissa talking to her? She couldn't be, Melissa couldn't even see her. The girl shrunk a little more into the wall as the Other misted and swirled near the tall chest of drawers, a black oily film trailing across the oaken top.

No! the girl moaned inwardly. The woman thought *she* was the one who had pulled out the drawers.

It wasn't me! It wasn't me!

The girl desperately thought of a way to tell her, to warn her, but there was no way she could. She couldn't speak. At best, she could manipulate the radio but even that had failed. And there was no radio in this bedroom for her to try again.

Glancing around the huge master bedroom where her grandparents once slept, she derided the couple. *What kind of people would not put a radio in their bedroom? If I were still alive I'd surround myself with music, just as I did before I died.* Seeing the Other swirl around the woman's legs and then return to the dresser, the reason for her anger dawned on the girl.

She fully understood now. Melissa was angry with the Other, The Bad One, the one who opened the drawers. But she obviously wasn't aware of the Other's presence in the room, could only feel the cold raising goose pimples on her bare arms. And the girl was blamed for it.

She listened, stricken, as Melissa ranted, her breath steaming out in a fog. "I don't need your help! I can pack just fine on my own. You needn't have opened the drawers for me. I can take a hint." Melissa flung her under-things into the burgundy suitcase.

Having shrunk so small, the young ghost no longer needed the energy from the lights; her attempt to communicate had failed. The antique bedside lamps stopped flickering and glowed softly. Melissa snorted and pointed at one of them, and then continued packing.

"Bill, you're not here all day. The lights doing a Morse code dance are only the half of it." Picking a pair of pants up off the floor, Melissa grunted as she tugged and pulled the pair of faded jeans over her ample hips, her gown bunched around her waist.

Bill crawled out from under the covers and stood shivering in his black and yellow smiley-face boxers. The girl couldn't help but giggle. She had never seen anything like that when she was alive. She'd never come across anything as funny as Bill's boxers when helping her mother do the laundry. Her dad's boxers had been bought in plain colors. *When did they start making such cute underwear for men?*

"Do you know how many times this week I've had to turn the stereo off?" Melissa fell backward onto the bed to zip her pants, exhaling and holding in her tummy.

"Uh, how many?" the blond man asked, rubbing his muscular forearms to warm them. The girl could just make out the fine blond hairs standing up on his lightly tanned back.

Melissa stood up, the tight jeans straining to hold her flesh inside. She'd obviously chosen an older pair that she'd not worn for quite some time, but hadn't the heart to throw away. The ghost fully understood this. She'd kept her favorite jeans until they were frayed and full of holes, and had only chunked them at her mother's insistence, and completely under protest. But that was a lifetime ago. She smiled at Melissa's retort about the radio. "Fifteen times!" she barked. "At least twice a day. And I'm tired of I'm running around the house closing drawers and cabinet doors. Something keeps opening them."

It wasn't Me that opened the drawers!

Boy, is she mad, thought the girl. *Her green eyes are spitting fire.* She could almost imagine smoke coming out of her nose and ears. Maybe she shouldn't have played the radio so much, but time was of the essence. *I did what I had to do,* she justified herself. If only she could aim those green livid eyes at the Other and let him have it with both sockets. Melissa, she knew, had a hot temper to match that fiery hair.

The girl continued to watched as a few shirts flew into the air and landed in various places: the bed, the lamp, the floor, and even on the high, wing-backed chairs angled near the unlit fireplace.

Having found what she was looking for, Melissa put on a bra and a white blouse, fastening the buttons, and added, "Know what was playing on the stereo?"

The man shook his head, wondering around the room trying to find his clothes.

"That old stuff. You know, music from the seventies. And sometimes that junk from the sixties. It's creepy being in the kitchen and the Bee Gees start blaring out "Tragedy" from the living room stereo. Bill, I hate disco. I just want to get out of here!"

The ghost drew her self up with indignation and almost floated completely out of the wall. *Old Stuff!* The woman obviously had no taste in music. But what did she expect from a grownup? Besides, playing the radio was serious business. She had been trying to communicate with them, not entertain them.

What was it with adults not listening to kids? Did nothing ever change? It had been years since she had died, and still, adults weren't paying attention to the younger generation. *Somehow I've got to make them understand that I need help.* The girl pondered her dilemma, trying to find a solution before it was too late; before they abandoned her, just like so many others had.

She could hear the man trying to reason with his stubborn wife, but it seemed to the girl he wasn't having much luck.

"Honey, we paid six months in advance to live here. We signed a lease agreement. Not only will we probably lose our money but how is it going to make us look when we tell that sniveling little balding man, Mr. Smedley, why we broke our lease?" Bill grunted as he slipped on his dark pants and polo shirt, and then hunted among the strewn clothes for his socks.

Yeah, Melissa, think of that. Stop packing. The girl silently rooted for the man. *Go, Bill, Go! Talk her out of it. Come on. You can do it. You're her husband for Pete's sake; put your size eleven foot down.*

Bill continued, as he slipped on his mismatched socks, "Here's the key, Mr. Smedley." He mocked as if talking to the real estate agent, jangled his keys, and then slipped them into his pocket. "Nice place, but it's already occupied. And after he pushes those heavy-wired glasses on that pug nose and says, 'Waddiya mean?' I'm gonna have to tell him, ghost man, ghost; the place is haunted."

Bill thrust on his brown loafers and ran his hands through his cropped sandy hair. "Honestly, Melissa, I don't think it's been that bad. I'd like to stay and figure out what's going on here." His blue eyes pleaded with his wife's stern freckled face. But even the girl could see there was no swaying her.

"Bill, I don't care about the money. I know it was a lot but I just don't care. I do care, however, about my sanity. And if you care about yours, you'll get me out of here. Tonight." Her arms were crossed in front of her heaving chest. She was standing firm.

Well, at least the *man* wanted to stay. The girl wished she had tried harder to communicate with him instead of her. Well, it was too late for that now. She was still trying to formulate a plan to try one more time with the woman. There was something else she could do but it would require a tremendous amount of energy. It was not going to be easy, nor was it going to be safe. And she'd better hurry; the crestfallen look on the man's face told her he had given in.

"Okay, Moppet," Bill said, as he took his wife's hand in his. "We'll leave tonight." Their eyes locked in mutual agreement (the girl was well aware that the man was only placating his wife) then he released her hand.

The girl watched him walk to the door, pause, and then turn. "Are you going to be all right while I pull the car around?" he asked.

Melissa tucked a red curl behind her ear. "Yeah, sure. Now that this specter knows we're leaving, it probably won't bother me anymore." Bill nodded and left, leaving the door open.

You don't know how wrong you are, lady.

The girl sighed heavily with dejection, as she watched the Other's black oily film slither out of the room. And with his leaving the temperature returned to normal. He had won, again.

She was angry but there was nothing she could do about it. He was much too strong for her to fight him. Besides having had more years to practice and gain strength, he obviously enjoyed frightening people. Derived real pleasure from it. He was a nasty character.

She couldn't bring herself to do the things he did to terrify people. She just wanted to communicate, but she couldn't convey to this couple that he also frightened her. He was bad and rotten to the core and she wished many times over that he would just simply give it up, go to sleep, and wait for his judgment to be handed down like everyone else. If he would go away, then perhaps she could rest, too.

But, she knew what tied him here. Although she felt no sympathy for him, she knew that he was also a victim but had gotten what he deserved. Now, she just wished he would move on. But that wasn't going to happen. He still clung to his revenge. He had no intention of leaving, at least, not on his own. She knew what needed to be done but it was going to be difficult and perhaps even dangerous and she was going to need help. She couldn't do this alone. Twenty years of trying had proven that fact, and it didn't look as if assistance would be forthcoming from this couple. They had chickened out on her, running scared at the thought of ghosts; the woman had finished packing. But, the girl had one more idea up her ghostly sleeve. She just hoped she would have enough strength to do it.

She watched as Melissa snapped her suitcase shut, grab her overnight bag and head for the bathroom down the hall. The master bedroom had its own bathroom but they were in the process of painting it.

Yuck! Yellow. The girl disapproved. *Who would paint their bathroom the same color as the outside of the house? And what am I doing lollygagging in here by myself? Get going!*

She floated out into the hall and went left, gliding along the paneled wall. She made a right turn, passing the closed door to the spare bedroom, heading for the bathroom. The oak wood panels were still in good shape and Melissa, she noticed, had polished them to a fine gleam. She'd even removed the dust from the wall light fixtures. A neat and tidy person except for the way she packed.

She stopped just inside the bathroom doorway. Hanging suspended behind Melissa, she waited as the young woman quickly swept everything from the medicine cabinet shelves into her bag. *Well*, she thought, *it's now or never.*

The lights in the hallway began to flicker, buzzing loudly, droning like a million honeybees in flight. The girl drank thirstily, drawing every once of energy into her translucent being. The light in the bathroom also flickered but stopped and blazed brightly. She left that one alone. This was going to be frightening to the woman and she didn't want to terrify Melissa out of her mind by leaving the woman in the dark, staring at the only thing left glowing, herself the ghost.

Looking in the medicine cabinet's mirror, she observed what Melissa saw reflected there. Melissa's pale reflection stared back at her, and just over her shoulder, she saw her own swirling mist, hovering in the doorway. She shimmered, coalescing blue and white. Why those colors, she couldn't begin to guess. Maybe because of her name. Oh well, now was not the time to speculate. This was difficult and took concentration.

She drank. The electric's energy fortified her being, strengthened her pale form, slowly giving her substance.

She could see herself in the mirror, something she hadn't done in a very long time. Her head was beginning to form and she could make out the dark outline of her long hair. With extreme force of will she formed one slender arm, minus her fingers, as the hall lights dimmed. *Can't have everything,* she thought. She raised it in wonder, fascinated. *I have an arm!*

In the mirror's reflection, Melissa's green eyes were wide and staring. Her freckled creamy skin paled by several degrees, mouth opened in a soundless scream. The overnight bag rattled in her shaking hands.

Darn! I'm scaring her spitless. Wait; don't shut your eyes. I need your help. Look, you goofy woman. I'm not the Bad One.

She tried to utter those words but all that escaped her distorted mouth was a low moan. *Great, I'm a ghost that moans. I just hope she doesn't faint. It's been twenty years since I've tried to speak, I don't know how to do it. Not like this.*

The ghost strained with effort and tried to form the word, "Help." But all that came out was, "E-e-e."

Frustrated, she began to lose hold on her shape. Shimmering and swirling once again, all that remained was her face and it glowed a cool blue with dark spots for eyes. The lights brightened. She wondered if she'd gotten through to the woman at all, but one look told her the sad truth.

Melissa had shut her eyes, lips moving as if talking to herself. She'd made a shaky half turn, facing the tub, her bulging bag clutched tightly against her chest. She was trembling violently. She muttered out loud the number two.

Good grief, she's counting. Melissa was bracing herself for a confrontation, counting her steps to turn and face the door, eyes tightly shut against the ghost's frightening image.

One more number and she'll be facing me. Good. Come on. I need to talk to you before I completely melt. Come on.

Suddenly the room grew cold, a chilling breeze blew through the hall. *Oh, no. He's coming back. I've gotta split. I tried,* she cried mournfully as she disappeared into the wall, but not before she heard footsteps pounding down the hall. Melissa's husband was running to the bathroom. She guessed he saw the lights flickering and hurried to keep his wife from freaking out.

The girl moved up toward the ceiling watching for signs of the Other, but there was no sign of his oily blackness, only the freezing cold he generated.

The girl observed Bill halting near the bathroom doorway, huffing air from his dash up the stairs, a puzzled look on his handsome features that lasted only an instant. She giggled silently as Melissa reached the number three and bolted through the doorway, slamming her husband against the opposite wall, eyes still tightly shut. Melissa had finally gained the nerve to exit the bathroom. Bill uttered a soft *"Oof"* when Melissa made contact with his chest, knocking the breath out of him.

It's a shame they're leaving; I kinda like them. Sometimes they're fun to be around, not like that old woman who'd stayed here more than a year ago. She sighed. *And now it will be the waiting game again until someone else comes along. I'm tired and want to move on. I wish it were Me leaving.*

"Jeez, Louise!" she heard Bill exclaim and gasp for air. "I always knew you were a corn-fed, stout woman, but you nearly broke my ribs."

"Oh, God! Bill! Thank heavens I ran into you instead of that . . . that thing." Her face was ashen as she sagged against him, the overnight bag crushed between them. She looked tentatively over her shoulder at the gaping bathroom door; there was nothing there.

Bill grasped her shoulders. "You know, you look like you've just seen a—"

Melissa's green eyes bore into his baby blues, cutting him off. "—Don't say it, Bill," she warned. "Just get our stuff so we can get out of here."

The girl slid down the wall, through the floor, and floated down to the living room, not wanting to witness another chance for help running with bags in hand out the front door.

She drifted near the couple's stereo. One more song couldn't hurt, one for the road. It didn't matter if it was a clue or not. She needed something to cheer her up. *That's funny,* she laughed to herself. It never crossed her mind before that ghost's got depressed. She had always been a cheerful and upbeat person in life. But this was death, and she was growing weary with the fight. She did get depressed. Maybe all ghosts did.

If only Mattie would come back. If only I hadn't made that impetuous vow. But she had made it, just before the accident. And a force greater than herself, greater than the Other, was holding her to it. It was that force, that higher power, that moves all things seen and unseen on this earth, in life, in death, in the universe, that kept her in this state of limbo, waiting for her to fulfill her oath.

She hovered over the silver and black state-of-the-art stereo, appraising the technology (she'd never seen a CD before, they came after she'd died), and then slid inside, turning on the power. At least this didn't require much energy. With the electricity turned on the stereo had an endless supply and she didn't require much to select a station. With a hiss of static the radio came on and she manipulated the digital numbers till she found an oldies station. *Humph. Oldies, indeed.* Turning up the volume she rocked back and forth between the circuits as she listened to "Another One Bites The Dust" by Queen. "That's an understatement," she muttered.

From overhead came the sound of heavy footfalls, moving with great speed. Yep, just as she figured, footsteps pounded down the stairs, and with bags in hand, Bill and Melissa Hayden flew out the door, slamming it shut behind them.

The girl turned down the volume, no longer in the mood for Queen. Sadness settled around her like a shroud. Manipulating the stereo again she found a station playing Gilbert O' Sullivan's "Alone Again Naturally." *How true and fitting*, she thought sadly.

Despondent, she left the radio on and floated upstairs, her essence growing dim. Turning to her right, passing the attic, the servants' quarters, and linen closet, she floated past the bay window overlooking the side garden, seeking solace in her old room at the end of the hall. She uttered a mournful wail and slid into her lonely room through the wall near the door. Why must she bear this alone? The soft strands playing on the stereo wafted upstairs to mingle with the piteous sound of the girl's cry of despair. Curling into a luminescent ball, sinking into the bare mattress of her old bed, her form dissipated, her wails grew weaker, and then were silent.

After the taillights on the Hayden's Mazda SUV were no longer visible from the house, inside the old Fitzgerald home, one by one an invisible hand, beginning with the downstairs rooms, turned off the lights.

"Wasteful brat!" the black oily shadow cursed from an even darker gaping hole that served as a mouth. *"If only I could get my sleek tendrils around that misty throat. I'd squeeze the afterlife out of her."*

The Bad One was frustrated. He was pleased he'd gotten rid of that cowardly couple, but frustrated just the same. Why could he not rid himself of that pesky girl? He seethed and roiled with hatred. Something protected the girl; she always managed to elude him, and he couldn't stand to look at her. Her essence was too bright, sometimes causing him pain deep in his center. But he would find a way, he vowed. Everything has a weakness. She was only a girl, a pathetic nothing, and soon he would squash her like the irritating bug she was.

And he would find *it*. Wherever she had *it* hidden, he would find *it* . . . and destroy *it*.

As the last light was extinguished upstairs, the music also died away into the silence of the night.

Grace Stone Manor stood alone once again, devoid of living inhabitants.

Chapter 2

April 26, Monday

Madeleine Martucci awoke to a bright sunny spring morning. She opened her soft blue eyes to the sun's rays streaming through the lace curtains, making patterns across her king-size bed. Madeleine loved the sunshine and spring was her favorite time of the year. Maria, her housekeeper must have crept in earlier to open the sage green drapes and the window, allowing the clean, fresh scent drifting in on the morning air to blow through the billowing curtains from the inner courtyard below her modern two-story Pasadena home.

Yawning and stretching she sat up to better arrange her white satin pillows behind her and said, "Come in," to the soft tapping at the door.

Maria, Madeleine's housekeeper and friend, entered carrying a breakfast tray, her white hose making a swishing sound as she crossed the large master bedroom. Her light blue uniform was pressed and clean, hugging her generous figure, and her apron was crisply starched as usual. Being of Spanish descent, in her mid-forties, her black hair was beginning to gray and she wore it piled on top of her head, slicked back from warm brown skin, accentuating her high cheekbones and wide set eyes. She approached the large bed and placed the silver tray across Madeleine's lap.

Madeleine inspected her breakfast. The coffee in the silver teapot was steaming, the eggs were poached and the toast lightly buttered. Maria had also, thoughtfully, placed a rose in a small vase on the corner of the tray. Madeleine poured the hot coffee into a china cup, fringed with blue flowers, and added cream and sugar.

"Thank you, Maria, and how is Mr. Martucci this morning? Did he eat any breakfast?" Madeleine inquired.

"Mr. Martucci did eat this morning Miss Mattie and he's in his office downstairs." Maria spoke in clear English but still rolled the letter R. Only when stressed would she pour out a torrential rain of Spanish that neither Madeleine nor her husband could understand. Her smile faltered for just a fraction of a second but not before Madeleine saw the change.

"Is anything wrong, Maria?"

"No, Miss Mattie." Maria's twitching hands belied her reply and she kept her almond brown eyes averted.

"Come now. We've known each other for almost ten years and I can tell when you're keeping something from me. You know you can tell me anything." Madeleine took a sip of her coffee and waited for Maria to collect her thoughts.

Maria Fuentes had lived in the Martuccis' home for eight of those ten years. When Madeleine learned that Maria was living alone in an apartment and raising a child by herself, coming five days a week to work for her, she had insisted that Maria and her son come live with her and her husband. At that time Maria's son, Carlos, was eleven years old. Maria's husband had been an innocent victim, killed in a drive-by shooting in front of a supermarket just a few short months before coming to work for Madeleine. Carlos was now nineteen and attending UCLA; Victor Martucci had paid his college tuition. It had been an honor and a pleasure to pay for his education since she and Victor could have no children of their own.

Although Maria was very close to Madeleine and possessed a loyal respect for her, she knew her place as housekeeper. She wasn't one to gossip about her employers and didn't believe in carrying tales. And she certainly didn't like discussing her employer with his wife. That was taboo. On the other hand, Miss Mattie was waiting for an answer; she was looking at her expectantly, coffee cup poised near her cupid-bow lips and questioning blue eyes fixed on her face.

She was just about to open her mouth when they both heard a male voice boom from downstairs.

"Damn!" Victor's baritone reverberated throughout the house.

"Miss Mattie, I just wanted to give you fair warning that Mr. Martucci is in a uproar." Maria spoke quickly and made a hasty retreat to the hall and down the servant's stairway to the kitchen. The one place she knew Mr. Martucci never visited and therefore would be left in peace. Maria didn't like to hang around when Mr. Martucci was in a temper.

Madeleine quickly rose from the bed, setting her breakfast tray on the table next to the open window. She grabbed her pink satin robe from the chair and put it on as she stepped out into the hall.

"Victor," she called out. "What's wrong?"

"That was Frank Smedley on the phone," Victor answered as he made his way up the stairs, breathing heavily. He was about thirty pounds too heavy for his five foot nine inch frame. He stopped midway to suck in three gulps of air and then continued to climb, moving just a little slower. Beads of perspiration broke out on his dark forehead.

As he reached the landing he paused to take a couple more deep breaths, leaning on the railing. *I need to get out and exercise more often*, he thought. *Maybe a trip to the gym. I'm only forty-seven.* He used to be able to climb these stairs without giving much thought about breathing.

Madeleine looked at her husband's flushed face. She knew when Victor was in a rage; an obvious sign was his booming voice. Another was his eyebrow knitting together making his dark eyes small pinpoints. This morning as he laboriously made his way up the stairs his bushy black eyebrows were saying hello to each other and his face was crimson. *Of course*, Madeleine thought, *the crimson color could be due to him pounding up the stairs. I must get him out to walk with me more often. The fresh air would do him well, not to mention getting him away from his business now and then. He needs a vacation*, Madeleine decided.

"Vic, come in and sit down. Remember your blood pressure. Tell me what's happened." Madeleine's voice was soft and soothing as she followed him into the bedroom.

"Another couple has left," Victor began between gulps of air. He was still huffing and puffing; he loosened his tie. "They left the house a couple of nights ago."

"Which house, dear?" Madeleine gazed at her husband in confusion. They leased many homes and she didn't keep up with them.

He took a deep breath and sighed. "Mattie, Grace Stone Manor, your family's home." *Ridiculous name*, he thought as he lowered himself down into a wicker chair, it creaked under his bulk.

"Oh." Madeleine said as she thought, *Again?*

"Oh? Is that it? That's all you have to say?" Victor trying to calm himself, tightly gripped the arms of the wicker chair. "I can't tell you right off hand how many tenants have come and gone since the middle eighties but it puts new meaning to the word nomad. None of those people seemed to want to put down roots. I just don't understand it. Are all Oklahomans that unsettled?"

"Of course not, Victor. I'm settled here with you and I'm from Oklahoma." Madeleine laughed at Victor but the irony of her statement was lost to her. She turned and went to the closet to pick out her clothes for the day. It was spring and she wanted something light and airy to wear.

Victor grunted and leaned back in his chair with an air of resignation and eyed his wife's breakfast; again she'd hardly eaten a bite. In fact, it looked as if she hadn't eaten at all. He sighed in resignation. It was no use. Mattie never saw anything as a problem. To her, people always have good intentions and never mean her harm. She didn't have a suspicious or malicious bone in her body. It was one of the reasons why he loved her so much. The other reason was that she was very beautiful. At thirty-nine she still had a slim figure but filled out in all the right places. Womanly. He worried sometimes though that she wasn't eating enough.

He stared at her back, noticing the graceful line of her neck and shoulders and pictured her tiny waist hidden beneath her robe. Her silky shoulder-length blond hair was pinned on top of her head. When she gave him a quick smile over her shoulder, he noticed a few strands had escaped the pins to frame her lightly tanned delicate features. Her cheeks were tinged with a slight rosy glow. He was glad his wife had the good sense not to cover her beautiful face with smelly make-up.

"Mattie, don't you want to hear why the Haydens left?" The conversation he'd had with Mr. Smedley still burned in his ears.

"Sure, dear. Why?" Mattie pulled a pale-peach chiffon dress from a hanger and held it up to her shoulders as she viewed herself in the full-length mirror that also served as the sliding door to the closet.

"Ghosts. Again we have lost tenants who gave the same excuse." Victor snorted air and ran his fingers through his salt and pepper hair. "Frank Smedley is as flabbergasted as I am. You know he's been managing and leasing out your home for years and he doesn't understand why people leave suddenly any more than I do. He's says people complain of drafts and flickering lights, stereos that turn on by themselves and TV's that turn off. If I were there I'd have the whole place checked out by professionals, electricians. It's probably faulty wiring."

Having removed her robe and gown, Madeleine put on a bra and slip, and slid the dress over her head while her husband talked. She now stood with her back to him and he automatically reached to zip up the dress, a soft flowing thing he'd paid a lot of money for but did not complain about. He loved spoiling her.

He watched her as she sat at her dressing table brushing her hair; it was all one length and tended to curl on the end, hugging her slim shoulders, and not showing any signs of gray like his own.

Already his anger was ebbing. Madeleine had that effect on him. He watched as she gathered her hair all into one hand and rummaged in a drawer with the other till she retrieved a golden hair clip with a pearl at its center. She put it on to keep her hair in place then found matching earrings to wear.

Victor came and stood behind her placing his hands on her shoulders, viewing her image in the mirror. "You always look so beautiful, Mattie. You calm the savage beast in me." He stooped to kiss her cheek.

"I'm going to the office now. I have some business to take care of and need to speak with Smedley again." He sauntered to the door adjusting his chocolate tie, his lungs working normally again, the redness having left his face.

Madeleine turned to face him. "Victor, please don't be late for dinner. I miss you when you're not here."

Victor smiled, "I'll try not to be late, dear. Love you."

She blew him a kiss. "I love you, too."

He left the room and softly closed the door.

Victor thought of his wife as he descended the stairs. At times life with Mattie could be exasperating and cause his blood to boil but he loved her dearly and had a deep abiding desire for her. He'd always felt a need to protect her, yet it was she who had the power to calm him. She had the uncanny ability to still the rage in him when his anger was reaching the breaking point. This problem with her family's old home had become a constant source of irritation and it seemed to keep him near the edge of total explosion.

But there was Mattie; sweet, gentle Mattie; always the buffer. He considered himself a very fortunate man to have her. There had been considerable hurdles to cross during their marriage and there had been times when he'd thought he'd lost her, but he loved her and had stayed by her side, never regretting for a moment for having married her. She was his Mattie.

Leaving through the front door, Victor was already thinking of his business. He had a very important deal to close today and needed to think of a way to settle the issue of his wife's family home. It was time to make permanent arrangements for that house and have done with it. He wished it had never come into his wife's possession.

Upstairs, in their bedroom, Madeleine sat at their little breakfast nook, enjoying the breeze drifting through the window and staring out at her flower garden below. The scents of spring and her conversation with Victor took her back in time, when she was still living with her parents and her younger brother, Paul.

Her father, Jacob Fitzgerald, had been very successful in the real estate business and when she was eight years old he'd started his own company. He'd moved his family from Oklahoma City to Pasadena where she was to grow up and one day meet her future husband. At first she had cried and thrown fits. She hadn't wanted to move away from her cousin, Skye, but in time she had adjusted and made friends at school.

Although she'd had a good life living in California, at times she missed the lovely home her grandparents had built. Her grandfather, Zedediah Fitzgerald had been somewhat prosperous raising cattle and began building a home for his fiancée, Sarah, late in the fall of nineteen thirty-five. When the house was finished in the spring of nineteen thirty-six they were married. Her grandfather had carried Sarah over the threshold of what was to be their home for only a short thirty-one years.

Her grandmother—Grammy Sarah, Madeleine had called her at the age of two—had been a very young seventeen-year-old whose head was filled with romantic notions, much like Madeleine, her father had teased. When she'd laid eyes on her new home for the first time, as she was carried over the threshold, she'd decided the house had to have a name; Grace Stone Manor, Sarah had dubbed the brightly painted, two-story home. Madeleine's father thought it was silly, but a dreamy-eyed, twelve-year-old Madeleine was of a different opinion and envisioned the romance that must have existed between her grandparents.

Moving forward in time, Madeleine's thoughts took her to nineteen eighty-one, the year she'd turned sixteen. Her family had returned to Oklahoma to spend the summer months in the house they'd inherited a year before when her aunt and uncle had died. She'd had a wonderful time camping with her family and although Grace Stone was like a second home to her, that year, staying in her cousin's bedroom, had been emotionally painful. It was fraught with so many memories of Skye.

Though the bedroom had been stripped bare of Skye's personal possessions, leaving only the furniture, her free-spirited personality still permeated the room. It was etched into the walls literally. At fourteen she'd talked her parents into letting her paint her room. She'd kept the door barred to everyone for several days that summer, including Madeleine. When she had finished, with great fanfare, the sounds of ABBA bouncing off the walls, she'd flung her door open wide to reveal her handiwork. She'd left the bottom half of the oaken wood untouched, but the rest of the room she'd painted a light sky-blue dotted with fluffy white clouds. In one corner, covering a portion of the ceiling and both adjoining walls, a blazing sun glared out across the room. Madeleine thought it was the coolest room she'd ever seen and secretly envied Skye for having a mother who encouraged her self-expression.

After the accident a year later, most of her belongings had been dispersed to goodwill. What was left, Madeleine had taken. Skye's records and tapes and sheet music were carefully stored in a special cedar trunk in her room. Music had been a big part of her cousin's life. She'd taught herself to play the piano at a very early age and her parents had bought her a new piano for her thirteenth birthday. It was still in the library at Grace Stone.

One night, about a week after arriving at the house in the summer of eighty-one, Madeleine had showered and dressed for bed, opening the window for just a hint of a breeze. It was a warm June night and her parents had left off the central air conditioning. She was sweating bullets, glad that she at least had a fan. She could not imagine her grandparents living here for years with no central air and wished her father had turned it on and cranked it up. But, he had grown up here without that modern comfort and saw no need for it while they stayed. She quickly turned off the lamp to keep the june-bugs and moths from pelting the screen and slipped in between the cool sheets. She'd turned the volume down on the bedside radio and lay there, staring up at the light blue canopy that matched the walls, listening to Blondie sing "Heart Of Glass."

Her thoughts had been of her day spent at the lake in Wister, a resort area her family had camped at many times before. She had swum and tanned and had even piloted the boat. It had been a glorious day and the only thing bad about it had been the two-hour drive home. She'd been bone tired from her activities and it hadn't taken long for sleep to overtake her.

She remembered having a strange dream. It was dark and shadowy and she was afraid. She'd heard her name being called out of the gloom, and echoing around her were the words, "You have to find it." She'd struggled wearily through the darkness as though it had substance; it was murky and thick and almost suffocating.

Blindly, her groping hands had touched things she could not identify, only hear; they rustled and crackled with her probing touch.

Suddenly, the atmosphere had become too thick to continue her search. She coughed and gasped, aching for a lung-full of fresh air. Trying to find a way out, she'd scratched and clawed at the shadowy dimness surrounding her, a deep panic tightening her chest. Then blessedly she was bathed in light.

She'd heard a click as a dull light illuminated the room and standing by the stairwell was her brother, Paul. He was naked from the waist up, wearing only his shorts. His brown curly hair, just like Dad's, was standing up on end and he had a puzzled look on his sunburned face. There were white lines across the bridge of his nose and at the corners of his hazel-green eyes from wearing shades. He'd looked like a raccoon. If she hadn't been so startled she would have laughed.

"Jumping Jehoshaphat! Mattie, what are you doing?" he'd exclaimed, stepping into the attic.

She'd blinked a few times in the sudden glare of the overhead light and then realized where she was. She was covered in dust and cobwebs and kneeling over an opened trunk in the attic. Sweat was running down her sides and dripping off her aquiline nose and pointed chin; it was stifling in the attic. She'd had no idea how she had gotten there. She only remembered dreaming. She had never walked in her sleep before and it had been a little disconcerting. As strange as it was, she wasn't frightened, only a little perplexed.

Looking back inside the trunk there was nothing of real interest to her, only some old clothes that her grandmother had worn, clothes that she and Skye used to play dress-up in, and some old photographs. She'd risen, dusted off the cobwebs as she walked past Paul to the small staircase leading down from the attic. She remembered laughing nervously as she passed her brother and him yelping when she'd slapped his beet-red bare shoulder. She'd told him she was just looking for something and it was no big deal.

Trailing after her down the stairs, he'd argued with her that it was a little weird to be digging around in some old trunk in the middle of the night, not to mention she had been doing it in the dark. She'd lied and told him she had lost her flashlight just before he came in and switched on the light. Then she'd told him to forget it, advised him to put some cold cream on his sunburn and to go back to bed and then returned to her room.

Something weird happened then. The radio had started making a hissing sound and then a jumble of voices mixed with various tunes issued from it as the dial turned on its own. When it finally stopped her breath had caught in her throat as hot tears coursed down her sunburned cheeks. The harmony of *ABBA* poured from the radio's single speaker as they sang "Chiquitita."

The grief she'd felt was like a punch in the stomach. She'd curled up in a tiny ball, hugging her pillow, missing Skye terribly, listening to one of the last songs her cousin had learned to play on the piano, one they used to sing together. Wallowing in sorrow she had cried herself back to sleep.

Not wishing to tumble headlong into that well of sadness that was her memory of Skye, Madeleine bit her lip, hard. The physical pain was effective. It smarted her eyes and she was able to push away those pain-filled thoughts. It would do her no good to dwell in that area of her mind for too long. The result would send her straight back to Dr. Irwin's leather sofa.

Banishing her thoughts of Skye to the void in the back of her mind, Madeleine couldn't help but laugh about her brother Paul, a safer area of the mind to remember. For a couple of years he had teased her now and then about her midnight stroll to the attic. For a while it was a joke between the two of them, when she was feeling well and could take it in good humor. That went on for a while, until her father caught wind of it and threatened to beat Paul within an inch of his life. Her father hadn't liked for anyone to bring up her somnambulism.

She'd asked Paul once what had made him visit the attic that night. Flashing her one of his goofy smiles he'd only replied, "I have heightened senses, you know. Just like Spider Man. I sensed a presence up there and went to check it out."

She'd always thought him silly collecting action figures and comic books but his boyhood hobby had turned into a moneymaking reality. He now worked for an advertising firm as a copywriter for the comic super heroes he'd loved as a boy. His office at work and at home was full of toys, no doubt, a veritable playground for his nine-year-old son Kyle.

Although Madeleine hadn't been to her grandparents' home for quite some time, she suddenly had a yearning to go. The house was about to be sold and she felt an inexplicable desire to see it one last time, a frightening and yet, gentle tugging at her soul.

She wondered if she could persuade her husband to take her there. It might take some doing, but she felt sure she could convince Victor that she was fine in making this decision. She could go alone but she really didn't want to rattle around in that large house by herself; she didn't want to be alone with her memories. Although she had grieved she couldn't help but feel there was something left undone. Maybe she just hadn't said good-bye to Skye and to . . . .

Madeleine mentally shook herself, casting off the clinging depression that was always attached to her memories of Skye and . . . little Antonia. She could not bear to think of Antonia. It was years ago that she'd lost her, but the memory still had the sting of a rattlesnake's bite.

Shifting gears to more pleasant things, she thought of her marriage and of her home here in Pasadena with her husband. They would never have met if her father hadn't drug her kicking and screaming to California. Thinking of Victor, her smile deepened as she remembered those highly emotional teen-age days before they'd married.

She'd met Victor when he came to work for her father. She was fourteen then and still a shy schoolgirl but had developed a crush on the man. Victor was twenty-two and had just begun working at her father's office. Her father had really liked him, said he showed great promise as a businessman in the real estate world and had often invited him to dinner at their home.

At that time Victor was only polite and had shown no romantic interest in her. He treated her with respect but kept his distance. By the time she was sixteen she noticed he was paying a bit more attention to her and, to be truthful, she'd had an all-out full-blown crush on him by then.

She'd stare at him when she thought he wasn't looking. And she looked as often as she could. He wasn't very tall, only about six inches taller than she and often she'd fantasized running her fingers through his wavy black hair. She knew he was of European descent, with olive skin, gorgeous dark eyes, a sexy smile, and a slight accent that made her heart flutter in her chest whenever he greeted her. He was the handsomest man she had ever seen and smelling his cologne was pure ecstasy. She could tell when he'd just vacated a room; his masculine scent lingered. And although his cologne had changed over the years she still loved his scent when he was near.

It had been painful and embarrassing to be sixteen and have a crush on an older man. Madeleine leaned back, caressing the rose from her breakfast tray as she remembered one such incident.

Sometimes during his visits she would avoid him but hover near the doorway just to get a glimpse of him. Her father caught her once and embarrassed her by openly inviting her to join them in the den. She hadn't wanted Victor to know she was standing there eyeing him and in that instant when she'd stepped out from behind the door, his brown eyes caught and held hers for what seemed like an eternity. Heart racing, palms sweating, and her face flushed to forty shades of red, she'd stammered a meaningless excuse and quickly made an escape to her bedroom where she'd cried from sheer embarrassment.

A few years later, during one of those mother and daughter talk and laugh sessions, after she'd married Victor; her mother confessed she had fussed at her father later on that evening for embarrassing their only daughter in front of the object of her affections. It was during that difficult teen-age time for Madeleine that her mother, Abigail, enlightened her father about their daughter's feelings for his aspiring apprentice. So, it came as no shock to her father when Victor came to him after her seventeenth birthday and announced his mutual feelings for Madeleine.

Victor was not allowed to date her at that time, him being so much older, but since his intention was now out in the open her father let him spend more time with her at their home under his watchful eye.

He had continued to come to dinner and was invited to their family cookouts and swim in their pool. The first few talks alone with him had been a little stressful for her but over time her palms finally ceased sweating when in his presence. A good thing that was, for there had been a few awkward moments when he'd taken her hand and pressed it to his lips, all the while holding her eyes captive with his own. He gently wooed her during her seventeenth year and by her eighteenth birthday her schoolgirl feelings had blossomed into a mature love. Well, as mature as an eighteen-year-old girl could get with no previous experience in matters of the heart, and hers belonged to Victor, always would.

Within six months after her high school graduation they were married. Her father had been upset to learn she was not going to attend college but she had been firm about that. Although her grades had been good in school, she'd had to struggle to maintain them and she just didn't want to face struggling through college. Besides, she had all she wanted. She hadn't wanted a career. Just to be Victor's wife was enough for her.

They had enjoyed twenty-one years of marriage and she looked forward to another twenty years or so with him. Her only regret was that she could bear no children for him.

Careful Madeleine, a voice whispered in her mind, *don't go too far.*

She would have loved to have a child with Victor, with silky dark hair and gentle brown eyes, like his.

Stop It!

Almost had a child, didn't you? Did have a child. But she was so cold, the voice whispered, *so cold.*

"Stop it! Don't do this to yourself," she murmured hoarsely, "It'll do you no good to remember."

Madeleine drew in a steadying breath. *Mustn't think about that. Not now, not ever. That's over and done with.* She bit her lower lip until tears smarted her eyes. *She's gone.* "Mustn't dwell on it. You weren't to blame. Dr. Irwin assured you, you were not to blame."

But I am to blame! She silently screamed at herself, eyes shut tight, lips trembling, fits clenched against her heaving chest. *Something's wrong with me, and it was MY fault! All my fault!*

A sharp pain jabbed in the pit of her stomach as bitter nausea rose to the back of her throat.

You went too far, Madeleine.

She hastily swallowed it back, fighting the urge to run to the bathroom as a light rapping sounded at the door. It was Maria coming to fetch her breakfast tray. Time had past so quickly she hadn't realized it was near lunchtime. Rubbing the tears out of her eyes she told her to enter.

Maria softly scolded her for not eating a bite when she surveyed the tray as she lifted it from the table. "You're too thin, Mattie," she admonished her gently.

"Well, then I'll eat a large lunch. I promise." Madeleine smiled and laughed softly with a mirth that didn't quite reach her eyes. "As a matter of fact," she added, "I'll join you in the kitchen. We can have lunch together." She was grateful for the interruption from her bleak turn of thought, and even more so that the voice was now silent.

"Great, Miss Mattie. I'll meet you in the kitchen." Maria was always glad to have her company, but as she left the room she wondered what had caused that hint of sadness in Madeleine's pale blue eyes.

Chapter 3

Over their dinner that evening Madeleine talked with Victor about his day, not that she paid much attention; her mind was elsewhere and she didn't understand much about real estate investing but she was eventually able to bring the conversation around to selling the house, which had been her ultimate goal. All day she had planned and rehearsed what to say to get her husband to leave Pasadena. The pull to return to Grace Stone had grown stronger as the day wore on.

She knew it would be more difficult to get him to take a vacation to Oklahoma than to take a business trip, something he was more apt to do, so she'd steered their talk more along the lines of money, wiring and plumbing, more specifically, the problems with Grace Stone. This was something he would readily chat about, not ghosts. He did not want to discuss things that go bump in the night. Balderdash, he'd called it. Nonsense and rubbish. Besides, Victor's idea of a vacation was leaving the country altogether. She just hoped he wouldn't balk at returning to Grace Stone after all this time.

"If the Hayden's had any sense they would have called Mr. Smedley the next day about the wiring instead of running off in the middle of the night. He would have called me immediately and I would have given permission to have it looked into right away." This was still a sore spot and Victor's bushy eyebrows were working furiously as he talked around his blackened chicken fettuccini. To his way of thinking, mid-westerners were lacking in higher education and so, after giving it much thought this morning, he'd come to the conclusion the Hayden's had acted within the bounds of their intelligence. But it rankled him just the same.

"Vic." Madeleine looked demurely at him across the dining table. "Why don't we go to Oklahoma and you can check it out yourself?" Madeleine held her breath for a second and then decided to move on quickly before he had time to react.

"Instead of losing the sale," she reasoned, "why not go and see about it yourself? My father leased it out for years and you've leased it out for the past four years and I agreed to sell it this time. Paul has no interest in it, doesn't want it. I know I don't understand much about investing but I've listened to you enough to know that we don't keep it rented out enough to pay for its upkeep." She slowed down for the jab at his money belt. "Isn't it costing money?"

Victor pinned her with his dark eyes, then glanced away thoughtfully, his wine glass poised near his lips. She was actually making sense about this problem. He'd found he could get more done if he handled things himself, and Madeleine knew this. But he wondered if after all these years she would be okay in returning to Grace Stone.

He hated the thought of being in Oklahoma; too many pastures with snakes, bugs, mosquitoes, and ticks, and everyone saying, "Howdy." One look at Madeleine told him she was serious about going. She was staring at him intently, soft blue eyes waiting for an answer. Maybe it would be all right. It had been a long time and she seemed fine to him.

She was right about one thing: her inheritance *was* costing him money. He paid Mr. Smedley a chunk each month to manage Grace Stone, and so far he hadn't seen much managing; the man hadn't convinced one person to remain at the house, most of them demanding their money back, and he was changing tenants like socks. It was way past high time to dispense with this noose about his neck and cut the rope. He swirled the Chardonnay in his glass and took a drink.

When he'd waited too long to answer, Madeleine continued, "We could meet with the Haydens and find out first hand exactly what's going on." Madeleine gave him a sideways glance, shrugging her small shoulders indicating she was only making a suggestion and then added, "I'm sure they're nice people. I bet you could get them to reconsider and buy it. You've told me many times there isn't a house you can't sell." She was playing on her husband's vanity but saw no shame in doing so. She wanted, needed to go to Oklahoma.

Victor paused a moment, twirling his glass as he eyed its contents and then downed the last drop. "As for what's going on, it's wiring, pure and simple. But, I have to agree with you, dear. I've always closed a deal when I've set out to sell. The Haydens obviously wanted to buy the house but Smedley just doesn't have what it takes to make it happen."

He blotted the corners of his lips, threw his napkin beside his empty plate, and pushed his chair back from the dining table. Maybe it was the Haydens who held the knife to cut him loose. Sell it to them? You bet he could. It would be a relief to get rid of that stupid house once and for all.

He was finished with his dinner and with this conversation. He had made his decision. "I'll make arrangements tomorrow to fly out to Tulsa. We'll be leaving in two days." He bent down to kiss Madeleine's cheek. "Are you sure you want to go there?"

"Of course," she said, and then added, "I'm fine, Victor. Really. I want to do this." She smiled up at him.

"All right. We'll go." He kissed her again and left the dining room.

Madeleine smiled at Victor's retreating back. It had been accomplished easier than she'd thought. She had rehearsed that small speech many times earlier in the garden and it had worked. She left the table to shower and dress for bed, murmuring a "Goodnight" to Maria when she came to clear the dishes.

She had gotten what she wanted; she was going to visit her family's old home, perhaps for the last time if he convinced the Haydens to buy it. She had little doubt her husband would do just that. She was a little saddened at the thought of losing it but it was time to let it go and with it her heartbreaking memories.

As Madeleine drifted off to sleep she was thinking of what needed packing and what she could do without. She would only need a few nice spring dresses and skirts for going out to dinner and shopping, but plenty of pants and shorts for cleaning and working in the flower garden. She imagined the house needed some spring-cleaning; it had been empty all winter before Mr. And Mrs. Hayden moved in and they'd only been there two weeks. *They must have busy schedules*, she thought, *and couldn't possibly have done it all.* She also longed to sit among the flowers her grandmother had planted long ago and where she and Skye had spent so many summers playing. And, she thought somberly, she was going to have to face her fear of the attic.

It had been an accident, she reminded herself, *just a stupid, unfortunate accident.* But one that had left her devastated, struggling to pick up the shattered pieces of her life, until finally she had gotten past the heartbreak and moved on. Or had she?

Stop it, Mattie! Just go to sleep.

With a sudden jolt, sitting upright in bed, Madeleine realized there was one other thing she could not do without: Maria.

Well, I'll just have to pack her too, she decided. She eased back onto the pillows and snuggled next to Victor's back. She heard him mumble something unintelligible, and then floated away into slumber.

Immediately, Madeleine was plunged into darkness. She was overcome with fear and wanted to run. She couldn't tell if she had legs or not but amidst the confusing darkness she had sense of movement, so she ran. Her motion was fluid as if moving through murky water and she strained to reach beyond the thick suffocating mist that felt slimy, like algae.

The smell of damp earth and something putrid assailed her nostrils. She choked and clawed, fighting for freedom. She didn't care what might be outside this damp and dark place; she only wanted to escape before it sucked her down into the muck that was dragging at her feet.

Suddenly, the dim fog swirled and dissipated revealing a large and forbidding outline. With a jerk she was free, pitching forward to come to a halt, her high-heels skidding on the rocks. She stood shivering in the cold, now aware of her limbs. A damp mist clung to her hose, but the upper air had cleared. She drew in a deep breath.

Up ahead in the distance, silhouetted against the backdrop of misshapen trees and a miniature moon she saw a large two-story house. Within seconds she recognized her grandparents' old home. It looked slightly lop-sided and a little disproportionate but she didn't care; it was better than being lost and blind in the dark.

Around her oppressing shadows roiled, like dark and bilious storm clouds with wings, weaving a dark trail between the blackened leaves of the oak trees and weeping willows lining the driveway. One large stump pointed jaggedly out of the damp earth and she hastily sped past it, blocking out the images of twisted metal and broken glass it conjured up. She shut her mind to that painful memory, looking beyond to the trees that were still standing. Against the pale night sky those eerie shadows moving there resembled nothing she recognized from this world and she wished the moon wasn't so tiny. The darkness had faded very little in the milky-light, but at least she could see where she was going as her feet crunched gravel.

Strange noises were emanating from the shrubbery as she made her way toward the house. Madeleine stopped and cocked her head sideways, listening. She could hear twigs and dead leaves crackling as if large animals were thrashing in the underbrush, fighting to see who would get to her first. Uttering a small cry, the hair on her arms and back of her neck standing up, Madeleine sped on to the safety of the porch. She glanced back once, but nothing was chasing her. She breathed a sigh of relief when she made it safely to the door.

Besides being tilted in that odd surrealistic manner, as if the foundation were giving way, the house was in disrepair and neglect. There were vines growing up the pillars, intertwining up and over the balcony. Some of the windows were completely broken out, the black shutters hanging in disarray, the once sunny

31

yellow paint chipped and peeling. Madeleine looked up to see the varnished plaque above the oak door hanging askew on a broken chain, the engraved words 'Bless All Who Enter Herein' barely recognizable. Madeleine wondered how the house had gotten in such bad shape.

She reached for the doorknob, afraid of what she might find inside. It was cold to the touch and the door moved inward on squeaky hinges.

Madeleine drew a deep breath and entered.

She quickly shut the door behind her and passed through the large foyer. Sorrow crumpled her features as she looked around miserably at the cobwebs hanging from the den and living room doorways and from the chandelier above the entry hall. *How could this have happened?* Had she neglected her family's home?

And then Madeleine saw the destruction. There were papers strewn everywhere like the house had been ransacked and abandoned. Thinking she recognized sheet music at the foot of the stairs, she took three or four steps into the entrance hall for a closer look and froze.

What was that?

She tilted her head. It was a pitiful low mewling cry coming from upstairs. Her heart skipped a beat and her mouth went dry. She didn't want to go up there but her legs moved of their own volition. She touched the banister and slowly made her way up.

Upon reaching the landing she stood there deciding which way to go. That heart-wrenching cry was low and muffled, permeating the walls. It seemed to come from everywhere, tugging at her emotions, drawing from her own well of despair and loss. It nearly broke her heart.

A child?

Could the person who caused the destruction downstairs have abandoned a child here? If only she knew where the crying was coming from.

In front of her was the playroom where her father and uncle had played as children; it now stood empty. To the left was the bedroom that Paul had occupied. Turning left and down the hall, was an alcove, a large sitting area with a brocaded lounger, a small cherry wood table and two matching chairs that were older than the house. Here, overlooking the west side of the house was a large leaded window. Further down from there were a bathroom, she remembered, and another bedroom. And then around another corner, its French doors opening out upon the front balcony, was the master bedroom where she knew her grandmother had shuddered her last grieving breath, alone.

Madeleine shrank from the thought of having to go there and hoped she didn't have to. If her grandmother was there, she would be a shrunken corpse and Madeleine didn't have the courage to face that.

To her right was a closed door, a small staircase the servants had used to enter the kitchen below. The next door was the staircase leading to the attic. The last place she would want to visit in this gloom. Turning right was another very short staircase going up to three small rooms that had been the servants' quarters; next to this was the door to the linen closet, one with enough space for three or four people to stand inside. After the linen closet was a large bay window containing a deep-red cushioned window seat, and beyond that, farther down the hall was the other bedroom, Skye's old room, completing the upstairs U shape.

Madeleine took a small step and let go of the railing. The mewling stopped. The house was quiet as a tomb. Madeleine listened intently but heard nothing.

She softly tiptoed past the playroom to peer into the open door of the first bedroom. It was still furnished as she remembered; a full-size four poster bed with a trunk stashed at the end, a small chest of drawers, a dresser, and a small writing desk placed in front of one of the windows overlooking the back garden with its water fountain and the pasture beyond. The bedroom was in the same state of disuse as she imagined the rest of the rooms looked, dusty and full of cobwebs. The only things missing were signs of personal use; the room could have belonged to anyone.

That's when she noticed there *was* something different, out of place. One drawer was pulled out half way from the chest of drawers, two pulled out part way from the dresser, and every drawer in the desk was wide open. *What on earth was this unseen, unknown person or persons looking for?* Even the chest was standing open. The only difference between here and downstairs was the forlorn and empty look. Here, there had been no papers to disarray and plunder through. Only those yawning empty drawers testified that someone had been searching for something.

Madeleine turned to go back the way she came, toward the attic staircase and linen closet. Passing the playroom door she thought she saw a shadow move but a quick glance confirmed there was nothing there. *Perhaps it's a bird flying across the window, or maybe one of those eerie things from the trees. Don't think like that*, she scolded herself. *Just keep going.*

As she neared the closet, the door slowly swung open. She paused a moment to control her rapid breathing and steady her nerves, then peered inside. There had been stacks of blankets, sheets, and towels on the shelves but now they were lying on the floor in a tangled heap. Someone had torn them off the shelves.

Somewhere, down one of the halls, a door slammed. Madeleine jumped, grabbing her chest. Her heart was pounding and there was a roaring in her ears from the rush of adrenaline. It sounded like it had come from the spare bedroom or bathroom on the other side of the landing, but she wouldn't swear to it.

She stood rooted to the spot, listening, willing her heart back to normalcy. The hall was bathed in a milky glow from the moonlight seeking refuge through the bay window, its light cut in strange oddly shaped squares on the floor. A few seconds ticked by, and then Madeleine slowly crept through the moon shadow toward Skye's bedroom. As she neared the door the crying began again.

It didn't sound as if it was coming from Skye's room but rather from the master bedroom. Madeleine shivered, moving forward on shaky legs. The door to Skye's room swung open as she approached it. She was about to step inside when it suddenly slammed in her face. Madeleine screamed a half-hearted squeal and jumped back. She screeched again when the opposite wall thumped against her back. *Dear God, what was making that awful sound?* The sobbing grew louder, resonating throughout the halls, and Madeleine's fear increased, sending a chill up her spine. With one hand clutched to her chest, the other sliding along the wall she cautiously made her way farther down to the end of the hall until she reached the corner. She didn't want to go there, but she was drawn. In fact, she didn't want to be here at all but it seemed she had no control.

Madeleine continued to be sucked down into fear; her legs were shaking.

She peeked into the next hallway. Just beyond another huge closet, the door to the master bedroom was slowly swinging back and forth.

Madeleine's entire body was shaking now.

A pale, bluish light was emanating from within the master bedroom.

Oh, God, please! I don't want to go down there.

Suddenly, there was a deafening boom, like someone beating on a bass drum. The crying turned into a frightful wail and then abruptly ended, choked, smothered out like a candle's flame. All the upstairs doors were swinging open, only to be slammed shut again and again. The noise was deafening.

Madeleine's terror mounted as she realized the loudest booming echo was drawing near, coming toward her from the opposite hall, making its way to the master bedroom. It was not the sound of a slamming door. It was the sound of something large, a menacing presence, and it was coming for her. She turned to flee back down the stairs.

Racing down the hall, she glanced behind her to see strangely shaped shadows slithering along the walls as she fled in terror. A strangled cry issued from her lips, for that was all she could force out of her fear-gripped throat. She flew down the stairs, grasping the carved railing for support as she tripped and nearly fell.

Making her way to the foyer across the littered floor, she ran to the front door and grasped the knob. In her haste, blind with terror, her hands slipped a few times before making a connection. She was sobbing uncontrollably now and only wanted out of this nightmare house.

This couldn't be her family's home! It just couldn't be!

The racket from upstairs continued, and that other ominous booming was quickly approaching, vibrating the walls. From the library came the sound of the old piano playing a strange but familiar tune, off-key.

"Let me out! Let me out!" Madeleine beat against the oak door.

Suddenly, a cold chill swept behind her, icy fingers brushed the nape of her neck, oily and cold. Sliding along her skin like several small reptiles, it felt like snakes. She sucked in her breath and let out a scream, grasping the doorknob in shaking sweaty palms.

It wouldn't turn.

In a state of panic, she pulled on the knob and beat on the door once more with her small fists. She had to get out. Her nails were breaking and her knuckles were bleeding but she paid them no heed. Escape was her only thought. With one last effort the knob turned in her hands as cold claws grasped her shoulders and spun her around.

Madeleine squeezed her eyes shut and screamed again. Then it was quiet.

Someone held her wrists, talking to her in a soothing voice. She blinked in the sudden light and the darkness faded from her eyes. Victor was standing before her, a concerned look on his lightly wrinkled, olive-toned face. And then her bedroom came into focus; the sheets were tangled and hanging off the bed and a lamp was burning. Her hands were in front of her, her fingers poised into claws, ready to scratch out his eyes; Victor was holding her wrists.

"It's all right now, Mattie," he murmured. "It's all over. Only a dream."

"Oh, Victor." Relief flooded her and she slumped into his arms.

Still talking in soothing tones he led her back to the bed, draped her robe around her shoulders and then put on his own.

"Do you know you kicked and punched me before you ran to the door?" Victor smiled and sat beside her.

Madeleine grinned sheepishly and passed a hand over her eyes. She checked to see if they were bleeding. They weren't. "I'm sorry, love. I've never done *this* before. I walked in my sleep once when I was a young girl but it was nothing like this."

"Care to talk about it?" Victor knew of her past history of somnambulism. Had witnessed it firsthand. He also knew she could only recall one instance of having walked in her sleep. The other times had been blocked from her memory. Maybe it was just as well.

"I don't think so," she answered him. "I can barely remember it now anyway. I just know that I was frightened. You know flying makes me nervous. Our upcoming flight probably triggered the bad dream. That's all." It was hard to put into words the feelings that her dream stirred up and she didn't want to try. And she certainly did not want to tell her husband the details of her dream. He would cancel the trip, and she couldn't let that happen. She couldn't explain why, even to herself, the reason she felt drawn to Grace Stone at this time. She only knew she could let nothing prevent her going.

She crossed her arms. Her gown was sticking to her skin. "I'm going to take a shower. What time is it?"

Victor glanced at the nightstand clock. "It's a quarter after three. Are you sure you're all right?"

He studied his wife's pale face; the corners of her mouth were turned down and a crease formed a jagged line between her worried eyes. He'd seen that look before and seeing it there now troubled him. But he knew he couldn't press her.

"Yes, I'm sure. It was only a bad dream." Madeleine moved to get another gown from her dresser, and then entered the bathroom.

She'd not had any nightmares since her father died and before that when she'd had the miscarriage years ago. She shut her eyes tight and clinched her fists as that thought came unbidden. She refused to let it take hold on her emotions. She was not going to think about it.

Adjusting the water as hot as she could stand it, she stepped under the spray. She dumped a handful of scented shower-gel into her hand and began to vigorously lather herself from head to toe, washing away the dregs of her nightmare.

It was only a dream, she kept telling herself. *See?* She pointed downward to the water and soap bubbles whirl-pooling, spiraling off her feet into the dark hole. *All that darkness and fear is disappearing down the drain with the soap.* "Just let it go, Madeleine," she murmured to herself.

When she'd finished and returned to bed Victor was lying there awake waiting for her. She crawled in beside him and nestled in his arms. She felt safe now. He turned out the lamp and pulled her closer, kissing her forehead.

From out of the dark a laugh rumbled deep in Victor's chest, escaping his throat. "Try not to pummel and kick me next time you go riding one of those night horses. To be so petite you pack a punch."

Madeleine smiled in the darkness and squeezed him affectionately. She snuggled within the circle of his arms thinking of her dream. It didn't frighten her as much now. She had mentally cleansed her fear in the shower just as her therapist, years ago, had suggested. But, she was still puzzled by the dream. Why on earth would she dream of someone ransacking her old family home? And why did that horrible nameless presence pursue her? What was it, anyway? She'd never had a nightmare about Grace Stone Manor before, at least not like this, and wondered fleetingly if it meant anything. And then she decided she was being silly. She was just keyed up about her impending trip. She had never been fond of flying and thinking of Skye earlier had brought back those old hurtful memories. That was why she'd had the dream.

But, as she lie in that state between consciousness and sleep, deep down in the recesses of her mind, something about it kept niggling at her conscience, gently tickling at some long forgotten memory; something she felt she should know.

Too tired to think about it anymore, she yawned a couple of times, watering her eyes, and then slowly drifted off to an uncomfortable sleep, listening to Victor snoring beside her.

Chapter 4

April 28, Wednesday

It had been four days since Bill and Melissa Hayden fled Grace Stone Manor. It was nearing midnight when he'd rented them a room at the Days Inn on the west side of Tulsa. The next day Bill had driven to Pine Ridge Realtor to talk with Mr. Smedley. It had gone better than he'd thought, although not at first. Mr. Smedley had scratched his balding head, pushed his glasses back on the bridge of nose countless times and rearranged the papers on his desk to the point of distraction as Bill explained the circumstances. At one point Bill had wanted to grab the man's hands and tie them behind his back. He figured he was making the little man a tad nervous with his theories about a ghost. It sounded a little crazy to *him*, but it was the truth as he saw it and was what he believed.

When he'd finished, Mr. Smedley surprised him by saying he'd heard it all before. This sparked Bill's interest. No one was crazy here if this phenomena had occurred with other tenants. Which, oddly enough, is exactly what Mr. Smedley related to him.

They weren't the only ones who'd left, scurrying away in the middle of the night. Other people had also complained of hearing music when the stereo had been turned off and lights coming on after they'd left a room. The scarier details included sudden drops in temperature in a room, doors opening and closing by themselves, and one hysterical older woman swore she saw books flying off the library shelves. That had been about a year ago. No one else had occupied the house since last summer and that family had beaten the record by staying a two full months. Bill was glad he could tell his wife that she hadn't been singled out for a haunting, maybe alleviating some of her fear. But, he wisely decided to leave out the part about flying books when talking to her.

Bill listened with great interest, leaning forward in the brown leather chair, and as Mr. Smedley talked, grew more intrigued and had half made up his mind to return to Grace Stone right then and there. The other half to be convinced was his wife. He would have to tread carefully when speaking to Melissa. She had really been frightened their last night at the house and he knew it might not be so easy to get her to return.

All in all, Mr. Smedley had been pretty understanding, told him since he'd paid in advance to keep the keys as long as he liked, to take his time to think things over before removing his belongings. Then he said he would have to place a call to Mr. Martucci, explain it all to him, and then they would proceed from there.

Bill gave him his room number at the Days Inn, he'd already given him the number to his new office downtown, thanked him for his time and for being understanding about the house, shook his limp hand and left.

That was three days ago.

He and Melissa were now having dinner at Ryan's Steakhouse on East 21st Street. The Days Inn was in a good location, if you wanted to spend your time in Tulsa gorging yourself. Memorial Drive and the surrounding area boasted more restaurants, fast-food joints, and Chinese take-outs than Bill could count. They had chosen a different restaurant each evening. Tonight it was Ryan's turn to feed them and take their money.

Bill was a steak and potatoes man and had ordered a rib-eye steak in the checkout line before being seated by a blond waitress in her early twenties. Her short black dress was cleanly pressed, with a nametag placed above her left breast that confirmed her name as Julie.

He'd spent the day at his office, getting the furniture arranged just the way he liked it, setting up his computer, and meeting the other employees. So, by the time he'd returned to the motel, showered and dressed for dinner, and had collected Melissa, he was famished.

While Bill waited for his steak to arrive, Melissa picked up her plate and headed for the buffet. The selections were mouth-watering, no way to sample them all but she finally decided on the most filling. She heaped her plate with roast beef, creamed potatoes, and sweet carrots, and returned to their table, her plate of food leaving a steam-trail behind her. She hoped she'd have room for one of the restaurant's delicious desserts; knowing she would regret it later as it settled around her already generous hips and thighs.

"Bill, have you decided what we're going to do? It's getting old living out of our suitcases. We need a place to live." She sliced a piece of roast beef, added a small carrot, dipped both of these in her creamed potatoes and carried the fork to her mouth.

"I understand how you feel, believe me." Bill looked over her shoulders, grinned broadly and rubbed his hands together. Weaving in and out of the tables was Julie, laden with a large plate bearing his rib eye.

She placed it before him. "I hope it's too your satisfaction. Enjoy your meal." Julie's smiled was pasted on, having to say these same words many times to other diners.

"Thank you, and I'm sure I will," Bill said. As soon as the waitress' back was turned he dove into his steak with gusto. It was juicy, medium well done and perfect. Just the way he liked it. He almost didn't hear his wife speaking to him.

"I checked with the answering service today. I got a position at St. Francis Hospital. They were impressed with my résumé and my references and I'll be rotated between the ER and the floor. They said I could start in two weeks, day shift. Also, the mechanic said my car wouldn't be ready for a few more days. They had to order a part." Melissa paused to take a drink of her iced-tea. "So, what have you got in mind about our living arrangements? I'm getting bored spending most of my day in our motel room."

Bill took careful consideration before answering. He chewed thoughtfully and took a slow sip of his Coke. *Well*, he thought, *might as well get it over with*. Bill knew he would have to tread carefully but not beat about the bush. If he ham-hawed around Melissa would grow impatient. Working as an ER nurse trained her for quick thinking and judgment, and she was fast on her feet. She was not the beat-about-the-bush type, but still, he needed to word this carefully.

"Honey, I've been thinking. The things going on in that house have really intrigued me. Working for a publishing company I've read a lot of manuscripts. You'd be surprised at how many are filled with extraordinary circumstances and strange phenomena. We've even published a book documenting true cases of the unexplained and the supernatural."

Melissa carefully lowered her fork. She didn't like where this may be going.

Bill continued between bites. "We have a great opportunity here to investigate something that's truly remarkable. This is something I've only read about but never experienced. I'd like to know more, first hand." He looked hopefully at his wife. But her tightly drawn mouth and the crease between those intense green eyes didn't offer him much hope.

"Oh God, Bill. Tell me you're not suggesting we go back." Melissa shuddered. "These last few nights have been the best sleep I've had in over a week. I admit I love the house, but it freaks me out." She angrily shoved a fork full of creamed potatoes into her mouth, the metal tines clinking against her small white teeth.

"Look, I know you're frightened of the place but in all honesty did you at any time feel threatened? Before you answer me, think about it. Were you ever in fear for your life? Did anything dangerous occur when you were alone?" Bill kept his gaze on her lightly freckled face; his optimistic blue eyes sparkled in the restaurant's lighting.

"No." Melissa held up her hand before he could respond. "But that doesn't mean it couldn't happen. Maybe we just hadn't been there long enough. And you're forgetting what I saw in the mirror." She leaned forward and lowered her voice. "Bill, that stuff just scares the crap out of me. I don't know how you can sit here and consider returning." She leaned back in her seat; glancing around at the other diners, making sure no one could overhear this ludicrous conversation.

"All I'm asking for is a chance to study the goings on at Grace Stone. I've paid for us to live there and we have five months left on the lease. I promise I won't let anything happen to you." Mr. Smedley had informed him the day before when he'd called Bill at his office that Mr. Martucci agreed to refund his money. It was a relief to Bill to know he could get his money back if he wanted it, and it gave him the freedom to choose to stay at Grace Stone if he could convince Melissa to return. He'd thanked Mr. Smedley for his help, silently thanked Mr. Martucci for being generous, and promised to get back with him tomorrow. He had one night to talk his wife into moving back into the house.

Studying his wife's face, he could almost envision the gears turning behind those piercing green eyes as she thought it over.

Melissa looked down at her half eaten dinner. Being away from the house and living in more normal circumstances (as normal as motel living could be) had lessened her fear somewhat but she still had misgivings about the place. She was still afraid to go back, but Bill seemed intent on making the acquaintance of a ghost. He was positively glowing with the idea. He reminded of her a child anticipating a trip to Disney World. *Yeah*, Melissa thought, *The Haunted Mansion being the main attraction.* She sighed. *I know I'll probably hate myself in the morning.*

"Okay, Bill. You win," she relented.

Bill exhaled. He didn't know he'd been holding his breath until she spoke.

"But, I have a condition."

"Sure, Moppet. Anything you want." Bill reached across the table to take her hand. This had been easier than he'd anticipated. She could name her terms. He would agree to anything she wanted as long as it put him back inside Grace Stone Manor.

"It'll have to be for only two weeks, until I start work at the hospital. I won't sleep well there and I need to rest when I return to work. That should be plenty enough time for you to do whatever you're planning, make contact, or whatever it is you're wantin' to do. And, promise me that you won't leave me alone."

"I think I can manage a week or two away from the office. I can have them send me manuscripts over the Internet to my PC at the house. I'll tell them there are a few problems with the house—"

"That's an understatement." Melissa snorted.

"—That," Bill finished, "need fixing. The old boss, Mr. Jensen, won't mind. He likes me." At this point, he jumped up from the table to kiss her on the cheek. "Thanks, hon. I know this was a difficult decision for you and I promise I won't leave your side, not for a moment." Bill was beaming. "I've read that the reason sometimes a place is haunted is because a person has unfinished business and died suddenly. Who knows, maybe there's a mystery here that needs solving."

Melissa's laugh floated across the table. "Okay, Scooby-Doo, heel."

"Ah, come on. It'll be interesting, you'll see. And which do you prefer to be as my sidekick? Daphne or Thelma?"

She shook her coppery curls. "Bill, you're nuts. But okay, I guess Thelma. Daphne is pretty but doesn't have a brain in her head. I'd rather have my wits." She considered what just came out of her mouth and made a correction, speaking more to herself than to Bill, "I guess I'm a Daphne after all. I don't have a brain in *my* head, either. I just agreed to return to Hell House."

Bill finished his meal with renewed vigor and didn't notice Melissa only picking at hers. She'd suddenly lost her appetite and her stomach was doing strange flip-flops.

That ghostly apparition that had showed itself to her in the mirror was slowly replaying over in her mind. It gave her the chills and made her want to cry. She'd never been terrified of anything in her life, but that night she'd thought she was going to die. Whatever had been reaching out to her seemed to want to consume her and bolting from the bathroom had been her only choice to keep her sanity. Hanging around to see what it would have developed into she was sure would have driven her insane. She wasn't positive that her decision to return to the house wasn't proof that she wasn't already losing her mind. She toyed with her food, feeling sick, until Bill was ready to go.

Back at their motel, Melissa showered slowly, letting the hot water ease her frayed nerves. She had been steadily growing edgy after their conversation, wondering what terrors awaited her at Grace Stone and getting angry at the thought of losing the chance to buy a beautiful home. Dammit, she *did* like the house. Why did it have to be haunted? And just what made Bill think he could do anything about it? He was no expert in the paranormal. What if the ghost became violent? There were just too many unknown factors in what they were about to take on. Hell, they honestly didn't know the first thing about ghosts; her mind reeled at the thought.

By the time they had gotten back to their room her stomach had twisted into knots and she'd rushed to the bathroom to vomit. *Well*, she'd thought as she'd brushed her teeth, *no calories going to my hips tonight.*

After dressing in a cotton nightgown and blow-drying her hair she crept to the bed. Bill was already fast asleep and breathing deeply. She eased under the covers and reached to turn off the lamp. At least here when she shut off a light it stayed off. She snuggled close to Bill and drifted off to an uneasy sleep.

Neither of the Haydens was aware that the Martuccis and their housekeeper had arrived at Grace Stone Manor late that afternoon. They'd caught a flight out of Burbank, California that morning, made a connecting flight in Denver, Colorado and arrived in Tulsa late in the afternoon. In the pouring rain, Victor rented a stale-stone colored Buick Park Avenue, loaded up their luggage, and drove straight to the house.

Passing through the outskirts of Broken Arrow, Victor was relieved that this trip was almost over. He was in a hurry to unpack and get a bite to eat. He didn't like to eat on planes and his stomach was complaining. Belatedly, he remembered he hadn't called Frank Smedley to inform him of his visit. Well, it didn't matter. He would just pop in and see him the next day and ask him to get an electrician out to the house, pronto. And then he would make an appointment to meet with Mr. And Mrs. Hayden. If anyone could get them to buy Grace Stone, he could.

Once out on the paved country road, with the rain slowing down to a drizzle, Victor pressed the accelerator and sped on to Grace Stone Manor. He'd decided this was going to be a quick business trip. An in and out job. He didn't want Madeleine at that house any longer than was necessary. He was pushing the car at seventy, but didn't care. A quick trip, he kept telling himself, glancing at his wife; a quick trip, a deal closed, and then back to California.

Chapter 5

It was a cool, Wednesday evening when the Martuccis parked in front of Grace Stone Manor. The setting sun, peeping through spent clouds, cast shadows across the porch, and the azaleas were glistening from the late afternoon rain. It was nearing five-thirty and Victor quickly unloaded their luggage and deposited them in the foyer. He left the women standing there with the luggage and parked the car in the garage located on the left side of the house. The old garage had been torn down and replaced by Madeleine's uncle over twenty years ago and painted yellow to match the house. Victor cast a disapproving eye at the chipped and peeling paint. It would need a fresh coat.

Victor entered the back yard through the white picket-fence gate and carefully made his way across the flagstones to the patio. The ground was soggy and he didn't want to ruin his expensive shoes. He grimaced in disgust at how tall the grass had grown and was glad to finally reach the patio floor.

He entered the mudroom using his key and let himself into the darkening kitchen. Even though Madeleine's Uncle Samuel had renovated much of the house in the late seventies, the kitchen retained much of its earlier décor. The glass-front cabinets and flooring were made of oak but had been refinished, and Samuel had wisely kept the cooking island, but had improved it. The top was made of marble with a sink stationed in the middle and burners to the left. There was a large cutting board near the stainless steel sink and a wooden knife holder filled with every shape and size tool of destruction a woman would need to cut and gouge meat and vegetables into something edible. This was not Victor's favorite room in any house. He liked good food but didn't want to know how it came to be, he just wanted it on the table. Cabinets and drawers were built into the island and hanging above it were various sized copper pots and pans.

Victor firmly closed the back door and gritted his teeth when the loose windowpanes rattled. That, he decided, would have to be fixed before someone shut the door too hard and broke out the glass. The house and grounds were in need of attention. It had been seventeen years since his last visit and he had no way of knowing it was in this condition. Smedley was obviously inefficient at taking care of the property and Victor may have to find someone else to fill his shoes if the Haydens didn't buy the house.

He pocketed his keys and wiped his feet on the mat, giving the kitchen a cursory glance. On his right, past the long counter, were a stainless steel stove and refrigerator. To the left of the refrigerator the door to the large pantry was standing open. Just inside the pantry, to the right, he remembered, were the stairs to the basement.

On the other side of the cooking island were a wooden table and four chairs. To his left were a deepfreeze, a small broom closet, and a tall cupboard.

In the dusky gloom he could see that the doors to the cabinets over the counter and the cupboard were hanging wide open and a few of the utensil drawers yawned in the gathering darkness. Just what *did* the Haydens pack when they'd left so suddenly? Pork-n-beans and a can opener? Is that what they'd ransacked the kitchen for?

The gaping cabinets gave him a creepy feeling of abandonment. Victor shrugged his shoulders to shake off the feeling and flicked on the light switch near the back door.

He strode across the oaken floor quickly and made his way to a wooden swinging door. He pushed through it and entered a small room that was more like a small hallway. He flicked on the switch. A single light fixture overhead buzzed a few seconds then remained on. *I'll definitely call an electrician*, he vowed. On his left was a dark and narrow staircase to the second story, on his right another swinging door into the dinning room. He continued on straight through an arched doorway and entered the main entrance hall.

The women stood waiting at the bottom of the stairs. Madeleine had turned on the chandelier lights, as it was growing darker outside, and was busy surveying the downstairs with a careful eye. She half expected it to be in a shambles as it had appeared in her dream. But, obviously the Haydens had taken care of her home; it only needed a little dusting. *It was just a dream*, she reminded herself.

She picked up the receiver of the old-fashioned black telephone at the bottom of the stairs, the dial tone buzzed in her ear. As she replaced it, the grandfather clock, nestled between two varnished tables near the living room door, rang out the half hour.

Moving past her and Maria, Victor went to the foyer to collect their luggage. He picked up Maria's large suitcase and overnight bag and looked at Madeleine, his eyebrows raised questioningly.

"Maria can use Paul's old room at top of the landing," she instructed him.

Maria made a move to retrieve her luggage from Victor but he shook his head and took a step back. "That'll be the day I let a woman pack her belongings up a flight of stairs." He moved past them and ascended the carpeted stairs as Maria thanked him.

"Well, Maria. What do you think? Shall I give you a tour?" Madeleine asked.

"Yes, but could we start with the kitchen? I'd like to familiarize myself. I've heard you speak of Grace Stone and can't wait to see the rest of the house but I would really like to start with the room I'll use the most." Maria was the true housekeeper and cook. She did not feel her station in life was low; on the contrary, this was her job, one she took pride in doing well. She was fiercely devoted to the Martuccis and although they never made her feel indebted for sending her son to college, she felt indebted to them just the same and repaid them with her loyalty and service.

Madeleine led the way past the stairs, under them she pointed out a large door that led into the library. Pulling her sweater tightly about her shoulders she crossed to the opposite wall and adjusted the thermostat. The chill she'd felt outside still reached her indoors. She was grateful it had stopped raining.

They passed through the arched doorway that Victor had emerged from and she pointed out to Maria the old servants' staircase and the door into the dinning room. Maria knew that the staircase was intended to save the servants time and energy when traversing back and forth. There was one like it in the Martucci's home, only not so dark and forbidding. She took note of a light-switch near the stairs and was thankful Madeleine's grandfather had the foresight to install lighting for the servants he'd employed.

They moved on through the swinging door.

Madeleine gasped when she saw the kitchen and immediately began shutting the opened doors and shoving in the drawers. It reminded her all too much of her dream. Closing the last cabinet door, she inhaled deeply to calm herself. It wouldn't do to show Maria how fragile her nerves had become in the last forty-eight hours.

Pasting a smile on her face she turned and led the housekeeper out the back door to the mudroom. With its concrete flooring, clay sinks and wooden tables for potting flowers, it wrought a deep sense of nostalgia inside her. She and Skye had played here; sometimes it became their veterinary office and they imagined themselves as doctors, bandaging the hapless, mewling kittens they played with. She smiled momentarily at the childhood memory then shook it off.

Here in the mudroom there was also a small bathroom that had first been installed in the thirties and later remodeled. It contained just a commode and a sink with a small chipped mirror. Madeleine gazed about the dirty mudroom; there were still old bags of potting soil and gardening tools lying about. Madeleine decided that since she was here she might as well do a little work out in the back garden one day this week.

Back in the kitchen, Maria admired the cozy pantry. It was well lighted and the tile floor gleamed with wax. A new washer and dryer were placed at the back of the room under a shelf still baring laundry soap and fabric softener. A folded ironing board was carefully leaning against the wall. *This must belong to the Hayden's*, she thought. There were shelves for storing can goods along the walls and a door to the basement. This she ignored and returned to the kitchen. No need for her to enter the basement since she would be doing the laundry in the pantry.

Walking past the double-oven stove she ran her fingertips over the counter top and the cooking island. For having been remodeled it still possessed the charm of another era. The appliances were the only modern things in this lovely kitchen. She decided she would like cooking here; it had a homey feel to it. The Martucci's kitchen in Pasadena was completely modern, almost sterile.

The cabinets were filled with dishes, some Madeleine recognized as belonging to her family, left here from summer vacations, and the rest, she guessed, belonged to the Hayden's. Her grandmother's china had been passed on to her a few years ago and was proudly displayed in a mahogany cabinet in her dining room back home.

She opened the huge refrigerator door and was mildly surprised to find it full of food. It had only been a few days since the Haydens had left; the food had not yet begun to spoil. There were only a few items she would need to buy, like milk and eggs and maybe some fresh vegetables; she made a mental note to shop tomorrow.

The freezer contained a few packages of steaks and pork chops, several bags of frozen vegetables and a box of vanilla ice cream. She would definitely need to buy ground meat and boneless, skinless chicken breast, and she mustn't forget Victor's pasta. First thing in the morning she would make a list and ride with him into town.

It would be nice to do the shopping instead of sending Maria. Madeleine rarely did the shopping at home. Sending Maria was out of the question anyway. Although she knew Pasadena like the back of her hand Maria had never been to Tulsa before. Maria had never left California nor rode in a plane either. Life at this moment was filled with many firsts for her housekeeper. She would need some time to adjust being here. She didn't want to overwhelm her with the shopping *and* the housekeeping in a strange place and decided it would be better if Maria stayed behind tomorrow and started on the cleaning.

"Well, shall we go upstairs? I'll show you your room."

"Yes, Miss Mattie. I'd like to unpack and get settled in." There would be plenty of time later the see the rest of the downstairs rooms. Passing through the swinging door Maria turned off the kitchen light.

Madeleine flicked the switch near the dark staircase and a single bulb hanging from the ceiling halfway up and around the corner cast eerie shadows down at their feet.

Maria was a little daunted by the poor lighting. A slight frown creased her dark eyebrows and a look of uncertainty passed over her deep-toned features as she followed Madeleine. The steps were very narrow, uncarpeted and in need of sweeping. She doubted two people could pass each other coming and going. *Were servants midgets in the thirties,* she wondered.

Maria guessed they had been used very little over the years; no one had servants these days in this area of the world, only housekeepers or cooks like she. From the looks of the dirty stairs this house hadn't seen a housekeeper for quite some time. She figured the people who had rented this house had only kept the service area clean. Why clean what you don't use and don't see? Or perhaps Mrs. Hayden just hadn't had the time. Well, Maria was here now and she would change that starting tomorrow.

Madeleine opened a small wooden door and they walked out onto the upstairs landing. For a fleeting moment worry sharpened her small features as her blue eyes darted left and right expecting to see dark slithering shadows on the walls but, the oaken panels were waxed to a high polished sheen and the light fixtures lining the walls were blazing; Victor having turned them on. She reminded herself once more that it had only been a bad dream and to stop being a ninny.

"Paul's old bedroom is the second door down." She gestured to Maria with her hand and then led the way. The door to the old playroom was closed. Madeleine couldn't suppress the shudder that rose from her spine and passed through her small shoulders. She hurried past the door.

"Miss, Mattie, it's a lovely older home. I love the woodwork. It has genteel class." Her Spanish accent was thick with appreciation. Maria slid her plump fingers along the wall, taking in the wainscoting and warm wood boarders, her brown eyes missing nothing. The banister was carved in intricate designs and curved down the red-carpeted staircase. Following it back up with her eyes she glanced at the chandelier and wondered how in the world she was supposed to dust it. And dust it she would just as soon as she learned how to lower it. It was going to be a pleasure cleaning this house.

Realizing she was lingering, she quickly caught up with Madeleine, her footfalls soft on the brocaded runners lining the hall, and entered the room that was to be hers for the next week or so. Looking around she decided it wasn't a very fancy room but it had lovely oak furniture. A full-sized four-poster bed was to her left and she was pleased to see a large cedar chest resting at the foot. The lid was raised but there was nothing inside it. There were a chest of drawers, a dresser, night stands on either side of the bed with antique lamps, and a writing desk placed under one of the windows. But she was sad to see the walls barren, naked without paintings or personal pictures to make it homey.

There was an old steam heater against the right hand wall near the chest of drawers. She knew it was no longer in use since the central heating and air conditioning had been installed years ago. Madeleine had told her it had been left there for the décor during one of her reminiscing phases. Her uncle had wanted modern conveniences without destroying the original look and feel of his parents' home. Maria readily agreed wholeheartedly with his decision to do so and inwardly approved.

"Well, best to get unpacked now. I'll prepare us a quick meal when I'm finished. You must be hungry and I know Mr. Martucci is probably famished." Maria hefted her suitcase onto the bed and realized it as bare as the walls. She also noticed that Madeleine was staring out a window, preoccupied. She had been distant throughout most of their trip as well and Maria wondered what was worrying her.

"Miss Mattie?"

"Oh. I'm sorry, Maria." Madeleine turned to face her. "I was wool-gathering. Goodness, me!" she exclaimed, taking in the bare mattress. "You have no linens." She hurried to the door, a little flustered, talking rapidly; her eyes had not missed the opened trunk. "I'll get you some from the linen closet. It's just down the hall, the second door after you turn. I'll be right back." Then she was gone.

Maria unzipped her suitcase and the first thing she unpacked was an eight-by-ten framed photo of Carlos. Her son's friend at college had taken it between classes. Leaning against a tree, his handsome dark features were crinkled into a smile, his light-brown eyes twinkling; obviously gazing at something or someone that he found pleasing beyond his friend's shoulder. *Probably a young lady*, Maria thought. *So much like his father.* This she set on the nightstand along with a framed photo of herself and her husband, and went to work putting away her clothes.

Nearing the end of the hall, Madeleine's heart picked up a beat. Her palms were perspiring, and her face was flushed. She averted her eyes and quickly passed the attic door, turning down the hall to the linen closet.

A voice whispered, *"that's the place, isn't it, Mattie?"*

She paused, but only for a second, screwing her eyes up tight to blot out the voice taunting her, and then moved on.

As Madeleine neared the linen closet she saw Victor exiting Skye's room. *Really*, she thought, *I've got to stop thinking of it as her room.* It hadn't been her cousin's room for over twenty years. But try as she might, she just couldn't see it as her room too, or worse, as a guest room. Skye had actually lived in it; Madeleine had only borrowed it from time to time.

Victor's face wore a scowl as he approached her and she wondered what could be wrong. She stood with her hand on the linen closet knob and waited as he strode purposely toward her, short legs taking long strides, his tie swaying side to side.

"Well, it looks as though we'll be sleeping under the heavens." Victor gestured behind him with a hooked thumb. The walls of Skye's room had been left untouched at Madeleine's insistence. "The wonderful Haydens left most of their things in the master bedroom. There are clothes and shoes lying everywhere. It looks as if one of your famous Oklahoma tornados swept through it. And you should see the bathroom."

Madeleine leaned against the door. She blinked slowly and then asked, "What's wrong with the bathroom?" She was steadily growing a little uneasy. Something was prickling the back of her neck. She rubbed it and shrugged her shoulders.

Victor hitched his suit-pants up around his wide girth and rested his hairy knuckles on his hips. "Everything is covered in drop cloths and the mirror is covered with brown paper and tape. There are a couple of buckets of paint on the floor and a few paintbrushes lying around with dried yellow paint on them."

Madeleine sighed with relief. She thought he was going to tell her the room had been ransacked and left in a shambles. As for the clothes left scattered around, she realized some people just weren't as neat as she. She had been untidy as a teenager but finally out grew it, maybe some people never did. Maybe the Haydens kept the house in order but liked their personal room disorganized. Who knows? She had to stop comparing everything to her dream.

"Victor, I had specified to Mr. Smedley a long time ago I did not want anyone doing anything to this house unless they were going to buy it. I suppose he gave them permission to paint the bathroom since they paid in advance with the intention of buying. I see nothing wrong in painting the bathroom. Did you say yellow paint?"

"Yes, dear, I did."

"Well, I think that's a lovely idea. It'll match the outside of the house as well as brighten the room. And they had the foresight to cover everything."

"And what if they decide not to buy the house?" Victor lifted his eyebrows in speculation.

"Then I'll finish painting it myself."

Madeleine sighed.

"Really, Victor. It's not that big of a deal. But, I'll have to see it later." Madeleine turned to open the closet door. "Right now I must get some linens for Maria's bed."

As she turned the knob the door flew open, forcing her to take a step back as a rush of cold air blasted her face, flinging her hair straight back. She had no time to react for just as quickly as it had come it was gone, leaving her and Victor both momentarily stunned. The door to the back staircase slammed shut in the draft's wake.

Madeleine nervously ran her fingers through her hair and glanced at Victor. "My, my. What was that?" Her voice twittered in her ears and sounded too high in pitch.

"That, my dear wife, was one of those drafts people have been complaining about." He peered into the dark closet, fumbled for the switch and flicked it on. Instantly it sizzled and popped and went dark. "And here we have a wiring problem. Ghosts, indeed." He chuckled. "I'll be seeing Smedley in the morning and I'll find an electrician. I'll replace the bulb tomorrow."

He sauntered back toward the bedroom. Continuing onward, sidestepping down the hall he said, "Oh, we also need linens for our bed. I'm going to unpack. Is there any food in the kitchen?" Seeing Madeleine nod he added, "I hope Maria can whip up something fast to eat. I'm starving." Then he disappeared through the door.

A slanted shaft of light from the hall reached into the closet, giving Madeleine just enough light to find sheets, pillowcases and pillows, and a blanket for Maria. Farther back into the closet it was dark and shadowy, and even though she had never had a fear of the dark, she would go no further than she could see. That blast of cold air had unnerved her. In fact, all the little things she'd seen out of place so far had her wondering if her dream had been a sort of premonition. If that were true, then the worst was yet to come.

"Get a grip," she muttered to herself, "You're not a psychic," and reached inside the closet. Her hands trembled as she collected the bedding for her housekeeper and she quickly retreated to the fully lighted hall, shutting the door with her foot. She chided herself for being foolish but hurried anyway to Maria's bedroom.

Forty-five minutes later, they were all seated at the wooden table in the kitchen. There had been enough eggs and cheese for Maria to quickly whip up some omelets and she'd brewed some coffee. Victor grumbled a little about eating breakfast food for dinner and in the kitchen, no less, but the rumblings in his stomach wouldn't wait for a dining room meal. He'd wolfed down his omelet before the women had half way eaten theirs and Maria jumped up to place another omelet on his plate that she'd already prepared. She wished she could have cooked something else but on such short notice it was the best she could do.

Her mind preoccupied with old thoughts, Madeleine ate most of her omelet and drank one cup of coffee, thanked Maria, and then excused herself to wander through the downstairs rooms.

Leaving the kitchen she turned right and went through the swinging door into the dining room. She flicked the light switch near the door and the room burst with light. Every wall fixture glowed softly against the paneled walls, and the chandelier hanging above the table blazed in glory. The matching sideboard and china cabinet had been polished to a soft shine.

Moving toward the majestic dining table she slowly reached out tentative fingers to lightly brush the smooth finish. In her mind's eye she saw her family seated among the ten high-backed chairs. Her Uncle Samuel was seated at the far end, the head of the table, where, she imagined, her grandfather used to sit. Behind him, the eight-foot tall window was wide open, the lace curtains billowing in a warm breeze. Madeleine could almost smell the scent of the new-mown hay that had been baled that day.

Laughter echoed in her ears from long ago, she and Skye regaling their parents with the story of Paul falling off his pony as they'd galloped across the pasture, hurrying home for dinner. She remembered Skye's waist-length dark hair flying out behind her as her buckskin horse pounded up toward the barn, his nostrils flaring. By the age of ten they were both riding horses, but being only eight, Paul still rode a welsh pony. Madeleine had stopped to let him ride double with her, while his pony trotted on up to the barn alone. After getting over the initial shock of being dumped, Paul giggled the rest of the way home and later joined in the laughter at the table, enjoying the attention he was getting.

Slowly, the scent of that summer day faded with the breeze as the late afternoon sunlight changed back into the glare of the chandelier. Her parents' and Aunt and Uncle's forms seated at the table diminished before her eyes and the empty chairs returned to her vision. The last one to fade away was Skye; her dark head flung back, eyes squinted shut, small, white, and slightly protruding teeth flashing in a hearty laugh. Three years later she had gotten braces to correct her over-bite.

Madeleine hastily wiped a tear off her cheek, opened the sliding oak panels and entered the dark living room. By the light spilling from the dining room she located a lamp on a low table to her left.

She surveyed her surroundings in the lamp's soft glow. On her left was the Hayden's entertainment center. The time, 7:23 p.m., flashed neon green on the stereo's face. Madeleine made her way to the large cream-colored sectional sofa placed in front of the fireplace. A low glass-topped table rested on the Oriental rug, supporting a vase of dying flowers; no one had been here for several days to freshen the water. Madeleine silently approved Mrs. Hayden's taste in furniture. The burgundy and cream drapes covering the tall windows on either side of the fireplace and at the opposite end of the room were drawn, keeping out the night pushing against the panes.

Madeleine strolled to the opened oak paneled doors to the entry hall and then suddenly stopped dead in her tracks. The back of her neck prickled ominously and a low hissing sound emanated from behind her. Her heart lurched in her chest and adrenalin rushed to her head, causing a roaring in her ears. She stood trembling, afraid to turn around. Her brain was working furiously trying to analyze the sound, her fear making her think the worst. Her first thought was snakes. This was the country and they'd been known to come inside.

Her next thought was more frightening.

Her imagination running wild, she pictured those dark slithering things from her dream, snaking around her ankles, cold and slippery. Her stomach felt icy and her legs trembled.

Madeleine Martucci! Get a friggin' grip!

She gritted her teeth and clenched her small fists. Gaining a measure of control she turned to face her fear.

Her blue eyes squinted, following the direction of the noise. To her right, near the lamp she'd left burning, the stereo had come to life. As she edged closer she could make out the digital numbers running larger then smaller, searching through the static. When it finally settled on a station she could hear music playing softly through the speakers.

Cautiously, drawing near the entertainment center, she played her fingers over the face of the stereo, her pink cupid-bow lips turning up at the corners.

One of Skye's favorite tunes drifted toward Madeleine, one of many her cousin had learned to play on the piano. Frank Mills' "Music Box Dancer" sounded as if it were being played on a tiny piano, or rather a small music box for which it was appropriately titled. Madeleine hadn't heard it for many years, it had always brought her pain, but now, here in this room, in this house, it filled her with warmth. How could this frighten anyone? Then an old memory slammed her between the eyes.

She jerked, as if stung by a bolt of lightening, remembering once again, this happening before. Was it possible? Could it be? Eyes brimming with unshed tears; she spun around.

"Skye?" her voice quivered. But the only answer she received was the sudden chill in the air, and the rustling of cloth.

Madeleine's smile faltered, and then completely fell as a cold breeze blew across the room, rustling the drapes and the dried out flowers in the vase, overturning it. It tinkled on the glass-top table then rolled onto the floor. Her breath caught in her throat, as the frigid gust played with her hair, blond stands whipping her cheeks, causing her to shiver. She crossed her arms, hugging her chest. Her breath came out in a fog.

This didn't feel right. There was evilness in that cold air as it touched the nape of her neck, icy fingers caressing her, just like they had in her nightmare.

She wanted to run but her legs wouldn't obey her commands and there was a lump in her throat. She couldn't call out to Victor or Maria. She stood frozen as those icy fingers made the descent to the small of her back. There was something frighteningly familiar about that cold touch, something horrible, and not because of the nightmare she'd had. It carried with it a portent of disaster and death, and of some deeply buried memory.

Cold claws dug at the recesses of her mind, digging at the memory she'd buried deep in darkness. She gasped in fear, clenching her teeth, willing it to stay buried, nailing shut the coffin of her mind.

Madeleine shook uncontrollably, willing herself to move. She felt dirty, violated. It was pure evil. This had to stop, she *must* move! Whatever was touching her wasn't going to sully her one second more!

Come on! Move!

With tremendous effort she took one small step, pushing against a cold, unseen force.

Suddenly, she was released. It was as if she had been held back by a giant rubber band, stretched taut and quickly snapped. She stumbled and pitched forward, but kept her balance. Whatever had gripped her had turned her loose with her force of will to move.

Behind her, the stereo crackled and hissed and then went dead. She twisted around to face it. The clock still flashed 7:23 p.m. as if no time had passed at all.

The air was still, the temperature back to normal; still yet, she shook, rubbing her arms, the chill going deeper than her skin.

In the silence that followed she thought she heard someone crying, and then it too was gone. She fought to silence her chattering teeth and took a slow, steadying breath, exhaling loudly. Out in the hall the grandfather clock informed her it was now seven-thirty. Only seven minutes had passed since she'd first entered the living room.

It had seemed eternal.

Madeleine took one step and then ran from the living room, not bothering to turn off the lamp or the dining room lights. She crossed the entry hall and rushed up the stairs, only slowing her pace when she reached the landing.

She had never been so frightened in all her life, except in her nightmares. Was this the horror those other people were talking about? Was this the reason they ran off in the middle of the night? She could now understand their feelings. Something evil was lurking here, she had no doubt of that.

Maybe her dream *had* been a warning.

Yes, Madeleine, and maybe you're losing your mind again? The voice inside her head taunted her.

"NO! No, I didn't imagine it! Something evil touched me!" she answered aloud. Something old . . . an evil she suddenly felt sure she had felt before. But that was impossible. She would have remembered.

Are you sure? The voice whispered.

She stifled a sob as she neared the bedroom. She heard water running and knew Victor was in the shower but she didn't want him to hear her crying. Her fear slowly ebbing, knowing Victor was near, she stood out in the hall, trying to understand what was going on.

She had never experienced anything like this before. Had she? This darkness? No, that was just a dream! Only a dream. Everything in her life was well ordered and perfect, full of light, love and happiness. Yes, yes it was perfect.

Except for . . . NO! I won't think about that. This is different. I didn't imagine what just happened down there. It was real!

There was definitely something wrong with her family's home, the home she'd loved as a child, filled with so many memories of the people she had cherished and lost. It was heartbreaking. She had to do something to make it right again.

For a brief instant a memory pushed at her mind telling her that she knew what to do. But it was gone in a blink of an eye.

What could she do? She hadn't a clue as to what was going on here or why. But, it must have been happening for a long time; all those years and all those tenants that refused to stay was proof of that.

At first, when the radio had come on, she thought it might be Skye reaching out to her. Just like she believed she had all those years ago. She'd missed her so much. Losing Skye at fifteen had been a cruel blow, almost as cruel as losing her baby. She and Skye had been more than cousins; to each other one was the sister the other never had. But this evil unseen presence was crueler. It had tried to trick her. And it had touched her. She shook her clothes as if to remove the evil residue she imagined was still clinging to her.

What was she to do? She was alone. Victor would be no help. He didn't believe in the supernatural and wouldn't even want to discuss it. He would think she had gone mad, needing therapy again. And Maria? That was out of the question. Maria was a good woman, a trusted housekeeper, but she couldn't burden her with this. Besides, she didn't think Maria would believe her. She and Victor both would probably think she was just holding on to this old house, emotionally tied to it, not wanting to let it go. And that was partly true. It was hard to say goodbye and she'd come here to do just that. Had come to say goodbye to Skye and to her little Antonia. But she hadn't counted on this evil presence. She didn't know what she was going to do, but she silently vowed to find a way and hoped that in the process she wouldn't lose her mind. She must remain strong.

Standing at the door, she looked down the lighted hallway. At one time it was warm and inviting but now it didn't seem the same. What was wandering down these halls? What was this darkness dwelling here? She wondered if that evil thing was watching her now, waiting to soil her with its cold black touch.

She trembled.

Quickly, she pushed open the bedroom door, seeking safety with Victor, and then paused, cautiously stepping partway back into the hall.

Footsteps were ascending the servants' stairway, a purposeful thump on each tread. Was it coming for her again?

Holding her breath, picturing a blackness that no night ever conceived, she shook uncontrollably, clinging to the doorjamb.

The wooden door to the stairs was suddenly flung back on its hinges, and . . . Maria entered the hall.

Air gushed out of Madeleine's lungs as she sagged against the doorframe.

"*Buenas noches*, Miss Mattie." Maria called out, shutting the stairway door behind her.

Madeleine lifted a weary hand. "Goodnight, Maria."

Before the housekeeper's back could disappear from view, Madeleine rushed into Skye's bedroom, firmly closing the door behind her.

Out in the back garden, the ground rumbled and shook. The crickets and frogs hushed their singing and scurried off into the dense bushes. A single burst of rusty water shot out of the cracked cherub's pitcher as the fountain rocked on its foundation. It splashed back into the curved bowl, raining blood-red droplets over the side, and then was still. A hairline crack jagged across the concrete. All was quiet for some time, and then the creatures of the night resumed their nocturnal wanderings, calling out to each other.

Chapter 6

April 29, Thursday

The sun had been up and shining for over an hour when Victor, dressed in a charcoal Italian suit, white shirt, and expensive light gray silk tie, pulled up to the front steps in the rented Park Avenue. Leaving the engine idling and the heater on low to relieve the early morning chill, he entered the front door and bellowed for Madeleine to get moving.

Heels clicking on the hardwood floors, Madeleine rushed from the kitchen, trying to stuff her grocery list in a light-blue handbag she'd chosen to carry because it matched her cerulean blue skirt and jacket, and high-heels. Over her shoulder she called out to Maria. "Feel free to start anywhere in the house. There's an old Kirby vacuum upstairs in the closet for the rugs and plenty of dusting supplies as well. Mrs. Hayden must be a good housekeeper. She'd bought plenty."

Maria emerged through the swinging door, armed with a broom. "Okay, Miss Mattie. I'll find what I need."

"Madeleine, let's go." Victor strode to the door, not looking to see if she were following him. He didn't need to. Her heels did a quick tattoo as she caught up with him.

"Aye. Blissful silence." Maria murmured as the front door closed.

Dressed in her housekeepers uniform she was ready to tackle those filthy stairs. The breakfast dishes were washed and she had made sweeping the stairs her first priority. Mrs. Hayden may indeed be a good housekeeper but she had neglected the back stairs.

Whistling a Latin tune, she made her way up to the landing, switched on the staircase light and opened the door. She attacked the first step with vigor, digging long-since accumulated compressed dirt out of the corners and flinging it out to the steps below. Having raised a cloud of dust she stopped whistling to keep it out of her mouth. Humming with her lips tightly compressed she continued on to the next step and then the next.

She was so deeply involved with her task that she failed to hear the front door open and close or the sound of footsteps ascending the stairs. She had already reached the central turn and was heading down when the door above her suddenly slammed shut.

Maria paused, listening, but heard nothing else.

That was no draft.

Flowing air did not reach this dark, cramped space. Someone was in the house with her. The hair on the back of her neck bristled as it dawned on her that she was alone, in a strange house, in another state, far from home, and from anyone she knew. She was alone with an intruder in the house.

She gripped the broom handle with plump tight fists, the only weapon readily available to her, and decided that since someone upstairs had closed the door her best direction was down. If she could make it to the kitchen she could call 911 and trade her broom for a knife.

She crept down slowly, one step at a time. Her ragged breath from the dust and exertion loud in her ears. As she neared the bottom she heard footsteps treading on the hardwood floor, coming in her direction.

Forget 911 and the knife, the broom would have to do.

Raising the handle higher in her sweating and shaking fists, intending to bash the first head she saw, she rushed out into the hallway, a torrent of Spanish rolling off her lips, and came face to face with a wide-eyed, pale-skinned young woman screaming her red curly head off. Their combined high-pitched screams seemed almost loud enough to shatter the windows and blow the roof off.

When the shrill screams reached Bill upstairs he thought Melissa was having another paranormal encounter and ran for the staircase; he didn't want to miss out on anything. Besides, he'd promised he wouldn't let anything happen to her. He silently cursed himself for letting her descend alone and flew down the stairs.

"Who are you?" the women demanded in unison when they'd both ran out of breath; Melissa in English, Maria in Spanish.

Melissa recovered first enough to speak again, although her heart had yet to recover and slow it's hammering. "I'm Melissa Hayden," she said breathlessly. "I live here. Do you speak English?"

Maria slumped against the wall, the broom sliding through her fingers at her side. She'd almost brained that curly mop. Her dark skin had waxed an ashen pallor and Melissa quickly moved forward, grasping Maria by the neck and forced her head down between her knees.

"You're going to be alright. You just need to get the blood back into your face." She talked in soothing tones as her profession had taught her. "That's it. You're getting your color back now." She removed her hand and stepped back.

Maria slowly raised her head and met Melissa's concerned eyes. They were the brightest emerald green she had ever seen but she had never seen hair like that. Flaming red Shirley Temple curls framed a full-cheeked, freckled face. She was not what you'd call a beautiful woman, she decided, but cute. On her pear-shaped body were white jeans and a green t-shirt. Maria guessed she was in her late twenties.

"*Gracias.* Thank you. Yes, I speak English." Having finally found her voice she introduced herself and went on to explain why she was at Grace Stone Manor.

Behind Melissa, Maria saw a tall, athletic looking, blond-haired, blue-eyed young man striding toward them. He was dressed in khakis and white polo shirt and was grinning broadly.

After accurately accessing the situation Bill suppressed his laughter as he drew near. "Hello there. I'm Bill Hayden. I see you've already met the wife." His easy-going manner immediately put Maria at ease; he had an aura of friendliness and calmness about him as he thrust out a large hand toward her. His handshake was warm and firm and he'd greeted her like she was the 'Lady of the Manor', not the housekeeper.

"Bill, this is Maria Fuentes." Melissa made the introduction. "She's the Martucci's housekeeper." The look in her eyes said they might have a slight problem. "Mr. And Mrs. Martucci are staying in the house. So, what do we do now?"

Bill looked at Maria. "Ah, when do you expect the Martuccis back?"

"I really couldn't say, Mr. Hayden." Maria shrugged. "Mr. Martucci has gone to Pine Ridge Realtors and Miss Mattie went along to grocery shop. My best guess would be around one o'clock or a little after. Miss Mattie told me they would probably eat out for lunch."

"Please, call me Bill. We're not formal."

"Very well. And you may call me Maria."

"Bill, is all the luggage upstairs?" Melissa was clearly uncomfortable. She was fidgety, trying to tuck an unruly curl behind one ear.

"Yes, honey, it's all in the bedroom." He placed a hand on her shoulder. "It'll be all right, you'll see."

Maria looked at them in turn and realized the awkwardness in their returning to the house unannounced. She knew her employers were not expecting them, Madeleine would have told her so.

"Well, if you'll excuse us, Maria, we have some unpacking to do. It was nice to meet you. Sorry, I frightened you." Melissa plucked at Bill's arm, heading back toward the stairs. He turned to follow.

On the way up Melissa leaned close and whispered in hushed tones; Maria could just make out her saying, "Bill, this is kinda embarrassing. I mean, God. I left our bedroom in a mess. I'm sure they've seen it. They've brought their housekeeper, for Pete's sake." Then she could hear no more as their footsteps retreated.

Now that the excitement was over, Maria grabbed her broom leaning against the wall and trekked back up the shadowy staircase. Things were going to get interesting around here and she was glad she could watch from the sidelines. She was the housekeeper, a spectator, not a player. As she resumed her sweeping she mentally calculated two more for meals in her menu.

Upstairs, Bill and Melissa continued their conversation, making their way to the master bedroom. Melissa glanced around nervously. It had been nearly a week since that awful night but she hadn't forgotten a minute of it. She cut her eyes to the right as they passed the bathroom door; it was bright and sunny, not dark and foreboding, as she'd remembered it. She wished she wasn't so nervous.

"Bill, are we gonna be allowed to stay, now that the owners are here?" she asked.

"I don't see why not. We haven't received a refund on our lease, so technically we have every right to be here. We'll just have to wait and see what happens when they return." Bill had decided not to inform her that he hadn't asked for a refund. Melissa would vehemently insist on getting it. For now, his lease was still in effect and if he could solve the haunting mystery of this house she would no longer be afraid to live here and he could still purchase it. That was the plan, anyway.

Melissa surveyed their sunny-bright bedroom with a critical and disbelieving eye as they entered through the doorway. "I can't believe I did this," she murmured to herself. God, what a disaster. And the owners of Grace Stone had seen the destruction she'd wrought in this lovely room.

She immediately began gathering up the shoes and clothes and putting them away. This was not like her at all. She was going to have to explain, but how? Tell them she had been frightened half out of her mind by a ghost? They would think she was crazy. She wished now she hadn't agreed to return.

Bill, on the other hand, was completely at ease. He calmly and methodically unpacked his belongings and then made himself comfortable in one of the high winged-back, overstuffed chairs angled in front of the large fireplace. Even unlit it had its charm. In fact the entire room was charming. The dark varnished wood panels were warm, the thick carpet a dark red, almost maroon, and the opened matching drapes had a fine flowered design etched with a gold thread that accented the chairs placed before the fireplace.

Bill's thoughtful gaze rested on a large pastel painting hanging above the mantel, depicting Grace Stone Manor as it had looked in the late thirties or early forties. The lane to the house had been only dirt back then but the house must have always been painted a bright yellow, sans the black shutters. He guessed those were added later and that the picture must have been painted in the summer for the few bushes lining the porch had been in full bloom even though they were much smaller than the ones now growing below the balcony.

He could just make out the figure of a young woman seated on a porch swing. Must have been Mrs. Fitzgerald. Her hair was dark and except for a soft curl hugging her brown cheek, the one exposed to the painter, it was swept back and loosely piled on top of her head. Even though she was depicted from a distance he could still make out the graceful lines of her lovely face and realized she was of Indian ancestry but he had no idea which tribe. Her mid-length dress and lace gloves were in keeping with the late nineteen-thirties.

The painting had hung above the mantle for more than sixty years. No one had ever bothered to take it down and store it in the attic with the rest of the Fitzgerald possessions. Bill was glad they hadn't. It belonged there. He sat staring at it, wondering what had happened between nineteen thirty-six and the present day to make this house a haunted site. Something traumatic must have occurred here during those years. But what?

According to Mr. Smedley the last of the Fitzgeralds to have actually lived here, were Samuel and Elise and their daughter, Skye. Samuel Fitzgerald, he'd told him, was the eldest son. Jacob Fitzgerald, his younger brother by two years, was Mrs. Martucci's father. There had been no daughters born to old Mr. And Mrs. Fitzgerald.

At this point, Mr. Smedley would go no further other than to say that Samuel and his wife and daughter were no longer living but would not divulge any details, only that they'd had a freak accident in June of nineteen eighty. When Bill had tried to question the realtor, he'd run into a brick wall; Mr. Smedley had been adamant in not discussing it. But he did tell Bill that Mrs. Martucci's father had passed away five years earlier, leaving Grace Stone Manor to Madeleine Martucci and her brother Paul.

Bill wondered about this tidbit of information. Here was a possible place to start. What happened to Samuel Fitzgerald and his family? What kind of freak accident had taken their lives? He only hoped that Mrs. Martucci would be willing to discuss what he knew must be a painful memory. He would have to wait for just the right moment to broach the subject and hope that she would be willing to talk.

Behind him, Melissa furiously labored to restore their bedroom to its immaculate state. Having put away her clothes, she then made up the king-sized bed and then rushed to the bathroom. Bill could hear paper tearing and cloth rustling.

He glanced back from the chair to the opened door. "What on earth are you doing?"

"I'm removing this stuff so we can use this bathroom." Arms loaded with the drop cloths she dumped them unceremoniously in a corner and then retrieved the paint cans and brushes. "I don't want to use the one down the hall. I never want to look in that mirror again. The painting will have to wait. Besides, I think the housekeeper is using that one."

"Are you about finished?"

"Yep. I just have to empty out my bag." She disappeared into the bathroom. A moment later she reemerged and stored her carrier on a shelf in the closet.

"I'd like to talk to Maria a few minutes. She might be able to tell me a few things about the history of this house. Maybe Mrs. Martucci has confided in her about her family's past." Bill's blond eyebrows bounced up and down as he asked, "Care to join me downstairs for a bit of sleuthing?"

"Well, I'm certainly not staying up here alone. Lead the way, Scooby-Doo."

Bill rose from his seat and together they left the bedroom. "Glad to see you still have a sense of humor, Thelma." He casually threw his arm over Melissa's shoulder as they strolled down the hall.

"So far so good. Can't promise you I'll be in good humor when I get scared out of my wits. And I know it's coming. It's inevitable. Just call me Shaggy when that happens, 'cause I'll be looking for a place to hide. Or better yet, call me in town. That's where I'll be." Although she joked about it, Melissa hated being frightened and was feeling a little disgusted for clinging to Bill. It was a sign of weakness. She had never felt so dependent on anyone until now. And didn't like it one bit.

Bill chuckled deep within his chest and gave her a quick squeeze. He was glad to be back. If everything went as well as he was hoping, he would be calling this house "home". Except for a ghost or two the house was great and he could picture himself living here the rest of his life, sharing this home with his wife and in the near future, their children. He kissed her squarely on the cheek and then released her to descend the stairs.

With Melissa trailing behind him, he glanced into the living room. Maria was not there so he crossed the hall to the den.

Maria was just giving an end table a final swipe with her dusting cloth and moved to clean the surface of the television when he and Melissa entered the room. Daylight was pouring through the opened drapes and through the dust Bill could see the windowpanes reflected on the screen and an eerie caricature of himself as he approached her from behind.

Maria gave the dark screen a vigorous wipe and let out a small yelp. Clutching her chest, she jumped up from her kneeling position and spun around.

"Mr. Hayden, you nearly gave this old woman a heart attack." She fanned herself with the cloth and gulped a few deep breaths, smiling nervously.

"I'm very sorry, Maria. Didn't mean to sneak up on you like that. And please, call me Bill," he told her.

"Is there something I can do for you?" Maria asked.

"As a matter of fact, I was hoping we could have a little chat. Why don't we sit down?" Bill gestured toward the green and beige plaid love seat and Melissa joined him. Maria settled into an upholstered matching chair, and nervously folded her dusting cloth.

Bill cleared his throat and began, "You must know that my wife and I plan to buy this house." Melissa's head whipped around; Bill ignored the steely green stare she was giving him. That argument would have to wait. "And," he continued, "I was wondering if you knew anything about its history. I'd greatly appreciate any information you could give me."

Maria silently digested this request. She really did not want to discuss her employer's family. It was too much like gossiping. But, perhaps just a few facts wouldn't hurt.

"Well, Mr. Hayden." She just couldn't bring herself to use his first name, it didn't seem right. "Miss Mattie's grandfather built this house in nineteen thirty-six when he married her grandmother. I believe his name was Zedediah and hers was Sarah. I'm told he made his living raising cattle and had employed many cattle-hands. There used to be an old . . . how do you say . . . um, bunkhouse. Yes, bunkhouse out in the back. It caught fire, was torn down a long time ago but Mr. Fitzgerald's cattle-hands use to sleep there. The old barn is still out there, though. He had also employed several servants. The cattle and most of the land were sold many years ago after his death . . ." Maria trailed off, not fully understanding what he was expecting to learn from her.

What became of the Fitzgeralds?" he asked.

"Um, let me see." Maria shut her eyes to recall Madeleine's words. "Oh, yes. I remember now. Mr. Fitzgerald passed away in nineteen sixty-seven. He'd had a stroke. Miss Mattie was two years old at the time." Maria fervently hoped this was all he'd wanted to know; delving deeper into Madeleine's tragic family affairs would cause her to enter that taboo zone; gossiping.

"And what about Mrs. Fitzgerald?" Bill's questioning blue eyes gently probed her brown orbs.

Maria was hesitant to answer, not because it was some deep dark family secret but because it was just plain sad. She wasn't sure Madeleine would want them to know that her grandmother had grieved so much for her dead husband that she hadn't wanted to go on living without him. Within days of Zedediah's funeral she'd passed away, upstairs, in her bed. She was only forty-eight years old. Maria decided on telling them a half-truth.

She looked away from Bill's gaze. "Um, Mrs. Fitzgerald passed away some time later. I think it might have been a bad heart or something. I'm not sure." She shrugged her shoulders, glanced down at her hands, and then at his face, but she couldn't meet his eyes.

Bill knew she wasn't telling the truth but wasn't going to press her. He had one more question to ask her but wasn't sure the answer would be forthcoming. He decided to ask it anyway. "Maria, do you know what happened to Mrs. Martucci's Aunt and Uncle and their daughter, Skye?"

From the reaction he got he might as well have slapped her in the face. Her coiffed head jerked back, air sucked through her teeth, her brown eyes darkened. Clearly she had no intention of answering. There was that same brick wall that Mr. Smedley had erected but with a few more bricks added to its thickness.

With a sinking feeling in his chest Bill knew this chat was over. What could have happened to these people that was so horrible that no one would talk about it? And how was he suppose to figure out what was going on here if no one would?

Maria rose hastily from her chair. "I'm sorry, Mr. Hayden. I really can't say more. Now, I really must get back to work." Stopping at the door she added, "I'll have lunch ready in an hour." But instead of leaving she hesitated in the doorway.

Bill stood up and waited. She seemed to be mulling over her thoughts. Then having made a decision she spoke. "I apologize for being so abrupt. It's just that I love Miss Mattie. She's lost nearly everyone close to her and I feel I would be disrespecting her by talking about the tragedies in her life. I hope you understand and do not take offence."

"No offence taken, Maria," he replied. "And I want you to know I respect you for your loyalty. I understand you're more that just a housekeeper. Mrs. Martucci is fortunate to have a friend in you." He hoped by this admission he had gained back some of her trust. For a minute there he had blown it.

There appeared the barest hint of a smile as Maria nodded and left. He figured he was somewhat back in her good graces but from now on he was going to have to tread carefully when asking questions.

"Well, that was a bust, Mr. Super-Sleuth." Melissa smirked, and then dark anger clouded her face. "And what do you mean, we're buying this house? When did *we* make that decision?"

Bill raised his hands in supplication, "Now, honey, I was gonna tell ya."

"Tell me!" Her raised eyebrows disappeared under her red curls as she glared at her husband.

"I mean, discuss it with you," Bill amended. "Honest. It's just that you were so frightened and dead-set against being here."

"You got that right."

"Ah, come on, Melissa. Didn't you love this house when we first walked in the door?"

"That was before I knew something else was already living here." Her arms shot out to encompass the room. "Bill, I don't want to buy this house, not like it is. It's haunted. It's too freaky. I agreed to spend just two weeks here so you could play ghostbuster and I don't intend to stay here any longer than that." Her chin pointed up at him defiantly, hands braced on her hips.

Melissa was in her stubborn witch mode and Bill knew it would be useless to argue with her now. Best to placate her for the time being. "I really like this house, Melissa, but okay. I know you have mixed feelings right now and don't want to buy it. But let me explain something. If we're going to be staying here I have to let the Martuccis believe we intend to buy it. Otherwise, they may not tell us anything about this house, and I need to know about everyone who lived here. So, please, for the time being just go along with me. Okay, Moppet?" Hands on her shoulders, his soft blue eyes gazing intently into her own fiery green ones, he enticed her with a boyish grin.

I wish he wouldn't look at me like that and call me by that silly pet name, Melissa thought as she tried to look away and failed. It was hard to stay mad at him when he cajoled her with those boyish blue eyes. *But if he buys this house, he's going to be one lonely man,* she sternly vowed. *He'll be single again.* Her shoulders slumped under his warm fingers; arms fell loosely at her side. "All right. I'll play along. But it's under protest."

Bill heard the gravel crunching outside as a car drove pass the front porch and receded around to the back. He glanced at his watch, 11:45. The Martuccis were early. "Well," he said to Melissa, "put on your best poker face. We're about to meet the owners of this fine haunted establishment." He was in good spirits.

Melissa was a bundle of nerves; her stomach was performing acrobatic flips.

Chapter 7

Madeleine and Victor were just coming through the back door, laden with plastic grocery bags, as Bill and Melissa entered the kitchen. Maria was busy chopping up the last of the lettuce for salad at the island, her deft hands moving quickly over the cutting board.

"Here, let me help you with those." Bill stepped forward, taking the bags out of Madeleine's hands. Little drops of perspiration had beaded on her smooth tanned forehead. She relinquished the bags gratefully. He took in her petite frame, shoulder-length blond hair softly framing her dainty features that were devoid of make-up, and kindly blue eyes. *Nice looking woman,* Bill thought. He couldn't fathom her age.

"Thank you, Mr. Hayden." Her voice was soft and slightly musical.

"Please, call me Bill." He offered his hand after setting the bags on the counter.

"I'm Madeleine Martucci, and this is my husband Victor." Her slender ringed fingers gestured toward Victor who quickly set his bags down and thrust out a beefy hand.

"Pleased to meet you, sir," Bill said, and grasped him in a firm handshake, meeting him eye to eye. Bill liked Mr. Martucci's grip; solid and commanding, a man who knows his own mind, not a nervous people pleaser like Mr. Smedley.

Victor's eyebrows rose in surprise at his greeting; he had expected a loud and hearty "Howdy" accompanied by an overly friendly slap on the back. *Well,* Victor thought, *I'll give the young man credit for having manners, despite the Okie accent.*

A strange rasping sound, like a muffled cough, grabbed their attention. Standing on the other side of the cooking island was Melissa.

"Oh. This is my wife, Melissa." Bill hurried to introduce her.

Victor greeted her with a charming smile but it was Madeleine who rushed around Maria to shake her hand, ever the gracious hostess.

She wasn't sure how to feel about the Haydens being here. Her thoughts were a little mixed up on that point; not that she didn't like the company, but after what happened last night she knew this was definitely not a good time. Her heart had lurched in her chest, sitting with Victor in Mr. Smedley's office, when he'd informed them of the Haydens return to Grace Stone. In fact, he'd said, they had already checked out of their motel and were on their way. So, there was nothing she could do but accept it and make the best of it.

In a way, she felt embarrassed. She owned this house and somehow that made her feel responsible for what was wrong with it. Like she had caused it all. It was a ridiculous notion and she knew it, but still she couldn't help feeling she was to blame. The burden of her family's home and all that came with it solely rested on her shoulders. And for all her tossing and turning last night she was nowhere near an answer or a solution to ridding Grace Stone of the dark malevolence residing here. She could only hope an answer would be forthcoming soon before another encounter took place. Meanwhile, she would bear the responsibility and make the Haydens welcome. After all, it was just possible; very soon, they would be the new owners.

She clasped Melissa's cool hand in her damp warm fingers. The humidity outside was rising with the threat of an impending storm, and the short walk from the car to the house had made her jacket stick to her back and her palms sweaty. She and Victor had hurried home to beat the rain after deciding to come home instead of eating out. They both had been anxious to meet the Haydens, but for different reasons.

Madeleine tried to keep from staring at Melissa, but she just couldn't keep her eyes off her hair. No salon created that color and style. On anyone else it would have been ridiculous but it suited the features of this young woman, framing her creamy skin and light dusting of freckles in a coppery halo. Melissa's emerald green eyes and red hair reminded Madeleine of Christmas and she wondered absentmindedly if the young woman were of Irish descent.

Watching her, it seemed to Madeleine that Melissa was a little nervous; one curly strand was being twirled around a finger and tucked behind a small ear adorned with a gold studded post, only to spring out and be tucked again.

She suddenly remembered her manners and looked away. "I suppose you've already gotten acquainted with Maria."

"Yes. We've met. We didn't know anyone was here when we arrived and I frightened her pretty badly. Shook me up a little too. We kinda ran into each other while she was sweeping the staircase. Gave us both a fright." Melissa laughed nervously and her eyes sought Bill. He had vanished.

Neither she nor Madeleine had noticed the men leaving out the back door to retrieve the rest of the groceries from the car.

Maria quickly put away what had been brought in, placing the can goods and packaged items in the pantry, and then set to work cooking spaghetti. Within a few seconds the men returned in a flurry of crinkling bags and two brown paper sacks. Victor hadn't forgotten to buy the wine.

Laying the food on the now cleared counter top Victor pronounced, "Mattie, I swear you bought out the store. There's enough here to feed an army."

"Well, when Mr. Smedley told us that the Haydens had decided to move back in, I figured I'd best stock up enough to last at least a week."

"Uh-huh," Victor grunted, and then growled, "You bought enough to last a month."

Melissa tried to steady her nerves but wasn't having much luck. Her stomach was rolling in an odd manner.

Being near to this petite and elegant lady, looking down on her from her five-foot seven-inch frame, made her feel awkward and clumsy; if she moved the wrong way she might send something flying with her large hips. Standing next to Madeleine she was feeling very much like a bull in a china shop. Not to mention feeling out of sorts in a kitchen she had come to call her own, but was now occupied with the owners and one busy cook. But why should she care? She no longer wanted the house, did she? Still it gave her an odd feeling of displacement, seeing Maria using her pots and pans and cooking utensils.

No one noticed her edging her way quietly through the swinging door. She suddenly had an urge to be alone, to sort out her conflicting thoughts, and she knew just the place.

Slipping out the French doors in the library, she welcomed the peace and serenity of the side garden as she eased into a large wicker chair, propping her sandaled feet on a matching stool.

This side of the house faced the east, and was quite shady with the sun reaching its zenith, weaving in and out of the white thunderheads above the veranda's rooftop. A warm breeze mingling with cooler air reached her from the south end of the house bringing with it the scents of roses and hibiscus, and various wildflowers. It was soothing to her troubled mind and calmed her senses.

With the breeze lifting her curls and gently caressing her cheeks, her discomfort began to ease somewhat. This was a lovely place to sit and forget your troubles. From the moment she'd seen this veranda she knew this would be the spot where she could relax and be at peace with the world, even if for only a few moments. But she couldn't push this distressing situation from her mind. Sitting out here, inhaling the fragrant air, it was hard to believe that there was anything wrong with Grace Stone. But she couldn't deny that eerie face in the mirror. And now the owners were here. What if she had another episode? Would they believe her when she told them it was a ghost? No, she decided again, they would think she was crazy.

Her kitchen. That was also bothering her. She admitted to herself she was no great chef, but she still enjoyed cooking in her own kitchen. Melissa made a wry face. She'd been kicked out of her kitchen and replaced by a hired cook. She had no doubts that Maria was competent in the culinary arts but she would miss that homey relaxing feeling of puttering in the kitchen. "I should go back to the motel." She muttered as she swatted at an insect buzzing past her face.

"Surely, you don't mean that." A soft voice spoke behind her.

Melissa jumped up from her chair, nearly overturning it, banging her knees on the stool.

"I didn't mean to startle you." Madeleine said as closed the glass door behind her. "Please, sit back down." She pulled another chair a little closer to Melissa and made herself comfortable.

Melissa regained her composure and resumed her seat as Madeleine went on to say, "I kind of figured I'd find you here. The kitchen *was* a little chaotic. This used to be my favorite place to come when I was feeling out of sorts. I can imagine what you must be feeling."

"Can you?" Melissa quietly asked.

Madeleine leaned back, completely at ease. "Of course. I didn't expect to hear that you and your husband had returned, either. But, I'm sure we'll get along famously after we're better acquainted. Victor only came to inspect the wiring and I wanted to see the house before it sold. I haven't been here in a long time." A dreamy expression crossed her sun-golden features. "It's such a lovely place. I was told my grandmother used to sit out in the back garden a lot, until she got the fountain. She loved flowers, planted nearly every bush herself. They've been growing for over sixty years and have weathered many storms. Did you know about the water fountain?"

"Yes. But I haven't seen it, yet." Melissa replied. Remembering to go along with Bill's pretense of buying the house she added in present tense, "It's become a little overgrown and I plan to have everything trimmed back when I get the time."

"It's funny about that fountain." Madeleine's brow knitted together as she reminisced. "My grandmother, Grammy Sarah I call her; Grammy was what I called her when I was two, anyway, she wanted that water fountain badly and was out there everyday, overseeing all the work; from the digging to the laying of the water pipes. She'd even planted those rosebushes surrounding it before it was put in. And the day they poured the concrete she refused to set foot near it. For years after that she tended the flowers nearer the house but had the servants take care of everything else growing near the fountain." Madeleine uttered a soft tinkling laugh, "My father said it was just like a woman; give them what they want and they'll change their minds. My father told me Grandfather Zed used to grumble and tease my grandmother about it."

As Melissa listened to Madeleine's musical voice she became more at ease, even peaceful. She wondered at herself for feeling uncomfortable around her in the first place. Madeleine Martucci seemed to be a nice lady, sweet in fact, but there was a sense of vulnerability about her pale eyes and small mouth. She looked as fragile as a bird's egg, and as harmless as a dove.

Melissa suddenly felt foolish and a little embarrassed for sneaking out of the kitchen like a scolded child running away with stolen cookies. She just hadn't been herself for a couple of weeks. This house, it seemed, had turned her character a little topsy-turvy. She'd always been confident and self-reliant, but here, she was insecure and at a loss.

Feeling angry and disgusted with herself she wondered what Bill had thought of her slinking off like she did.

"So, what are the men up to?" she asked.

"Not sure, but knowing Victor, he's showing him the plumbing, the wood-moldings, lighting fixtures, and telling him how well the house is insulated. He's a real estate investor and enjoys showing off a house. But he'll probably get the grand tour after lunch. When I left them they were getting on like a house afire. I must tell you that he's very determined to sell you Grace Stone Manor." *I just hope I can figure out what's wrong here and correct it before they buy it,* she silently prayed. But deep down, subconsciously, a little knot of fear coiled within her mind at what she may have to do. It made itself known by a tiny feeling of unease that she didn't understand.

Madeleine couldn't help but notice the frown crossing Melissa's pale face. It made her a little nervous remembering that this woman and her husband had fled in the middle of the night. They obviously had experienced something frightful. If that was the case, she couldn't blame them for leaving. But what had given them the courage and incentive to return? "Do you like it here?" she asked tentatively.

"Um. It's a lovely house. Yes, I like it." Melissa cleared her throat. "May I ask you a question?"

"By all means."

"Why do you want to sell it?"

Madeleine gazed off toward the increasing storm clouds, carefully considering her answer. "I'm nearly forty years old," she replied, "and outside of just visiting Grace Stone I've never actually lived here. My home is in Pasadena. For the most part this house has stood empty for many years. It seems a shame to let it sit here and ruin. People who love it and want to take care of it should inhabit it. It should be filled with the sound of children's laughter, just as it was long ago." *And not with the dark force that had invaded it.* Madeleine blinked back tears burning her eyes. *Antonia's laughter never had the chance to grace its halls.*

She quickly pushed the thought away. "I do hope you and your husband purchase it and I hope you plan to have a family." Her last words were almost a question as she gazed at Melissa's face.

A slight flush filled Melissa's cheeks but she saw no harm in answering. "Actually, we had that in mind when we saw the place. We've been married for five years and although I love my work at the hospital, I'd been considering giving it up for a while to have a child. Purchasing this house was to be a turning point in our lives. I plan to work for another year while we settle in, before trying to get pregnant." Melissa couldn't believe her own ears; not only was she opening up to this woman but she was talking like buying this house was still an option. *Stay focused, Melissa.* She silently warned herself. *Don't forget this lovely house creeps you out.*

She remembered why they were here and decided to risk asking a sticky question. Bill had failed with Maria; perhaps she could do better with Madeleine. A woman will usually confide in another woman. Right? *And if she doesn't, well, all she can do is tell me to mind my own business.* Anyway, it's worth a try. Why wait? "Um. Mrs. Martucci, Bill and I "

"Please, it's Mattie. I'd prefer that. Mrs. Martucci makes me feel old."

"Okay. Mattie. We're very interested in the history of your family's home and who all lived here." Melissa hesitated. It suddenly didn't seem like such a good idea to ask this painful question. Maybe she was rushing things a bit. What if she blew it, questioning her now, and Mrs. Martucci never tells them? She suddenly felt like a nosy busybody.

"It's all right, Melissa. You should know about the history of the home you plan to buy. Anything you ask about Grace Stone is perfectly legitimate." Madeleine steeled herself. She had a feeling she knew what Mrs. Hayden was going to ask and she also knew she would have to talk about it sooner or later. Might as well be now. After all, she came here to face these painful memories and put them behind her.

Melissa nervously tucked her unruly curls behind her ears and clasped her hands tightly in her lap. "This is very uncomfortable but I have to ask. This house is still filled with some of your family's possessions, and we can't help but wonder . . . we've heard . . . well, we've heard some things about your family but no one will talk about your aunt and uncle and your cousin-about what happened to them. I know this has to be hard for you but I must know if they died here. Here in the house." *There I've asked.* Melissa expelled the rest of the air from her lungs and waited tensely. Maybe she should have waited until they were better acquainted. But patience had never been her virtue.

She noticed the sad expression that crossed Madeleine's delicate features and then be replaced by a look of stern determination. "You're right. It is painful but it's time I talked about it and let it go." She straightened her back, uncrossed her slender legs, and braced her feet flat against the veranda's wooden floor; bracing herself mentally as well. The air swirled around them, much cooler, and the sky had darkened with black rain clouds, obliterating the sun's light.

Madeleine took a deep shuddering breath and began, "My cousin, Skye, and her parents came home late one night; June 17th to be exact, in nineteen eighty. They'd been camping down at Wister Lake. I'm sure you know where that is. They had just turned into the lane . . . " Madeleine paused a moment to collect her thoughts and then continued, "They hadn't gone very far when a bolt of lightening struck one of the oak trees. It crushed their car, caving the roof in. My . . . my aunt and uncle died instantly."

Madeline tried to blink back her tears but they were too full. A few escaped to roll down her cheeks before she regained her composure and checked their flow. "Skye, managed . . . God, I don't know how she did it, she was only a young girl, but she managed to crawl to the house and call for help. No cell phones back then. The Sheriff arrived within fifteen minutes, but it took half an hour for an ambulance to get here. They found her broken and battered body in the library. God only knows why she had crawled in there. I used to think it was because she loved that old piano that sits there now and knew she would never play it again. But, I don't know. She was so badly banged up she couldn't have been thinking clearly. She'd had a concussion. But that wasn't the worst of her injuries. I think she knew she wasn't going to make it."

When Madeleine trailed off, obviously pained by the memory, Melissa gently prodded her. "Mattie, did Skye die in the library?"

Madeleine wiped her tear-streaked face with the back of her hand and replied, "No. No, she didn't. The paramedics worked to stabilize her, and thought they had succeeded. But, she passed away on the steps as they were wheeling her to the ambulance. The Sheriff told my father that she kept rambling on about a red book, but he couldn't make any sense out of it. The library has many books with red bindings and quite a few of them Skye enjoyed reading. I've looked through them all but I haven't found anything that would have been significant to her; one that would have been so important that she would have used her last dying breath to tell someone. I've never been able to understand it."

Madeleine gazed off in the distance toward a bruised and swollen sky, remembering her father's words; "There was no storm that night," she whispered, "how could lightening strike a tree?"

She turned back to Melissa and sniffled, drawing a handkerchief from her skirt pocket. "Just a tragic freak accident they'd said."

Drawing Madeleine away from that long ago night she asked a needless question. "Which room did Skye occupy?" Melissa was pretty sure she already knew.

"The third largest bedroom, around the corner from the master bedroom. The room Victor and I are staying in." Madeleine confirmed the answer, softly blowing her nose.

Overhead, the sky began to rumble with the first sounds of thunder, and the leaves were rustling in the wind as the first drops of rain pelted the roof. Melissa had one more question and quickly asked before the wind could slant the rain and drive them indoors.

"What did Skye look like? Did she favor you much?" she asked.

"Heavens, no. We looked nothing alike. We were born just a week apart and I couldn't help but rub it in that I was the eldest." She smiled at this childish memory. "She was just a little taller, a little more filled out. She had these brown doe eyes and long dark hair. I was told she favored my grandmother a lot; Grammy Sarah was Indian, a Choctaw woman.

Skye was very intelligent, excelled in school whereas I struggled, and had taught her self to play the piano. She had a favorite tune she often played. Well, actually she had a couple she loved to play. Have you ever heard of "Music Box Dancer" by Frank Mills?" She went on when Melissa shook her head. "Anyway, Skye loved music. Any music. Even Mozart. ABBA was a favorite group of hers, among a few others. And my Aunt Elise, Skye's mother, still clung to her old sixties tunes. There was always a radio playing in this house or an old cassette playing. Skye and I had a lot of favorites we shared back in the seventies. But ABBA was her favorite."

Melissa's face blanched at that last bit of information. Seventies music. How often had she heard that old music playing on her stereo? Could it be possible that the ghost of this fifteen-year-old girl was the one haunting this house? And then, just like the thunderbolt that suddenly clapped above their heads and rattled the windows, it hit her; that face she saw in the mirror had dark hair! She was sure of it. Gooseflesh appeared on her arms with the realization. Seventies music, dark hair! It fit. She was positive that it was Skye's ghost haunting Grace Stone and she needed to tell Bill. He would be excited to gain this piece of information.

Although it was Bill who wanted to ghost hunt, her curiosity was now piqued. Maybe there was nothing to fear from the ghost of a teen-age girl. Maybe there was no danger in staying here. Well, that at least answered one question. The who. She was glad she had taken the risk and asked.

She looked at Madeleine who was now gazing at the bushes being whipped by the wind, her blonde hair obscuring her features. How was she going to tell this nice lady that her dead cousin was haunting her old family home and had been for a long time?

Twenty-three years! That *was* a long time. What was so important that a young girl would hang onto this life for twenty-three years, roaming through a lonely empty house? And why scare the few tenants who came and went?

Wait a minute! Didn't Bill say that sometimes a ghost would try to communicate if it was about something very important to them? He'd also said that they don't speak. At least, not in the books he had read, not without help. How would a young person talk to you if they couldn't speak?

A flash of insight and understanding made her sit up straight. Of course! Skye had loved music. Songs were filled with words and meanings, and not to mention feelings of emotions. Maybe she hadn't meant to frighten them. Had Skye been trying to communicate with them through music? All those times her stereo had come on by itself and she hadn't known to pay attention, had been too scared. It made sense now to Melissa. But just what was this girl trying to relate through those old tunes?

There were so many questions that needed answers. But the most important question of all was . . .why? Maybe Bill *could* figure it out. She would have to tell him everything. And maybe, just maybe, she wouldn't mind purchasing Grace Stone Manor after all.

Just then, Victor and Bill poked their heads out the French doors. "Come on ladies. Stop gabbing. Lunch is getting cold and I'm starving," Victor bellowed above the thunder.

"Victor, you're always starving." Madeleine laughed and patted his tummy, slipping past him into the library.

"I have something to tell you after lunch," Melissa whispered to Bill in hushed tones as they entered the library following the Martuccis. The driving rain, now in full force, was muffled behind the French doors.

Chapter 8

A soft soothing darkness, nothing like what the Other generates; dark and cold, but a darkness as warm as a blanket enveloped her. How long this time, a day, a week, months? Maybe a year. Time has little meaning when you're dead. All else around you grows old; books layered in dust, the pages parched and crinkly; clothes from a by-gone era rotted, hanging in tatters; pictures of remembered loved ones faded with age. But you remain the same. Unchanged. Never having a birthday, you remain the same age as when you died. Time doesn't matter when you can no longer count your heartbeats, or have a need to draw breath. Everything around you ages, but you are constant.

Skye slowly became conscious of her being. She glowed faintly and floated near the ceiling. It was dark, but not oppressively so. Soothing in fact. A comfortable feeling of security enclosed her as the vague shadow of old wooden rafters melded with her body; a cobweb hung through what would have been her shoulder if it had substance. She watched it, mesmerized. Wispy, barely swaying in an almost imperceptible draft through her essence, it didn't even tickle.

I'm in the attic. As usual.

Always, over the years, after moments of unconsciousness, she would awaken in the attic. After being drained she would fall asleep, almost ceasing to exist. It wasn't the same kind of sleep she experienced while living. She never dreamed. Dreams were for the living. One moment she would be manipulating the radio or hiding from the Beast and the next she would find herself in the attic, not knowing how long she had been in stasis. She stopped pondering why a long time ago. It was just the way things were. And that was okay. Surrounded by the odds and ends of Fitzgerald possessions she was comforted. It was always warm and inviting here.

The Ogre, as she sometimes called him along with a few other colorful nicknames, her favorite being Mr. Worms, was nowhere around. For some reason he didn't hang around the attic. Which was great for her. It gave her time in a place of peace to re-group and plan her next strategy.

At the moment nothing came to mind. Just the remembrance of a vow she had made long ago. Her oath. She hadn't known that it was going to cost her twenty-three years of unrest. She had kind of thought it would become null and void at her death. But God, it seemed, was keeping her to her promise, even after death. By swearing impulsively an oath to reveal the truth she had sealed her fate. She wished she didn't have to fulfill it alone. She couldn't. She remembered her father telling her that God places no more upon a person than he or she can bear. But why must she bear *this* alone? Why hadn't she told her father before that terrible night? She wouldn't be facing this alone or at all if she had told her father before the accident.

Wait a minute! She was not alone!

Mattie!

Remembrance shot through her like a high voltage current of electricity. Mattie was here!

Skye shimmered with excitement, her essence gaining strength. Losing control she shot through the roof. Swirling in the late afternoon glow of the setting sun, peeping through the spent yellow-orange and purple clouds painting the sky, she gazed upon the raindrops clinging to the garret rooftop, shining like diamonds. *Beautiful!* She didn't know it had stormed; didn't know how much time had elapsed since Mattie arrived.

Darn that Ogre! She cursed, remembering how he drove her out of the stereo in the living room, just when she was making contact with her cousin. Mattie had even spoken her name. No one had called her by name for more years than she could count and she only knew how many had past by the calendars placed in the house by the people who came and went.

She wished she could speak, actually use words. She hadn't had a decent conversation with anyone since her accident, except for that awful goof-up with Melissa Hayden in the bathroom. But, she had never tried before that night. It took a lot of energy. Perhaps, if she practiced she would learn how to speak and use less energy. But it would take time and she didn't know how much time she was going to have with Mattie. She didn't know how long her cousin was staying. And what if she went into stasis again, only to awaken a year later and find new owners in residence and Mattie never to return?

This time, she was sure, was her only chance. It was going to be a challenge, and tiring, to accomplish what needed doing. She couldn't afford to spend too much energy at once and she would have to be careful and always on the lookout for the Bad One. She didn't know if he was aware that Mattie was related to her. If he didn't know, he would figure it out soon enough. And he wouldn't like it one bit. He didn't like the Fitzgeralds. Mattie could very well be in danger for her life. His power had grown stronger over the years, feeding off his own hatred. She feared for Mattie.

Skye swirled and turned to face the south, looking toward the lane leading to the front of the house and the circular drive. The sun had nearly set, pushing its dying rays against the trees to cast long shadows across the drive. In the distance someone was walking toward her. She drew near the front balcony for a closer look. Mattie, with her eyes downcast was briskly making her way to the steps. *Must have gone out for an evening stroll,* she thought.

Skye was careful not to float too far away from the house, for some reason she was not allowed any farther than that. She'd tried many times to leave but always ended up back inside the attic. She was literally housebound. She gazed down at Madeleine as she drew near.

She marveled at how well her cousin had aged. She was still as beautiful as ever, still slender and small-framed. Only the tiniest of lines lacing the corners of her soft blue eyes and around her mouth showed she was no longer in the prime of youth. Her dear, sweet, cousin Mattie, whose hair was the color of corn silk and just as soft. Never had an unkind word for anyone and as gentle as a lamb. How she missed her! Missed sharing secrets late at night by phone. Giggling until 1 a.m. over her silly crush on the man she eventually married. Victor, she decided, wasn't bad looking for an old guy, just a little thick around the middle. She never got to tell Mattie about her date to the movies with Brad Wilson, the coolest boy at her school. Well, it wasn't important now.

Skye felt regret at the pain she was causing her best friend and cousin, had never intended to torment Madeleine. But somehow she must reach her. If only Madeleine wasn't so fearful, so fragile minded. If only she had some help, someone Madeleine could rely on.

She folded in upon herself, seeping into the master bedroom, as Madeleine disappeared from view, entering the front door below.

In the master bedroom, Skye stopped short, hovering above the French doors. Twilight had darkened the room, leaving just enough light to see. Not that she needed any light, she could see just as well in the dark.

Oh my God! I don't believe it! My favorite couple has returned.

Skye gleefully hugged herself within her mist. Here was the help Madeleine needed. She couldn't believe her good fortune in this turn of events. She was thrilled. Her hope soared. If she could reach them as well as Mattie, she would have the reinforcements she desperately needed to expose that nasty Mr. Worms once and for all.

Skye had no idea just how brightly she glowed in her excitement. For an instant, she suddenly felt rejuvenated; a small tingling surged at her center. But it was short-lived. It ebbed quickly, leaving her with a deep feeling of loss and a profound craving for more.

"Good heavens! Did you see that?" Bill jumped from the bed.

He and Melissa had been resting after dinner, chatting once more about the information she had gained from Madeleine earlier that day. Melissa had showered and changed into a pair of white cotton shorts and another green t-shirt. He still had on the khakis he'd put on that morning.

They had just been discussing how to approach Madeleine when from the corner of his eye, for just a second or two, he saw a bluish-white light fixed above the French doors. He fairly flew off the bed, heart racing, for a closer look. But it was gone.

"Bill, don't move so fast, yelling like that; you nearly scared me to death." Melissa chided him, sitting up hugging her pillow. She was shivering. "What did you see?"

Bill stood, gazing up at an area just above the French doors, his fingers gently rubbing his creased forehead in a slouchy mock salute. Had he actually seen something sparkle there or was it his imagination? At any rate, it was no longer there, if it had been there at all.

He returned to Melissa and lowered himself onto the bed. "I thought I saw some kind of light up there. But it happened so fast I'm not sure I saw anything now." Sighing, he stretched out, tucking the pillow firmly beneath his head. Elbows bent, he clasped his hands above his mussed blond hair.

Melissa stared at Bill's features. He seemed to be studying the ceiling, his blue eyes squinting, deep in thought. She grimaced. For some reason her stomach was churning. "So . . . it was just a light? That's it?" she asked.

"Well, I don't know. It happened so fast. But, I swear, it was kinda bluish." He reached out to switch on the bedside lamp. The sun had finally set.

Melissa's stomach twisted into a knot and she swallowed hard. She felt as if she had eaten a rock for supper instead of the linguine Maria had served. She wondered dismally if she were doomed to eat nothing but Italian food for the week the Martuccis would be here. She hadn't been able to keep down the spaghetti she'd eaten for lunch either.

"Bill?"

"Hmm."

"That thing I saw . . .in the mirror . . ." Her stomach lurched. Was she going to be sick? Again? " . . . It had a bluish tint." She murmured the last as a wave of dizziness hit her and her stomach heaved.

She didn't hear Bill's reply. With a hand clamped over her mouth she sprang from the bed and ran to the bathroom, silently praying she would make it to the commode before she lost her dinner. Falling on her knees, her hands grasped the cool porcelain as she retched into the bowl.

Bill, concern creasing his brow, had followed her and stood just outside the bathroom door, feeling inadequate and helpless. Doing the only thing he could think of, he grabbed a washcloth, ran it under the cold water tap, wrung it out, and gently laid it on the back of Melissa's hot and perspiring neck.

When Melissa began vomiting, Skye quickly made her exit and escaped to the dark and quiet attic. Being a ghost didn't change the fact she had no desire to watch someone toss his or her cookies. Disgusting! Besides, she needed time to ponder what just occurred and figure out how in the world Bill had gotten a glimpse of her. She had not drawn any energy from another source; there had been no lights on in the bedroom. She settled in among the old dusty trunks containing stored and forgotten treasures of the Fitzgerald's, to think.

Melissa rose shakily to her feet, flushed the commode, and moved to the sink. She wiped her face with the cool cloth Bill had given her and then proceeded to brush her teeth. When she had finished she looked at her ashen face in the mirror. Bill still hovered near the door.

"Gawd, Bill." She glanced away from his reflection. "Don't stand over my shoulder. That still freaks me out a little."

"Are you okay? I mean, well, you're hardly ever sick. You threw up after lunch too."

"Yes, I'm alright. It's just nerves."

"Are you sure?"

"Yes! It's probably PMS too. It's near that time of the month for me."

"It's never made you sick before, that I know of." He continued to stare at the ashen pallor of her skin. "Are you sure that's all it is? Do you want me to take you to a doctor or something? Is there anything I can do?"

"For Pete's sake, Bill! It's just PMS and nerves! I don't need a doctor!" Melissa voice rose in pitch as her hands clutched the sink, her knuckles as white as a bone.

She was getting irritable and Bill knew to back off. "Okay, okay." He held up his hands.

He backed away from the door as Melissa turned to face him. "I'm sorry, Bill. I don't mean to snap at you. I love you and I appreciate your concern. It's just that I haven't been myself lately. It's . . .it's the situation we're in. It's like I don't have control over my life anymore. We're dealing with something we've never dealt with before. And I don't like the pretense of buying this house. And I hate the fact that I really wanted it and it's haunted. It isn't fair! We're alive and need a roof over our heads. That damn ghost just needs a grave!" She felt herself growing a little hysterical with her outburst. Appalled at her tirade, she clamped her mouth shut. What was wrong with her?

Not wanting to see the confused and hurt look on Bill's face, she moved past him to lie on the bed. She was tense and irritable and was feeling a little shaky and didn't think her legs would hold her up. She collapsed onto the bed, pressed her throbbing head into the pillow and draped an arm over her eyes. *Okay, Melissa, calm down*, she told herself. She smiled thinly as Bill eased beside her.

"Sorry, Bill," she muttered contritely. "So, what did you and Mr. Martucci do all afternoon?" Changing the subject seemed like a good idea at this point.

"Well, Victor gave me a grand tour. More like an inspection of the premises. I learned that in nineteen seventy-five Samuel Fitzgerald began remodeling the house. He replaced a lot of the old water pipes and wiring, added insulation, and by nineteen eighty, just before he died, he got rid of all the window units and installed central heat and air. He had also refinished all the woodwork during the years he lived here. All in all, except for the foundation, most of this house is only about twenty-eight years old. I didn't try to argue with him about a possible wiring problem. You and I know that's not what's going on here. He's determined to have that checked out. As a matter of fact, an electrician is coming out tomorrow. Someone Mr. Smedley recommended. Can't wait to see what he has to say. Betcha he won't find a thing wrong." Bill was positive of that.

Peeping out from under her arm she saw the smug look on his face. He was a good husband. He'd already forgiven her for her outburst. "Bill, you are so caught up with this ghost business. It almost frightens me how obsessed you've become. You're actually enjoying yourself."

"I love a good mystery. You know that. I read for a living and now I'm living a mystery right here. Yes, I'm enjoying myself. It's like taking a vacation to an island where you participate in a mystery script, becoming one of the characters. I wish you could relax and enjoy it too." He gently patted her thigh and glanced at his watch. It was nearing 7 p.m. "Are you feeling any better?"

"I'm just a little tired but my stomach seems to have settled down Just a slight headache. I'm all right."

"I'd like to go downstairs and have a go at those library books. Since it was where they found the girl, and she obviously tried to tell them something before she died, I figure it's the best place to start. Feel up to joining me?"

"Mattie said she already looked through those books and didn't find anything significant. She knew her cousin better than anyone else. I don't think you'll find anything useful, probably a waste of time. Anyway, I'm tired. Honestly Bill, I'd rather rest for a while. But you go ahead."

"I'm not going if you're not. I promised not leave you alone. Remember?"

Melissa sighed. "I'm not as frightened now that I know it's a young girl haunting the place. I mean, yeah, it would shake me up a bit to have another encounter with her. But, I don't think I have anything to worry about. I'm not really afraid of a twenty-three year old ghost of a fifteen-year-old girl. Besides, except for a flash of light, which you may or may not have seen, it's been pretty calm around here. I get a little jumpy but I'm not terrified. You go on and do your sleuthing. I want to rest. After a while, if you're still down there and I feel better, I'll join you."

Bill leaned over to kiss the exposed part of her cheek beneath her arm. "I have an idea." He sprang from the bed to rummage around in the closet.

Melissa heard him unzipping one of his bags. A few baseballs thumped to the floor, one of them rolled toward the fireplace, bumping against the fender. She uncovered her eyes to see what he was doing, as Bill turned around with a triumphant grin plastered under his nose.

"Ah-hah!" he shouted.

Melissa giggled. He held a Louisville Slugger baseball bat high in the air and swung maliciously at an imaginary baseball.

"And just what are you going to do with that?" She laughed at his antics as he made his way to the bed, swinging the bat and thrusting it like a sword.

"I'm not going to do anything with it, my little Moppet. You are." He stopped beside the bed with a flourish, leaning on the bat, bowing deeply.

Melissa stuffed a couple more pillows under her back and head, leaning against the oaken headboard to get a better view of Bill. Her eyes were a shining glass of green and out-matched the color of her t-shirt. "And just how do you suppose I'm going to fend off a ghost with that? It'll go right through her."

"Well, actually I thought you could use it as a sort of call bell." He demonstrated by thumping the floor with the bat a couple of times. "You see. I'm leaving this with you. If you get frightened or if anything happens, you just pound the floor with this. I'll hear it and come running. Promise. Cross my heart and hope not to die till I save you." He extended the handle toward her and made the sign of the cross over the region of his heart.

"Bill, you truly are a nut; one of the reasons why I married you. Thanks." She smiled up at him, taking the bat, and he leaned down to plant a resounding kiss on her lips.

"Don't forget," he admonished as he strode to the door. "First sound of distress, you pound, I'll run." Flashing her a toothy grin he disappeared out into the hall.

Melissa stood the bat against the wall, leaning it beside the headboard, and then removed all but one pillow from beneath her head. Her eyes were beginning to feel heavy and her mind fuzzy. A little snooze was just what she needed. She hoped she wouldn't awaken scared witless, having another ghostly encounter.

She looked at the bat reassuringly and blessed Bill. Then she grabbed the comforter from the opposite side of the bed and flung it across her body. Snuggling down deep in its warmth she quickly nodded off.

Bill heard the shower running as he neared the hall bathroom. Maria, having finished her last chore of cleaning the kitchen was getting ready for a quiet evening, the time being her own. He rounded the corner, moving on past the housekeeper's room, and headed for the stairs.

The door to the old playroom stood open and he spied Madeleine, her back turned to him, staring out a window. She had showered and changed clothes before dinner. She was now wearing pleated white dress slacks and a pink pullover. She was unaware of his presence, and not wishing to intrude, he moved to the first step. It creaked under his loafer.

"Oh, Mr. Hayden. Hello there." She called out to him.

He turned and entered the room. It was clean and completely empty. He wondered, briefly, where her thoughts had taken her while gazing outside to the darkened garden below.

"Please, it's Bill." He looked around at the empty room. He could make this into his office, he thought, or perhaps a playroom again when he and Melissa had children, or a game room. Or even an extra bedroom when his or her parents came to visit. Not to mention, brothers and sisters with their children.

The house had so many possibilities and he was delighted at the prospect of entertaining company. He'd already envisioned converting the old servants' quarters into bedrooms his nieces and nephews would enjoy. With some carpeting, bunk beds, a few dressers and nightstands, they would be as cozy as toast. And it wouldn't cost that much. Even Melissa's younger cousins would love it. Inviting their myriad relatives for Christmas warmed him down to his toes. He would love to do it this Christmas, christening his and Melissa's new home with cheer and laughter and closeness of family.

Bill drew himself back to the here and now.

Madeleine stood in the center of the room with her arms folded across her chest. "Of course. Bill." She acquiesced.

Staring out the window she had felt lost and alone. Then she'd heard someone on the stair. She had been grateful to see Bill Hayden there, dispelling her gloomy thoughts.

"So, tell me. This couldn't have always been just a playroom for children. What else has it been used for?" He moved further into the room looking up at the glass light fixture sporting four light bulbs. It was very bright, not casting shadows, one bulb pointing at each wall. There were also other more modern fixtures on the walls and track lighting running across the ceiling. Madeleine had them all blazing. "Someone had wanted a lot of light in here, like a studio." Bill observed.

Madeleine slipped her hands into her pants pockets. A smile brightened her thoughtful features. "You're very astute. I wish you could have met my Aunt Elise. She was one of a kind. She'd turned this room into an art room, her place for self-expression when she'd lived here. For several years these wooden floors stayed covered in drop cloths. She loved to paint. Since this part of the house faced the north and didn't receive a lot of natural light, she'd had my Uncle Samuel install those extra light fixtures you see on the walls and the track lighting. And she had left the windows bare of blinds or curtains."

"Did she ever sell any of her paintings?" Bill's curiosity rose. Mrs. Martucci was finally talking to him about her family.

"Oh, goodness, no. Well, not professionally. She painted for fun and relaxation. She'd tried to give away a few to people she knew and had admired her work, and wouldn't dare ask for money but, they'd always given her money for them anyway. A couple of my Uncle's business associates bought some of them too."

"What did your Aunt Elise like to paint?"

"Oh, daisies, sunflowers, vases. You know, still life. Sometimes she painted portraits of people. Of course, when she was in a mood she painted these outlandish abstracts in bizarre colors." Madeleine laughed. "You have to understand. Aunt Elise was a product of her time. She was young in the sixties. She wore tie-dyed t-shirts, her own that she'd dyed herself, low hip-hugger jeans that were wide and frayed at the bottom. And occasionally she even wore a leather hippy headband. I have a lot of pictures of her taken back then. She was fun and exciting to be around and I just loved her to pieces." She smiled, remembering the nickname Aunt Elise had given her one day while painting Madeleine's portrait: Sunflower.

In the portrait, Madeleine was standing among a patch of tall sunflowers, wearing a pale green dress. The sun was very bright, making a halo about her golden hair, and it looked as if she were looking off into the distance, when in reality she had been watching Skye make bubbles out of dish soap. She was seven years old at the time. The framed painting now hung in her private sitting room in Pasadena.

"Was she also into bra burning?" Bill joked, breaking in on her thoughts.

Madeleine laughed. It was honest laughter, musical and full of mirth. It brought tears to her eyes, and it felt good. She had forgotten that a merry heart did a person good, like medicine.

"Are you kidding?" Madeleine's face glowed with happy warmth. "She was probably the first one to strike a match. In the seventies she was still very much a sixties woman. I stayed many summers here with her and my Uncle Samuel and my cousin Skye. She encouraged both of us to join her and paint. And it didn't matter what our paintings looked like, she always remarked how great they were. She was a unique and lively person. Skye was just like her." Madeleine paused a moment, then asked, "You really like this house, don't you? I can see it in your eyes."

"As a matter of fact, I do, very much. I was just mentally picturing my young nieces and nephews visiting. I love the chaos they cause. They're so rambunctious and full of life. It would be great to have them here for holidays."

A thought suddenly struck Madeleine. Victor had shown him around the house today but there was one place she knew Bill Hayden hadn't had the pleasure of seeing. Not even Victor knew about it. Since they had only leased the house to strangers, neither she nor her father, before he'd passed away, had seen any reason why anyone should know about the room she was about to reveal to Bill. The truth was she rarely ever thought about it, should have told Victor, had meant to, but had never gotten around to it.

"Bill, there's something I'd like to show you. It's downstairs." There was a gleam in her soft blue eyes as she led the way to the stairs. She went on to explain as they descended. "I don't know if you are aware my Uncle Samuel was an architect. It's what he did for a living. He remodeled this house and made many improvements."

"Yes, you're husband explained that to me," Bill said, nodding of his head.

They reached the entrance hall and Madeleine led him to the library through the door underneath the staircase.

She clicked one of the light switches by the door and the light from the desk lamp softly illuminated the room. They rounded the huge mahogany desk on their left where Bill had placed his computer and printer and fax machine. Farther down from the desk the tall upright piano stood against the wall. Its dark varnished wood shone warmly from the polishing Maria had given it that afternoon. Madeleine glanced at it and quickly averted her eyes.

Striding to the far wall she frowned, deep in thought. The entire wall was one huge bookcase. A few of the shelves were empty. Bill was surprised when she told him, "My uncle designed and built a small room just behind this wall." She slowly moved down a couple of feet, located the spot she remembered, and then stopped.

She removed two books from the end of a shelf above her head in the middle of the wall. Standing on tiptoe she reached inside and pushed. There was a faint click and a small portion of the bookcase swung inward a fraction. She replaced the books and then pushed. Swinging it further inward she slipped between the slanted bookcase and the other stationary shelves.

She felt along the inner wall and located a light switch. She flicked it. The room remained dark. "I guess the bulbs have gone bad from too many years of disuse."

"Hold on. There's a flashlight in the desk drawer." Bill quickly moved to the desk, dug through two of the drawers, located the flashlight, and returned to Madeleine. He turned it on and followed her into a small cobwebby room.

Bill shined the flashlight from left to right. The single beam revealed a small metal desk, a drafting table and a filing cabinet. All were covered in a layer of dust, and cobwebs clung here and there. One big cobweb trailed from the bent light on the drafting table down to the floor. Over in a corner he spied an aging rope ladder and an aluminum pole.

"What's that for?" he asked, shining the light in the corner.

"If you'll shine that light up to the ceiling I'll explain."

Doing as she instructed, Bill saw a skylight situated in the center of the ceiling flanked by burned out fluorescent lights. He could just make out the moon's glow shining through it.

"If you've walked around the outside of the house, you've noticed there are no windows at this end." The beam of the flash played across Madeleine's features for a moment, moving slowing from wall to wall.

"Yes," said Bill, "and that explains why the dimensions on the outside don't match the dimensions inside. I was a little curious but hadn't given it much thought. I also hadn't bothered looking out the old servants' windows. I imagine you can see this from up there, and probably from the upstairs bay window."

"Yes, you're right." Madeleine continued, "In case of fire, should my uncle become trapped in here, he could open that window with the pole. It has a hook on it just for that purpose. Then he could stand on the desk, hook the rope ladder to the windowsill and climb out. Once outside, he could pull the ladder through the window, leave it hooked to the sill and dangle it down the side of the house. It was his fire escape."

"Your uncle was a smart man." Bill was impressed with the construction of this little room, and pleased. It would be perfect for him as a private office just as it had been perfect for Samuel Fitzgerald.

Directing the beam back to the metal desk he saw an old beige telephone. So there *was* a phone line here. Perfect for his computer. He would have to come back in the morning and take a better look. He couldn't wait to see what else had been left behind, prowl in the desk drawers and dig in those filing cabinets. Madeleine's voice brought him out of his thoughts and he gave her his attention.

"My uncle built this room for peace and privacy," she was saying. "When Aunt Elise and Skye were blaring music, he would escape to the tranquility and quiet of his personal haven." Madeleine laughed. "He and Aunt Elise were so different; I wondered how they ever got together. I guess it's true that opposites do attract. They were fun to be around."

"Sounds like you had quite a time when you visited."

"Oh yes. Always." she murmured and slipped back into the library, Bill following. She turned and pushed the bookcase back into place, then pivoted to face him. "I've really enjoyed talking with you about my aunt and uncle. I thought it would hurt me but, really, it's been nice. It's refreshing to remember them and smile at how wonderful they were."

"I'm glad you felt you could share this with me. It makes me appreciate this house even more." Bill went to the desk and returned the flashlight to its place in the drawer. He sauntered over to the piano and leaned his elbow on top, crossing one foot over the other. "So this is the piano your cousin used to play?" He hoped to draw Madeleine into a discussion about Skye.

He was perfectly at ease, casually propped against the large piano, until the sound of the keys plunked out a few notes by unseen fingers.

His heart skipped a beat, then the hair on the back of his neck bristled, but he wasn't frightened, he was excited. It had to be Skye touching those keys.

He stepped away from the piano and turned to stare at it, fascinated. A few more notes issued from the keys and he began to make sense of a tune being played. It was slow and halting and every so often just a little off key.

The desk lamp began to flicker. He turned to see Madeleine's reaction.

She had gone quite pale. Grasping the edge of the desk, her terrified eyes stared at the piano, her mouth open.

The keys moved a little faster, picking up the tempo. The lamp continued to buzz and flicker.

"Mattie, do you recognize that tune?" From the look on her face he was sure she did.

But Madeleine could not answer. She was chilled and frozen from head to toe, but not from an outside source. This chill permeated from the inside out.

Her hammering heart pounded in her throat as a teen-aged memory surfaced. Slowly her lips began to move. No sound came out at first, and then she began to whisper the almost forgotten lyrics to the tune issuing from the piano.

Bill rushed to her side and grasped her upper arms. She seemed to stare right through him. On the desk, the lamp flickered crazily.

"Mattie, what's the name of that tune?"

Her eyes were glazed as she softly whispered words too low for Bill to hear.

"Mattie!" Bill shook her in his excitement. "This is important. Don't you see? It's your cousin! Skye! She is trying to communicate."

Madeleine slowly fixed her shimmering blue eyes on Bill's. And then laughed. It was not a musical humorous sound.

My God, thought Bill, *she's hysterical.* He'd never dealt with a woman in the throes of hysteria before. All he could do was shake her, try to reach her in that lost place in her mind. She had slipped off somewhere into the past. A stinging blow to a cheek might work, but he couldn't bring himself to slap her.

"Madeleine!" he shouted, but she paid him no heed. The maniacal laughter died, replaced by singing. Madeleine was not aware of his presence.

She was staring beyond him once again. The lamp was growing dim; the tune on the piano was slowing in tempo, still hitting a discordant note, and Madeleine's voice eerily matching the pace gave him a chill.

He released her to turn on the overhead light. It blazed brightly, but did little to remove the chill in his spine.

He looked toward the piano. It was eerie watching the keys moving alone. If only he could see the fingers depressing the keys.

He almost laughed out loud at that crazy thought. *Oh yeah, Bill, hands chopped off at the wrists, tickling the ivory, would definitely be better. Why not picture the entire ghostly girl seated at the bench?*

He made a wry face, corralling his inane thoughts. Overhead, the lights began to buzz and flicker, the tempo picked up a beat.

Madeleine, standing stock still, was softly singing, her voice now clear and bright.

He moved toward her, intending to swing that vacant gaze away from the piano but he didn't have to. The music abruptly stopped as a chill descended over the library, freezing him in his tracks just as he reached her.

Madeleine shook her head, her silvery blond hair cascading around her small shoulders. "Bill?" she murmured uncertainly.

He stepped in between her and the piano. "Mattie, please. You must tell me the name of that song. It's important." Bill gazed into her eyes. She gazed right back at him. Her blue eyes focused on his, no longer glazed. She was with him now. She had returned to the present from that far away time deep in her memory.

"No." She shook her head. "That wasn't Skye." She folded her arms, goose pimpled from the cold. She shivered. "Can't you feel the cold?" Her breath fogged as she spoke.

"Yes, I feel it. But, I'm telling you that was your cousin playing the piano. What was the name of that song?" He released her.

Madeleine grasped the sides of her head, her fingers splayed through her hair. "No, it wasn't!" Her voice rose in pitch. Bill feared she was nearing hysteria again. "There's something evil residing here and it's cruel. It pretends to be Skye to hurt me!" She covered her face with her hands. "I don't know what to do." she wailed. "Maybe you should leave. You haven't felt what I've felt. You don't want to. It's evil!"

"Please, listen to me." He gently placed his hands on her trembling shoulders, lowered his voice. "I honestly believe your cousin is haunting this house."

Madeleine shook her head violently. "No, no, no! I can't listen to this. I won't! You don't know what you're talking about!" She broke from him and ran to the door.

"Madeleine!"

She stopped at the door and turned, tears glistening her eyes. ""S.O.S.",," she whispered.

"What?"

""S.O.S." The song. It's by ABBA. Skye . . ." But she couldn't finish what she was going to say. She turned and fled, biting back the sobs with her knuckles.

Bill rubbed his hands together, the temperature in the library had returned to normal, the lights burning as if nothing had happened. He ran his hands through his short hair, making it stand on end. He sighed, wondering what to do next. He was thrilled that Skye had tried to communicate with them. He just wished he understood what it was she was trying to say.

Everyone knows that S O S definitely means 'help', especially in Morse code.

Bill felt immensely sorry for Madeleine. No doubt, this was hard for her. But, it was going to be harder still, convincing her of Skye's presence. No matter how painful it was going to be, he would have to make her understand. Her cousin was here for a reason, and couldn't move on until they found out why and helped her.

He pondered Madeleine's statement; 'You haven't felt what I have felt.' He needed to ask her what she meant by that. She was terrified of something. Maybe she just didn't want to face the fact that her cousin had died so young and had never really dealt with her grief. They must have been very close. She had talked openly about her aunt and uncle but, was evasive when it came to discussing her cousin, skirting around Skye's name like she was trying to avoid falling into a deep chasm.

This whole thing was like a jigsaw puzzle, some of the pieces he felt sure he had, the others were still missing. Skye had those and seemed to be doling them out one at a time. He needed to be analytical and methodical about this. He couldn't go about it willy-nilly.

He turned off the overhead light and sat at the desk. He withdrew a notepad and pen from the drawer and placed them before him. He began to write notes, facts he knew.

He was positive the ghost was a fifteen-year-old girl. He wrote her name. Before she died she made her way to this room. He wrote library. She had spoken of a red book with her last breath. He wrote this down. He needed to find it, find where she'd hidden it. She loved music. He wrote manipulates piano and stereo under the heading of communication.

Bill absently scratched his head, deep in thought. He must ask Melissa if she could recall the names of the tunes she'd heard on the stereo or if she had some idea what they were called. They could go over the list of billboard hits he'd managed to obtain this afternoon from the Internet. He thought they might be of help. He was glad now he'd had the foresight to get them. Now more than ever they had meaning. Bill took a deep breath; he wished he hadn't decided to wait until tomorrow to study the list with her. For some reason he felt the urgency of figuring out what was going on here. He couldn't explain it. He just knew they had to do it soon.

On the next page he wrote; must chat with Mattie about any incidents she had experienced, now and in the past. What did she mean by 'what she had felt'?

He was flipping the pen in his fingers, considering what else to write when he heard a low wailing sound. It was piteous and sad, not coming from any particular direction; it just hung in the room and gave him chills. It was the voice of a child, one crying in despair.

He lowered his pen to the desk. Should he speak to her? Could she even hear him if he did? He cleared his throat.

"Skye?" He paused, listening to her weep.

"Skye. I can hear you." He waited, but all he heard was that pitiful wailing sound. It sent shivers up and down his spine.

Then, without warning, the French doors blew open with a loud thunderous crash. Flung back on their hinges they banged against the walls. An arctic wind, worse than any winter night he had ever felt, entered his bones, chilling his marrow.

The crying had stopped but he hardly noticed.

"My God! What *is* this?" Bill was suddenly frozen to the core.

The papers on his desk rippled with the wind, some falling to the floor. It played with his notepad, fluttering the pages, nearly lifting it off the desk. He covered it in both hands to keep it in place and noticed his hands were shaking. Where was this wind coming from? *It's not that cold outside*! He thought wildly.

He felt a chill rippling up and down his forearms; fingers of ice slid down to his hands. Then the notepad began to slide away from him. He stared in amazement; it had moved on its own. Grabbing the notepad he stood up.

It nearly flew out his hands.

He grasped it tighter, leaning over the desk, playing tug-of-war with an unseen force, and stared in horror and fascination as he lost. It slipped through his fingers and flew across the room, landing on the veranda outside. Some of the pages had been torn out and lay scattered, leaving a trail from his desk to the wicker chairs outside.

Bill stared in disbelief at his hands. A crumpled blank page was all that was left in one hand, still flapping in the cold wind.

And then, with great force, the air sucked outward, momentarily pulling the air from his lungs. He tried to gulp in some life saving oxygen but it was like trying to breathe in a vacuum. His face turned red and his blue eyes bulged with the effort, and just when he thought he was going to pass out, suddenly, the room made a collective popping sound, like something had simultaneously hit every object in the room, each with its own distinctive sound; the crackling of the leather chairs, the thumping of wood and books, the clinking of the glass bulbs overhead and in the desk lamp, the electric pop of his computer screen.

And then as quickly as it had come in, the last of the frigid cold went out, slamming the French doors shut with its passing. Overhead, one bulb exploded within the glass fixture.

Bill collapsed into his chair. "Sweet Jesus, help me!"

All was still and quiet as Bill stared straight ahead, sucking in great gulps of the wonderful air he had coveted just seconds ago, wondering if he were having a bad dream.

What was that?

He couldn't believe what just happened. It was incredible, and yet at the same time frightening. It was an experience he would definitely put down as a first.

Finally, his breathing returned to normal and his heart quit slamming against his rib cage.

Looking down at his desk, and seeing no sign of his notepad was proof that he had just experienced what he, up till now, had only read about in books. A poltergeist. No Dream. It happened. And this one, it seemed to Bill, attacked with malicious intent. It had taken his notes, and his air!

He rose slowly from the desk on somewhat shaky legs and crossed the room to the French doors. He hesitated and then firmly grasped the knob, opening one side. He opened it wide for a poor shaft of light from the lamp, and stepped outside to retrieve his notes.

There was a faint breeze stirring the bushes, clean and cool from the afternoon's thundershower. Fireflies danced near the railing.

He gathered up his notes in trembling hands, hoping he got every page of his notepad and re-entered the library, shutting and locking the door behind him. On his way back to the desk, he stooped to gather the rest lying on the floor.

This was an interesting and eerie turn of events, a twist to the situation. This was no longer just a simple haunting by a young girl. There was something else here. Something malevolent. Somehow, there was a connection between the two. Had to be. It seemed to Bill that they went hand in hand. He reasoned out his jumbled thoughts; Skye plays the piano, the room grows cold and she suddenly stops. He hears her crying and speaks to her, and then he is attacked. Definitely a connection.

He looked at his torn notepad lying on the desk. Whatever it was that had entered this room, didn't want him getting involved. It was the only thing it had tried to destroy.

Poor Madeleine. No wonder she was so terrified and confused. Was this what she had meant? 'You haven't felt what I have felt.' He could now sympathize. It had frightened him more than he cared to admit, but it hadn't dampened his curiosity. Now more than ever, he wanted to solve this puzzle.

Bill shoved his torn papers into a desk drawer. Rising from the desk, he switched off the light as he passed through the door. It was nearing eight-thirty and he hadn't heard a sound from Melissa above.

"My God. Melissa!"

He quickened his pace up the stairs. It was no longer such a good idea to leave her alone. It never had been. From now on, he vowed, they would be joined at the hip. He couldn't leave her alone to face a possible attack. What if it could do worse things than what it had just done to him? What would "it" do if "it" deemed it was necessary? And what could he do about it? At the back of his mind, he wondered if he had bitten off more than he could chew in returning to Grace Stone Manor.

He quietly entered the bedroom and was relieved to see Melissa sleeping soundly. She had turned on her side, holding his pillow close; her red curls framing her cheeks glowed softly in the lamplight. His bat stood near the bed.

He felt guilty for dragging her back to the house. Maybe he should have listened to her. But no, he had to have his adventure. He felt like an insensitive heel, only thinking of himself and what he wanted.

It wasn't too late to back out. He didn't owe the Martuccis anything. They were free to leave. They could pack tomorrow, shake the dust off their feet, and never look back. *And*, he thought miserably, *I would forever wonder what had become of that poor lost little girl*. He really wanted to help her.

Bill groaned in his frustration and indecision. He crossed to the chest of drawers and withdrew his blue cotton pajamas and a pair of boxer shorts. He would not be sleeping in just his boxers tonight, as was his habit. If anything happened, he at least wanted to have some kind of clothing on. He couldn't just run around in his underwear if the girl or the other entity decided to pay him another visit. If for some reason he had to run out into the hall, he couldn't risk doing so half naked in front of Madeleine or Maria.

He quietly bent over Melissa, nightclothes in hand, and gently kissed her cheek. He really loved his wife, and she deserved an account of what had happened in the library, and if after telling her, she wanted to pack and leave, he would do so. He had to be fair to her. A part of him still wanted to stay but he would not force her to remain if she were afraid. He would discuss it with her first thing in the morning. He went to shower and dress for bed, leaving the bathroom door open.

Down below in the back garden, once again, the fountain shook. Another crack appeared along the foundation and bits of plaster chipped off the cherub holding the pitcher that adorned the center. It rocked, spurting a stream of rusty water in the air. From the basement up to the second floor of Grace Stone, the water pipes gurgled ominously and then all was quiet. Not even the crickets dared to sing near the old and decaying fountain.

Something dark, unholy and inhuman slithered from the fountain's moss-covered bowl, fell on the ground. At first it was gelatinous, blob-like, darkening a patch of weeds. It pulsated in a rhythmic pattern like the heart that once beat within it, and then it grew, coalescing into the thing it had become; cold, black. And full of hate.

It's time to have a little discussion with the brat, the black writhing mass that was once human decided. *Bill Hayden is getting too close. He now knows who she is. And worse, he believes. After all these years she's finally managed to reach someone. And the other woman, the blonde; something about her seems very familiar.*

A disturbing feeling deep in his core gnawed at him but he pushed it away savagely. He wanted to remember last night, how he enjoyed caressing her and making her shiver. He wanted to feel the warmth from her small perfect body and draw the life right out of her. So sweet and good, and he wanted to crush her. In life he had preferred brunettes, but something about the blond woman drew him to her; he could ignore the silvery hair if she gave him the life-force he craved.

But first, find the brat. It's time for a chat. It's time she learned what being a ghost is all about. It's time for her to climb down off her high and holy loft and come down to my level.

He glided through the overgrown garden and slithered into the house. His black filmy substance shadowed the kitchen walls for a few seconds and then he disappeared through the ceiling, moving upward. In his passing, a few of the cabinet doors slowly swung open.

Chapter 9

April 30, Friday, 4 a.m.

"Skye." He spoke with a gravelly voice that only she could hear. His shadow slid across the attic doorway. He waited, pulsating. "Come on Skye." *Brat!* "I'm not going to hurt you. I know you are afraid of me, but don't worry. I just want to talk to you." He drifted slowly into the room a few feet and stopped.

The temperature dropped.

His shadow thickened, pitch black against the darkness in the attic. He would go no further. This room still permeated with the stench of the Fitzgerald belongings; he could still feel some of their essence clinging to old clothes and useless trinkets. He shivered.

A dusty old trunk resting further back in the gloom shook and bumped against the wooden floor. He stared at it warily. A blue mist was slowly forming over it and he waited as a small form ascended through the lid.

He shook involuntarily and took on the shape of the body that once housed his being. The girl also was taking on her old form as she rose up from the trunk.

Something over the region where her heart would beat if she still had one was shining just a little too brightly. He squinted his eyes against the glare and took two steps back when the pain struck his bowels. He had anticipated this but still it caught him off guard when it slammed into his being. With great effort he held his ground, determined not to let her see his pain.

He had a vague notion why this was so and knew that she had no knowledge of the pain she caused him, was unaware of it. And he wanted to keep it that way. All these years of playing cat-and-mouse, she with her little useless tricks of trying to communicate with the living, and he, always the aggressor, chasing her, had grown old and tiresome. He wanted to finish her. Keeping her fear of him alive was only a game. He knew it. She did not. But he must change this situation without her knowing the truth. He must change her to destroy her.

Skye trembled and opened her mouth to speak. She was afraid that nothing would come out except for a ghostly moan. She closed her lips.

"Go on, Skye. You can speak. I know it's been a long time for you. But we can speak to each other. It's just the rule of our kind. Go on. Give it a try," he coaxed her.

"I . . ." Skye stumbled at the first word she'd heard herself utter in over two decades. She hovered above the trunk, in the dark, and trembled; something wet was tickling her cheeks. She lifted her hand and touched her own tears for the first time. Without form she had wept and wailed, but without tears, without substance.

She glanced down at her body; she was bare-armed, clad in the purple spaghetti-strapped sun dress she had died in and she could feel the soft material of the black bathing suit she'd worn home that long ago night beneath it. And for once, in over twenty years, her long dark hair was heavy, cascading down her slim back just as she remembered. Her large brown eyes trailed up the dusty floor. Once again she was looking at her nemesis.

"There are many things about this kind of existence that you do not know." He spoke softly, trying not to frighten her and at the same time fighting the rage within himself. He wished he could destroy her now. "I know a lot and I could teach you."

Trying her voice once more, Skye spoke, "Why? Why would you be willing to teach me anything? You hate me." She heard the distrust in the timbre of her teenage voice.

"I know we haven't exactly been friends." He blinked and tried to concentrate on her face or her feet, anywhere but her heart. The brightness there smarted his dark and smoldering eyes. "But, I realize, you are very young," he continued, "and inexperienced. Our twenty-three-year-old fight, shall we say, hasn't been a fair one. I can do many things you have not even dared to try. Fun things. But this little game we play is bothersome. It took you over two decades just to make yourself heard. Don't you want to be done with this?"

"Of course, I want to finish this. I'm tired and want to rest. But I can't. I pledged an oath." Skye looked wearily down at the floor. "What do you want? What do you propose we do?"

She looked up at the man he once was. His face was lined from too much sun and his unruly dark hair hung in clumps over his high forehead. She would not look into his eyes; they were as black as the night. His brown work pants and long-sleeved shirt were rumpled and dirty and he looked like he was in bad need of a shave. There was an ugly dark stain in the center of his chest and a ragged gaping hole in his shirt.

So, this is what he looked like when he died. Just a stupid, evil, immoral man, she thought, shaking with disgust. *No*, she amended; *he's more than that*. He was a rapist and a baby killer and he had killed her parents! He had killed *her*! She wasn't sure she should listen to him. In fact, she knew she shouldn't. But still, she was intrigued. Why was he here? She remained guarded and waited for him to answer.

He glanced away from her to the darkened window, barely able to hold himself in the attic. Something, other than her presence, was digging hot needles into his being and he strained with the effort to keep his stance. He wanted to get this over with and escape.

"The way I see it, you have two choices." He stared once more at her young face; one that looked too much like her grandmother. So innocent and sweet looking. It made him sick! He envisioned himself ripping out her eyes and smiled a black-toothed grin. He shook with the anticipation, his fists clenched at his sides. *Not yet! But soon!*

"What are they?" she asked suspiciously.

"One: you could renounce your oath, or two: you could learn to fight me on equal terms. I will give you a chance to fight me fairly." *Come to my level brat, and I'll destroy you.*

"I cannot renounce my oath." Skye didn't need to hesitate in answering. Renouncing the vow she made would surly mean eternal damnation. She believed this with all her heart. She considered the other choice. Fight him on equal terms? What did he mean by equal? What would constitute a fair fight? He was evil, full of tricks and lies. What did he know about being just? She couldn't understand why, all of a sudden, he wanted to be fair. She voiced her thought.

"Let's just say I find it beneath me to carry on a war with a young girl. One who hasn't found her potential yet," he answered. "I'm gonna tell you a secret about our kind. You know, everyone feels anger. You feel anger at me, but you don't use it to your advantage. You shouldn't hold back what you feel. Anger is a powerful generator. You would be surprised at what you can do if you would allow yourself the freedom to feel."

Somewhere in his lower region the pain was lessening, losing its grip on him. He could feel her interest growing. *Yes, that's it!* He'd learned in life, at a very early age, that deception and corruption were useful tools. He wished he'd tried to reason with her a long time ago.

"You've noticed that I don't need to draw energy from this house's electricity. And if you listen to me, you won't need it either." He smiled at her slyly, his deep-set eyes so dark that he seemed to be staring out at her with a skull's empty sockets.

"What about going into stasis?" she asked, glancing away from his dark visage. She couldn't bear to look at his eyes, she wasn't sure he had any.

"What do you mean?" *What was she talking about?*

"You know. When I feel drained, I kinda fall asleep."

So, it happens to her too. He just hadn't understood the word she'd used. "That never happens to me." He lied, keeping his secret from her. He wasn't about to inform her of any weakness he had. He wouldn't give her the pleasure of knowing that sometimes he suddenly found himself locked inside a dark and damp place and only escaped with tremendous effort. It was the only time he felt real fear.

"Are you saying that I can draw energy on just my anger and do things and not feel drained later?" she asked doubtfully, wondering if he was telling the truth.

But wasn't it wrong to feel anger? She thought of scriptures in the *Bible* about anger, scriptures her father had read to her whenever her temper flared. Then she remembered reading about Jesus getting angry with the moneychangers in the temple and overturning their tables. He had shown His anger back then. Maybe releasing it, instead of holding it in, was better. Maybe it wasn't wrong. Maybe, just maybe, he was telling her the truth.

"Skye, you have known me in this state for over twenty years. In all that time, have you ever noticed me weak or growing tired?" Although the pain had lessened in his mid-section, still he hurt and was growing impatient with her questions.

"Give it a try," he urged. "Practice. I will leave you alone for twenty-four hours. I know you don't wish to frighten the people in this house but, you must practice to be any good. And if you want to gain strength you're gonna have to scare someone. Try it on the redhead or that Spanish maid. Pick someone. But do it soon," he warned her. "Who knows, maybe you'll win in the end."

His form began to quiver, losing its substance. To Skye, it was like watching a melting snowman, a dirty one.

His voice suddenly grew harsh. "But I won't stop fighting you and right now I'm stronger!" *I hate you, you miserable brat!* He roared with the fury of an insane animal.

All he could think of, all he wanted, was to crush that pious face and drain the life-force out of her being. He bellowed and lost his shape, turning into a black writhing mass of oily shadow, and despite the intense pain that pricked his very being, he flung himself at Skye, no longer able to contain his rage.

She had no time to react. He'd changed shape so quickly and he was coming for her throat. She could only stare, frozen in fear.

Tentacles of black reached for her. This was the end. She hoped it would be over quickly. Hoped beyond hope that she would at last be reunited with her parents. Maybe she should have given up long ago. But deep down, she knew better. She knew that if he took her, she would be forever lost.

She shut her eyes, expecting the coldness to engulf her, obliterate her, but it never came. In an instant, something gripped her feet and drug her down into the dark trunk as he flew past her head and out through the attic wall to the garden below.

Skye stayed inside the trunk, among her grandmother's things, trembling, becoming a blue mist. She didn't know what had saved her but she was grateful. In another split-second he would have had her. She didn't want to imagine what would have become of her if he had gotten to her. Perhaps she would have been swallowed up in his eternal darkness, forever trapped with him in his dark soul. It was a horrible prospect, and she was too frightened to continue this train of thought.

She sighed, unaware that the dust surrounding the trunk stirred, as if her very breath was gently blowing away the traces of his presence.

Agitated and confused, she thought about his visit. This was the first time he had ever approached her just to talk. Why now? After all these years? Maybe he *had* grown tired of the games, cat-and-mouse, hide-n-seek, and chase.

He was right about one thing though, she *was* angry. She was angry at his cruelty, at his tenacious grip on this existence, at his black evil ugliness. Everything about him made her angry. And she was angry with herself for being scared, being weak, being stuck in this house, unable to reach anyone for twenty-three years. And she was angry with herself now for making that stupid oath, trapping her here.

Skye felt her anger rising, boiling within her, and she let the emotion come. Welcomed it. She *was* tired of holding it in.

Her being shook with hot fury.

The trunk in which she hid began to rock, thumping the bare attic floorboards, sending up a plume of aging dust. Why should she have to be the one to cower in fear? Why not instill some of that fear in her adversary? It was time to stop hiding. She was sick of the games. She wanted to be the cat for a change and he the trembling mouse. She felt hot with rage.

Unable to feel the comfort and security of her grandmother's clothes, her essence boiled and flared a flaming red. She thought she would explode, burning everything in the attic in the flaming inferno of her fury. No longer able to contain the consuming fire burning within her, she flew out of the trunk, sending it skidding across the floor behind her.

She stared at the musty old trunk she had moved three feet from its place and felt deep satisfaction. She had accomplished this feat under her own steam. It was amazing. All she had to do was get mad and let it out. So, he'd told her the truth after all.

Her newfound strength felt glorious but, she noticed with some small trepidation, the color of her essence was no longer the bright, pretty, cool blue that housed her being. Instead, she was glowing an ugly reddish-orange, and as her anger dissipated, her center grew dim, like a fire banked into dully glowing embers.

Looking at herself, she thought back to earlier this evening, when she had entered the Hayden's bedroom. She had been surprised to see them and greatly pleased. She had felt hope and joy. They had returned to help her. She remembered a wonderful feeling surging through her and of Bill exclaiming, pointing right at her as he'd jumped off the bed. For a moment, he had seen her and she hadn't even tried to make her presence known. She still did not know why. It had been a feeling that had ended all too soon.

Well, that didn't matter now. She had finally reached someone. Bill knew who she was. All that remained was to convince Mattie. After that would come the task of telling them about Mr. Worms, the Other, the Bad One, the Ogre, the Beast John Sneed. And more importantly, helping them find the red book. Somehow she would have to convey the message of where to look to find the answer. *Mattie should know. But she just wasn't paying attention.*

Now that Skye knew she could manipulate objects, maybe it would be easier for her to communicate. And finally, with her newfound strength and their help, Sneed would be defeated and the truth would be known. And then . . . she could embrace the much longed-for and over-due rest.

It was late, the living were in bed, and tomorrow she would try to give them more clues, and yet again try to make her presence known to Mattie.

Skye floated through the dressmaker dummy. One of her grandmother's dresses hung on its frame in tatters. It was over forty years old; if she could touch it, the material would disintegrate.

She moved to the window, staring out at the blanket of stars overlooking the back garden. Her attention drew to the old water fountain far from the house. *Soon,* she thought, *soon.*

Then she turned and drifted down to her old bedroom. Drawing near to Madeleine, she hovered near her cousin's ear and began to whisper, *"Find it, Mattie, you must find it. Remember. Remember my hiding place. I need your help. Please, Mattie."*

Beside Victor, Madeleine began to whimper, feverishly tossing beneath the covers.

Chapter 10

April 30, Friday

Madeleine awoke, blurry eyed, from a restless night. She rubbed her swollen eyes gingerly and stared through the watery haze up at the light blue canopy overhead, slowly bringing it into focus. She'd had Mr. Smedley replace it several times over the years to preserve the look of Skye's bedroom as time and dry rot left the previous canopies in tatters; the matching curtains as well.

She stretched upon the firm and comfortable mattress she and Victor slept on which had also been replaced a few years ago as well as the mattress in Maria's room and the master bedroom. The rest of the furniture at Grace Stone her grandparents had bought new after they were married and had remained within these paneled walls, except for the few pieces the Haydens had brought with them from their apartment in Oklahoma City when they'd relocated to the Tulsa area.

The white dresser, chest of drawers, vanity, and matching nightstands adorned in soft blue lace and antique lamps had once belonged to Skye. These, her parents had purchased when Skye was very young. They were very much a part of her cousin as had been her clothes, her music, her hairbrushes, and everything else she had once touched and made use of. There was still the imperfection in the vanity's wooden top where Skye had once thrown a porcelain figurine of a black rearing horse in a fit of temper. It had shattered, cutting the cherry wood beneath the paint, leaving a deep scar etched in the white finish. All of her personal items were gone now but the furniture remained, naked, silently giving voice to the echo of her beloved cousin's memory.

Madeleine moved slowly to sit on the edge of the bed. She felt fatigued, didn't have the energy to stand, and wasn't sure she wanted to. Her bedside clock read 8:45a.m. She had overslept. And no wonder; she had lain next to Victor and sobbed piteously until, emotionally exhausted, her tears finally spent, she fell into an erratic fitful sleep.

She wished she had lain unconscious all night, but the throbbing behind her red-rimmed eyes told the truth. She had hardly slept at all, merely dozing and tossing, plagued by strange and twisted dreams of Skye, only to awaken to the remembrance of the living nightmare that had taken place in the library, and then dozing off again to face more sporadic haunted dreams. She couldn't even recall what they had been about, just that Skye was a part of them, and they had left her in a state of depression and immovability. She did not wish to get up.

She did not want to face Bill Hayden.

Victor, a firm believer in early to bed, early to rise, had risen from bed, showered and dressed impeccably as ever, and had raced downstairs for breakfast well over an hour ago, anticipating the arrival of the electrician.

Maria, she knew, would soon be upstairs to check on her, no doubt bearing a breakfast tray laden with food, which she had no desire to eat. Maria always set aside a tray for her if she didn't show up for a meal. But this morning she had no appetite.

She forced her legs to stand, and moving slowly, wobbled to the bathroom. It had also been painted to resemble the great outdoors; Aunt Elise's idea and handiwork when she saw what her daughter had done with the bedroom, but this she had painted as green rolling pastures dotted with trees, horses grazing in the background, and a waterfall flowing down toward the huge porcelain tub and shower. Madeleine had also insisted that the bathroom be left unscathed by a paintbrush or wallpaper when leasing out the house. She was pleased to see that her wishes had been respected.

When she had finished in the bathroom she returned to bed, bringing with her a cold washcloth to place over her swollen, burning eyes. The cool damp cloth was soothing and helped blot out the sunlight prying its way through the blinds and blue sheer curtains. She had just tucked the quilt up around her waist and covered her eyes with the washcloth when, right on time, Maria knocked on the door, entering with an old wooden tray.

Maria placed the tray on the dressing table and went to Madeleine's side. She didn't like what she saw as Madeleine removed her washcloth to peer up at her through haunted blood-shot eyes. "Oh, Miss Mattie, are you ill?" she asked with great concern, kneeling at her side.

Madeleine gazed into her housekeeper's warm brown eyes, seeing the worry in them. Her gentle concern was touching and comforting. She looked down at her hands toying with her washcloth. Afraid she might cry, she bit her trembling lip.

With more surety than she felt, she replied, "Oh, I'll be all right. I . . .it was just one of those bad nights. Headache, you know. Honestly. I just haven't had enough rest, that's all. I'm not ill."

Maria wasn't certain that Madeleine was entirely truthful with her but had to take her at her word. "I've brought your breakfast tray. Shall I bring it to you?" she asked. With confident hands she carefully tucked the downy-soft blue flowered quilt around Madeleine's tiny waist and smoothed the rest down to the foot of the bed. She was reaching for extra pillows to place behind her head when Madeleine stopped her with the wave of her hand.

She said, "I appreciate your thoughtfulness, Maria, but I don't think I could eat just now. Would it be too much trouble to bring me a cup of hot tea instead?"

"Of course, it would be no trouble at all. And it might go down better than the coffee I brought." She crossed the room and lifted the tray; the familiar sound of her white hose gave Madeleine a peculiar feeling of comfort, a secure feeling of home and familiarity. Maria was a solid, grounded person, not given to flights of fancy and imagination, and right now her presence reminded Madeleine of home. Her Pasadena home.

Madeleine had to admit she leaned on Maria as much as she leaned on Victor. They both had been and were still her mainstays in times of emotional anguish. She wished greatly that she could confide in them now but she dare not. This distressing situation was beyond the realm of normalcy. She could barely face it herself. She couldn't expect Maria to do more than look after her everyday needs.

"Thank you very much, Maria. I may not be down for lunch either. Would you bring up a bowl of soup about one o'clock?" Madeleine felt pathetically childish making the request but she didn't want to face Bill and Melissa for a while. She wasn't sure she could face Bill at any time today. For now, she was content to hide behind the closed door of Skye's bedroom, at least until she could collect herself and coax the puffiness out of her eyes.

Maria lifted the unwanted tray, said, "Of course I will, and I'll be right back with your tea. In the meantime, you have the right idea. Keep that cold cloth on your eyes. It'll help." Then she was out the door.

Madeleine closed her eyes and replaced her washcloth. She felt drained and sleepy. Her arms lay at her sides like limp dishrags, her legs to heavy to move beneath the light quilt.

She wanted to go home. Maybe it hadn't been a good idea in coming after all. Nothing here had changed. If anything, it had become worse, and Madeleine didn't want to think about what had happened in the library. It was too scary.

She sighed deeply and settled into the warm and comfort of Skye's bed.

Behind her eyelids she pictured herself in the garden in Pasadena, far removed from Grace Stone and its trouble. She envisioned herself seated on a cushioned wrought-iron chair, reading a book, and enjoying a warm California breeze carrying the scent of roses and wildflowers. Overhead, birds were singing prettily and dancing across an azure sky. She felt warm, safe, secure, and free of turmoil.

Madeleine began to float dreamily.

She did not hear Maria softly calling her name when she'd returned carrying a steaming cup of Jasmine tea laced with honey. She did not hear the door closing behind her when she left, taking the cup with her.

Downstairs, Victor Martucci, and Bill and Melissa Hayden had finished a warm and filling breakfast of eggs, their choice of poached or scrambled, hot buttered crescent rolls, creamed oatmeal, bagels with cream cheese, and sliced oranges. On the table, Maria had also placed various jams and marmalade and sliced toast, a cold pitcher of milk and one of orange juice. When they had nearly finished their meal, to top it off, she'd brought a steaming pot of coffee and three mugs.

Victor sat at one end of the dining table near the swinging door. One seat away on his right, sat Bill, across from Bill sat Melissa who had thoroughly enjoying her meal.

Victor had glanced at her generous hips and thighs as she had taken her seat and was not surprised at the way she had filled her plate. Melissa, on the other hand, had cared less what he or Bill thought. Since she had failed to keep down her dinner last night, this morning she was famished, and Maria had laid out a delicious breakfast. She'd dove in heartily, only glancing now and then at Bill who seemed to be in a brown study.

For the most part they had eaten in silence, each deep in their own thoughts.

Victor was anxious for the electrician to arrive. He wanted to quickly settle this little problem of wiring and get on with making the sale of Grace Stone Manor. Having that done, he could make a hasty retreat back home to sunny blue skies, modern homes with well-kept yards, sensible people who didn't believe in ghosts, and his successful business in downtown Burbank.

And Mattie. He took a drink of his coffee and sighed. He shouldn't have brought Mattie, but she had been so adamant about coming. He'd thought she was stronger now, but he had been wrong. Best to hurry this up and be done with it before her condition worsened. He had not been oblivious to his wife's restlessness during the night.

He liked the Haydens well enough and had been pleased with the conversation he'd had with Bill about the renovations done to the house. Bill had not mentioned anything about ghosts, in fact, acted as if he had not run off in the middle of night, but had chatted rationally and amicable as they'd made their rounds throughout the house.

It was obvious to Victor that the young man wanted to buy the house but he couldn't help but get the feeling that he was holding something back. Maybe it was the price. Victor thought two hundred thousand dollars was reasonable but to get this noose off his neck he was willing to negotiate. He would concentrate more on that after hearing the electrician's diagnosis.

The other thing he was pleased about was Bill having shown him Samuel Fitzgerald's private office. He was a little peeved that his wife had chosen to show it to Hayden before confiding in him, but he could let that slide since it obviously had an appeal to Bill, a carrot to dangle in front of his nose when negotiating the price. Maybe he wouldn't have to lower the price by much. He was anxious to clench this deal and had eaten with the harried zeal of a man late for an appointment.

Occasionally looking at his wife, Bill had played over in his mind his conversation with her that morning before coming downstairs to breakfast. Although the food looked delicious and he had eaten enough to be filled, he had done so absently, barely tasting it.

He was deeply concerned at Melissa's stubborn refusal to leave the house. He had expected her to immediately begin packing after relating the frightening incident that had occurred in the library the night before. Instead, she had surprised him by saying she had no intention of leaving. She wanted to take back control of her life. She had fallen in love with this house the moment she'd seen it and nothing was going to drive her away from it. 'Houses are for the living,' she'd said, 'not the dead.' As far as she was concerned the ghosts could pack up and leave. They were supposed to at death anyway.

Bill had admired her bravery and tenacity but was worried that she had failed to understand just what she getting into. He'd tried to tell her that it could be dangerous but she wouldn't hear of it. She was not the same Melissa he'd slept next to the past week, the one who was frightened and had needed to be cajoled into returning to Grace Stone.

It seemed to Bill that sometime during the night Melissa had found her self-confidence and this morning was much like her old self; secure, self-reliant, and sure. In light of last night's events he wasn't sure if it was a good thing or not. It seemed the tables had turned; now he was the one who was worried about staying and it was Melissa who was now gung-ho about solving the puzzle. He was glad she was willing to help him now but still, he was worried. He slowly sipped his coffee and wondered what was going on behind his wife's calculating green eyes; she was grinning like a Cheshire cat.

Melissa had slept like a baby. No interruptions by ghosts, no bad dreams. She had risen from bed feeling renewed and vigorous like the last three weeks had never happened. Gone were her uncertainty and her fear, replaced by self-assurance and strength of will. Today she was taking back control of her life.

Today was the day for honesty, she'd decided. No more hedging the truth with the Martuccis. If asked a point blank question of what was going on here they were going to get a straightforward answer from her. She didn't get where she was by being a wimp. When a doctor had criticized her for a mistake she had made she had taken it like the stalwart woman she was, no crying self-pity did she allow at any time. She was not going to be timid now.

She glanced at Victor Martucci. She'd felt intimidated by him yesterday, but not today. So what if he's rich, lives in California, and wears expensive suits. Strip him down to his skin and he's like any other man, and she would handle him in the same steely professional manner she'd learned from handling egotistical, and sometimes chauvinistic, Oklahoma City doctors. Victor Martucci wasn't any different; just rich and use to getting his way. Well, like it or not, he was selling a haunted house. She grinned over the rim of her coffee cup at her resolve to set him straight and then remembered her talk with Bill.

She had showered with the door open to listen while Bill related what had happened in the library. Instead of frightening her, it had bolstered her determination to stay. It was time to do something about the haunting and she wasn't about to keep her thoughts to herself. The Martuccis needed to be told everything that she and Bill knew. And Madeleine was going to have to face facts; her dead cousin was haunting the house. As for the other one, she was confident they would figure it out soon. They had learned about the girl, hadn't they?

She had argued with Bill as she'd put on a pair of khaki pants, a v-necked white t-shirt, and thrust her red-painted toenails into her sandals. She was not going to run. She was not going back to a motel. The rent was paid and she intended to stay until this house was cleared of spooks. She had wanted to buy this house from the beginning and she was tired of being frightened. They had enough clues to get them started in figuring out what was going on and she was sure they would soon have more. It was only a matter of time.

She had waited impatiently as Bill dressed casually in jeans and a light blue t-shirt, and then practically dragged him out the door before he could put on his shoes. He'd had to hop on one foot, quickly donning his other loafer, as she'd pulled him down the hall. It had been nearly 8:00 a.m. She hadn't wanted to talk anymore; it was breakfast time and she was starving.

Now, deep in thought, she was startled when he spoke.

Halfway through his cup of coffee, Bill cleared his throat and said, "Would it be alright to have a look at those files again?" That morning he had found the file cabinet in Samuel's private office still contained drawings and diagrams, left there by Madeleine's father after his brother's death, blueprints of the house and grounds.

Victor dabbed at his lips, replaced his napkin and replied, "I don't see why not. Look all you want."

Bill looked at Melissa and raised his eyebrows. "Care to join me in the library, Hon?" Despite her arguments, he still did not want to leave her alone. She didn't have a clue just how bad the other ghost could be.

"Why don't you two go ahead?" She gave Bill a don't-coddle-me look and then smiled at Victor. "I'm sure I saw a blueprint that had a layout of the wiring. That might be useful to have when the electrician arrives."

"I believe you're right. Good thinking," Victor said as he got up from the dining table. "Come on, Bill. Let's get a closer look at those papers." He pushed in his chair. Not waiting for Bill, he strode through the swinging door.

"Melissa, please. Come with me to the library." Bill implored her, sliding his empty mug away from him.

"Bill, I'm a grown woman. I'll be perfectly all right." She began stacking her empty glasses onto her plate. "I have other things I want to do. Giving in to fright and following you around takes away my freedom. I told you, I can't live confined and restricted. That's what's been eating at me."

She rose from the table, picking up her plate, cups and glasses clinking against each other. "I'm going to do something ordinary, like helping Maria clear this table and wash the dishes. And this evening I'm going to help fix dinner, because if I have to eat and upchuck one more Italian dish I'm going to scream."

She backed out through the swinging door, leaving Bill standing by his chair, his face flushed with irritation.

"God, what a stubborn woman!" Bill exclaimed to the empty dining room. There was just no reasoning with her this morning. He slammed his chair up to the table. *Oh, well*, he thought, *might as well get to the library*. No doubt Victor was probably wondering what was keeping him. He strode silently out of the dining room and headed for Samuel Fitzgerald's private office.

Maria was just placing a steaming cup of coffee on Madeleine's tray as Melissa entered the kitchen. She frowned as Melissa stacked the dirty dishes in the sink. "Please, Mrs. Hayden. I'll take care of those. I'm just taking this tray up to Miss Mattie, and then I'll clear the table and wash up. You don't have to do that."

Melissa drew a deep breath and turned to face Maria. "I'm going to put this as honestly and as delicate as I can. There are some things I'm not use to, being waited on is one of them." Maria stood at the cooking island, her face expressionless. Melissa continued, "You're a terrific cook and I want to thank you for that delicious breakfast. But, I'd like to help with dinner tonight. And I want to help with the washing up. It what's I'm used to doing. Quite frankly I don't know how you can stand to eat all that Italian food. I mean I like Italian food, just not everyday. So, I'd like to help with dinner tonight."

A slow smile spread across Maria's dark features and understanding lit her eyes. "Mrs. Hayden I'd like to tell you a secret. I haven't touched Italian food in years."

"What?" Melissa wasn't sure she heard right.

"It's true." Maria went on, her brown eyes beaming with her confession, "I got burned out on that a long time ago. Since I never eat with Mr. And Mrs. Martucci I cook for myself, whatever I want, usually enchiladas or tacos. I make my own Spanish rice and guacamole. You see I also do the shopping."

"Maria, you surprise me. I thought you ate whatever you cooked for them." Melissa grinned from ear to ear.

"Oh, no." Maria shook her head. "So, you see, I understand just how you feel. And I understand about doing things for yourself. I knew when you first arrived here you were a little uncomfortable. And when you had quietly left the kitchen yesterday I figured you were probably feeling awkward. I mean, there I was, taking over your place, in your kitchen. I'm the one who brought it to Miss Mattie's attention that you'd left."

Melissa was modestly embarrassed, a pink tinge rose in her cheeks. "I didn't think anyone had noticed me sneaking off like that. And to be truthful I *was* a little resentful at you taking over the kitchen. I'm sorry for that. It was childish of me."

"Oh, don't apologize. I do understand. I don't have a problem with sharing the kitchen duties if you don't. I'll still have to cook Mr. Martucci's pasta dishes though."

Melissa nodded her head in agreement. "I don't mind sharing. Just so long as I get to eat something different tonight." She smiled in relief at how easy it had been to talk with Maria. "Well, I'll start clearing away the dining table. I hope Mattie isn't ill. Let me know if there is anything I can do."

Maria lifted the tray and headed for the swinging door. "I'm sure she's all right. She sometimes gets these headaches and stays in bed for awhile." Maria paused, and then added, "I'm glad we had this talk. I like being comfortable and at ease with others."

"Me too," Melissa said, as Maria slipped through the swinging door.

"Well, I'm glad that's out of the way," she said to the empty kitchen she'd just reclaimed. "I feel much better."

Leaning against the counter, she thought of Madeleine. After what Bill told her this morning about last night Melissa could understand why she was staying in bed. But, it seemed to Melissa that Madeleine was maybe just a little bit spoiled and used to being pampered. Obviously Maria had brought food to her many times before and thought nothing of it. "I'd like someone to bring me a breakfast tray just because I have a headache," she muttered. Then she thought better of it. *No, I wouldn't. I'd disgust myself.*

Melissa went to the dining room and began stacking that morning's dirty dishes. She made several trips to get it all cleared and then made water to wash them. She quietly hummed to herself as she worked, feeling very much back in control of her life. Now this was how she was supposed to feel. Normal. Performing ordinary everyday functions in a beautiful house she would soon call her own. Hers and Bill's that is.

She was thoroughly relaxed, gazing out at the overgrown backyard, absently washing the dishes when Maria returned to make a cup of tea.

"So, how is Mattie?" Melissa asked, rinsing soapsuds off one of her own black plates that were trimmed in gold. It wasn't very expensive but elegant enough for special dinners. Mr. Martucci, she figured, was used to eating off better dinnerware even for breakfast, and Maria knew how to set a fine table for him. She'd used her best plates.

"Oh, she'll be fine in a little bit. Just like I said, one of those headaches. I'm going to make her a cup of tea." Maria set the untouched tray on the table. She ran water into a teakettle at the island and then placed it on the stovetop to heat it. She retrieved a tea bag from a box in the pantry and placed it in a cup she had taken out of the cabinet.

Yep, Melissa thought derisively, *she's a little spoiled.* If Melissa stayed in bed all morning Bill would think she was dying. And after finding out she only had a headache he would smack her large derriere for making him worry. And then the fun would ensue. She smiled to herself.

Her eyes twinkled at the mental picture she conjured up. A little slap on the rump would lead to a little slap-and-tickle under the covers. It had been weeks since they'd last made love. The last time had been upstairs in that king-size bed. They had taken the bottle of wine upstairs with them after dinner, and since it had been a chilly spring night, Bill had built a small fire in the fireplace. It had been a very romantic night. She vaguely remembered having had a little too much wine; she had been slightly hung over the next morning and beset with a vague feeling she had forgotten something important. It still nagged at her now and then. But no matter how hard she tried she just couldn't put her finger on what that something might be.

Melissa shook herself out of her reverie and realized she had been rinsing the same pan for quite some time. She placed it in the overflowing drain board and saw she was finished except for the dishes on the tray. She began emptying the now cold untouched food into the trash bin. "Maria?"

"Hmm?"

"What's for lunch?"

"Oh, I thought we'd have a cold lunch today. I made a meatloaf last night for meatloaf sandwiches and there's plenty of cold cuts and cheese in the fridge. I also made Mr. Martucci a pasta salad, but there's enough for everyone." Maria threw away the used tea bag and measured out two teaspoons of honey into the cup.

"Lunch sounds great." Melissa washed up Madeleine's unused breakfast dishes and let the dishwater go. "How would you like to sample some of my cooking tonight?" she asked as she dried her hands. Since she had done the washing she would leave the drying and putting away to Maria.

"Okay. But only if tomorrow night you try one of my Spanish dishes." Maria's wide smile matched the twinkle in her eyes.

"Deal." Melissa thrust out a hand and shook Maria's in one hard jerk; nearly sloshing the tea Maria held in her other hand. They both laughed.

With her back to the swinging door, Maria paused and asked, "Where you looking for something last night in the kitchen?"

"No. Why?"

Maria shrugged, cradling the steaming cup near her bosom. "No particular reason. It's just that this morning when I came down to fix breakfast most of the cabinet doors were open. I thought perhaps someone had gotten up in the middle of the night for a snack." She opened the swinging door with her hip, "Well, it doesn't matter. It was probably Mr. Martucci." She departed with Madeleine's tea, the door swinging slowly back and forth, and then finally coming to rest.

Melissa took several pork chops out of the deepfreeze, placed them in a pan, and set them on the counter to begin thawing.

She vaguely remembered having to close a few dresser drawers this morning that she hadn't opened. But she'd shrugged it off thinking Bill had probably forgotten to close them when he got dressed for bed last night. Now she wasn't so sure.

A creepy feeling stole up her spine. She'd also found doors opened when she and Bill were the only two people in the house. It unnerved her just a little but she wasn't going to let it bother her. She'd attained freedom of movement this morning and wasn't about to let it go now. It was odd, yes, maybe even a little spooky, but it was harmless, and besides, she reasoned, Maria was probably right, someone had probably returned to the kitchen last night for a late-night snack. Yeah, she decided, that explanation was good enough for her.

Digging around in the deepfreeze again she pulled out a large package of frozen corn. She placed these in the refrigerator to thaw slowly. She must remember to put the meat in the fridge in a little while to keep it from spoiling. Tonight the Martuccis were going to get a taste of country cooking. And maybe in the morning she could help with breakfast and put biscuits and chocolate gravy on the table, just like her mother use to make when Melissa was a little girl, and still made whenever she and Bill visited her folks. She smacked her lips and smiled. It sounded good to her.

Having accomplished an ordinary chore she was now ready to tackle the extraordinary: Ridding the house of their otherworldly guests. She and Bill needed to get down to business and assemble the clues they had so far.

She left the kitchen and headed for the library, her head held high and a bounce in her step, her red curls bobbing with each footfall. It felt good to *choose* to go to the library and be with Bill, and not because she was afraid of being alone. It seemed silly to feel triumphant over making such a simple decision, but it was how she felt as she entered the library. She was back in control of her life.

Chapter 11

Melissa peered into the walnut shelf, eyeing the almost invisible lines of the section that would open the secret door when gently pushed. The old books that had concealed the small panel had been moved to another shelf when Bill made known this private office to her and Victor just before breakfast.

She had just placed her fingers on the polished wood when she heard a soft click. She stepped back as Victor swung the door open and entered the library carrying one of Samuel Fitzgerald's rolled diagrams in his hand.

"Thank you for reminding me of this," Victor said, patting the blueprint. "It'll be useful to the electrician." He made his way to the desk and proceeded to unroll it, pinning the curled corners with a brass paperweight and a glass penholder. He was so engrossed in studying the drawings he didn't hear Melissa's reply of "Your welcome," as she disappeared inside the small room.

Bill smiled up at her from the dusty metal desk. Forgetting his earlier irritation at her stubbornness to join him, he was pleased to see her now. On the desk before him were several more rolls of drawings like the one Victor was now studying.

"So, how did you and Maria get along? Did you fight over who was washing the dishes?" he gently teased her.

"Yes, and I won." She joked back at him. "Actually, we had a very nice conversation and came to a mutual agreement. I'm helping with dinner tonight," she announced, eyes twinkling.

"Oh? And what are we having?"

"Not telling you. You'll have to wait for the dinner bell." She grinned impishly.

"So, did you find anything interesting among those blueprints?" Placing her palms gingerly on the edge of the desk she leaned over to see what he was looking at. From her point of view they were upside down and didn't make much sense.

"Well, I found the specs for this room and how he made the mechanism to open the door." Bill unrolled the diagram. It protested at being unfurled after years of untouched solitude, crinkling and breaking off at the corners. Bill pointed with a forefinger at a section that was squared off and enlarged. "There's a bar running through it with a spring-loaded catch at either end. Pushing the panel releases it. It's very simple. Samuel was an intelligent man and was meticulous in everything he did. Wish I could have met him."

"Bill, if you had met him we wouldn't be buying this house." Melissa straightened her back and rubbed her hands together to dust them off. "This place needs a thorough cleaning." She moved to the drafting table and blew a cloud of dust into the air. "Yuck. This room's been closed off for years. I'll have to vacuum the dirt and cobwebs before I can actually start cleaning."

At the desk Bill unrolled another diagram. "Know what this is?" he asked.

Melissa skirted around the desk to peer over his shoulder. "Uh-uh. Oh. Wait a minute. That looks like a drawing of a water fountain." Melissa pointed near the bottom. "Are those pipes?"

"Sure are." Bill glanced at her over his shoulder. Returning his eyes to the drawing he said, "It looks as though he was planning to replace the old water pipes and install a new water-main for it, and possibly a new fountain."

"What do you mean plan to? How can you tell he didn't have it done before he died?" she asked.

"Simple deduction, my dear." The aging paper curled back around itself when he released it. He opened the drawer beside his right knee and withdrew a cracked and faded black leather date book. Samuel's personal planner.

"I've been looking this over," he said, carefully thumbing through the yellowed pages. "Here's a dental appointment for Skye." He turned a few more pages. "And a lunch date with someone named Robert Hopkins. Either a friend or business associate." He turned the dry crackling pages to the month of June. Written in Samuel's backward slant on June 20th were the words: Begin digging pipes. Remove fountain. "Do you see what I'm getting at?" He gazed up at Melissa.

Her eyes squinted, furrowing her brow, as she tried to reason it out in her mind. What was so important about June 20th? Try as she might, she still didn't understand. It just didn't ring a bell. "I give up. How did you figure it out?" And then, enlightenment came just before he spoke. "Oh! I remember now."

"That's right, Thelma, old girl. Now you're using the old bean." Bill beamed at her. "Samuel never got the chance to start digging. He was killed on the 17th. Three days before breaking the ground." He closed the book and returned it to the drawer. "I don't guess it has anything to do with our problem but I thought it was interesting. Anyway, most of the pipes had been replaced inside the house, but the ones outside are very old. We may have to have them replaced ourselves." Bill tapped the rolled blueprint. "We could use his plans. It shouldn't be too hard since we won't have to try and figure out where all the pipes are laid. He'd already done that."

Melissa stood, arching her back to get the kinks out from stooping over his shoulder. "Is that all that's here?" she asked.

Bill swiveled around in the squeaky chair to face her. "Yeah, that's about it. Except for some old dried out pens, a few stubby pencils with nasty looking erasers, and some bill receipts. The filing cabinet was practically empty but for these diagrams."

Looking appreciatively at the paneled walls and low-lying light-blue carpet dressing the floor, he envisioned himself ensconced behind a new desk, working at his computer. "Hon, this will make a great office for me. It's private. It's quiet. I might be able to start that book I've wanted to write. Once we get it cleaned up I'll move my computer in here."

Bill rose and stretched his long legs. He would have to buy a new office chair. Not only was Samuel's chair outdated but also it sat uncomfortably low for his six foot five inch frame. He glanced at the useless drafting table. "I won't be needing that," he said, pointing at it. "Man, that spot is just crying out for a new stereo sound system. God, what a house!"

He turned to Melissa and took her in his arms. "Have I told you lately that I love you?" He stared intently into her eyes. They had a shine he hadn't seen for quite some time; they reflected his own happiness, and mirrored his love, there was no fear there now, no insecurity in their emerald depths.

"No, not lately." Her fingers were entwined behind his neck. She was smiling up at him, enjoying his closeness.

"Love ya," he said.

"Back atcha," she replied, staring into his eyes.

He bent to kiss her, brushing her lips gently with his. Her musky perfume tickled his nose and he inhaled her scent deeply, kissing her once more, his lips lingering. He longed to continue this conversation upstairs but he remembered they were not alone in the house.

Thinking of the Martuccis reminded him of the predicament they were in. They couldn't fully lay claim to the house until the otherworldly occupants had found lodging elsewhere; like eternal rest. He pulled back from Melissa, but still held her loosely in his arms.

He said, "Care to talk about our ghosts?"

"Why not," she sighed, reluctantly stepping back from him. She had not mistaken the desire in his kiss and the feeling had been mutual. Again, that nagging feeling that she had forgotten something tugged at her conscience. But she realized they needed to get down to the business of solving their ghost problem and brushed it away impatiently. "Want to talk here or elsewhere? I'd prefer elsewhere. It's too dusty in here and I've no place to sit."

"We could sit in the living room." Bill suggested. "How about getting us a glass of iced tea? I've got some papers to get from the desk in the library, and then I'll meet you there."

"Sounds good to me." Melissa turned and slid through the bookcase door.

A few minutes later she met Bill in the living room. Seated on the sectional sofa, their glasses of tea resting on coasters to prevent the condensation from pooling on the glass top, Bill handed her a thick pile of papers.

"What are these?" she asked, glancing at the stack in her hands.

Bill took a sip of his tea and returned it to the coaster. "That is a printout of the Billboard Top 100 hits dating between 1960 and 1980. I thought you might be able to recall some titles to a few of those tunes you heard playing on the radio."

Melissa leafed through them doubtfully. "God, Bill. That's twenty years of music. Music I've never paid much attention to, even though I had to endure listening to it all those days I worked for Dr. Maxwell Remer on my days off. Remember? One of his nurses was on maternity leave and I agreed to fill in for her until he'd found someone else. He always had a radio playing in the back tuned in to some oldies station."

She smiled, remembering with fondness the middle-aged doctor who looked like a hippy reject from the sixties; he was tall and thin with a long face sporting a full mustache, and although his graying hair was long he'd kept it neatly pulled back into a ponytail. He was a caring and humorous man and she'd spent some interesting funny days working in his clinic. Some of his regular patients, on routine visits, would often join in singing a chorus to some old tune with him as he breezed into the room. And, foregoing formality, most of them just called him 'Doc'. It wasn't hard to see why his patients loved him to death.

"I got there early one morning," she told him with a wide grin, "and there he was, drinking his coffee and snapping his fingers and singing "My Guy." I couldn't help myself; I busted out laughing. He just smiled and said that the best tunes ever recorded were between 1950 and 1980. Said he couldn't stand to listen to the junk the music industry put out these days. Anyway, he'd told me that someone named Mary Wells sang "My Guy." If he'd been here the last couple of weeks he could tell you exactly what the names of those songs were and the artist. How are these lists supposed to help me? About the only thing I like from back then is Pink Floyd."

"You and your Pink Floyd." Bill grinned. "Well, if you can recall any of the words to those songs, especially the chorus, you might stumble upon a title. Usually you can find the title to a song in the chorus."

"Where did you get these?" she asked, rifling the lists with her fingers.

Bill answered, feeling pretty smug, "When I got away from Victor yesterday, I got on the Internet. There's a place where you can download music and chat with the people you get them from. I'm not sure it's entirely legal, but they're a friendly lot and were very helpful. I downloaded their play lists and printed out the billboard hits."

"Okay, smarty-pants, since you went to all that trouble, I'll give it a try." She threw off her sandals and tucked her feet beneath her.

"Start with 1970. I think it's best to begin there and it may save you some time," he suggested.

"You're right. Most of them I heard, I think, were from that decade." Melissa leafed through the top stack, noticing that he had stapled them into sections, separating them, one section for every five years. She removed the top two and began scanning the billboard hits for 1970. She gasped. Right on the first page she found two that she recognized. "Bill, here's two right here."

She pointed and read them aloud, ""Raindrops Keep Falling On My Head" by BJ Thomas and . . ." she giggled, "Norman Greenbaum? What kind of a name is that?"

"I remember that one," Bill said, as he wrote down the titles on his yellow, legal-sized, crumpled notepad with a ballpoint pin. "It was a one-hit wonder. "Spirit In The Sky." Right?"

"Yeah, that's it. Oh, I get it. Skye. Spirit. Well, I'll say one thing for her, she's clever." A look of dismay crossed her features. "Oh, Bill. I wish I had known. But I didn't. I was too annoyed and frightened to think these tunes meant anything."

"It's okay. We know now. That's the important thing. Keep looking."

"Here's one on page two. "Rainy Night In Georgia."" Melissa was thoughtful for a few seconds, and then said, "That's two that mention rain. I wonder what that means?" She turned the page and smiled, "And here we have another winner. "Fire And Rain." Hmmm. Curiouser and curiouser."

Scanning the fourth page, nothing jogged her memory. Then she sat staring at the fifth page for so long she forgot Bill was sitting next to her until he gouged her rib cage with his elbow.

"Yoo-hoo. Anybody home? Did you find something; you looked kinda dazed?"

"Ye-e-s," she said slowly, frowning. "This one I heard several times. It's a melancholy tune." She stared at the title, remembering one occasion when she'd heard it.

She'd been washing the windows in the living room when the stereo had suddenly come to life. She'd frozen in place, afraid to move, her hands pressed against the pane, a paper towel beneath one hand. It was a sad tune and it had held her spellbound. She hadn't moved an inch until without warning, with not even a hiss, the stereo had gone silent.

Bill nudged her again and asked, "What's the name of the song?"

"Oh, it's "If You Could Read My Mind" by Gordon Lightfoot. Bill, it gives me goose-bumps when I think about her playing it on the radio." She rubbed her arms, feeling chilled.

"Go on. What else can you remember about the song?"

"Bill, I don't know. I can't remember the words. I didn't pay attention. I just don't know how I'm going to be of any help to you. I don't listen to oldies," she muttered, shaking her head, coppery curls bouncing. "She really was trying to get through, wasn't she? And I just didn't know."

"It's all right, keep looking," Bill said, as he continued to scribble the titles on his notepad.

"And here's another one containing the word rain. "Rainy Days And Mondays" by the Carpenters. On page six is another one called "Here Comes That Rainy Day Feeling Again."" She quickly scanned the page and moved on to the next. "Here's one I remember but it's different. Not about rain. "Slippin' Into Darkness" by War. That's an odd one if you compare it to the others that mention rain. Hmmm, "Time Passages" by Al Stewart. I wonder what that one means? Well, that bring us up to 1979. I just don't get what she was driving at."

Melissa paused to take a sip from her glass of tea. Throwing her head back, she snorted a short laugh when she got to the 1980s. "Here's that one that was playing the night we left. "Another One Bites The Dust" by Queen. Well, I know why that one was playing now. She has a sense of humor, doesn't she? Or should I be saying *had*? Anyway, I'm surprised I remembered these. I didn't think I could. I've probably missed quite a few though. Oh, don't forget to put down that one by the BeeGees, "Tragedy."" She took a long refreshing sip and replaced her empty glass on the table, the melting ice tinkled. "I'm sorry I can't help you with the lyrics."

"Moppet, you're doing great." He encouraged her, patting her hand. "And don't worry about the lyrics. Remember, I can Google with the best of them. There's a Web site on the Internet where I can get the lyrics. No problem. Some of the clues are probably in the words."

Melissa continued to scan the pages, then found one printed out of place, a list of ABBA tunes that were recorded during the seventies. Of course, Madeleine had said that ABBA was Skye's favorite group, and Bill would want to know all those.

They were unaware of Skye having entered the living room a few moments before, settling on the sunny window seat at the end of the room. Bill sat facing the fireplace, furiously scribbling on his notepad, while Melissa had chosen to curl up in the sofa's deep-cushioned corner. From Melissa's vantage point she could see over the back of the sofa into the front hall as well as the window seat at the other end of the room that faced the front circular drive. She would have seen Skye if she were visible.

Bill absently scratched at a tingling sensation at the back of his neck, but paid it no mind. It wasn't a very strong feeling, just a little tickle, like a loose hair teasing his skin.

The sound of the doorbell pealing startled the couple. Bill halted his writing, his pen poised over the yellow legal pad. They heard Maria's quick footsteps as she hurried to answer the door with Victor following behind, right on her heels. Skye also had been startled at this new arrival. She hadn't known they were expecting anyone. She wondered who it could be and slipped into the hall.

Melissa continued to search for titles going back to the 1960s list. They heard Victor's anxious voice echo from the hall.

"It's alright, Maria. I'll get the door." Victor nudged past her in the foyer and she turned to go back to the kitchen.

Opening the door, the first thing that caught Victor's eye was a white embroidered patch on the man's left breast pocket. Wheeler's Electric was stitched in dark blue to match the color of his shirt and pants. It was about time, Victor thought. The man was late. It was nearly 10:00 a.m.

Victor thrust out his hand, "Hello. I'm Victor Martucci." His friendly grin was replaced by a sardonic look when the man spoke and grasped his hand.

"Howdy!" the man greeted him loudly, giving Victor's hand a good pumping in a firm grip. *Does he think he's drawing water?* Victor thought sarcastically, extricating his palm from the man's sausage-sized fingers, noting with disgust that the electrician's fingernails were in need of a manicure. Victor quickly scanned the man from head to toe.

Although the man's work clothes were clean, they were slightly rumpled and the buttons on his shirt were straining across his mid-section. His pants hung low on his hips, giving him that baggy look in the crotch and his scuffed boots had seen better days. Victor hoped he was more competent than he looked. The electrician also wore an old leather tool belt. It too hung low on his hips beneath his large belly, almost too low, giving him the appearance of an old western gunslinger. He seemed to be in his fifties, maybe mid-fifties, Victor judged, and probably liked John Wayne movies.

The lines in the electrician's craggy, sun-darkened face deepened when he smiled and introduced himself. "I'm Ralph Wheeler," he announced, speaking in a deep baritone, his Oklahoma accent heavier than Bill Hayden's. "Mr. Smedley sent me, said you folks have a wiring problem."

He lifted his fading blue cap, with the matching insignia of Wheeler's Electric on the front, to scratch his head and unsuccessfully smooth his unruly graying brown hair. It was a little to long and stuck out like wings above his ears when he replaced his cap.

For a split-second Victor thought about telling him there had been a mistake, send him on his way, and find another electrician. But he was impatient to have this taken care of and the man was already here. So, with not a little apprehension, Victor opened the door wide and asked him to come in.

Ralph Wheeler's tool belt jangled loudly in the hall as he entered the house and followed Victor into the library. Skye also followed them and hovered in the doorway as Victor unrolled the blueprint on the desk, displaying the layout of the house's wiring for Wheeler.

"Well, it seems to me like you have two breaker boxes. One in the basement and one in the attic." Wheeler observed the blueprint, hitching up his weighted tool belt.

"Yes. You see, my wife's uncle remodeled this house and replaced most of the wiring over twenty years ago." Victor explained.

Wheeler peered at the blueprint. "Lookie here." He pointed with a large index finger. "It looks like he replaced the old fuse box in the basement with a breaker box and added one in the attic to help carry the load when he installed the central heat and air. It's kinda odd having them in different places but . . . well, whatever floats your boat. If you'll just show me how to get to the basement and attic I'll be 'bout my business."

Victor released the blueprint, rolled it loosely and handed it to him. "Follow me," he said and headed to the kitchen, Wheeler jangling noisily behind him.

Passing through the doorway, they entered and exited through Skye's mist. Although Victor showed no signs of having felt anything, Wheeler passed a hand across his forehead and removed a bead of sweat. He felt like he'd just passed through an oven.

Skye shuddered at the thought of what just passed through her invisible body. Unknowingly she shared Victor's feelings about the electrician. There was something untrustworthy about the man. She didn't want him here and decided to follow him.

In the pantry, Maria was just filling up the washer with a load of soiled towels and washcloths as Victor and Wheeler entered the room. Ignoring the housekeeper, Victor made a right turn, switched on the basement light and opened the door. A set of wooden creaky steps led straight down to the concrete floor below.

Having shown Wheeler where to find the basement, they left. On the way out, Wheeler tipped his hat and flashed uneven, coffee-stained teeth in Maria's direction. She returned a sickly smile and quickly looked away, pouring a cup of laundry detergent into the washer. Knowing that the electrician would be returning, she closed the washer lid and made herself scarce. The library, she decided, could use some more dusting and polishing.

Victor took Wheeler upstairs by way of the servant's staircase, taking note that not one of the lights he'd switched on had flickered, not even for an instant. But that didn't really mean anything. Faulty wiring could sometimes be tricky.

He opened the door to the attic and switched on the light, illuminating the whitewashed steps. He took a deep breath and steeled himself against an unbidden memory, shook it off, and climbed the stairs.

They went up for a few feet and then made a sharp left turn. Over the years the steps had been repeatedly painted white along with the walls and the railing near the top of the staircase, but the attic floor had been left in its natural state, bare and dusty. He explained to Wheeler there was another light-switch at the top of the stairs for the lights in the attic.

Wheeler turned, hitched up his pants and tool belt, and headed back down to the servant's staircase saying over his shoulder, "I'll jus' get a quick look in the basement first and finish up in the attic. You jus' leave everything to ole Ralph. I'll have it taken care of in a jiff." The sounds of his tools swinging low on his swaggering hips were muffled as he disappeared down the narrow steps to the kitchen, with Skye hovering above his head.

As Victor made his way down the front stairs he wondered if he'd made a mistake. Shaking his head and muttering to himself, he had a feeling deep in his gut that he shouldn't have let 'Ole Ralph' cross the threshold. Why couldn't the man have scrubbed his fingernails? And why couldn't he purchase better fitting clothes? Victor made a mental note not to stand behind the man if he were stooping or bending over.

"Ugh!" He shook himself in disgust at that mental image as he neared the bottom of the stairs. He fervently hoped Mr. Wheeler could and would fix the problem quickly and be on his way.

Victor wanted to return to Pasadena as soon as possible. He had a growing concern for his wife's mental being. She'd roused him from sleep several times during the night with her tossing and turning, sometimes crying out her dead cousin's name. His flesh had goose pimpled when she'd muttered something unintelligible about the devil and her soul. But the worst had come just before dawn when she'd cried out, "My baby!"

It was a mistake coming here. No, he amended, he'd needed to come to clench this deal and be done with it. The mistake had been in bringing Madeleine; she was too emotionally tied to this house and it had only taken forty-eight hours for the tragic memories of her dead cousin to resurface, not to mention that other awful night long ago. They were already taking an emotional toll on his wife's mental state; sleepless nights, nightmares, and migraines were just the beginning. He needed to get her back home before the sleepwalking started again, and worse, the hallucinations.

He feared that in a very short time she would be reduced to the emotional basket case he'd witnessed before. More than once. It pained him to think of his beautiful loving Mattie stretched out on the therapist's sofa, reliving her life's tragedies once again as Dr. Irwin probed into her fragile mind. After her father's death, it had taken a year for her to finally face each day without the help of medication. He wouldn't let that happen again. Time was of the essence. He wanted to get those papers signed, the deal closed. And afterward, he never wanted to hear the name Grace Stone Manor again.

Victor, the repugnant memory of Wheeler's low-riding britches making him a little self-conscious, hitched up his own tan dress pants and straightened his coffee colored tie. It was time to talk turkey with the Haydens and make this sale. He'd done his part in getting an electrician out to the house, even though 'Ole Ralph' had just arrived and hadn't had time to come to any conclusions, Victor didn't think he was moving too fast. It wouldn't hurt to at least begin discussing the sale, and perhaps negotiating the price. He cleared his throat and entered the living room.

Twenty minutes after Wheeler's arrival, Madeleine awoke. Although she felt rested, the evidence of last night's sleeplessness still showed in her bloodshot eyes; the swelling was markedly reduced thanks to the cold washcloth, but dark circles still marred the loveliness of their soft blue hue.

She peered into the bathroom's gold-framed mirror in despair at the paleness of her skin. She rarely wore make-up but decided a little concealer might help, and perhaps some fresh air and sunshine would fully restore her mental state and drive out the horror of last night's nightmares. A visit to her grandmother's flower garden was just what she needed.

After showering, she dried her hair and pulled it back into a ponytail. Dressed in a pair of jeans, white cotton shirt, and her white leather trainers, she looked more like a teenager than a mature woman pushing forty.

Peering out into the hall, seeing the coast was clear, she left the sanctuary of the bedroom, striding purposefully toward the back staircase.

As she passed the opened attic door she could faintly hear the sound of clanking tools and a man muttering unintelligibly. At first, it gave her a chill, and then she remembered the electrician was coming today. Not wishing to encounter Victor or the Haydens, she hurriedly made her way to the kitchen using the servant's staircase.

She was relieved to find the kitchen empty of Maria's presence. Quickly downing a glass of orange juice, she placed her empty glass in the sink and went to the mudroom. She found an old basket with a carrying handle and a pair of rusted pruning shears. Cutting fresh flowers for a centerpiece for the dining room would be relaxing and was just what she needed to clear her mind. Retrieving her small gardening gloves from her back pocket, she pulled them on, picked up the basket and shears and strode out into the bright April sunshine.

The heat from the sun felt good on her bare skin, warming the back of her exposed neck and her arms. She breathed deeply, inhaling the confusion of scents. She could even smell the pine from the trees growing between the hibiscus and wild honeysuckle. Everything was green and richly dotted with an explosion of color.

She carefully followed the overgrown flagstones toward the trellis. It was covered in yellow climbing roses. She paused to caress the soft petals before cutting a few of the velvet buds and placing them in her basket. She then passed on through to the shaded garden.

It was much cooler here in the shade. Interspersed throughout the pines were weeping willows and mimosas gone wild. She preferred the warmth of the backyard but longed for the quiet and solitude of her grandmother's garden. She turned to stare up at the gabled rooftop of Grace Stone; secure in the knowledge that no one could see her from the house at this point.

She followed the winding path and reached a small clearing; sunbeams sparkled on an old concrete pond filled with lily pads and algae. A startled bullfrog bounded into the murky water and she jumped aside from the edge giving a small laugh. "Sorry I disturbed you," Madeleine said, continuing onward at a leisurely pace. Around another bend she stopped to sit on a rusting wrought-iron bench, setting her basket beside her. She sighed wistfully, filled with contentment. A gentle breeze played in the swaying weeping willow behind her. Overhead, a cardinal warbled in song.

She and Skye used to play hide-n-seek here. The bench she now sat on had been their home base. At other times, they would rummage through the trunks in the attic and dress up in Sarah Fitzgerald's old dresses and return to the garden to play. Madeleine laughed out loud, startling the cardinal; it flapped away on angry wings. Skye, she remembered, sometimes very much the tomboy, put on Zedediah's old pants and coat, his hat, and stuck his pipe in the corner of her mouth and pretended to be an old southern gentleman, lord of all she surveyed. And when the summers became too warm, they would cool themselves at the fountain, splashing each other in the running water pouring from the cherub's pitcher.

Madeleine reluctantly rose from her seat, leaving the bench and her memories of Skye and continued to stroll down the ivy-covered path, stopping along the way to cut flowers for her centerpiece.

Without realizing how far she'd gone she suddenly found herself facing the moss-covered fountain. She eyed it in dismay; it was so old and had begun to crack at the base. Water no longer poured from the pitcher in the cherub's hands and it too was crumbling. She sighed and looked away.

All things change with time, and as sad as it made her feel she had to accept the changes. Skye was gone. Her aunt and uncle were gone. Her father was gone. And her mother, bless her heart, had accepted life as it came. She knew the secret of moving on.

Madeleine's mother stayed busy after Jacob's death; she'd taken up pottery and beadwork and discovered she enjoyed traveling. Madeleine couldn't count the times her mother had advised her to broaden her horizons as well. Abigail Fitzgerald—Abby, she preferred to be called—was a spry and healthy sixty-year-old woman and had many friends, traveling companions. Madeleine almost envied her mother for her love of life but she loved her too much to be jealous and was very happy for her. Besides, Madeleine felt she kept busy enough without traipsing around the world with her mother. What else was out there that she couldn't find in Pasadena, with Victor, or at Grace Stone?

She breathed deep. This was her last visit to her grandparents' old home. She was sure of it. So she needed to make it count, enjoy it while she could for the last time.

Madeleine contemplated the old rosebushes that her grandmother had planted so long ago. They were of the Don Juan variety. A deep, rich, crimson red, and sweetly scented with soft velvety petals. Dense foliage and weeds had grown up between them, nearly choking them out, but they were hardy, and still grew strong in a perfect concentric circle around the old fountain with only one small opening leading up to the concrete base. She admired their resilience and decided a little help was in order.

Setting her basket, overflowing with flowers, down at her feet, she took out the pruning shears and began cutting and pulling the weeds away from the rosebushes. She worked fastidiously, careful not to harm a single rose, reveling in the thought that perhaps she was touching the stems her grandmother had once held in her graceful fingers as she carefully and lovingly planted them in the ground.

Madeleine struggled for a minute with a thick weed whose roots had a firm grasp in the soil. Not to be outdone by a plant, she grasped the stubborn weed with both gloved hands, leaned back on her haunches, and pulled with all her might. She landed hard on her backside as it came free, roots and all, dirt flying into her face and hair. Dangling the ugly weed between her knees she laughed at herself, feeling young again, and was just about to fling the offending intruder away, when a glint of something shiny caught her eye.

Curious, she brought it closer to her flushed face, wiping the dirt from her check with a raised shoulder. Entangled in the roots was a tarnished chain, its small links filled with dirt.

Gingerly she cut the roots, freeing the broken chain. She gasped in surprise. She dropped the forgotten weed and stared at the dirt-encrusted cross hanging between her dirty-gloved fingers. She rubbed it vigorously to remove the dirt, wishing the fountain were still flowing so she could rinse it off.

She removed her gloves to feel the cold metal between her fingers, scraping the back of the cross with a thumbnail. Cleared of age-old dirt she saw an inscription on the back. She squinted, bringing it closer to her eyes. Her breath caught in her throat and tears burned the backs of her eyelids. She couldn't believe it. On the back was inscribed, *For Sarah 1936*. This was her grandmother's necklace!

From the date on the inscription she knew her grandfather had given it to

Sarah the year they were married. She stared at this wondrous find, enthralled, mesmerized, and wondered how her grandmother had lost it when all thought suddenly ceased.

Without warning, the day turned unusually bright. Madeleine gasped. She couldn't breathe. The air had grown impossibly thin. She gulped for a breath of air but her lungs seemed frozen in her chest and her heart beat so loudly she thought it would burst. Her ears had a strange buzzing sound in them, humming, throbbing. A wave of dizziness overcame her; she would have fallen if she were not already sitting down.

What was happening to her? She looked up and tried to focus her eyes but they had begun to glaze, no longer able to follow the trees as they spun around her in a crazy, dizzying dance. The world had gone topsy-turvy and way too bright.

With her hands clutching at her throat, she struggled to breathe, the necklace dangling between her fingers. Was she dying? Was this what if felt like to have a heart attack? *I'm too young!* She thought wildly. But no, that couldn't be it. Her heart was thumping wildly, but she felt no pain in her chest. Only the constriction around her lungs caused some pain in her ribcage, but that now seemed to be easing. She drew in a deep, shuddering breath.

Mingled with the sound of her pounding heart was a rumbling noise coming from behind her as the ground shook; the old fountain was rocking on its cracked and peeling foundation and she feared it might collapse upon her.

She rolled over on to her side and tried to crawl away, but she found she couldn't move; a heavy weight pressed her to the ground and she gasped a short breath as the chain in her outstretched hand began to burn in her fingers.

Shocked and terrified, her pale blue eyes wide, she raised it before her ashen face. The last thing she saw was a shimmering glint from the cross, blinding her for a split-second as a ripping pain stabbed her lower abdomen.

A loud, savage howl erupted from behind her, barely registering in her ears, and then everything went dark.

Chapter 12

In the attic, Skye's attention was arrested. She'd been intently keeping a watchful eye on Wheeler as he set about tracing down the wiring to the breaker box.

The man disgusted her; how many times did he need to scratch his crotch or pick his nose? And too many times she'd nearly been mooned when he'd bent down to his knees. She'd quickly looked away and only returned her gaze when she deemed it was safe to do so. One quick glance at a hairy crack, caught off guard, and she'd learned her lesson. It was during one such time, when looking away, her eyes fell to the window.

Outside, Madeleine was passing through the trellis to enter the back garden. Skye wished she could leave the house to join her cousin for a long-missed stroll through the trees. She missed feeling the wind blowing through her hair and she longed to inhale the fresh air she knew was riding on that spring breeze. But, she was stuck here in the house, and even if she could venture outdoors to the garden, she could not enjoy it. Those pleasures had long since passed away from her with the passing of her death.

She sighed and turned her attention back to the electrician. She didn't like the way Wheeler fingered her grandparents' belongings, taking his sweet time doing his business, greedily touching the things she cherished with those over-sized, calloused hands. She was growing agitated with each moment. A fire was slowly building inside her, heating her mist. She also longed to leave the attic and listen in on the Hayden's conversation with Victor, but didn't dare. She feared the electrician might steal something.

She watched Wheeler move deeper into the attic, the wire he was following taking him into the section that was situated over Maria's bedroom. He skirted around a cobweb-covered rocking horse, his dangling tool belt setting it in creaky motion, and stopped at an old chrome kitchen table thick with dust. Here he deposited Samuel's blueprint.

On the table was an old Victrola with a crank handle. Wheeler rubbed a dirty finger around the rim of the metal horn, simultaneously pushing his cap to the back of his head with his free hand. Stacked beside the antique phonograph was a collection of old Benny Goodman records along with a few of Glenn Miller, The Andrews Sisters, and Frank Sinatra. What lie beneath these, Skye didn't know?

She seethed in anger as he carelessly lifted one of the albums and blew off the dust. He tilted it sideways to get a better look at the title; the bare bulbs hanging from the ceiling cast many oblong shadows, Wheeler's own being the largest. He snickered out loud and pitched the album back onto the table; it slid and fell to the floor. He ignored it. "Junk," he muttered and continued on.

Junk! Skye's anger flared. How dare he? *I'll show him junk.*

Focusing her anger inward she felt the familiar burn she'd experienced last night. She drew near the old phonograph and concentrated on the handle. It protested at first, creaking, and then slowly began to turn. She strained with the effort and almost gave up the struggle, but seeing the old Victrola's handle crank around and around gave her a mental high. When she felt it was enough, she then lifted the arm, concentrating fiercely, and placed the needle on the spinning record. She didn't know what had been left on the turntable but was extremely pleased to hear the scratchy tune wafting out of the single speaker. It sounded small and tinny, monotone, as if coming from a single headphone filtered through a tin can.

A few feet from the table, she saw Wheeler stiffen as the sound of "My Blue Heaven" broke the silence of the attic; Glenn Miller was playing in top form on the scratchy record.

Wheeler froze, bent on one knee, then slowly rose, turning to stare at the antique gramophone. How did that happen? He took out a soiled red bandana from his back pocket and mopped his sweating face. The temperature outside was a comfortable seventy degrees but inside the attic it was a hot and stuffy eighty-five.

Wheeler wiped the sweat that was running down his neck into his collar and moved slowly back to the table. He couldn't understand how the temperature had jumped so quickly, and nervously reached out a shaky hand to remove the needle from the record. "Must have bumped it," he muttered, stuffing the damp bandana back inside his hip pocket.

He moved uncertainly toward the front of the house, a chill creeping up his spine despite the heat. He glanced over his shoulder several times and quickly made his way to the breaker box. The hair bristled at the back of his neck; he no longer felt alone. It was absurd to feel this way; there was no one but him in the attic, but just the same the feeling was there. He couldn't shake the feeling that he was being watched.

He shoved a box full of old novels out of his way, not caring the box tilted over, spilling the dry and dusty books. He was in a hurry to get finished and get out. He kept muttering to himself as he quickly checked the wiring and the inside of the breaker box. There was nothing amiss here that he could see. "Rich people, go figure," he mused. "Always needin' someone else to do the work for 'em.'"

Near the dusty table Skye fumed. Those were her mother's old books that he'd just tossed aside like so much garbage. It was time for Mr. Wheeler to make his exit; there was nothing wrong with the wiring, her father had done a terrific job working on this house and she wasn't about to let that man spend one more minute pilfering with contempt her family's belongings.

Skye stood staring at Wheeler's back, seething in anger. It was alien to her being to be overwhelmed by so much emotion; she had never felt so much fury and loathing in her natural life, had never given in to these base feelings before. Last night had been her first taste of real rage and the release it had brought her was liberating. It still amazed her; these intense feelings were animalistic and bordered on hatred, but they allowed her to do things, powerful things she could never do before. Sneed had not lied to her on that score.

Boiling within, burning like fire, she became frightened of her own feelings but was unable to quench the desire to exercise her new power and expel this sticky-fingered idiot from her house. Here was her chance to experiment and focus this energy on the living, without frightening the people she cared about.

Unaware that she was glowing so brightly, she moved toward the electrician, becoming visible.

Her center burned with a blaze of dazzling red, fiery like a ruby, churning, radiating outward to her arms and legs becoming a dark orange with tongues of flames licking outward from all points of her now visible body. Her lower legs and forearms were as bright as the noonday sun, a burning yellow. And her dark hair fanned out around her, a deep magenta, moving in the conflagration as if being blown by a solar wind.

She looked down at the over-turned box of books. They shimmered in a haze just as a blacktop on a desert highway seems to dance in the heat. She raised her right hand and pointed at the thickest of her mother's books. She couldn't read the title but it didn't matter; the book was a good two inches thick and would make a formidable projectile. It rose in the air, spinning. She pointed at

Wheeler's head. In an instant the book flew, obeying her silent command, zeroing in on its target.

Shutting the breaker box door, Wheeler withdrew his damp bandana to mop his sweaty brow. Was it possible the temperature had risen another ten degrees? Facing the wall, he tilted his head inquisitively as he noticed the area surrounding his shadow had become brighter, thinning his outline on the wall.

He had no more time to wonder about his diminishing shadow; something hard slammed into the back of his head, knocking him off-balance. He fell against the wall, losing his cap.

Everything went dark for a few seconds as the pain exploded inside his head but he did not lose consciousness. White-hot needles pierced the backs of his eyes as they slowly came back into focus. Leaning with one hand against the bare grimy wall for support, he massaged the back of his head with the other one; the pain was excruciating. A lump was already forming and something warm and wet covered his fingers.

He blinked a few times, rubbing the sore spot, and then slowly turned to see what had hit him. His worn boot scuffed the dirty floor as he turned and it thumped against the book lying at his feet. With arms hanging, he looked down at the large paperback book, wondering how it hit him.

Something warm and red dripped off his dangling hand and splashed on the floor near his leg, and then another drop fell. He brought his hand up to his face and stared unbelieving at the blood smeared on his fingers.

Immediately, he then saw the flames glowing between his spread fingers. He forgot about the throbbing in his head and the blood on his hand as his gray eyes fastened in fear upon Skye's visage.

"Sweet Mother of God! A devil!" Wheeler began to whimper and tremble. His body shook so badly that his tool belt nearly vibrated down to his knees. He grasped it in his bloody hand and hitched it clear up to his navel, unaware that he'd lost control of his bladder.

A low, animal moan vibrated in the back of his throat to escape from his dry, cracked lips as the strong smell of fear and urine assailed his nostrils. His eyes, staring wide at the horror before him, showed the whites completely, making the irises small gray points.

He frantically tried to think of a way out as he gasped for air. The conflagration before him was greedily eating up his much needed oxygen. His lungs burned within his chest; it was like breathing in a furnace, and sweat poured down his craggy cheeks. His only thought was to escape this hellish nightmare, and his only route to safety was through that fiery thing that was looking at him like it wanted to consume him. And he very much believed that it would, bones and all, if it got close enough.

Desperately, he averted his eyes just long enough to seek another way out, a window perhaps. He knew there was one located further to the front of the attic but didn't know if it would even open.

Cautiously, he took a step in that direction while keeping his eyes focused on the she-devil. What if that thing followed him? His imagination running wild, he pictured those tongues of flames licking at his body, burning his clothes and hair, toying with him, torturing him. And just as he was home free, climbing through the window, that she-devil would pounce and fully consume him. He laughed hysterically at the thought of his charred bones, frozen in the act of escape, climbing half in and half out the attic window; a blackened, skinny caricature of his former self.

Skye saw Wheeler hesitate and take a step away from her, and then heard that deranged laugh escape from his panic-stricken face. It was then she knew he could see her form. Looking down she saw what the electrician was staring at; she could barely recognize herself. She looked like a fiery demon from hell.

Feeling ashamed, but still enjoying the freedom she felt, she slowly backed away from Wheeler, moving toward the back of the attic, past the stairs, leaving him an exit.

God, what had she done?

She'd hurt him badly. The man was scared to death and bleeding. She had never frightened anyone like this before. At the time it had given her a wild rush to feel the release of power, but now, her anger dissipating, she felt only shame and regret. She hadn't meant to hurt him like this, hadn't meant to terrify the man. He looked like he was about to fall down dead of a heart attack.

With her center only glowing a dull orange, she made herself smaller, less threatening, and glided toward her grandmother's trunk. She hovered over it for a few seconds and watched as Wheeler, seeing his opportunity for escape, make a bee-line for the attic stairs, mumbling incoherently, his tools jangling loudly all the way down. She shrunk herself as small as she could and followed.

She was invisible once again.

Hovering outside the attic window, Sneed had watched the change in Skye's appearance. It no longer hurt him to look at her. Now he had her right where he wanted her. She could no longer draw upon her innocence, her pure heart. Her goodness could not sting his soul. Perhaps he could destroy her now.

As Skye had approached the trunk, orange and vulnerable, Sneed gathered his writhing darkness, ready to spring. He floated backward a space, and with a roar flung himself at the window. But before he could make contact with the glass, an unseen force sucked at his tentacles, drawing him backward. Back to that damp, dark place.

"Nooo . . . ." He wailed, but his cry went unheard.

Downstairs, Victor had made himself comfortable at the end of the sectional sofa. He had immediately broached the subject of the sale of Grace Stone, secretly hoping to get the papers signed today. Although Bill hadn't argued the price, he still hadn't made the commitment of buying the house.

Victor crossed his leg, giving the appearance of a man at ease, but drummed his fingers impatiently on the back of the sofa.

"So, tell me, Bill. What's the problem?" he asked, getting down to the business at hand. "I know you and your wife like the house. You've paid a handsome price for the first six months and I'm letting that count toward your down payment. To be honest, you're the first tenant that didn't demand a refund and actually returned to the house. So, let me in on what's going on. Maybe, it's something we can work out."

Bill cleared his throat. He would like to discuss this ghost issue maturely and coherently but he knew that Victor Martucci was a no-nonsense kind of guy, strictly a businessman. He would be a hard man to convince that Grace Stone was haunted even if he'd had a paranormal encounter himself. Victor, he knew, was the type to always look for a reasonable, normal explanation. Bill just wasn't ready to get into this discussion yet.

He cut his eyes toward Melissa, and just in time gave her a silent warning not to open her mouth. She was just about to speak when she caught his look. Exasperated, she flung the play lists she was looking at onto the table in front of her. Clearly, she was itching to spill her guts and never mind the consequences.

Bill expelled a sigh of relief. For once, she took the hint to hold her tongue. He relaxed as she settled deeper into the cushions and tucked her hair behind her ears. For the moment, she was willing to let him handle this his way.

He leaned back into the cushions. "About the furniture, does it also come with the house?"

"Of course," Victor replied. He forced his fingers to still their tattooing. It wouldn't do to have Bill Hayden notice how anxious he was. "Everything is included in the purchase price." He draped a hand causally over his crossed leg.

"I noticed that the library contains some very old books. Nothing real expensive, but a few are worth more than fifty bucks. Are you sure you would like to let those go as well? Some of them are classics. Originals. First copy printing. They're a little worn, but a wonderful addition to any library. There's Rudyard Kipling, Robert Louis Stevenson, Washington Irving, Charles Dickens . . .there's even a collection of poetry books that's over a hundred years old. I consider them all a great asset and would love to have them but, are you sure you'd be willing to part with them?"

Although Bill was stalling for time in making a commitment to buy the house, he knew he was asking legitimate questions and hoped that Victor wouldn't see through him. He sincerely wanted to buy the house. But if he were unable to rid the house of ghosts there was no way he and Melissa could make it their home.

Another thought crossed his mind; it seemed as if Victor Martucci was in a hurry to be rid of this house. Whatever happened to his original contract of leasing it for six months and then deciding to buy? Why was Victor pushing the sale? The sound of the older man's voice broke in on his musings.

"Well, my wife *might* want to look through them one more time." Victor conceded. "I believe there may be one or two she would like to keep. But, for the most part, I think it's safe to say that you'll be getting the bulk of whatever is in there."

Victor would love to sell it all to him, lock, stock and barrel. If only he could get him to commit and sign the damn papers. Then he and Mattie could pack and get out the hell out of here. If Bill Hayden backed out now and decided to continue leasing the house, within six months he and his wife would probably move out and Victor would be right back where he started, trying to find a buyer. And that was almost next to impossible. He had no illusions about that. They hadn't had much luck keeping it rented out to people, much less sell it to anyone.

For the first time in Victor's life he'd hit a brick wall in making a deal. Of all the homes he'd sold, this was the one he wanted to sell the most. It was a millstone hanging about his neck. *Damn this house!* He silently cursed. Feeling as if a noose were tightening around his throat he loosened his tie. *Come on, Bill.* He urged within his mind. *Say you'll buy it. Put me out of my misery so I can go home.* But instead of hearing Bill say, 'I'll take it. Where do I sign.' he heard him asking another question.

"Will you be clearing out the attic or leaving it all behind? I figure you're wife will probably want to spend a little time going through her folks' things. I don't want to rush her. You're going to be here a week or so, aren't you?" Bill affectionately patted the top of Melissa's foot.

Leaving him to master this conversation, Melissa had stretched out on the sofa, lying supine and languid, a thick cushion cradling her head, wriggling her toes against Bill's thigh. She gave the appearance of being bored with the discussion but inwardly she followed every word, acutely watching the body language of each man. She noticed the tenseness about Victor's shoulders, the lines around his mouth tightly drawn and a tiny vein ticking in his forehead. He was definitely on edge. He reminded her of a sensitive ticking time bomb; the slightest jar might set him off. Bill, on the other hand, gave her the impression of a small sailboat gently gliding on a calm sea. It didn't surprise her. No matter how tense a situation could become he always managed to appear at ease, hence the nickname she'd dubbed him after they'd married, *Cool Breeze*.

She stretched, digging her toes playfully into her husband's leg.

Bill was thinking it would probably take Madeleine a couple of days to sort through the attic and decide what to keep, and that would buy him some time for ghost hunting.

He cast a quick look at Melissa and then at Victor. He was slightly taken aback at the coldness he saw in those dark eyes. No, that didn't quite describe what he saw there. Forget cold. Try frost. Did he say something to piss the man off? He didn't think so. Again, Bill wondered why he so was so anxious to sell. Other than being haunted he hadn't found anything else wrong with the house. In fact, it was in better shape than the newer homes he and Melissa had looked at before seeing this one. So, why was Victor moving so quick to unburden himself of Grace Stone? And why the cold stare?

Victor was about to answer Bill's question about his length of stay, when they all heard a clamoring noise of heavy thundering footsteps pounding down the front stairs and Wheeler bellowing in a shaky voice, "Mr. Martucci! Mr. Martucci!"

The men jumped up, leaving Melissa to roll off the sofa. She quickly caught up with them in the entrance hall. Forgetting to don her sandals, her bare feet slapped the polished oak floor.

They stopped short at the sight of Wheeler, stumbling down the stairs, whimpering, looking over his shoulder as if the hounds of hell were baying at his heels. One beefy hand was sliding down the rail for balance, leaving a trail of blood, the other firmly grasping his tool belt. His cap was missing. His face was flushed and he was gasping for air like a man who had just narrowly escaped drowning.

"Mr. Wheeler—" Victor began, but the electrician's terrified voice cut him off.

"Mister, you ain't got no wiring problem! But you got a problem all right!

There's a she-devil livin' in your attic!" He grasped the back of his head and then thrust his bloody hand in Victor's face. "It tried to kill me!"

He rushed on past the stunned group to the foyer and flung open the front door. He whirled to face them. Pointing a bloody finger and making a declaration born of fear, he flashed a parting shot before flying out the door, "I'm gonna sue! You'll be gettin' my bill!"

Through the opened door they watched in stunned silence as the electrician gunned his truck and flew recklessly down the drive, throwing gravel.

Victor raised his hands in resignation. "Is everyone in this state crazy, teetering on the verge of a collective nervous breakdown?" He whirled around to face Bill, an angry look plastered on his olive features. "What's going on here? You don't seem to be the type to run off in the middle of the night because of a simple wiring problem. What happened the night you packed and left? And why did you return? You're the only ones who did, you know." He planted his fists on his hips. "I want an explanation. And none of that ghost stuff! I want the truth. Do you plan to buy this house or not?" he demanded, huffing and puffing, the commanding tone in his voice leaving little room for doubt that he would put up with any nonsense.

Next to Bill, Melissa raised her eyebrows, peering at him as if to say, "Now, can we tell him?" She glanced at Victor, a little fearfully. *I think the bomb has reached critical mass*, she thought somberly. *We'd better start talking and try to defuse him.* Which was fine with her. It was about time.

Bill rubbed his chin thoughtfully and then ran a hand through his hair. He wasn't ready to talk about it but circumstances beyond his control had dictated the timing. He exhaled loudly, "All right, Victor. The truth. But, you might not like it once you hear it." He turned to Melissa, "Honey, will get me a fresh glass of tea. No, make that a glass of wine . . . better yet; just bring the whole bottle and three glasses. This is going to take a while."

Feeling a slight prickle behind his head, Bill rubbed the short hairs standing up on the back of his neck. He closed the front door and followed Victor into the living room. And right behind Bill, Skye trailed after them. Melissa headed to the kitchen in search of Maria to clean the blood off the banister and to retrieve the wine. This was the moment she'd been waiting for all morning.

Chapter 13

Madeleine grasped the soft warm soil in her fingers and tried to rise. She made it to her knees, struggling with the folds of a long skirt. *Skirt?* What happened to her jeans?

Something fleshy and unyielding slammed her back down to the ground, knocking the breath out of her. She tried to turn her head but a heavy hand pulled her hair, keeping it straight.

"Don't fight me." A harsh male voice rasped in her ear.

Her attacker moved to lie upon her back, pinning her to the ground. She could feel and smell his hot stinky breath just behind her ear. It smelled like rotting, putrid vegetation and something else she couldn't identify. It was nauseating. *Oh God!* she thought fearfully. *I'm going to be raped?* She fought with the panic gripping her heart. Immobile, frozen to the ground beneath her attacker's weight, dirt in her nostrils, she stared at the loose earth stirring with each labored breath she took.

This can't be happening! Madeleine wriggled; drawing her hands beneath her chest and shoved, screaming, "NO!" Upsetting the man's hold, catching him off-balance, she frantically scrabbled forward and gained a few inches of freedom before he was on top of her once more.

"You know you want this as much as I." He laughed, gripping the back of her dress.

Dear God, what was that odor? Madeleine gagged.

"It's going to be fun, you'll see. Isn't it thrilling to know that at any minute someone could catch us?" His fingernails scraped the back of her neck. Something tightened around her throat but only for an instant, it felt like a thin chain cutting into her windpipe. It jerked free as he gave a hard yank, and she heard the tearing of threads as he ripped the cloth down her back, exposing her skin. "But, don't worry," he rasped, "No one will. They can't even hear us. So, it'll be all right when you scream out in ecstasy. And believe me, you will. I *am* gonna make you scream. Scream, you whore!"

Madeleine stiffened and screamed as sharp teeth bit into the soft flesh of her shoulder. She had never felt pain like this before. She felt the skin tear as his teeth sunk into her soft flesh. Tears smarted her eyes and ran down her cheeks. The pain was unbearable. She twisted sideways trying to grab his hair and throw him off, but she was helpless in this position. He was too fast and stronger, pinning her to the ground. Mercifully, he un-clamped his jaw. With mounting terror she felt the air stir between her legs as he hiked up her dress. She screamed again and kicked her legs but her only reward was evil laughter filling her ears, and that pervasive revolting odor making her want to wretch.

"Victor!" She screamed wildly over and over. *Oh God, please let him hear me!* Why was there no one to help her? She was going to be raped, right here in her grandmother's garden and there was no one to save her. No one to hear her screams. No one.

For one maddening moment she became confused. She wasn't Madeleine, and didn't have a husband named Victor. Maria did not exist. She had a servant named Annie, and Annie had told her she shouldn't be alone just now out in the garden. She should have waited for Annie's help. She should have *asked* Annie for her help in planting the rosebushes. Oh, God, where was she? Where was Annie? *Where are the servants?* She wondered in confusion. *Why do they not come?*

"Please, somebody help me!"

But no one came. No one could hear her cries.

Who was Annie?

Madeleine shut her eyes tight, and shook her head to clear it.

Panic filled; bewildered, and desperately longing for this nightmare to end she looked wildly about. Her gaze fell upon the rosebushes. Something was wrong with them. They didn't look the same. They were smaller somehow and looked more pronounced, sharply outlined, but their center wavered as if moving under water, like seaweed in an aquarium. And that wasn't all that was strange about the garden. Where were the weeds? It was crazy, but somehow the trees had shrunk, they looked younger. Beneath her hands there was only fresh, softly dug earth, no overgrowth. And everything seemed hazy; she felt as if she was looking through smoky glass. The bright sunshine had darkened suddenly to a late afternoon glow, but her thoughts had cleared. She was no longer confused. Frightened, yes, but aware of her identity.

Madeleine made another effort to throw off her attacker, but she was now moving in slow motion. In fact, every moment in this hellish nightmare was moving slowly.

Even sound.

How could that be?

The clinking of her attacker's belt buckle being released was loud in her ears and it seemed to take forever for him to unzip his pants. The sound dragged and rebounded within her mind. Echoing. It was horrifying to have her fate prolonged and at the same time it gave her a twisted comfort to know she had a few more seconds of her life intact, inviolate.

Knowing it was no use to struggle any longer, she lay motionless. Blocking her mind to the rasping, heavy breathing she felt upon her exposed back, she concentrated on her surroundings trying to ignore the sharp, searing pain in her shoulder and that awful smell. Slowly she turned her head to the left and couldn't believe what her eyes told her was not there.

The fountain was gone!

A pile of dirt lie next to the deep hole where it should have been and glinting in the sun was her pruning shears. Her only viable weapon if she could reach them.

Careful not arouse her attacker's attention, she cautiously snaked her hand toward the shears. She dug her fingers into the warm soil, filling her fingernails, willing her arm to stretch another inch. Her fingertips brushed the wooden handle as the man above her grunted in anticipation. It was an eerie sound, as if a reel-to-reel tape were being played at a slow speed.

Her dress was now bunched up around her hips and she could feel a calloused hand sliding up her thigh. As his rough fingers found the waistband of her panties, her own fingers found a grip on the handle of the pruning shears.

The heavy weight was no longer pressing her to the ground; her attacker had gotten to his knees and was wedged between her legs. His calloused hand on her back had slackened its pressure. Now that she was no longer fighting him, he could take his time. There was an awful dragging, tearing sound as he ripped her panties, and threw them aside.

Madeleine swallowed the nauseous bile that had risen in her throat when he massaged her bare buttocks. She was deeply ashamed at her nakedness and a loathing unlike any she had ever experienced filled her heart. She hated this vile man that had dared to degrade and humiliate her. She gritted her teeth and moved ever so slowly.

Finally, she held the handle in a tightly clenched fist, willing herself to move before he could thoroughly violate her.

Now! She told herself. *Now!* Don't cower here and let him do what his sick mind desires, she coached herself.

MOVE!

With a sudden burst of strength she didn't know she possessed she rolled onto her back, slinging the shears at his head. She missed the mark by mere inches and produced a glancing blow to his collarbone, slashing his shirt, scoring flesh. He grunted in surprise and pain when he lost his balance and his right shoulder hit the ground. Madeleine wriggled away from him, crab-like, in slow motion, but he recovered quickly. Sitting up and bellowing in rage, he slammed a fist into her mid-section. And then again another fierce blow slammed into her.

Sharp pain exploded within her abdomen, radiating down into her hips and legs. A wild, frantic thought filled her mind, *"He's killed my baby!"* She screamed in agony and fear as he dove for her yet again.

"I hope you rot in hell!" she shrieked in a voice that was not her own. Did she say hell? She'd tried to say jail. She'd never used profanity before. And what happened to her voice? It was not her own. It was deeper, richer, laced with an accent. Nothing like her soft, musical, California tone.

Forgetting she still held the shears, she brought her hands up to ward off another blow and heard the sickening sound of breaking bone as it plunged into his chest. It droned in her ears forever, mingling with the sound of escaping air as his lungs collapsed. A slick darkness spread across his tan shirt and she stared in revulsion as blood ran down the handle, staining her hands.

"What have I done?" she whispered.

In shock, she forced her eyes to travel upward to see the face of the man who had attacked her.

That's not possible! Her mind screeched.

Air filled her lungs, traveled up her burning esophagus, momentarily wedged in her constricted throat, and then suddenly burst through.

Her scream shattered the stillness in the garden, reverberating throughout the trees; her attacker, just inches from her eyes, had no face.

She screamed again, ear piercing, and threw the faceless man off to her side. He landed on his back with a thud, the handle of the shears pointing skyward at the late afternoon sun. There was only a crawling black mass of worms where his face should have been.

Madeleine retched, catching bile in her throat, and crawled backwards on her hands and knees away from the horror before her, whimpering deep in her throat.

She'd killed a man! A faceless man! A thing! A demon! It had touched her flesh, had bit her with those crawling things!

Madeleine rolled over and vomited. The only thing in her stomach was the orange juice she had drunk, and it burned her throat. When she was spent, and the dry heaves under control, she crawled away, and sat upon her knees, shivering and shaking her head.

It didn't happen! It couldn't have happened! Her mind reeled, seeking denial. *It's not real! It's not real! I'm losing my mind! It's happening again, and I'm losing my mind!*

But the pain in her stomach was real enough. She wrapped her arms around her abdomen and bowed her forehead to the ground. Curled up in a fetal position, she fell onto her side and wept convulsively until her tears abated, and she was dry-sobbing hoarsely.

She lost all sense of time as she lie there, jerking, bringing the hiccupping under control. Her thoughts began to drift as if in a dream. Within the dream she heard a voice calling out to her, begging, pleading. It was the same voice she had spoken with when she'd killed her attacker.

"Madeleine. Madeleine," it pleaded. "You must help Skye. This is my doing. All my fault. I'm sorry. Please! Help Skye, help Skye, help . . ." The voice faded, being carried away on the wind.

As Madeleine became aware of her surroundings, the words '*Help Skye,*' echoed within her and danced upon the rustling leaves on the trees, gradually disappearing with the current of air until she could no longer hear them. Now they only whispered within her heart.

Help Skye? How could she help her cousin? She was dead. Dead and gone from her years ago, forever beyond her reach. Dr. Irwin said so. Skye was not trying to reach her from beyond. Dr. Irwin had assured her it was all in her mind. People do not come back from the grave.

But still, what if Skye needed her? What if she was in trouble?

NO! She mustn't think like this. Mustn't!

Madeleine fought to hold onto her sanity.

I'm well, she told herself. *I'm well. Skye is dead. And I'm well now.*

Slowly she opened her eyes and moved her stiffened legs. It was hard to straighten them out. Her muscles ached. They twitched. She felt as if she'd been body slammed and then beaten with a board.

She rested among the weeds, panting, until she brought her ragged breath under control. Her left shoulder felt as if it were on fire. What happened to her shoulder? Memory tugged at her conscience like a current, flowing and ebbing, rising and falling, frothy with fear. She'd done something. Something awful.

A cold knot of fear sunk into her belly. There was ice in her veins. What had she done? And what was pricking her palm? She opened her trembling hand. The necklace had been so tightly clenched in her fist that the cross left its imprint in her palm. *Grammy Sarah's necklace.* She'd found it. And then . . .

Something evil had found her.

Oh, God!

She remembered.

Madeleine pushed herself up into a sitting position, a sharp intake of breath burned in her lungs. She covered her face and screamed, "I've killed a man! Dear God in Heaven, I've killed a man! I didn't mean to do it! I didn't mean to do it!"

The floodgates had opened; memory came crashing in on a tidal wave, drowning her in fear. She shook uncontrollably, rising on shaky legs.

The garden now seemed sinister, vines and weeds reaching out to smother her, to punish her for the crime of murder she'd just committed. She cast her eyes about fearfully, desperately wondering what to do.

Help. She needed help.

Victor!

Yes, dear, sweet Victor! Victor would help her. He would know what to do. Had always been there for her. He would keep her safe. He'd always protected her during the worst times of her life, giving her his strength to lean on, giving her his love.

Suddenly, she needed the safety and security of his arms.

Forgetting her basket of flowers, she turned and fled back down the path toward the house, her grandmother's cross dangling from the dirty chain clutched within her fingers.

Chapter 14

Victor sipped the amber liquid from the wine glass Melissa had handed to him. "But, this is preposterous! I don't believe in ghosts." He settled deeper into the cushion, cradling his glass.

Was this man serious? He'd thought Bill had better sense than to believe in this nonsense. He squirmed a little on the sofa, crossing his legs. A strange feeling of unease quietly stole in at the back of his mind; he wondered where it had come from. He shrugged his shoulders to shake it off.

He sat with his knees crossed, nursing the warm brandy as the couple related the events that led up to the night they'd packed and left. What, five, six days ago? Or was it seven? He studied Bill's face, looking for a sign that this was some kind of a joke, but there was no twinkle in the young man's eyes, no tell-tale sign of mirth playing about the corners of his mouth, and he'd spoken in earnest as he'd explained his theory about Victor's wife's cousin haunting the house. One thing Victor was certain of: He was not going to let them mention this to his wife. It was the last thing she needed to hear.

It was all so ridiculous! *A fifteen-year-old girl haunting this house?* There had to be another explanation. And Victor believed he'd hit upon it. Now he knew why they were hesitating to commit to buy. If Bill could convince him that Grace Stone was haunted, the young man probably thought that he might be willing to lower the purchase price. Well, that just wasn't going to wash with him. He would need proof. And since he didn't believe in ghosts he knew there would be no proof made available. He was not going to lower the asking price of this beautiful, solid-built home based on a gimmick. If it had real problems, like bad plumbing or termites, then he could see negotiating. But, ghosts? Victor wondered why he was even surprised at the their suggestion. Of course, *they* believed in superstitions. What did he expect from backward mid-westerners?

Still, he was disappointed. He had begun to respect Bill Hayden. The young man had seemed intelligent enough when they'd met. And honest. His wife was a bit of an over-fed bumpkin but she wasn't stupid. She was a licensed nurse, after all. She'd gone to college. There had to be some sensible brains inside that curly head somewhere. But, at the moment, Victor thought disparagingly, both of them had taken a leave of absence where their intelligence was concerned. He straightened his tie, trying to push away that uneasy feeling that had returned and crept up his spine.

"Honestly, Victor. The clues point to Skye," Bill was saying, touching the back of his neck once again. That tingly sensation was still there, announcing an unseen presence. He was growing more aware of Skye's aura and was sure they were being watched. He just wasn't sure if the other ghost was present as well, listening in on their conversation. Although he'd told Victor about Skye, he didn't think the older man was ready to hear about the Other. From Victor's posture he could tell the man was a little uncomfortable. Was he also aware of the heaviness pervading the room?

"Here, look at my notes." He handed the slightly rumpled yellow notepad to Victor.

After glancing through several pages Victor handed it back. "I can see where you would draw that conclusion but I still don't believe in spirits. Skye's or anyone's. There's always a logical explanation for everything."

Next to Bill, Melissa could hold her tongue no longer. She suddenly stood up and glared at Victor, "Just because you don't believe doesn't make it any less real, and ignoring it doesn't make it go away! Believe me, I've tried. It doesn't work. If you could have seen what I saw in that bathroom mirror . . ." Her eyes sparkled with emotion.

Bullheaded man! She should have known he was going to be obstinate. The man had a closed mind. Did he even believe in the after-life? Probably not. *He probably thinks that without money there is no after-life.* Had he never experienced anything out of the ordinary? Melissa didn't think so. Maybe that's why they were having a hard time convincing him.

Abruptly, she regained her seat next to Bill. "Have you ever encountered anything supernatural? Something you couldn't explain?"

Victor looked her full in the face, "No, I can't say that I've had the pleasure." He glanced down at his watch then lifted his face to Melissa once more, making eye contact. It was near lunchtime and he felt he'd given them enough of his ear to bend and fill with this baloney. Besides, he wanted to go upstairs and check on Mattie. He was worried about her. And after that he was going to have to get on the phone and find out exactly what had happened to Mr. Wheeler in the attic.

"That figures." Melissa returned his stare, her manner decisive. "But whether you believe or not doesn't change one thing. This house is haunted." She drained the last of her brandy and pursed her lips. No one said a word.

An eerie stillness had settled over the room. Subdued, but pregnant with anticipation. Something was about to happen. Melissa and Bill passed a knowing look at each other. They both felt the presence. Bill exhaled a breath, checking for fog, but the air was not cold. In fact, it was quite warm.

On the table before them their empty tea glasses began to shake, and Victor straightened in his seat.

"I believe, Mr. Martucci, that Skye is about to make her presence known to you," Melissa whispered as she huddled closer to Bill. This was her first encounter since returning to the house. She had expected it but still it chilled her blood.

All eyes were focused on the glasses as they shook violently, the melted ice sloshing.

Bill sat grinning, staring at the tinkling glasses, not moving a muscle, but Victor's dark eyes widened and his mouth gaped open in surprise. He loosened his tie nervously and felt perspiration staining his armpits. *Why was it so hot in here?* Was this some kind of a joke? How were they accomplishing this parlor-room trick? For that's just what it had to be. Just a trick. Yes, that's it. An optical illusion. He'd almost convinced himself of this belief when something even more fantastic happened.

Victor pushed back deeper into the cushions as the tinkling glasses rose into the hot still air, circling each other.

Seated near him, holding her breath, Melissa reached out and grasped Bill's arm. His hand closed reassuringly over hers.

Suddenly, the glasses flew and crashed into the fireplace. Victor jumped up, spilling his brandy down the front of his shirt and tie as Melissa let out an ear-splitting scream. And then they heard a frantic voice, calling out from the hall.

"Mr. Martucci! Come Quick! Mr. Martucci!" Maria's shrill voice rose above the expletive that flew from Victor's mouth. The panicked housekeeper rushed into the living room from the entrance hall. Her dark eyes were brimming with tears. "It's Miss Mattie, sir! Come Quick!" She lifted her apron to dab the moisture off her cheeks, she'd been crying.

Victor made a mad dash toward the stairs but stopped and flew back down when Maria told him that Madeleine was in the kitchen. Bill and Melissa followed, rushing behind Victor and Maria to see what had happened.

They entered the kitchen to find Victor kneeling before Madeleine, holding her tightly in his arms. She was sitting at the table sobbing hysterically on his shoulder. She kept repeating the same words over and over again and it took Melissa a few moments to understand. Then it became clear; Madeleine was confessing to a murder. She kept saying that she had killed a man.

Victor reluctantly released his hold to pull her back from his shoulder and look at her distraught face. "Mattie, tell me what happened."

"Vic . . ." She hiccupped, her entire body shaking, trying to gain control of her tears. "Victor, I . . . I killed a man." She burst into tears afresh, leaning her dirty forehead against his chin, her fists pressed against his stained shirt.

He let her cry for a few seconds longer then pulled her head up again. "It's all right, Mattie. Take a deep, even breath. That's my girl. It's all right; you're safe. Now, slowly, tell me all that happened."

Madeleine sniffled and then blew her nose on the handkerchief Victor pressed into her right palm. She seemed oblivious to everyone else in the room. Taking a deep breath to steady herself she gazed into her husband's concerned face and began in a shaky halting voice. "I went to the garden to cut some flowers . . . For the dining room. I went down to the water fountain. I started weeding out the rosebushes and . . . and I found this necklace." She lifted up the cross dangling in her other dirt-encrusted palm. "It's Grammy Sarah's. I found my grandmother's cross." She gazed at it intently as it swung to and fro between their faces, just as she had stared at it in the garden.

Fresh tears welled up in her pale blue eyes. "Oh, Victor. I was attacked! A horrible man attacked me!" She shut her eyes and went on in a rush between sobs. "He knocked me on the ground. He bit me! Oh, God, Victor! He *bit* me!" Her right hand crossed to her left shoulder.

Victor held her close, softly murmuring to calm her, telling her that she was safe now, that she was all right. When her tears subsided a little, he lifted her chin. "What happened, dear? What happened next?"

"I . . . I grabbed the shears." Madeleine pressed the handkerchief against her mouth trying to bite back the words but they rose with her hysteria and flew out of her mouth, "I Stabbed Him!" She shook her head violently as if to shake loose the memory of her attack, but kept screaming, "I stabbed him! I stabbed him! I stabbed him!"

Standing next to Melissa, Maria was softly crying and made the sign of the cross. Tears ran unchecked down her brown cheeks. Melissa placed an arm around the housekeeper's shoulder to comfort her and Bill caught her eye above her head. He gestured toward Madeleine who was now crying silently, her emotions exhausted and nearly spent.

Melissa released Maria and stepped toward Victor. "Mr. Martucci, give her to me. Maria and I will take her upstairs. I've dealt with sexual assault many times in my work. She'll be all right. Let us get her upstairs."

She gently laid a hand on Madeleine's back as Victor lifted her up from the chair. He caressed Madeleine's disheveled hair, her ponytail hung limply down her back; the front strands had escaped its hold. He tenderly kissed the top of her head, and then turned her into Melissa's waiting arms. Madeleine went willingly, and as meek as a lamb allowed Melissa and Maria to lead her through kitchen door.

Passing by Bill, Melissa whispered, "Maybe you should call the police." He assented with a nod.

After the kitchen door slowed its swinging motion, Victor suddenly picked up the wooden chair his violated wife had just vacated and flung it across the room. It skidded to a stop near the pantry door, but amazingly had not broken.

He could not conceal his rage. Hot blood pounded in his temples, blurring his vision. His breath came in short bursts and he saw everything in a red haze. He wanted, needed, to destroy something. Seeking release, he punched a copper pot hanging above the cooking island and sent it flying into the refrigerator. But that wasn't good enough; he wanted to hurt the man that had dared to touch his wife.

"If that bastard is not dead," he hissed, "he's going to be!" He then whirled on his heels and flew out the back door.

Bill witnessed the older man's rage from a distance near the swinging door. He couldn't blame him. If this had happened to *his* wife he doubted very much that he wouldn't react in the same manner. He knew he should call the police now but he couldn't let Victor face the man who had attacked Madeleine alone. If the man weren't dead, he would be if Victor got to him.

Hurrying his footsteps, he followed him down the garden path, hoping to catch up with Victor before any more violence took place.

Nearing the fountain he began calling out Victor's name, begging him not to make a mistake. He reasoned with him, telling him he would do Madeleine no good behind bars. They should call the police and let them handle it.

When he reached the circle of rosebushes, Bill stopped short. Victor was leaning against the water fountain, the shears dangling from his hand, his eyes staring at nothing. He drew near and placed a hand on the man's shoulder, then dropped it when Victor spoke.

"There's no one here," Victor said quietly. "I'm not sure there ever was." His voice was low and dispirited, devoid of emotion. His rage had died a quick death the moment he'd arrived at the fountain and found it deserted.

"What do you mean?" Bill asked in confusion, looking around. But he could see the man was right. There wasn't anyone else present. Alive *or* dead. No corpse lie upon the ground. No spilled blood. Taking it all in, Bill could see no evidence of there even having been a struggle. He was thoroughly baffled.

Victor raised the old pruning shears. "There's no blood on these. Just rust and dirt. She didn't kill anyone." He flung them into the weeds. Nearby he spied Madeleine's basket. It was filled with an assortment of wilting flowers. A look of profound sadness crossed his dark features. *So it had begun again.*

"Victor, I don't understand. Something had to have happened to your wife for her to be in the state she was in. She was hysterical, for Pete's sake. What happened here?" Bill could just make out the impression left by Madeleine where she had lain upon the ground amid the now dying pulled and cut weeds. But there was no sign of a struggle. *Had she fallen asleep and dreamt it?*

Victor pushed himself away from the fountain and slowly began to make his way to the path, shoving aside the tree branches that hung too low to the ground.

"Come on, Bill. There's nothing to see here. But I need to talk to you. I want to explain. I need to tell you something about my wife."

Bill followed Victor down the path, dodging the branches before they could snap back into place and slap him in the face. The way the older man's shoulders sagged, as if the weight of the world was dragging them down, was not lost on Bill. In front of him walked a sad man; his commanding posture and purposeful step were gone. Something was wrong in the Martucci household; all was not as perfect as Bill had believed.

He thought as he walked.

Bill had questions and they spun in his mind. What was wrong with Madeleine? What happened to her out here? Why was Victor anxious to sell the house? Why was Madeleine's dead cousin haunting the place? Were Skye's ghost and what happened to Madeleine related in some way? Did all this tie in together? Bill wished he knew.

Somehow, this simple ghost-hunting adventure of his had turned into a deeper, more meaningful mystery. It wasn't fun anymore. It wasn't a game now. Reality had finally hit him. Something serious was going on at Grace Stone and Bill had a strong feeling that Madeleine could be the key. The answer. After all, this was *her* family's home. She was the blood-tie. One thing he felt sure of: Madeleine's relative's had woven secrets into the very heart of this house. How was he, a stranger, going to unravel them?

As they neared the back patio, Bill wondered how he was going to get close enough to Madeleine to talk with her. Victor was now probably going to watch his wife like a hawk. If he were in the older man's shoes he would do the same. But, somehow, he would have to find a way to get Madeleine alone.

They entered the kitchen after stopping in the mudroom so Victor could wash his hands at the clay sink. Coming in behind him, Bill was mildly surprised when the older man went straight to the refrigerator and began pulling out food to pile on the table.

Sure, Bill mused humorously, *dealing with a hysterical and imaginative wife could give a man an appetite. Old Vic could probably eat during a funeral.* He decided to help by setting the table. He figured Victor planned on filling him in on his wife's problems over a cold lunch.

Upstairs, Melissa carefully helped Maria undress a dazed and sluggish Madeleine. At first, she kept rambling incoherently about planting rosebushes and pouring concrete for the water fountain, as they removed her socks and shoes and her soiled pants and shirt. She wasn't making much sense; for a while she kept referring to Melissa as someone named Annie. Eventually, as Melissa examined her, Madeleine became somewhat more lucid and finally recognized who she was.

Melissa checked every inch of her exposed flesh for cuts and bruises and gave a close examination to the alleged bite mark on her left shoulder. Puzzled, she could find nothing that would indicate a struggle between the small woman and an attacker. She had seen the aftermath of plenty of sexual assaults at the hospital, with all kinds of injuries, but she could find no evidence of anyone having laid a hand on Madeleine. There were no teeth marks in her skin, either. Nothing matched the older woman's description of the events that took place in the back garden. Not a single bruise or scratch.

She allowed Madeleine to take a shower after having learned that penetration had not occurred. She would have preferred to wait until a doctor had examined her but Madeleine's placid demeanor had grown near hysteria when she'd told her she couldn't bathe. Although Melissa did not want to doubt the woman, she was having a hard time believing that she had even been attacked. Something happened to her; that was obvious. But, Melissa was sure it had been an attack on the mind, not the body. She supposed the shower wouldn't make any difference; it wouldn't destroy any evidence of an attack. Melissa didn't think there had been one. At least, with a shower taken, Madeleine would feel cleaner and perhaps be able to rest.

Madeleine had clutched her grandmother's cross in a tight fist while being undressed, only relinquishing it to Melissa when she stood naked near the shower. She made Melissa promise not to lose it while she bathed. When she turned on the faucet it gurgled ominously, spitting out rusted water, and then cleared. Melissa frowned and left the bathroom after Madeleine stepped under the spray. Something was wrong with the plumbing and if Mr. Martucci wouldn't get it fixed, she and Bill would have to. But it was odd; a couple of weeks ago the plumbing had been fine. What next, she wondered?

In the bedroom, Maria had nervously tidied up, straightening the bedcovers and placing the soiled clothes in a corner to take downstairs later, and had laid out a cotton gown for Madeleine.

"It's a lovely old cross," Melissa said to her, handing the necklace to Maria.

Maria took it from her and gently removed the broken chain. She crossed the room to the vanity and opened the jewelry box Madeleine had brought from Pasadena. After a few moments of searching, she found what she was looking for. A tiny gold chain with a pendant she had gotten Madeleine for Christmas two years ago. She carefully removed the cameo pendant and affixed the cross to the chain. She knew her friend well enough to know that's just what she would want. Madeleine would want to wear her grandmother's necklace and perhaps by doing so would feel closer to the grandmother she'd never gotten to know in life.

Maria wiped a tear from her cheek. She took the gown and the necklace to the bathroom to help dress her Miss Mattie for bed. She was not going to leave her side until she was tucked in and fast asleep. If everyone were hungry, they would have to fend for themselves. Her sole duty at this moment lay in caring for her friend.

Melissa stayed long enough to watch Maria lead Madeleine to the bed. She looked vulnerable and as small as a child in the pink cotton gown. It nearly dragged the floor. Her eyelids were half closed and she moved like an automaton as Maria settled her in the large canopy bed. She had to lift her legs for her and gently push her head down onto the pillows before tucking the quilt around her narrow shoulders. Maria clucked and cooed to her like a mother hen but Madeleine didn't make a peep. Melissa stared a moment at the cross lying on her pale throat, nestled in the hollow of her collar bone, rising and falling with each small breath Madeleine took, and then turned to go downstairs.

The atmosphere in the kitchen was subdued. Melissa eased herself into a chair. Both men had stopped chewing and were looking at her, waiting to hear her diagnosis. Before them was a spread of food fit for a small army. On a huge platter were four different kinds of cold cuts; ham, turkey, salami, and roast beef, surrounded by sliced cheddar, Swiss, Colby, and mozzarella cheese. The bread sack lay open next to several containers of condiments and opened jars of sandwich spreads. Wads of plastic saran wrap littered the table in any available space they'd found to tuck them in and both had tall glasses of wine at their elbows, the bottle of Chardonnay stationed between them.

Melissa picked a slice of Colby cheese off the platter and nibbled at the corner. "Your wife is resting comfortably," she said. "I examined her as thoroughly as I could. She told me she wasn't raped, Mr. Martucci." She looked at Bill. "You haven't called the police, have you?" He shook his head and bit into his sandwich. A chunk of lettuce plopped out onto his plate and he silently tucked it back in among the lunchmeat bulging out of his wheat bread.

"Mr. Martucci, I'm not sure how to tell you this." She took a deep breath and opted for being straightforward. "I don't think your wife was attacked by anyone. She doesn't have a scratch on her and I couldn't find any teeth marks. And to be honest, I think she experienced some kind of a hallucination. She was in a fugue-like state upstairs. She was kind of delirious, talking like she was someone else and calling me Annie. She kept going on about having to plant rosebushes and something about pouring concrete and getting a new water fountain. She didn't make much sense for a while. Then she calmed down enough to take a shower. By the time Maria put her to bed, she was silent. She didn't even know I was there."

Victor took a drink of his wine and slowly lowered his glass. When he offered no comment, Melissa asked, "Has Mattie experienced anything like this before?"

His face bore the expression of a tired man, haggard and drawn. Melissa suddenly felt sorry for him and compassion rose in her heart. She'd been blinded by his opulence and had forgotten that he was human. Being wealthy wasn't a buffer against tragedy; misfortune could strike anyone, anywhere, anytime. God made his sun to shine on everyone, and let the rain fall on us all. Rich or poor didn't matter. Just as everyone has a measure of faith, we also have our share of grief and our burdens to bear. None of us are impervious to pain when we love someone and Melissa knew that Victor loved Madeleine with all his heart and soul and that at this moment his heart was wrenching in his gut. To her chagrin, she felt tears burning her eyes, suddenly overcome by emotion.

She swallowed hard and blinked her eyes, embarrassed for Victor to see her lose control. This wouldn't do. She rose from the table to get a plate and fork, and a roll of paper towels while she put her emotions in check.

Returning to the table she helped herself to a slice of cold meatloaf, neither of the men had touched it, and then went to pour a glass of milk. Seated once more, she remained quiet while Victor gathered his thoughts.

He toyed with his sandwich a moment, arranging it beside a helping of pasta salad. But instead of taking a bite he lowered his fork and leaned back in his chair. He cleared his throat. This was not at all what he had expected in coming here, to expose his deeply cut wounds to people he hardly knew, and discuss his wife's mental problems. But, whether he liked it or not the young couple now knew something was wrong with his wife. It was best to explain than to leave them to draw their own conclusions.

He took a deep breath, his gaze resting upon his wine glass, instead of their faces. He cleared his throat. "My wife is a very sweet and gentle woman. She's always had an innocence about her. She can be stubborn when her mind is made up, but she is also very fragile. She's had three breakdowns in her life and I've witnessed them all. Her first was at the age of fifteen." Victor stole quick glances at their faces and was relieved to see understanding written there.

"She took Skye's death pretty hard. And, of course, the deaths of her aunt and uncle. I worked for her father at the time and deeply respected him. I was a young man of twenty-two when he'd become my business mentor and I'd spent a lot of time at the Fitzgerald house.

"I've known Mattie since she was an awkward and shy fourteen-year-old girl. I watched her grow and blossom day by day, month after month, year after year. One thing I learned about her early on was that this house was her favorite place to be in the entire world. But after Skye's death her family only came here for two summers and then stopped coming. They discovered it was too hard on Mattie being here, too many memories of Skye that haunted her.

"After Skye's funeral, Mattie sunk into a deep depression and her parents put her in therapy. She'd suffered from bad dreams and swore that Skye was trying to reach her from beyond the grave. She'd stayed in therapy all that summer and by the time school started she was almost back to normal. She didn't need therapy again until her family brought her here the following summer for vacation. Afterward, through the winter months she was fine, and the following summer they came once more, but they returned home early. Mattie's nightmares had returned and she'd begun sleepwalking.

"She doesn't remember doing it except for one instance. At sixteen her brother found her in the attic rummaging through one of those old trunks. And at seventeen, the last time her family was here, they'd found her several times out in the back garden, clawing at the dirt with her bare hands, like she was looking for something. God only knows what she was doing out there. She has no memory of it."

Here Victor paused to take a drink. He wondered if he should continue. The worst was yet to be told and he didn't know if he could tell it without becoming emotional. Once more, he wished he had not brought his wife back to this house. It had been years since it happened, and he'd thought that was all behind her. But he'd been wrong. Dead wrong.

"Bill, I can't explain what happened in the living room. But please, I'm begging you; don't mention this ghost business to my wife. It may send her over the edge. She's already begun to display the symptoms of a nervous breakdown. I'm afraid if that happens again, she may never return to me. Whole. Please don't tell her."

The sorrow in his dark eyes touched Bill deeply. It was not easy for a man of his standing to beg for understanding and compassion, and Bill knew it took guts for Victor to bare his soul about his wife to a near-perfect stranger.

"All right, Victor. I won't say anything to your wife." Bill had to bite his tongue to keep from telling the man about the encounter he and Madeleine had the night before. Was it only last night? It seemed like ages ago. Madeleine was very much aware of something not right with this house, but in light of what Victor had just shared with him, he decided it was best to keep his mouth shut for the time being.

Victor sighed with relief. "Thank you, Bill. There is something else I think I should tell you. It was a long time ago, seventeen years ago to be exact, but it may help you understand Madeleine's state of mind."

At the other end of the table, Melissa had remained quiet, silently nibbling her lunch but paying close attention to everything Victor was saying. She was shocked to hear him blurt out, "My wife had a miscarriage seventeen years ago."

"I'm sorry to hear that," Bill said.

"Thank you. It happened long ago and I've come to terms with being childless, but for Madeleine, sometimes it's a fresh wound. For the most part, she's accepted she will never be a mother and after a couple of years of therapy she found ways to occupy her time and mind. She organizes fund-raisings for various charities and volunteers her time at a women's shelter. Most days you would never know she'd ever experienced any tragedies and had needed professional care. Her last breakdown was five years ago, after her father died. It took a year of intense therapy and medication to put her back on track, but she's been fine for the past four years. Since it was her idea to come here I thought she was stronger and would be all right. But, after today, I know I was lacking in good judgment. I shouldn't have brought her here."

"Mr. Martucci?" Victor was startled to hear Melissa's voice. She'd been so quiet he'd forgotten she was in the room. He inclined his head in her direction and asked her to please call him Victor.

"Victor, where was Madeleine when she had her miscarriage? I mean, were the two of you in California at the time or some place else?" she asked on a hunch.

"Your ability to pick up on these things is astounding, Melissa. You're quite right to ask. We weren't in California."

Bill slapped his forehead, catching on. "My God! You were staying in this house at the time, weren't you?"

So, he was right. Madeleine was the key. He didn't exactly know how, but he knew he was right. All of this pointed to the connection between Madeleine and her cousin and everything tragic in their lives. Puzzle pieces. That's what he had. A few puzzle pieces construed from tragic events. They were beginning to fit in odd little places and Bill wondered what the entire picture would be once he put them all together. The centerpiece was going to be the worst of them all, he was sure. And at the heart of it all was this house. He shivered and thought of that old saying of someone walking over his grave as Victor explained what happened to his wife seventeen years ago.

At the age of twenty-two Madeleine had been deliriously happy to discover that she was going to be a mother. Her first trimester had been without difficulty and at four months along she glowed with the promise of a new life that only expecting women possess, and Victor had thought she couldn't be more beautiful. At five months she discovered she was having a girl and wanted to name the baby Antonia Skye. Antonia was Victor's mother's name.

Then, for some strange reason Madeleine wanted to visit Grace Stone. She hadn't been there for five years, not since she was seventeen. She'd nagged Victor for a month, until he'd relented. So, during her sixth month they'd packed and come to Oklahoma. It was October and the house was empty, no one was leasing it at the time.

For a few days, everything had been fine. Then Madeleine began sleepwalking again. A couple of times he'd found her in the library, seated at the piano. When he'd touched her arm, she'd slowly risen from the bench and allowed him to take her back upstairs to bed. Never uttering a sound, moving like a zombie, she had not awakened. It was as if she'd been under a spell. The next day, she'd acted as if nothing had happened. She never knew she'd even left the bed. After a few more days he'd noticed she was no longer smiling. She always seemed deep in thought and the light of joy that marked her pregnancy that once blazed in her eyes had dulled into a glazed faraway haunted expression.

He'd known then that it had been a mistake to come. Without telling her, he'd booked them a flight home. And many times during the weeks that followed, crying alone, he'd wished to God that he'd taken her home sooner. But he had waited one day too late.

The night before their scheduled flight home he'd awakened to discover that Madeleine was missing once again. Throwing back the covers he'd raced out of the master bedroom, taking the hall that led past Skye's bedroom.

Before he'd even reached the linen closet, he'd heard Madeleine moaning. His heart had nearly stopped when he saw her sprawled at the foot of the attic stairs. Her nightgown was soaked in amniotic fluid and blood and there was a gash in her forehead. Fearing the worst, he'd gently lifted her, carried her downstairs and laid her on the sofa. Then he'd called for an ambulance. She'd remained unconscious all the while. It had seemed to take forever for help to arrive but they had come quickly.

After loading her into the ambulance they'd told him which hospital they were taking her to and he'd quickly dressed and followed. By the time he'd arrived, it was all over. His daughter hadn't survived and his wife was in critical condition; she'd lost a lot of blood during delivery. She'd regained consciousness long enough to hold their daughter for just a few precious moments, and then blacked out. After that, she had lain in a coma for three days and had made a slow recovery.

Victor had returned to the house only once, to clean up the attic stairs and pack. He'd checked into a motel but spent most of his time at Madeleine's side. Within two weeks she was well enough to travel and he took her home. He had also taken his daughter home to be buried in one of the plots he'd bought for himself and Madeleine. What followed was two years of intensive therapy and many sleepless nights. Eventually Madeleine grew strong and that's when she became involved with doing charity work. After a while, she'd donated the entire contents of the nursery they'd made for their daughter to a shelter for abused women and children and became involved with their organization.

Victor emptied his glass. "We haven't set foot in this house since then. And I never want to again."

Bill pushed aside his empty plate. No wonder the man had given him that cold stare when he'd mentioned the attic earlier. "Now I understand why you are so anxious to sell. I'm really sorry."

At the end of the table, Melissa hastily wiped the tears off her cheeks and took her dishes to the sink. How awful! That poor woman, she thought. Meeting her yesterday, she'd had no idea what this lady had been through and she was so sweet. She would never again think that Madeleine was spoiled. It had taken guts to come back to this house, to face the tragedy of losing her only child. No wonder there had been tears in her eyes when she'd asked Melissa if she'd planned to have children.

"Bill, I'm sorry for pushing you to make a decision to buy the house," Victor was saying, "You paid a six month lease. If you still want to stay, go ahead. You're not under any obligation to buy. But, after you leave, I'm closing this house up for good. I don't care if sits here and rots. I'm not going to deal with it anymore and this is the last time Mattie will ever set foot in it." He rose to leave. He needed to be by Madeleine's side, to assure himself that she was all right.

"Well," Bill said to Melissa when they were alone, "What do you think?"

She returned to the table to collect their dirty dishes. "I think there's a lot more going on here than we'd thought. And I think we may be in over our heads." She went to the sink to start washing up.

"So, you don't believe we could solve this problem?" he asked, clearing the table, putting away the food.

"Bill, I'm just not sure. One thing I am sure of is that Skye has been trying to reach Mattie for years. Why? I don't know." She shivered, her hands in the hot sudsy water. "I wonder if all the times that she was sleepwalking if Skye had been directing her steps. Telling her where to go. She'd been found in the library, out by the water fountain, and in the attic. These seem to be important places."

Bill put the last of the condiments in the fridge, and then began rinsing the dishes. "Okay, lets assume you're right, and I think you are. What have we got? Skye is found, dying in the library, talking about a red book. Let's assume the red book hasn't been found, but there was a reason why she crawled into the library. She had to have hidden it somewhere in there. So we need to find it. A year later, Mattie is found in the attic. The next year she is found outside at the water fountain. Five years later she's found in the library *and* she had an accident on the attic stairs and lost her baby. And this year, something terrifying happens to her out by the water fountain and in broad daylight. I don't think she walked out there in her sleep, she had to be awake to find her grandmother's necklace, plus she had dressed herself." He dried his hands and leaned against the counter. "What do you think so far?"

"I think the ghost or ghosts of Mattie's relatives are trying to tell her something and her mind is too fragile to take it." Melissa suddenly gasped. "Bill! So many of her relatives died here on this property! What if they are *all* here? What if one of them was evil? You said there was a bad one here. Are we doing the right thing? I mean, in buying the house? What if we can't make it livable?"

Bill shook his head. "We don't have to buy it. But we've got it for six months. Less, if you decide not to stay. We don't have to, stay that is. Victor will refund our money if we leave."

"Oh, you think so?"

"Yeah. He'd already told me he would. I just hadn't mentioned it to you. Until now. So, anytime you want out, let me know. I'd like to stay a little longer and try to figure this all out."

Melissa sighed, and then grabbed the pork chops she'd left out and put them in the refrigerator. It had been a long morning, nearly two in the afternoon now, and she was feeling a little tired. It was strange, but she had been feeling a little less energetic lately, sluggish. She hoped she wasn't coming down with anything. Come to think of it, she was starting to feel a bit queasy, too. She fervently hoped she wasn't going to face another bout of vomiting.

She stopped, her head poking into the cold fridge. She held her breath for a few seconds and then slowly straightened. Madeleine had been pregnant the last time she was here. A baby! It had been a girl and it had died. Skye was just a teenager when she had died. An only child. Madeleine, as far as she knew, was the only Fitzgerald female left in the family. Old Mrs. Fitzgerald had given birth to only two boys. And tragedy had struck the daughters of the Fitzgerald men. One with loss of life, the other the loss of a child.

She slammed the refrigerator door, rattling its contents. What did it all mean? Something, surely. Women. Girls. Babies. Why did Madeleine imagine being attacked? Why? Why at the water fountain? Why not inside the house? Melissa grabbed a handful of her curls. "Oh, Bill, this is so aggravating! I feel like it's staring me in the face and I'm too blind or stupid to see it. It's so close, I feel I can almost touch it, but it's eluding me. Ugh!" She crossed the room.

"Where are you going?" he asked.

"Upstairs to take a nice, long, hot bubble bath and clear my head. I suddenly have a pounding headache."

"Don't forget to use the bat if you need me!" he called out after her.

Chapter 15

On his way to the library Bill met Maria coming down the back staircase. She was carrying Madeleine's soiled clothes and offered only a tight-lipped smile as she went into the kitchen.

He stopped at the library door, remembered he'd left his notepad in the living room, and went to retrieve it.

He gave the fireplace a passing glance. The shattered remains of his and Melissa's tea glasses lay scattered among the unlit logs. It seemed that Skye's ability to manipulate objects had improved. He didn't know if that was a good thing, or not. *Were* they getting in too deep? In over their heads? He wondered where the other ghost or entity had been during this show of her powers as he gathered his notepad and play lists.

In the library, he was a little disconcerted to find that all the desk drawers were open, as well as the drawers in the two tables positioned between the leather chairs that provided cozy reading corners. Who had done this?

A little aggravated, he rammed the drawers home in the mahogany desk. Had Maria done it? Or had Madeleine performed a sleepwalking search before going out to the garden? Possibly. Who knew what she had done between the time the electrician arrived and Skye's little performance?

He crossed the warm and inviting room to shut the table drawers. The light from the French doors and windows had darkened, and outside the glass Bill could see a few thunderheads gathering for another deluge. Wheeler might have done it, he thought, as he switched on a table lamp. But had the man had time? Bill wasn't sure. Besides, what could have ol' Ralph Wheeler been looking for?

He went into the private office and retrieved Samuel's blueprints and date book. Returning to the library, he placed them by his computer. He'd just sat down at the desk when he heard a strange thumping sound on the ceiling. Melissa was calling him. Jeepers! What now?

He jumped up and ran, taking the servant's stairs two at a time.

In the bedroom, he was relieved to see Melissa waiting for him, unharmed, dressed only in a yellow bathrobe. Apparently she wasn't frightened, but the knitted pattern between her brows informed him that she was irritated about something.

"What's wrong? I came as fast as I could," he said, a little out of breath.

Shoving her hands into the robe's deep pockets, she answered irritably, "Bill, there's something wrong with the plumbing. It's starting to come out all rusty looking. It's gross!"

He crossed to the bathroom feeling a little irritated himself. "Is it doing it now?" he asked, looking down at the rust stains collecting near the drain.

She followed him, peering over his shoulder as he tried the cold faucet. "No. Not now. It clears up after a few minutes. But it shouldn't be doing that. And it wasn't doing that when we were here before."

"Well, I don't know what you expect me to do about it. I can't fix it right this minute!" Why was he getting so uptight? He felt as if little needles were pricking him all over, making him want to lash out at anything that moved or talked. There was a slight chill in the air too, but he couldn't decide if it was emanating from the air conditioning vent or Melissa's frosty glare.

"I know that!" she spat at him. "I just wanted to tell you about it, that's all." She had a sudden urge to slap his face, and shove him against the wall. God, she was angry! She felt like an old witch in heat, with no takers around. What was wrong with her?

Her fists curled into tight balls, nails digging into her palms. Not trusting herself, she kept them hidden in her pockets. *I shouldn't have called him up here. I wish he would leave.*

Bill strode to the door, as if reading her thoughts. Speaking in strident tones, he said, "Call me the next time you have a *real* problem. I've got some thinking to do." He slammed the door behind him.

Melissa stood in the center of the room, dumbstruck and seething. She let out a small screech and flung her slipper at the door, wishing it had hit Bill's head instead. She stood stock-still and took in a few deep, calming breaths. What was wrong with her? She hadn't been angry a few minutes ago. And she'd never wanted to hit Bill before. He'd never snapped at her before, either.

She shivered inside her robe, feeling a chill that went down to the marrow. She went to the bathroom and began filling up the tub, switching on the overhead heater-vent for extra heat. It was cold in the bathroom. She grabbed a bottle of Vanilla scented bubble bath from off the shelf and dumped half of it into the hot, steamy water. She was cold, tired, and queasy, and wanted to soak in those hot bubbles. So what if the water was a little rusty at first? It was nothing to get pissy about. She wished she hadn't bothered to call Bill.

Removing her robe, she eased into the tub. She turned off the water and settled down into the foam until it covered her shoulders. Ah, this was what she needed. Shutting her eyes, letting the hot water massage her muscles, she forgot about being angry.

In the bedroom, the sound of wood scraping wood did not penetrate through the closed bathroom door.

Melissa soaked, unknowing, and undisturbed.

Striding down the hall, Bill ran into Maria. "Mr. Hayden, there's a man downstairs. A police officer. I didn't want to disturb Mr. Martucci. Will, you talk to him? He's waiting in the den."

"Okay. Thanks, Maria." They parted company, she going down the back staircase, he going down the front to the den.

He made a wry face, trying to put aside his annoyance at Melissa as he descended the stairs. What had that been about, anyway? He hadn't understood her summoning him in the first place. He'd exhaled loudly in disgust. She was acting like a child, demanding satisfaction now. 'Fix the water!' he imagined her whining in a childish voice. *Jeez, Louise! Okay, let it go,* he chided himself. Just let it go.

Wondering why the police should be paying them a visit, he entered the den.

A very tall, middle-aged man, wearing a uniform, was just straightening up from leaning over the coffee table. He paused, as he was about to pop a dinner mint into his mouth. "Ah, hope you don't mind," he said, gesturing with the mint pinched between his thumb and forefinger. His voice was a rich, deep bass, strong but friendly.

"No, not at all. Help yourself," Bill said, coming further into the room. "It's what they're there for."

The man held out a hand to Bill. "I'm Sheriff Hopkins. Bob Hopkins."

Bill shook his hand. "Bill Hayden. What can I do for you?"

"Well," Sheriff Hopkins shifted his weight; his policeman's leather belt creaked when he placed his hands on his hips, one huge hand resting above his holster.

He wasn't obese, but he was a large man and seemed to fill the room. Bill was tall, but this man looking down at him was at least 6' 10", broad shouldered, and compact. Beneath a gray felt cowboy hat, he was pale skinned and looked to have permanent sunburn on his nose and cheeks. Bill was sure those keen steel-gray eyes would miss nothing during an investigation. Although Bill wasn't worried about his presence at the house, he would bet money the man's stature would put the fear of prison into any criminal.

"I got a call a little bit ago," he was saying, "from a man named Ralph Wheeler. He's an electrician. Said someone or *something* attacked him while he was up in your attic. Do you know Mr. Wheeler?"

"No, not personally," Bill said. "But he was here this morning to check on the wiring. Is he all right?"

Sheriff Hopkins scratched his forehead nonchalantly. "Since you asked, I'm assuming you know he did receive an injury when he was here. He had to have a couple of stitches put in his head. Know anything about that?"

The man was shrewd. "Sheriff Hopkins," Now why did that name sound familiar? "My wife and I are leasing the house, possibly to buy it. Mr. Martucci and his wife, who own the house, have come from California to make sure it's up to code and discuss the purchase. Frank Smedley, at Pine Ridge Realtor, sent Mr. Wheeler over. I wasn't actually introduced to—"

Sheriff Hopkins cut him off. "—Are Victor and Madeleine here? Well, I'll be . . . I haven't seen Madeleine in years." A grin cracked his large jaw, exposing well cared-for teeth. "Nice woman, that Madeleine. Of course, our last meeting, about sixteen or seventeen years ago, was under terrible circumstances." His smile faded. "Is she here now, I'd like to see her?"

Bill hesitated for a moment, then replied, "Uh, Mrs. Martucci is feeling a little under the weather at the moment. She's upstairs in bed. Mr. Martucci is with her."

"That's a shame. I'm sorry to hear that. Hope it's nothing serious."

"No, nothing serious. She'll be back on her feet in no time." Bill saw absolutely no reason to go into details. He wasn't about to tell the sheriff that Madeleine's mental state of mind might not be up to par and was in no shape to receive visitors, even if they were old acquaintances. At the back of his mind was that little niggling feeling again that he should know whom this man is. Bob Hopkins. Maybe not Bob. But something like it. *Why* was it so familiar?

"Glad to hear it." The sheriff broke in on his thoughts. "I'd heard her father passed away a few years ago. He was a good man. His brother was too."

"Have you known the Fitzgeralds long?"

"All my life." He shifted his weight again.

"Where are my manners?" Bill moved toward the loveseat. "Would you like to sit down, Sheriff?"

"If you don't mind, and you don't have to let me, I'd like to take a look in the attic. Just to get an idea of what Wheeler was talking about." He bent down and took another dinner mint out of the candy dish. "Just a formality."

"Sure," Bill said, turning to toward the entry hall. "It's this way."

"Yep. I remember the layout. It's been a while, but I remember." He followed Bill, his tread heavy on the stairs.

They walked in silence until they reached the top of the attic stairs. Bill flipped on the attic light. It wasn't very bright, but it was enough to keep him from tripping over boxes and banging his knees.

The sheriff carefully made his way to the old table Wheeler had told him about and eyed the Victrola. Well, Wheeler was telling the truth about what was on the turntable but he just couldn't picture the old thing actually working. It had to be at least sixty or seventy years old, maybe older, probably had belonged to Zed's or Sarah's parents.

Moving further into the shadowy dusty gloom, he nearly tripped on the overturned box of books. Grunting a little, he bent down and picked up a thick book. He blew the dust off the cover and tilted it sideways to read the title and checked the binding for blood. There was a dark reddish stain at one corner that could have been blood, but he wasn't sure. It was a pretty hefty book, one about painting with perception, and he guessed it had belonged to Elise Fitzgerald. He was about to turn around when his foot made contact with Wheeler's cap. He picked it up. The white patch on the front verified that it belonged to the electrician.

He laid the book on the table and moved back toward Bill who was perched upon an old trunk.

"I've dealt with complaints on Mr. Wheeler before; people saying he stole things, but this is the first time *he's* made a complaint." Sheriff Hopkins lifted the cap for Bill to see. "To tell the truth, I didn't believe him. But, here's his cap. He was up here all right. But the rest of his story gets a little crazy." He tilted back his cowboy hat, scratched his forehead, apparently not sure how to tell Bill Wheeler's story. Then seeming to come to a decision, he adjusted his hat back on his forehead and spoke. "He said that old phonograph played on its own. And when that book hit him in the back of the head and he turned around, he said he saw a she-devil, whatever he meant by that. He described something that couldn't possible exist. Something like a witch with flames shooting out of her. Scared the daylights out of him. Crazy, ain't it? But the man admitted to wetting himself. I just don't know what to make of it."

Beneath Bill's legs, the trunk moved a fraction of an inch and something thumped within it.

He stiffened and slowly rose, dusting off his jeans; he didn't want the sheriff to notice the trunk. He hoped the man hadn't noticed the startled look that must have crossed his face.

Willing his features back into passivity he said, "I really don't know what Mr. Wheeler was talking about. None of us saw what happened. Uh, could we go back down and get out of this dusty place?"

Bill moved toward the attic stairs and was relieved when the man followed him down. He had a hunch Skye was hiding in the trunk and she'd heard the sheriff give him Wheeler's description of herself. He wasn't sure how she, being a ghost, would take being described so horribly and didn't want to stick around to find out. He wanted to get the sheriff out of there before she made an appearance and gave credence to Wheeler's testimony. The last thing they needed was the local sheriff having a ghostly encounter and asking embarrassing questions.

Bill closed the attic door and followed the big man down the front stairs. He was saying over his shoulder to Bill, "It's a lovely old house. Been a long time since I last had dinner here."

"Were you here frequently?" Bill asked, as they reached the bottom of the stairs and the sheriff turned to face him. Bill had to look up to make eye contact. God, the man was huge, only a very slight paunch around his middle. Probably worked out in a gym, too.

"Oh, yes. Samuel was an old buddy of mine. That wife of his was something else. What you'd call a free spirit. I still have a couple of her paintings hanging on my walls. It was a shock when they'd died. I came out here with my dad when he got the call. He used to be the sheriff. Guess I followed in my old man's footsteps. He's Senior, by the way. I'm Junior."

What happened to Wheeler was unfortunate, but was propitious for Bill. The arrival of the sheriff was a blessing in disguise. Bill believed he'd just gotten lucky and tapped into a well of information. He silently thanked the Lord, and decided to dig a little deeper.

"Ah, sheriff, would you mind staying a little longer?" he asked, when the man made a move toward the foyer. He stopped, re-adjusted his cowboy hat, and followed Bill into the den.

"I'll only take a few minutes of your time." Bill sat in an upholstered chair while Hopkins eased his bulk onto the plaid loveseat. He pitched Wheeler's cap onto the coffee table.

"My wife and I are interested in the history of this house. As I said, we're thinking about buying it."

"Glad to hear it, Mr. Hayden. It's been empty too long."

"You said you knew the Fitzgeralds all your life."

Hopkins picked up another dinner mint and popped it into his mouth, nodding his large head. "I was just a boy when my dad started bringing me out to the house. He and old Zed Fitzgerald were close friends. I used to ride horses with some of the cowhands' sons. Jacob and Samuel were a little older than me, about eight or nine years difference in our ages; they tolerated me pretty well when they were teenagers, but we became good friends when we reached adulthood. I was about seventeen years old when Zed passed away, and a few days later, his wife Sarah, followed suit. Sometimes it happens that way. My dad said Sarah just couldn't face life alone without Zed. She passed away quietly, upstairs in her room."

Oh, jeez, thought Bill. In the very room he and Melissa shared. It didn't take Bill but a second to decide that telling her would be a bad mistake.

"About two years before their deaths," the sheriff continued to reminisce, "Madeleine and Skye were born. Sarah fussed over those two when they were here and spoiled them rotten. She hardly let them out of her sight. I got a good tongue lashing one afternoon for taking them out to play in the garden. She'd turned white as a sheet when I'd told her we went out to the fountain. The girls loved it out there."

The sheriff's face broke into a huge grin. "What a pair they made. One as pale and as delicate as a flower like her mother, Abby, and the other as dark as Sarah and as free spirited as Elise. Together they made a formidable pair, inseparable. Went hand in hand as night following day. For years they insisted they were sisters, not cousins." He paused a moment. "Samuel and his wife and Skye were killed in a bad accident, out there on the lane."

"Yes, I'd heard. Was there anything unusual about the accident?" Bill was hoping to learn more about that.

"Aside from the fact that they'd been crushed by a tree, no." The sheriff's eyes looked introspective for a moment, as if recalling a faded memory, and then he said, "About a week before the accident, I got a strange phone call from Skye. She was asking me all kinds of legal questions. Strange ones. Like, if someone in her family had committed a crime and it wasn't discovered until they'd passed away, what would happen? Would it go to court? Would her father have to pay for a relative's crime; like restitution to surviving members of the victim? Things like that. I didn't get anymore out of her. She'd made me promise not to mention the call to her father. Assured me that nothing was wrong and that she would talk to Samuel herself. I'll never know what that was all about. And there have been a few nights it kept me up, wondering. I finally had to quit thinking about it. No point now." His gray eyes seemed to dim for a moment, and then brightened.

Suddenly, he heaved himself off the sofa. "Well, I'd best get going." He snatched Wheeler's cap off the coffee table. Bill stood up and followed him to the foyer.

"I wouldn't worry about Wheeler too much," he assured Bill. "The man probably tripped and fell, and to cover his clumsiness claimed somebody bonked him on the head. Probably thought he could make a quick buck filing a lawsuit. I'll head him off. At least he didn't claim that one of you attacked him, so I think this concludes my investigation."

Bill opened the front door for him and followed Hopkins out to his white Ford pickup. A sheriff's star decorated the door beneath the window.

"Thanks for talking with me, Sheriff. Before you leave, I have one more question. Did your dad ever talk about anything unusual going on out here years ago, when the old Fitzgeralds were alive? Any problems?" He hoped for more info and wasn't totally disappointed.

Sheriff Hopkins opened his truck door, threw in Wheeler's cap, removed his cowboy hat and pitched it in also, but turned to face Bill instead of getting behind the wheel. He ran his hand over his thinning sandy brown hair.

"Now, that you mention it. Yes. Zed filed a missing persons report. Oh, somewhere about nineteen forty-two or maybe forty-three. Dad said it was the one time he was glad he'd failed in his duties." He leaned a muscular arm through the opened window and rested a booted foot on the running board.

"You see, a man that worked for old Zed went missing. Dad said it was the best thing that could have happened to this county. He was an unsavory kind of fella. Always getting into trouble. Dad had arrested him on several occasions for being drunk and disorderly at a bar in Broken Arrow. And once, the man came up on rape charges, but they were dropped. It was hard to prove a rape case back then, and the girl's family didn't want to put her through it. Anyway, he up and disappeared one day. Was never heard from again. I honestly don't think dear old Dad looked very hard. And I don't think the man had any relatives, well, any that would have cared if he went missing. No one contacted Dad looking for him and that was that."

"Do you know the man's name?" This might be useful, Bill thought. But, the sheriff couldn't recall the missing man's name and his father wouldn't be of any help; Sheriff Hopkins Senior passed away a good number of years ago. Dead end.

Hopkins cast a keen eye skyward, scrutinizing the clouds converging there. It was looking pretty bad toward the west, the clouds running dark blue and lower down, black. "Better keep your ear tuned in to the weather news. We're entering tornado season and those clouds don't look too friendly. Take shelter if it gets bad. It was nice meetin' you, Bill Hayden."

Bill shook his proffered hand, and Hopkins got into his truck. Leaning out the window, he said, "Give my condolences to Mattie. Her father was a good man. And I hope she's feeling better, soon. Let her know I'd like to see her and old Vic before they head back out to California." He fished into his shirt pocket, found his card, handed it to Bill. "Don't hesitate to call if you ever have a problem." He switched on the ignition, put it in gear, and followed the circle drive back out to the lane.

Bill looked up at the threatening sky. The black-shuttered house stood out against the backdrop of white thunder heads, and sneaking up toward the back garden, seeming to crawl up and over the tumbling barn, blacker, more ominous looking clouds were coming in fast from the northwest. The weather couldn't be more fitting for the mood he was in. His thoughts were filled with death and despair and the mystery of one missing *unsavory* man. The plot was getting thicker and tangled up within his mind. He felt disorganized.

He studied the sheriff's card a moment, and then headed back to the house.

Back indoors, crossing the foyer, once again the sheriff's name teased him. He looked at the card again. He'd either heard it or seen it somewhere before. Seen it, he decided. Yes, definitely seen it. Or something like it. But, where?

He went back into the library and sat staring at the mess of papers lying on the desk, wondering how he was going to sort out everything he had learned so far. Without thinking, his hand reached for Samuel's planner. He began to thumb through it. And then, it leaped out at him. Robert Hopkins, written in black and white. A lunch date Samuel had made years ago. Next to the word Hopkins was written Sr. Bob was short for Robert. So, Samuel had made a luncheon date with Sheriff Hopkins' father. As far as he knew, it meant nothing. There was nothing else written on the page for that date. Another dead end.

Bill tossed the black book back onto the desk. That hadn't gotten him anywhere.

Outside the windows, the bushes were being whipped by a gust of wind, and the panes rattled with the first rumblings of thunder. Bill rose to return to the attic. Although it went against his Christian upbringing, he intended to try making contact with Skye. He couldn't just sit and wait for another encounter, doing nothing.

He grinned derisively, as he climbed the attic stairs once more. If his mother knew what was going on here, she would lecture him on conferring with ghosts, digging out her large-print Bible to read to him the scriptures. Bill knew just which ones she would expound on, too. He could recall them from his Sunday school days. 1 Samuel chapter 28, verses 3-20. Of all the lessons he'd learned, this one had held his interest the most, had kept him from fidgeting in his seat for the duration of Sunday school one morning and had stayed with him the rest of his life.

The scriptures had been about a ghost.

Settling once more upon the trunk, Bill remembered his old Sunday school teacher. At the age of thirteen he'd finally been moved to the older boys' class and Brother Moore had made learning the Bible fun as well as interesting. On that particular morning, he'd read them the story of Saul and of the prophet Samuel.

Samuel had died and the Lord no longer communicated with Saul. Seeking a word from God, Saul sent his servants to find someone who could communicate with the dead. They found a woman living in a place called Endor. Some people refer to her as the witch of Endor, someone who could summon the dead to speak. Saul had disguised himself to meet with this woman; he knew she would be afraid of him because he had killed all the others like herself and she feared he would put her to death as well.

He met with her at night, promised that nothing would happen to her if she complied, and asked her to summon Samuel's spirit. She became afraid and told him she saw a divine being ascending out of the earth. When she described what she saw, Saul knew it was Samuel. And Samuel had spoken to him.

Ever since that day in Sunday school, Bill strongly believed in the afterlife, and he believed that ghosts existed. But, he'd also learned that communicating with the dead was a sin, and herein lay his conflict in talking to Skye; he was fascinated, afraid for his mortal soul, but couldn't curb his curiosity.

Bill had grown up in a religious household, never missing church, and so all he'd learned was ingrained into his being. Although he'd slacked off going to church as an adult, much to his mother's displeasure, he couldn't change the fact that he feared doing wrong. It was part of the fabric of his soul, sewn up tightly within his heart and mind. Still, he reasoned, the ghost of this girl was the one who'd made first contact, not him. She was the one reaching out for help. Maybe it *was* wrong. But how could he ignore a plea for help?

Sighing, he stood up. A rumble of thunder shook the attic eaves and the first drops of rain pelted the windows.

"Skye?" His voice was barely above a whisper. He cleared his throat and spoke a little louder to be heard above the thunder. "Skye, it's Bill. I'm not sure if you can hear me or not, but I'm here. I want to help you. Are you still here?" Bill shuddered, standing near the trunk he'd rested upon earlier, remembering the earlier thump he'd heard and felt within it. Heaven have mercy, this was giving him the willies.

He called once more. A hushed silence answered him; it was too quiet. Then a rumble of thunder vibrated the eaves again, making him jump; the storm had arrived at last. Lightning flashed, dimming the bare bulbs.

The back of his neck tingled, but this time it felt different, sinister. It made his flesh crawl. Maybe this wasn't such a good idea after all. The rumble of something moving within the stillness of the attic blended with the sound of thunder. A crash deep within its dark recesses, punctuated by a bright flash of lightening, seemed to stop Bill's heart.

He suddenly grew cold. Icy fingers of fear danced along his nerve endings, shaking his entire body. Something dark and menacing was floating toward him and he knew he'd made a mistake. A terrible mistake. He *was* in over his head. Way over.

It was not a benevolent Prophet Samuel coming toward him. He wished to God that it were, and silently offered up a prayer of protection for his life, for his soul, and for his sanity as things began to move about the gloomy room.

Chapter 16

Melissa was feeling decidedly better after her bath, but experienced a little irritation at seeing all the drawers pulled out in the dresser and night tables. *Bill!* Why couldn't he shut them after digging through them! She slammed them shut after finding her comfortable terrycloth dress and had pulled it over her head. It was sleeveless, orange and lime green in horizontal stripes, clung to her wide hips, and hung to her shins. She'd had it for years, and although it was a little worn and slightly faded she couldn't bring herself to throw it away. It was just too comfortable.

Her eyes fell to the growing darkness outside. Through the lace curtains hanging on the French doors and windows, she could see the trees bending with the wind, and as the thunder rattled the panes, Melissa crossed the room, turned on a lamp, and then shut the heavier drapes, immediately enclosing the room, giving her a sense of security from the onslaught of the storm beginning to rage outside.

Although it was a little early to start dinner, she headed to the kitchen anyway. During a storm the kitchen was a cozy place to be and she could keep her mind off the weather while she piddled. On the way down the back stairs, she decided while she was piddling among the pots and pans, she would make a peach cobbler to serve for dessert.

Upon entering the kitchen she heard a male voice, but saw no man. She stood still, near the table, straining to hear where it was coming from above the storm. It sounded funny, like someone talking through a tin can. Was it the ghosts of the Fitzgeralds having a tête-à-tête in the late afternoon storm? She followed the voice, cautiously moving toward the pantry. The voice grew louder.

Standing at the threshold, she laughed at herself for being silly. A small boom box was perched on the shelf above her washer and dryer; an announcer was giving the latest details on the weather. Melissa heard him mention strong rotation and a good chance that this storm system would produce a tornado.

"Stay indoors and stay tuned in for the latest details," the man warned. *Great!* She thought, *just what they needed.*

"I hope you don't mind." Melissa jumped when Maria appeared at her elbow. She had just emerged from the basement with an armload of candles. "I thought we might need these," she said, moving past Melissa to the kitchen.

Maria opened her arms and dropped the load of candles onto the table. Some rolled away and she deftly caught them before they could hit the floor. "I searched everywhere for extra candles before going down to the basement. You have a few scented ones placed about the house, but in the basement I hit the jackpot. There's a box full of them down there. They're a bit dusty," she said, cleaning them off with her apron. "But they'll do."

Melissa helped her dust them off and then searched the cabinets in the kitchen and the shelves in the pantry for candleholders. She'd found several old ones in the pantry, faded brass and dusty looking, and one large candelabra that was usually placed on the dining table. It could hold six candles. Well, this is nice, she thought, they could have a candle-lit dinner tonight. She hoped they wouldn't have to use any of them, but was glad they had plenty. She didn't relish the thought of being plunged into sudden darkness, on a stormy night, with otherworldly visitors lurking about. Candlelight could be romantic, she mused, remembering a better time with Bill, but in other circumstances, like a bad storm and a haunted house, they just made the atmosphere spooky, not reassuring.

On the radio, the announcer switched tunes and she couldn't believe she heard a man singing about raindrops falling from his eyes. She crossed her own green eyes in disgust, looking up at the ceiling, ineffectually blew the curls off her forehead, and then returned to the table with the candleholders. The man must be crazy to play that kind of tune on a day like this.

She and Maria worked, side by side, placing the candles in the holders. Melissa placed a fat white candle in a single holder, it was held in place by a sharp metal point protruding from the base. From the pantry came the announcer's voice for a few seconds and then a woman singing about her mama, saying she was going to have days like this.

Melissa hooted and snorted at that one.

"Maria, do you usually listen to golden oldies?" she asked, a grin tugging at the corners of her lips.

"No, not usually," she smiled in return. "But, with this weather, and the reception I got in the pantry, it was all I could pick up. I was hoping for a Latino station, something to keep me company. Plus, I wanted to keep up with the weather. You don't mind, do you?"

"No, not at all. It was a good idea."

"I hate storms and I heard you get really bad ones here." Maria cast a worried eye at the window above the sink. A small branch, nearly stripped of its leaves, flew past the glass. Lightening flashed, followed immediately by a crack of thunder. Maria started; the lights flickered, dimmed, and then brightened.

Without a word they both scrambled, digging through the cabinet drawers. The lights flickered again. Within seconds Melissa held up a box of large kitchen matches, "Got 'em!" she shouted triumphantly.

She raced back to the table and lit the largest candle. She pushed it toward the center of the table, tucked a curl behind her ear and looked nervously at Maria. For a split-second they didn't breath, and then both exploded with laughter.

"Look at us, acting like a couple of scared five-year-olds." Melissa tossed the matches onto the table. "Well, we've got our security light burning. Let's cook something. It'll keep us busy."

"Good idea. What have you got in mind?"

"I thought I'd make a peach cobbler for dessert."

"Sounds good to me. That'll take a while."

Melissa shook her head. "Not the way I make it. I know a short-cut." She took out a large baking dish and a mixing bowl. "It's real simple." She went to the pantry and returned with two large cans of sliced peaches and a bag of brown sugar. "This is the easiest way to make it. My sister gave me the recipe. She looks for a short-cut in everything she does."

She explained as she worked. "You melt two tablespoons of butter in the pan and sprinkle a little brown sugar over it. Or you could use plain sugar. It doesn't matter. Next, you just add one cup of milk, one cup of self-rising flour, one cup of sugar, and a half cup of peach juice into a mixing bowl and stir it up." With this done, Melissa dumped the peaches into the buttered pan after stirring the cobbler mixture. This she poured over the peaches. It was milky-white and swirled around the fruit. "Now, for the best part." She generously sprinkled ground cinnamon over the cobbler.

Maria opened the oven door for her and Melissa slid the full pan inside. "You bake it at three hundred and fifty degrees for about thirty minutes. After that, I usually start checking on it until it gets golden brown. Doesn't take long."

Maria looked doubtful. "That's it?"

"That's it." Melissa grinned at her. From the pantry, the announcer was warning everyone in the area to take shelter. A tornado had been spotted over Broken Arrow.

"Do you think it'll come here?" Maria couldn't hide the trembling in her voice.

Melissa didn't want to frighten her, but thought it best to be honest and keep her alert. "We're a little ways off from there, but you can never tell with a tornado." When she saw the stricken look on the housekeeper's face, she added, "But, hey, this house has been here since the middle thirties. It's weathered many storms and its still standing. Besides, down in the basement there's a door connecting to a storm cellar, and it has a door going to the outside. We'll be safe enough if it comes to that. Don't worry." She patted her hand. "We'll be fine. My biggest worry is the lights going out." She gave her a reassuring smile, which Maria returned.

Melissa wondered how Mattie was doing and asked Maria if she were resting.

"Yes, she seems to be feeling better," Maria replied. "She dosed off for a while and I stayed with her. She woke up asking for a bowl of soup; the poor thing hadn't eaten a bite all day. Mr. Martucci stayed with her while I got the soup. When I'd returned, he'd showered and changed clothes and had fallen asleep next to her. She'd dozed off again but woke up when I brought the soup. She assured me she was fine, so I left her the soup and came looking for candles."

"I'm glad she's feeling better." Melissa switched on the oven light and peered through the glass door. The cobbler was heating up nicely; the mixture had started to bubble. She poured two glasses of iced tea and returned to the table.

"What happened to her out there?" Maria's dark brows wrinkled and her eyes darted to the window. It was as dark as midnight outside and the wind was howling fiercely.

"I don't really know." Melissa took a sip of her tea, feeling the cold liquid coating her esophagus. "She was a little confused. But, don't worry. Bill said there wasn't anyone out there. She didn't kill anyone." Relief crossed Maria's features, smoothing out the worried line in her forehead. "She may have fallen asleep and had a bad dream. At least, I think that's what might have happened." Melissa thought it best not to tell Maria what she really thought had happened.

She wondered if the housekeeper was aware of Madeleine's somnambulism and her bouts of depression. She didn't know how long the Spanish woman had been with the Martuccis. She reasonably assumed the housekeeper hadn't been in their employment seventeen years ago but, could very well have been with them when Madeleine's father passed away and had needed to see a professional. At any rate, it was easy to see that Maria cared for Madeleine as a friend, not just as an employer.

Melissa glanced at her watch. Thirty minutes had nearly passed, time to start checking on the cobbler. A delicious aroma of peaches and cinnamon filled the kitchen, making her mouth water. A scoop of vanilla ice cream would be perfect to top it off.

After checking the cobbler she glanced at her watch once more. It was just past four-thirty, time to start on that dinner she promised Maria. She decided that homemade mashed potatoes would go nicely with the corn on the cob and oven-fried pork chops, and making it would occupy her time, taking her mind off the storm. She moved to the potato bin under the cabinet.

Maria rose from her seat to help and got out a colander for rinsing the cut potatoes, and a couple of paring knives. She paused at the window above the sink. The rain pouring down the pane blurred her vision; she could barely make out the trees being whipped by the wind as the lightning flashed. All that water, she thought. Would they get flooded out? She blurted, unaware that she had spoken out loud, *"Mucha agua!"*

"Yes," Melissa agreed, "That is a *lot* of water." She cast a disgusted look into the pantry, that idiot of an announcer was playing another one of those tunes, this time a man was singing that he wished it would rain to hide his tears. She dug her knife under the peeling and nearly sliced her thumb. The man had a twisted sense of humor. Who in their right mind would play all those songs about rain in the middle of a thunderstorm? Who wants to be reminded of all that water and the damage it could do? What a dingle berry! What a dolt!

And then an idea slammed her between the eyes. She jerked her head back, as if it had been a physical blow. Wait just a darn minute! *Water, not rain!* All those songs had been about water.

Melissa sucked air between her teeth. The paring knife made a perfect small cut in the thumb she'd managed to spare just seconds ago. She threw down her knife and sucked on her thumb, turning on the water faucet to rinse the wound.

"Dadgummit!" she hissed under her breath. Blood-red water spat out of the faucet in fits. She'd nearly stuck her thumb under that nasty-looking gunk. But within seconds the water cleared and flowed smoothly.

"Are you okay?" Maria put down the potato she was peeling and leaned across the cooking island. "I'll get you a Band-Aid. There's some in the bathroom." She went out to the mudroom.

The cool water now running over Melissa's thumb, went un-noticed. At first, she'd watched her blood mingle with the clear water, pooling in the sink like dark cherry kool-aid before disappearing down the drain in the stainless steel sink. Then the sight of it blurred. Her emerald-green eyes widened and glazed over as her thoughts turned inward.

Outside, the storm raged in the now pitch-black sky, branches snapped and fell like kindling. The patio was flooded; water seeped under the back door, making mud on the dirty concrete floor of the mudroom.

Upstairs, the sound of breaking glass went unheard.

Chapter 17

Madeleine stirred, becoming aware of the bedcovers lightly pressing against her legs and torso. It was comforting. Where was she? Her eyelids rose slowly and she focused on the blue canopy overhead. Skye's room. Yes, of course. Skye. She had dreamed a surreal dream. She had seen Skye. She hadn't wanted it to end. But what had awakened her? As if in answer to her question, thunder boomed outside the window near her bed.

A thin stream of light inched its way through the partially closed bathroom door. Someone had left the light on for her. She moved her legs and made contact with Victor. Then she heard him softly snoring. The room lit up for an instant, in strobe-like effect, and then dimmed once more. Thunder boomed. It was storming. So that's what had awakened her.

She had dreamed the dream again. One that she'd had several times before, and she knew with every fiber of her being that this was so, but in the past she could never recall what the dream had been about. Only this time, it was different. She *could* recall it. She finally remembered.

She sighed deeply, feeling a small piece of metal resting against her throat. Her fingers sought out the prize she'd retrieved from the ground. Making contact with the cross, she smiled in the semi-darkness. What was once her grandmother's cherished possession, now belonged to the last female Fitzgerald. Madeleine reverently caressed her grandmother's cross, fingering it like a talisman, as if to ward off evil. It was warm in her palm and radiated hope.

It was meant to be that she should come to Grace Stone. The desire had always been there, but drowned by fear. It all made sense to her now. She was not going crazy. She'd never been crazy. Skye truly had reached her from beyond the grave. There was something she had to do. Her dream told her. All those dreams she'd had in the past told her, but she'd blocked them from her mind, afraid of going insane. She now understood what they meant. She must finish what Skye had failed to do, had died before she could. She must find the book.

Careful not to disturb her sleeping husband, she rose. She tucked the covers around Victor's shoulders, kissed his cheek, and then reached for her robe.

Quietly, she stole out into the dark hall. She belted her robe and then cautiously moved toward the stairs. Lightening brightened the bay window casting paned shadows on the wall beside her. She froze, remembering the moon shadow from her nightmare. She took a deep breath and crept on past when it darkened once more. She knew where she had to go. She knew where she had to look; Skye's favorite hiding place. The one place where she'd always hidden things that were precious to her, things she didn't want anyone else to see. How could she have forgotten? How could she not understand what Skye had been trying to tell her? It was all so clear now.

The dream. As Madeleine crept down the stairs, she remembered the dream. She and Skye were little girls again, playing hide-n-seek down by the fountain. Suddenly the sky grew dark, the fountain shook and made a roaring noise. They were afraid. They ran indoors, screaming, and hid in the linen closet. And then, suddenly, it was no longer dark, it was bright and sunny again, and they were older.

Madeleine turned at the foot of the stairs. The clock chimed. It was four o'clock in the afternoon, but there was no sunlight pouring through the windows on either side of the front door, nor was there any light coming from the den and living room. A soft glow emanated from the library leading her to the very room she needed to enter.

She paused at the threshold. The dream swirled in her mind's eye, coming into focus. She and Skye were now fourteen years old. They sat, side by side, at the piano. Skye was playing "Chiquitita" and they were singing. They harmonized; Skye's alto to her soprano, just as they had harmonized in life, opposites, and yet, perfectly balanced.

Madeleine moved further into the library, her slippers light on the hardwood floor, her pink cotton gown and robe swaying softly. Thunder rattled the French doors and lightning brightened the corners that the lamp failed to reach. She cocked her head to the left, her silvery blond hair draped around her shoulders. The piano. She moved toward it and sat upon the bench. The lamp flickered, dimmed, and then glowed softly.

In her mind's eye, Madeleine saw her cousin touching the ebony and ivory keys, those small hands with the slender fingers, moving expertly, never missing a note, nor losing the beat. Their voices rose during the chorus, and fell, slowing in tempo as the song ended. Skye turned to her, smiled, her teeth gleaming with the braces although they'd been removed before the accident.

Skye's form began to thin, as if she had no substance, and she began to glow a brilliant blue hue. Madeleine could see the bookcase beyond, showing through the shape of her small body. Then Skye spoke, "I have to leave you, Mattie. But, there is something I need you to do. Something I should have done the minute I learned about it. Now I can't. Now, it's up to you. It was too late to tell Dad. He would have done the right thing, but now, you have to. You're the only one who can." Skye held Mattie's blue eyes, penetrating her very soul with her own dark irises, she never blinked, and her child-like palm stole upward, gently touching the top of the piano.

Madeleine's gaze broke away from Skye's, trailing up her cousin's translucent arm. She saw the polished wood gleaming through her cousin's palm. Skye's hiding place.

Madeleine stood up. She lifted the top of the piano; it was heavy and creaked eerily on hinges badly needing oiling. She dipped her hand inside. Running her fingers across the strings, they plunked discordantly. Midway across the strings she made contact with what felt like dried leather, small and compact. She grasped it and drew it out, closing the top. It was smaller than a book, but a book just the same. Its red binding was cracked and faded.

She blinked back her tears. This was the red book Skye had so desperately tried to tell the sheriff about twenty-three years ago with her dying breath. This was what her beloved cousin had been trying to tell her about all these years. And this was why the piano had sounded funny, like it was out of tune.

Madeleine sat back down at the piano, Skye no longer beside her.

She pressed the book to her chest, savoring the moment. Skye's hands were the last to touch the leather binding. She caressed the cracked, dry cover as if to caress and hold Skye's hand once more.

Madeleine sighed deeply. She was not crazy. Had never been crazy. Skye had been trying to reach her all along. This was what Skye had wanted her to find. And now, it was time to learn why.

She opened the book, careful not to destroy the old crinkly pages. On the very first page, the words *Property of Sarah Fitzgerald* leaped out at her. She gasped in the lamplight. Her grandmother had kept a journal and Skye had found it long ago.

The wind roared and howled around Grace Stone Manor. Thunder boomed, and lightning flashed, the driving rain threatened to bring down the roof as Madeleine read.

For a while, Skye hovered above her, smiling with love for her cousin, and then moved on toward the attic, her task almost complete. She was glowing a brilliant blue, and almost wished Madeleine would look up. But, it was more important that her cousin learn what had happened to Sarah, to learn what had happened to all of them.

Madeleine sat, ramrod straight, holding the journal with both trembling hands. Gently she turned the pages, learning about the best days of her grandmother's life: Her marriage to Zedediah, and then the birth of her son, Samuel, coming with blessedness and joy in the fall of nineteen thirty-nine. Sarah had been thrilled to have a son by her beloved Zed, and the following year had learned she was going to have another child. Secretly she'd hoped for a daughter, but wasn't the least bit disappointed when she was blessed with another son in nineteen forty-one, Madeleine's father, Jacob.

Her days had been filled with raising her children, and overseeing her home, Grace Stone Manor. Annie, her upstairs maid, had increasingly become her friend, not just a servant, helping her with her sons. They had grown very close.

Madeleine paused, the lights flickered, and then she sighed. Just like her grandmother before her, Madeleine's housekeeper, Maria, had also become her friend over the years. The similarity was startling.

She turned the next dry and crinkling page. In March of nineteen forty-two her grandmother was pregnant again. She had written that within her heart of hearts she had no doubt that her baby was going to be a girl. She was positive that her prayers had been answered and she was finally going to have a daughter.

Days, weeks, months passed by as Madeleine turned the pages and read of her grandmother's life. Her grandmother had not yet informed Zedediah of her impending birth. Instead, she had chosen to wait until she was further along. Had wanted to wait until she was finished with the garden and tell him when everything was in bloom. Sarah had written about her garden. How she loved flowers, their fragrance, and their color. She boasted how Zed was spoiling her, giving her anything her heart desired. And out in the back garden she had wanted a water fountain surrounded by roses. She would tell Zed the good news of her pregnancy when the fountain was in place. Madeleine turned a page . . .

June 13, 1942

Today, Annie and I have planted hibiscus and hyacinths. She enjoys the feel of the soil as much as I. She is a treasure and I am so glad to have her near me. Tomorrow the rosebushes arrive. I am so thrilled. All week the men have labored, digging and laying the water pipes. I am planning to plant the roses in a circle but will leave an opening for a path to the fountain. That disgusting man, John Sneed was there, ordering the men about like he owned my home and had the right. I am quite sure I was not mistaken of the leer I received from him while

Annie and I watched the men work. He makes my skin crawl. Annie pulled me away, suggesting we return to the house for a glass of lemonade. Glad we did, the boys had awakened from their nap and were looking for me. I wish my husband had never hired that John Sneed. Must go now, Jacob is crying for me.

June 17, 1942

My soul is destroyed. I have committed a great and terrible sin. I have taken a life. My heart pounds in my chest, near to breaking, as I write this. And write it I must. The roses have been planted, but I shall never enjoy their beautiful fragrance. While Zed was away, gone to get the fountain I so desired, I worked in the garden. I planted all the rosebushes, and as I finished, that horrible man, John Sneed, came upon me. He tried to force himself on me, and Dear God in Heaven, I didn't mean to do it. I swear it. I grabbed my pruning shears. I only wanted to warn him away from me, but he lunged for me, punching my stomach over and over. I am bruised and sore, and nothing can fill the emptiness I now feel deep within my womb.

Oh, God, how can I live with what I have done? All is lost to me. My baby is gone. She fled my womb with the blows he dealt to me. I fear I will never have another child. My daughter is dead. I can't help but feel that if I had not murdered John Sneed, my baby would have lived. It is my curse, a curse upon me as a woman. There shall never be any Fitzgerald women born to this family. He cursed me with his dying breath. And to seal my fate, I have vowed silence. There is only one who knows what I have done. And I trust her with my life. Annie helped me bury him. It was she who came to my aid, but arrived too late. She had also suffered at the hands of John Sneed. We both wept, right there in the garden. She has vowed to keep my sin a secret. And I have taken an oath never to tell Zed what happened, nor to reveal where we have laid that evil man to rest. But, I doubt that he shall ever find rest. I have denied him a proper burial.

No one knew I was going to have a child. I was going to tell my beloved husband first. Now he will never know. Zed will never know of the child I have lost. Will never share my pain. That I must endure alone. I abhor that wretched fountain now. I will never go near it again. During the struggle with John I lost the cross that Zed bought for me our first Christmas together. So that too has forever passed from my hands. It is as if God has turned His back on me, and I cannot blame Him. I will not search for my necklace. I don't deserve to wear it.

This is the last time I will write in this book. Nothing I can say will erase what I have done. There is a loose board behind the shelf in the linen closet. I will place this book there for safekeeping. It will remind me that God witnessed my sin, and I am not worthy of his love. Sarah Fitzgerald

Madeleine slowly closed the red journal and wiped the tears from her cheeks. The anguish her grandmother must have suffered in silence was almost more than she could comprehend. But one thing she fully understood, could empathize with her grandmother, heart and soul, was the loss of her child. It's the single most greatest pain a mother can ever feel. The death of her own Antonia had ripped a hole in her heart as wide as empty space, and had left a permanent aching deep within her being.

Drawing her knees up to her chest, clutching her grandmother's journal close to her heart, Madeleine wept. She wept for Sarah, for her anguished soul; she wept for Skye, losing her life so young and not able to rest. And she wept for her daughter. That tiny, fragile, beautiful creature that had grown cold in her very arms as she'd held her close to her breast right there in the delivery room.

As the onslaught of wind and rain beat against Grace Stone Manor, an emotional storm beat against Madeleine. She wailed aloud with the rising wind and her tears fell profusely as the rain pelted the house. She thought she had grieved, crying with Victor as he offered comfort, crying on her therapist's sofa as she pressed tissues into her palm. But she hadn't grieved. Not like this. Not this gut-wrenching, soul-tearing, heart-breaking anguish. Now she understood why in some cultures they rent their clothes and beat themselves. It was pure unadulterated soul-pain that threatened to rip you apart, and there was no way this side of Heaven to bear it while it was trapped within your heart.

Madeleine held nothing back. She let it all out, grieving for her father and her Aunt Elise and Uncle Samuel as well. Her muscles grew weak from the shaking and she slid off the bench onto the floor. She lay there curled in a fetal position until, finally, her tears were spent.

The lights flickered again as she labored to rise off the cool hardwood floor. She moved to a small table and plucked a handful of tissues from the box to blow her nose, discarding the used wad into the wastebasket. She drew in a deep steadying breath. It was time to end this. Time to make things right. John Sneed would have to be dealt with. She knew now that it was his ghost that had soiled her two nights ago with his cold evil touch.

Madeleine squared her shoulders, pulling herself up to her full five foot, three-inch height. She was a Fitzgerald and this was the Fitzgerald home. That evil menace was the interloper. He did not belong here. It was time to expose him. It was time to finally send him on to his eternal rest where he would await judgment. And it was time to reveal her grandmother's crime, whatever the consequences may be.

"John Sneed!" she summoned him aloud. "I know the truth." She stood alone, listening to the storm violently beating against her grandparents' home. "I know where they buried you! It's not a secret anymore." Although there was no response, she knew down deep in her bones that he was here, somewhere in the house. She would find him, unless he found her first. Either way, this was to be his last night in this house.

She held on tightly to Sarah's journal. This was what he had been looking for. That's what her nightmare had been about. For years he had stolen inside the house to search for it. He hadn't wanted anyone to know what kind of a sick perverted man he was. He had been a rapist and a murderer and had gotten away with it until Sarah ended his life. He'd killed her grandmother's baby and somewhere deep in her heart she felt he was responsible for the death of her little Antonia. He had to be. And Madeleine felt sure there had been other victims years ago, falling prey to his sadistic desires just as Annie had once fallen prey to his filthy hands. No wonder she had stood by Sarah's side in shared silence.

Madeleine blew her nose again and straightened her back. There was one place she had yet to visit, had avoided since arriving. A place she had not been for seventeen years, since that awful night. It was time to face what had happened to her in the attic the night she'd lost her baby.

Chapter 18

Maria quickly shut the back door, rattling the panes. "I found a Band-Aid for your thumb. And I found this." She set a dusty old hurricane lantern upon the counter, kerosene sloshed in its bottom. She hoped it would still work. She looked up at the dimming lights overhead; they flickered but remained steady, at least, for now. She grabbed a damp cloth and wiped the dust off the lantern.

Melissa tossed the soggy, red paper towel into the trashcan and wrapped her thumb in the Band-Aid, staunching the blood flow. The cut was throbbing. She must have sliced it pretty deep and hoped she wouldn't need stitches. She thanked Maria for her help and asked if she wouldn't mind finishing the potatoes. There was something she needed to do and it couldn't wait. She would only be gone a few minutes. Maria nodded.

"Oh, and would you take out the peach cobbler? I'm sure it's done. Thanks. Be right back." Melissa trimmed the wick and lit the old lantern, taking it with her as she left the kitchen. The swinging door closed behind her, drowning out the sound of the radio. She was glad to be spared another golden oldie of someone telling her to listen to the rhythm of the rain.

The light to the servant's staircase was burning dimly and Melissa thought she heard a light tread upon the steps. She stopped to listen. Yes, there it was again, the sound of a soft-soled shoe upon the step, slowly ascending. She stood at the bottom of the dimly lit staircase, and from above came the unmistakable sound of the staircase door being opened. Someone definitely had just passed this way.

She knew it wasn't Maria. She'd just left her in the kitchen. And she knew it couldn't be Bill or Victor, they had a heavier tread. That left only one possibility, no, perhaps two possibilities. But Melissa didn't think ghosts made the sounds of footfalls. Didn't they glide? Or float? So, if not a ghost, then it had to be Madeleine.

At that moment the clock in the hall chimed out making her jump. "Stupid clock!" she cursed and moved forward.

Hoping it was a flesh and blood Madeleine she was following, she began to make the ascent. She'd only gone five steps when the lights dimmed and went out. She lurched against the paneled wall for balance. *Great!* Just what she needed! No electricity in a haunted house! The fury of the storm raging outside wasn't helping matters either. Thank goodness she had the lantern. Within the circle of its soft glow Melissa continued to ascend the stairs.

After reaching the hall on the second floor, she paused to listen. Besides the rumbling coming from the outside, she heard scraping sounds coming from the attic above that made her hair rise. Dear God, where was Bill when she needed him. She believed she had a piece of the puzzle figured out and wanted to discuss it with him. She hoped it was Bill she'd heard in the attic. She took one more step out into the hall and froze, heart racing.

A slight flutter of movement caught her eye. She turned her head to the left and almost fainted at the sight of a small ghostly figure, dressed in a soft flowing garment. Her palms grew sweaty and her heart slammed against her ribcage. Her throat constricted. She would have screamed if those imaginary hands were not squeezing her throat so tight.

The blood drained from her face as the ghostly figured turned toward her, its shimmering blond hair glowing in the lantern's light. *Dear God, is that the ghost?* But this one didn't have dark hair. A small squeak jumped from her throat and she sagged against the wall in relief.

"Mattie, you scared me to death." She exhaled loudly, finding her voice.

"Melissa, Skye is here. I feel her presence in the attic." Mattie whispered, almost monotone, bereft of emotion. Melissa shivered.

Under the circumstances, what with the wind howling like it was, trying to tear the house apart, that pronouncement was spooky coming from the ethereal form floating toward her, and Melissa wondered briefly if Mattie was in her right mind, or maybe sleep-walking. She certainly looked as if she was.

Madeleine paused, shifting her pale blue eyes upward at the sound of something crashing to the floor. It had to be Sneed, looking for the very thing she now clutched in her bosom. She stood there for a few thunderclaps, undecided, then finally moved on.

It was with some trepidation that Melissa watched Madeleine glide toward her, her slippers making no sound. She still resembled a ghost in the eerie light but her eyes were alert, not glazed like a sleepwalker's. Okay, Melissa conceded, so maybe she wasn't sleepwalking. But how was her state of mind?

Madeleine drew close to Melissa and held out Sarah's journal to her. "Read the last two entries." Thunder boomed overhead, mingling with the sounds coming from the attic. Melissa felt it vibrate in her chest.

She exchanged the lantern for the journal and quickly read the pages Madeleine indicated. Her mouth remained in a silent O until she'd finished, handing the red book back to Madeleine. Comprehension had dawned while she'd read. Well, now she understood why Madeleine had called her Annie while in that confused state. And she now understood the significance behind the music.

"I knew it!" she exclaimed excitedly. "It just hit me a minute ago. I knew it had something to do with that fountain." She rambled on loudly. "Skye kept playing old tunes about rain. It threw me off for a while, and then I realized she meant *water*. It was her clue to lead us to the water fountain. That, and I remembered just before your Uncle Samuel died he was planning to replace it. He would have dug new water pipes and found that man's bones! I . . ." Melissa firmly closed her mouth, curbing her zeal. Madeleine could only feel sadness at what had befallen her family, not enthusiasm for its discovery.

"Mattie, I'm so sorry. Forgive my callousness." She laid a gentle hand on the older woman's shoulder. *Me and my big mouth!* Melissa wished she could stuff a sock in hers right about now.

"It's all right," Madeleine whispered softly. "This doesn't touch you the same way it touches me. I understand. At least now I know I'm not crazy, Melissa."

"I know that, Mattie. You never were." Melissa's voiced softened.

"What happened to me, out in the garden . . ." Madeleine began.

"It was an instant replay." Melissa interrupted her, sure of what she now knew. "What happened to your grandmother was acted out in your mind. It's what happened to her long ago. You're tied to her, Mattie. She was trying to show you what took place."

Melissa reached out and touched the cross hanging around Madeleine's throat. "Perhaps finding this opened a door. She hadn't felt worthy to wear it and left it out there. Now it's yours. You're a good and sweet person, Mattie. It belongs with you. You're grandmother was obviously a religious person, a kind person. But she forgot something important about God." Melissa's eyes glistened with unshed tears. "She forgot that God is merciful and forgives us when we ask Him."

Madeleine's features crumpled at the generosity of Melissa's compassion. She didn't think she had any tears left to cry, but there they were, just the same. "But, Melissa, my grandmother killed a man and hid the deed."

Melissa wiped her own tears with the back of her hand. "Oh, Mattie, don't you know? The same God that forgives us for telling a lie or stealing or committing adultery is the same God that can forgive someone for taking a life. There are no big sins or little sins. It's all the same. A sin is a sin, and his forgiveness is the same. I wish your grandmother had known that. She needn't have suffered all those years with her guilt. And as for committing a crime, what she did to John Sneed was in self-defense. She wouldn't have gone to jail. She suffered in silence needlessly."

Madeleine sniffled, reigning in her tears, drawing the journal closer to her chest. "If Sarah hadn't hid his body, none of this would be happening now. Skye would be at rest; Sneed would not be here. I would have had my daughter. She would have lived. I'm saddened at what happened to my grandmother and yet at the same time I'm angry with her. All I know is that I have to fix this. The truth has to be told and that man will have to get a proper burial."

She looked back toward the attic doorway. "I have to go up there now. I believe Sneed is there." She took a step, Melissa's hand dropped from her shoulder. "Is Maria in a safe place?"

"She's in the kitchen."

"I hope she stays there. The attic is not a safe place to be right now, and I don't want her involved." Madeleine padded softly in her slippers, stopping at the bottom step. Melissa was right behind her, holding the lantern aloft. Looking over her shoulder, Madeleine said, "Maybe you shouldn't go. It might be dangerous."

"Are you kidding? I lived with that thing for a couple of weeks, scaring me half to death. I wouldn't miss rousting him out of here for anything in the world." The determined look in Melissa's green eyes sparkled in the lantern's light. "Besides, you shouldn't have to face this alone. I admit I'm scared. Who wouldn't be? But I'm not leaving you."

Madeleine offered her a weak smile. "I appreciate that. But, I won't be alone." Her gaze focused upward. "Skye is there."

"Just the same. I'm coming up." Melissa was not to be deterred.

Madeleine turned and began her slow ascent. Her thoughts playing back to the last time she had climbed these stairs.

She vaguely remembered hearing her name being called out long ago within the darkness of her grandparents' bedroom. She had followed the voice to the attic stairs that terrible night. And then from there everything was a little hazy. She struggled to recall those events, latching on to those psychological triggers that her therapist had told her about.

She drew upon her senses.

She had felt coldness sweeping down the steps that night, swirling around her feet, just as she was feeling the cold now. It chilled her bones; she shivered as her gown flapped against her legs. Her thin robe offered little protection. Only this chill was different, forceful. It was as if someone had opened a window to the storm outside. She could smell the rain.

Her steps were painstakingly slow, and her hand shook as it glided up the railing. Melissa dogged her footsteps but didn't crowd her. She was grateful that the young woman had had the foresight to bring the lantern. Otherwise they would be making this ascent in a pitch-blackness that was only relieved by the sudden flashes of lightning.

Up ahead, she heard scratching noises, and things bumping against the bare floor, like something being dragged. And that night, seventeen years ago, she remembered hearing the same kind of noises.

Heart thumping against her ribcage, she neared the turn that would take her on up to the attic floor. She steeled herself for what was to come next.

Before she had even reached the doorway and the platform of the last step, the wind was whipping her hair. It was damp and smelled of the outdoors. It put ice in her veins and caused her to shiver as she remembered that frosty cold snake-like finger slithering around her body and playing with her hair, just like it had in her nightmare, and just like it had years ago.

In a sudden gust, some old Christmas wrapping flew into her face and she let out a small cry, losing her balance. She would have fallen back down the stairs if Melissa had not been behind her to steady her. She snatched at the old paper and flung it aside. A horrible memory surfaced. Madeleine closed her eyes. Something had also slammed into her head years ago, something hard and yet squishy, like a cold fist or a dead fish. Someone had wanted her to fall down these stairs. And she knew now who it was, and what he had become.

She remembered.

Out of the depths of sleep Skye had called out to her seventeen years ago. She had arisen in the dark of night, following that ghostly voice, a young voice from her past. It echoed eerily from the depths of the attic and she'd followed unafraid, her steps ungainly. She'd waddled down the hall, pregnant with the joy moving within her womb, lightly resting a hand on her swollen abdomen. Her little Antonia had been restless, digging into her ribs. As she'd neared the turn in the stairwell, a gust of artic air had lifted her gown and played with her hair. She'd shivered from the cold but moved on up. Skye no longer called out to her, instead a heart-wrenching wail tore at Madeleine's emotions. She should have fled then, but she could not dessert her cousin who was in obvious distress.

Near the top, she'd stopped dead in her tracks, a scream frozen in her throat.

A faceless fiend, whose body resembled a writhing mass of blackened worms, blocked her entrance. Her legs had turned to jelly when a few of those horrid tentacles reached out and touched her hair, moving slowly down her arms, leaving a trail of cold slime. An icy knot had formed in her stomach, radiating outward, freezing the blood in her veins. She'd nearly wretched at the stench of rotting flesh emanating from the beast before her.

All she could think of was fleeing this horror, but her weakened legs refused to move. An insidious laugh issued from a black gaping hole where a mouth should have been as the thing floated toward her.

The stairwell began to sway under her feet and she knew she was going to faint or die of fright. She took one step backward and the evil thing that John Sneed had become flew at her, bellowing from that blackened hole, "All you Fitzgerald whores shall die!"

Madeleine had staggered backward under the blow the thing had dealt to her head. She'd wrapped her arms around her belly in a vain attempt to protect the life within her as she fell. She vaguely remembered pain screaming through her hips as she made contact with the first step, the dull thud as her body tumbled and rolled down the stairs. Her last conscious thought had been a plea for God to save her baby. And then, there she was, in the hospital, holding that tiny fragile soul in her arms as the life ebbed out of that small battered body.

John Sneed had tried to kill her, but instead had caused the death of her baby.

Madeleine opened her eyes.

Long-held guilt lifted off her shoulders; she hadn't killed her Antonia. It hadn't been her clumsiness, and it hadn't been because she was mentally unstable. All these years she had blamed herself and it hadn't been her fault. John Sneed had destroyed the living soul within her womb, just as he had destroyed her grandmother's baby.

It was time for him to vacate the premises. He would no longer be free to haunt the Fitzgerald home.

Madeleine squared her shoulders, held her head up high, and stepped boldly into the chaos destroying the attic. She thought of the old saying 'Hell hath no fury like a woman scorned' but to Madeleine, at that moment, 'Hell had no fury like a woman deprived of her child!' He was going to pay for what he had done, for what he had done to all of them. She said a silent prayer for her grandmother, standing on the last step.

The air was so cold; they could see their breath. Melissa sidled up to Madeleine on the top step, shivering in her sleeveless dress, and set the lantern on the floor. The light flickered in the wind coming from a broken window but the globe protected the flame. Rain was making a puddle beneath the broken window frame, soaking the old clothes piled there. Next to them an old steamer trunk gaped opened, its lid creaking in the gale force.

Loose papers were flying about the room, slapping their bodies with dampness. Neither of the women could believe what they were witnessing, nor what they were hearing. The sounds of a major struggle reached them from the left, toward the front of the house, and the old Victrola was ridiculously playing "My Blue Heaven".

In her peripheral vision, Madeleine made out a faint orange-reddish glow. She moved further into the attic, detouring to her left, dodging flying debris. A small branch struck the side of the house and finally found an entrance. It flew through the broken window, landing near her feet. Madeleine ignored it and continued moving toward that strange orange glow.

Startled by the branch, Melissa moved to her right and stepped closer to the window. Outside, the wind had changed pitch, it sounded as if a locomotive were bearing down on them. It had also suddenly changed direction. The air in the attic was now being sucked outward, instead of being blown in; crumpled paper and old sepia photographs went with it, out into the storm.

Down at her feet, Melissa kicked at the pile of rotting, damp clothing. Her flip-flop did little to protect her toes from making contact with something more solid. "Crap!" she muttered.

She bent down to rub her pinky toe and was caught by surprise when her large derrière connected unexpectedly with the soaked floorboards when she lost her footing. "Crap!" she muttered again and rubbed her toes, looking at the rotting, soggy pile. Protruding from beneath the clothes was a leg clad in blue jean material.

"Oh my God! Oh my God!" She frantically dug at the wet clothes, tossing them behind her. Her hair was now soaked, damp curls clung to her cheeks and neck.

"Bill!" she screamed. "Bill! Oh God, please let him be all right!" At last, she grasped his damp shoulder. She shook him. In her panic, forgetting her nurses' training about moving an injured person, she tried to turn him over onto his back. As she rolled him over he began to moan. She silently gave thanks to God. He was alive! With relief flooding her heart, her training kicked in. She deftly touched him everywhere, looking for broken bones. Except for a knot on his forehead that was oozing blood he seemed to be intact.

She ripped an old dress into a long strip and tied it around his head to staunch the blood. She worried briefly about infection from accumulated grime in the rag but decided it best to stop the bleeding and worry about infection later.

By the time she'd finished, Bill was conscious and had managed to sit up. Something big was lying next to him and he picked it up. It was heavy and gray in color, mottled with moss, and some of his blood. It looked like plaster. He handed it to Melissa. "I think this is what hit me. Something flew through the window; hit my head, and then goodnight Irene. This must be it." His voice rose in her ear.

Melissa tossed it aside. "It's a chunk of that stupid water fountain. I hope the storm tears it to pieces!" They had to yell to be heard above the cacophony of noise filling the attic. "Can you stand? I want to get you to the stairs."

"I think so." The orange glow to his right barely registered through the pain throbbing in his head. What was going on over there? It was as noisy in the attic as the storm outside.

Bill placed an arm around her shoulders and she heaved him to his feet. He was glad he'd married a strong, sturdy woman. He didn't think he could have managed on his own. A wave of dizziness almost caused him to collapse, and were it not for his wife, he would have been back on the floor.

Melissa settled him down into the well of the second step near the lantern. At least he was out of the rain and somewhat sheltered from the wind. She had little doubt that just beyond the back of the house, a tornado had come calling, done its damage, and was moving on to some other poor family's house. It still continued to thunder, and brief flashes of lightning lit up the mess in the attic, but the wind seemed to be dying down.

Unfortunately, the sounds of a struggle were still going on in full force somewhere toward the front. There was a loud crash when the old Victrola was smashed against the wall. Where was Mattie? She wondered fearfully. And what was making that strange light?

Melissa stood near the top step trying to decide whether or not to search for Madeleine, if she should get Bill downstairs, or if she should fetch Victor. She was still pondering this when she heard harried footfalls ascending the stairwell. Whoever it was, they were in a hurry and were sure to trample Bill. In the split-second it took her to decide to move him and for her legs to obey the thought, someone flew toward her, sprawling at her feet.

Chapter 19

In the bedroom, Victor stirred. A sleepy fog clouded his mind, slowly lifting. He couldn't believe he'd actually fallen asleep. It was not his habit to sleep in the afternoon, but the events of the day had exhausted his nerves. He'd lain next to his beloved wife, watching her sleep, worrying about her, and longing to help her. He'd held her small hand, until, without even realizing it, he had drifted off to sleep.

Outside the window, thunder rumbled and a branch slapped the glass. Victor suddenly came fully awake. Something was wrong. He sensed he was alone, but shouldn't have been. The sound of Madeleine's soft breathing he expected to hear beside him was silent. He reached for her in the darkness.

Fear gripped his heart; cold empty sheets met his groping hand. She wasn't there.

He flung aside the bedcovers and scrambled to his feet, looking for his misplaced shoes. It was pitch-black in the room except for brief flashes of lightning. He tried the lamp and cursed when it wouldn't come on. The power was out. He finally found his shoes under the bed, thrust his bare feet into them and raced to the door, banging his knee against the tall chest of drawers in the darkened room, fumbling for doorknob.

Where was Mattie?

There was a stirring in his chest, a tightening of his muscles. Warning bells were ringing inside his head. Mattie was in trouble! "Where's the damn door!" he cursed, sliding his hands along the carved wood, finally making contact with the cold knob.

He flung open the door and rushed out into the hall. Thunder shook the walls. Was it happening again? This felt too much like the night they'd lost Antonia.

Fear spurned him into action. He ran blindly down the hall. The darkness was relieved for a brief second as the lightning flashed through the lace curtains in the bay window, giving Victor his bearings.

Up ahead, out of the darkness, he detected a faint glow filtering through the attic doorway.

Oh no! Not again! Was Madeleine sleepwalking? She might injure herself.

Heart pounding in his chest, he flew up the dimly lit stairs as thunder rumbled throughout the house. He rounded the turn, puffing for air, not watching where he was going in the poor lighting. His only thought was to find Mattie.

Suddenly, he lost his footing and landed face down upon the top step, the lantern blazing near his ear. Unbelievably, he found himself staring at some rather large feminine feet with painted toenails. The yell he'd heard as his chest connected with bare wood barely registered through his fear for Mattie. What had he tripped over? He stiffened when a hand gripped his ankle.

"Victor! Are you all right?" Bill was tugging at his pant leg.

Victor rolled over and sat up, stunned. Bill looked like something the proverbial cat drug in. His clothes were damp and dirty and clinging to his body. Above his round blue eyes, blood had seeped through an old filthy rag.

"Good God, man! What happened to you?" So that's what he'd tripped over. Behind him, Melissa moved to sit beside him. She was shivering in her thin dress.

Bill gingerly touched his wound. "This I got when a chunk of that water fountain smashed through the window. I think it got hit by lightning. I'm pretty sure a tornado passed this way."

"What are you doing up here? And have you seen Mattie?"

Bill shook is head no and winced as fresh pain struck his temples. He shifted, trying to get comfortable. "As silly as it sounds, I came up here to try to make contact with Skye. But she wasn't here. Something else was. It was dark and ugly and it started flinging things around. Scared the crap out of me. I moved next to the window, dodging flying books. Bad mistake. That's when I got hit in the head. I blacked out, thank God. Who knows what that thing would have done to me?"

Victor wondered if that knock on the head did something to Bill's reasoning capabilities. "What do you mean, *something* was up here? What was it?" *Was Mattie up here in this mess?* He fervently hoped he was wrong and that Madeleine had gone down to the kitchen.

"I'm not sure. Haven't figured that out yet. But he's one nasty customer." Bill gingerly touched his forehead.

Melissa cleared her throat. "I know."

"Know what?" Victor asked. Bill was eyeing his wife curiously.

"I know what it is. Or rather, who it is. Or was. Mattie found her grandmother's journal. In it, Sarah wrote how she'd killed a man and buried him without telling anyone except for a servant named Annie. Bill, she buried him under the fountain before they poured the concrete." Melissa hugged herself. She was very cold, her teeth were chattering. "I bet his bones are underneath the water pipes." She gestured to her right, "I think Mattie is over there somewhere. We came up together." A loud crash echoed from deep within the attic.

"Good, God!" Victor exclaimed, fearfully. "I have to find her!" He rose to his feet leaving Bill and Melissa sitting on the steps.

Another loud crash came from the inner recess of the attic and he moved in that direction. He'd only gone a few steps when he found himself on the floor again. Fragments of books, clothing, old lampshades, and various discarded items that the Fitzgeralds had banished to the attic made for treacherous footing.

He rose laboriously; kicking loose an old bucket he'd stepped in, sending it across the room. His shoe went with it. "Damn!" he cursed under his breath and carefully began picking his way through the clutter on the floor; one foot protected, the other stinging as sharp objects pierced his bare sole.

The light from the lantern barely reached him now but, strangely enough, he could still see. A reddish-orange light guided his steps toward the front of the house.

Chapter 20

There is something eerie hovering in the air of an attic. It's dusty, ancient, and out of sync with time. You walk in the present, live in it each day, it flows with you, matching your every step, until you enter that room of forgotten time: The attic. Here you leave the present at the threshold to rummage through old relics of by-gone days, wallowing in your memories. When you leave this place you leave the past behind you, taking up the threads of your present life in the here and now. But in this place of forgotten time, in the attic, past and present clash with each other. Old and new cannot be joined. Like sewing on new material to worn, faded out old clothing, the old and new cloth disagree and the tear you mend only worsens.

It was at this moment in time, as he moved further into the attic of Grace Stone Manor, his heart saturated with fear, Victor believed that the past had collided with the present, leaving a gaping hole that could not be mended. And after this night, he would firmly believe that the twain should *never* meet. *Ever*. What is dead and buried in the past should remain there.

What met his eyes in the uppermost floor of the old Fitzgerald home that night was a horror beyond Victor's belief or comprehension.

Chapter 21

There was a strange wind blowing, but it wasn't natural. It came from everywhere and nowhere that Victor could pinpoint. He only knew that it blew with a foul odor. An odor of death and decay. He gagged, swallowing the bitter bile that burned in his throat, and stopped dead in his tracks, unmindful of the sharp, stabbing pain in the sole of his wounded bare foot.

This couldn't be real. It just couldn't be happening.

Mouth gaping, Victor stared in disbelief at the gruesome image that would forever be permanently etched into his eyeballs, sometimes waking him up in the middle of the night in a cold sweat. There was a darkness in the shape of a man, but grotesquely misshapen at the arms and legs, locked in battle with the figure of a girl glowing in hellish flames. The girl could only be described as what Victor remembered Wheeler saying, "A She-Devil." So this is what the frightened electrician had seen. No wonder the man had urinated on himself.

Victor hastily checked his own pants, feeling the crotch for dampness. Although he felt a burning in his bladder, thank goodness his were still dry. He still had control of his bodily functions, but his intestines seemed to be twisted into a knot. Staring at the spectacle before him, he wasn't sure for how long he would remain unsoiled.

Black oil met red fire and swirled. The writhing tentacles the man-like thing had for arms were intertwined with the fiery ones belonging to the girl. They danced around the cold room, locked in a death grip, crashing into the walls, sometimes floating off the floor. Although both wore the faces of humans, they were contorted with fury.

The man-like being Victor did not recognize but knew that it was male in gender. It was hard to conceive but Victor swore later that the man had no eyes, only dark holes where his eyes should have been. He had the cheeks and forehead of a man, even dark hair, but he bore a skull's grin. On his torso Victor could see outdated tan work clothes from another era, but there was a jagged hole near the center of the man's chest. Black wiggly things were dripping out of it, falling onto the floor. They coalesced, black and oily, floated, and then returned to the thing's body, seeping up into its legs, or what passed for legs. Victor could only stare in shock and horror; at the elbows and the knees, the limbs disappeared, to be replaced by those slimy, black, writhing tentacles. An octopus from hell!

Suddenly, the ghastly creatures swung too close for comfort. Victor fell back, banging his head against an old iron bedstead.

He remained where he was, looking up, wild-eyed at the girl, as the beast flung her around with a roar. One tentacle was locked around her fiery throat and when she let loose a hideous skull-shattering scream, he thought his eardrums had burst. The screech rebounded off the walls, shattering a small, round attic window at the front of the house.

It took Victor only a second to recognize the ghostly face of the girl from the pictures his wife had of her cousin placed about their home in Pasadena.

"Sweet Mother of God!" Victor crossed himself with a shaking hand. This just wasn't possible! It couldn't be real! Ghosts do *not* exist! And certainly not monsters. The man-thing before him vaguely resembled the bogeyman from his boyhood imagination; the stuff nightmares are made of the monster from his closet. But this was ten times worse. This was not his imagination.

Victor rubbed his eyes with the heels of his hands, grounding out the horrible image still playing behind his lids. He thought he might go mad and argued with himself that it just wasn't possible, it wasn't happening. He removed his shaking hands.

"I *am* going mad!" he murmured. "It's still there!" He laughed hysterically and then clamped a hand over his mouth. He mustn't lose control, mustn't give in. He *must* stay sane, if only for Mattie's sake.

He crawled to his left as the two unearthly creatures crashed into the bedstead above his head. It fell with a thunderous crash, barely missing his legs as he brought his knees to his chest. Then he got a closer look at the girl's glowing face. Reason told him he was seeing the ghost of Skye, but his sanity screamed it wasn't possible. Skye was dead! He'd never believed in ghosts. And the other one! Dear God in Heaven, the other one, his Catholic mother would have proclaimed was a demon from hell. He *was* the bogeyman, come to eat them all! Victor laughed again, harsh; a raspy sound deep in his throat, and then clamped his lips shut, biting his bottom lip.

He didn't want to believe what he was seeing with his very own eyes, but no matter how hard he blinked, the image remained. Ghosts, the bogeyman, and demons did exist after all. And the smell! He brought a hand up to cover his mouth and nose. The stench assailing his nostrils was nauseating. He imagined the smell was like the lids of a thousand coffins, pried open, laying bare the rotting corpses of bodies that had missed out on the embalming process.

Victor held his breath, shut his eyes, worked up some saliva, and swallowed the sour lump in his throat, bringing his gag reflex under control, and blotted out the image his mind had conjured up.

He pushed himself backward, putting as much distance between this living nightmare and himself as possible, which turned out to be a scant four feet. His retreat was suddenly blocked when his back pressed into an old dresser. Victor winced as his neck snapped, banging his already throbbing head against the old wood. From there he could only watch in horror as the two otherworldly beings locked in battle, destroyed everything that crossed their paths.

With dread filling his heart he wondered if Mattie had crossed through the center of their battlefield. For the attic had indeed become a battlefield from hell. These apparitions from the past had crossed the threshold from death back to life, into the present. The combination was unmitigated destruction. They did not belong here. Why they were here at all, Victor couldn't fathom. He only knew that it was imperative that he found his wife.

With fearful savageness he tore his gaze away from the grisly sight and began crawling over broken furniture, calling out Madeleine's name. He prayed within his heart to find her alive and cursed himself out loud for having brought her back to this damnable house.

"Madeleine!" he yelled above the commotion, ducking just in time as an old painting flew past his head. It crashed into the dresser behind him, splintering the frame and ripping the canvas in two. "Madeleine! Where are you?"

To his left, an old mattress, laying half against the wall and half on the floor, moved. A low moan issued from beneath it. Victor scrambled to it on hands and knees. It was musty and rotted and looked as if it had been clawed by a giant hand. Rusty, broken springs were jutting through the fabric, gutting out the fiber filling.

Victor stood up, taking the mattress in both hands; he flung it aside like it was made of cardboard. His heart skipped a beat.

He'd found Madeleine.

She was pale, bruised, and barely moving, but alive. Near her right temple the skin was split and bleeding, but it looked superficial. Bruises were already forming on her cheeks and forehead. There were scratches on her slender arms and her pink robe was dirty and torn at the side.

His heart thudded deep within his chest as he knelt beside her, gathering her small frame into his arms. She moaned and opened her eyes. They were the prettiest eyes he'd ever seen. Never mind that he'd been looking into them for more than twenty years. He'd been so afraid to find them glazed and empty. But those baby blues had the light of life in them. Tenderly, he kissed her cheek.

He held her close for a moment and then helped her to her bare feet. Her slippers were nowhere in sight. Sneed had knocked her out of them. She held onto Victor's arm for support, reaching down to the floor to retrieve the journal. She rose, holding it tightly to her chest, remembering how she came to be on the floor.

By the time she'd reached this part of the attic, Skye and Sneed were already locked in battle. She couldn't believe that the fiery being before her was her cousin. Her beautiful, long, dark hair billowed out like it was being blown by a hurricane and glowed a deep magenta. Her slender young arms were flames of fire and she shimmered in the red heat radiating out from her body. The only thing she recognized was the sundress Skye was wearing. (She'd been with her cousin the day Skye had picked it out, during Spring Break when her family had visited long ago.) But the sight of her face frightened her most of all. Skye's brown eyes were bulging, her mouth was open and contorted out of shape as if frozen in a screech of fear and rage.

Madeleine did the only thing she could think of to save her cousin. She held up Sarah's journal, grasping it in both hands high above her head. She waved it like a signal flag. Just as she suspected, Sneed released Skye. She fell to the floor, weakened from the fight, like dying firelight. Sneed swayed from side to side like a hypnotized snake as Madeleine moved the book over her head. She had his full attention.

"Is this what you've been looking for?" she taunted him. "I know, Sneed. I know everything. I know what you tried to do to my grandmother. I know she killed you. And even though she doesn't say in these pages, I know she and Annie buried you under that fountain." A hot burning rage was seeping into her skin.

"Give it to me!" he snarled at her, drawing closer.

"Never!" she screamed at him. "But I *am* giving you notice, John Sneed!" she hissed, and then screeched, "You're being evicted! Get out of my house!" Madeleine had never felt fury like this before. The attic was saturated with it, seeping into every fiber of her being, burning deep within her gut, and igniting her nerve endings. This wasn't like her. She wanted to claw at Sneed just like Skye, but deep within she knew this wasn't the way to defeat him.

She squeezed the red book tightly, struggling to bring the fury under control. She shook with the effort. It would have been easier to give in, but she didn't dare.

Sneed roared with hatred, dripping black worms onto the floor. How dare she speak to him like that? Like she had the right? She had spoken to him with authority and without fear of him. It puzzled him, and deep within his rotting soul he felt something he almost couldn't identify. A twinge of fear. Fear from a living being. And then it grew, but only just a little.

He could sense the struggle going on inside Madeleine. Good and evil vying for control of her soul. Her fury brought him pleasure, but as she gained control of her anger, his fear stabbed him like a branding iron. He couldn't understand it. Other than the damp, dark place under the fountain, the only thing he feared was that good thing glowing within the brat now lying upon the floor. *And she no longer possessed it*, he thought, looking at her; elated at the corruption he'd wrought in Skye.

This woman, he decided, should join her cousin. She was one of those rotten Fitzgerald women, and his only desire was to rip the life out of her. He wished he had finished her off on the attic stairs that night long ago. But he'd been drug back to that miserable fountain before he could kill her. And this time, he hadn't known who she was until this morning. She was the one out in the garden, making him suffer through his death yet again. He despised her for it.

His rage deepened and grew; drowning out what little fear he had of Madeleine. "I'm going to rip out your heart and eat it!" he snarled. He drew himself up, gathering in strength, and flew at her.

Skye, lying upon the floor, watched helplessly as Sneed lunged at her cousin, knocking her against the wall. She watched Madeleine slide to the floor, dropping the journal, slowly losing consciousness. Sneed flew to the ceiling, roared with all the rage of a rabid animal, and plunged downward, the ends of his tentacles becoming talons.

The last thing Madeleine remembered was Skye's flaming arms throwing a mattress on top of her bruised body. She'd barely felt its weight before the darkness had claimed her. Then, there was the frantic sound of Victor's voice, calling out her name, the heavy mattress being lifted, and Victor's strong arms holding her close.

But the horror wasn't over.

Skye had saved her life. And now again, her young cousin was fighting for her very soul.

Back toward the attic stairs, a faint glow was moving toward them. The light bobbed and weaved awkwardly, making strange shadows. Melissa and Bill were carefully making their way toward Madeleine and Victor. As they came into view, Madeleine could see Bill leaning on Melissa for support, her arm around his waist, his around her bare shoulder. In her free hand Melissa carried the lantern.

In the center of the debris littering the floor, Sneed and Skye still clawed at each other. But it was easy to see that Skye was losing the fight. Her color had diminished, fading to a soft orange, as she grew weaker. Her frightened eyes rolled, casting a pleading look at Madeleine.

"Skye," Madeleine called out to her, tears coursing down her bruised cheeks. "You can't fight evil on evil's terms. You know that. You're not like him. You were never like him. You don't have to do this," she pleaded. "You're not alone anymore. *I'm* here. We're all here. You're task is finished now." She held up Sarah's journal. "I've read Grammy Sarah's journal. I know the truth. Tomorrow the authorities will be called. They'll dig up his bones and remove him from the property. He'll get a proper burial, a Christian burial. I promise. I'll see to it myself. Remember who you are and what you believe." But Skye was disappearing, fading, her color growing dark, a vanquished fire.

Anguish struck Madeleine. She was losing Skye all over again. "No," she whispered, falling to her knees beside Victor.

Skye had grown smaller, dimmer, being sucked into the blackness of Sneed's being. She was being stretched, folded. Her barely discernable legs had already disappeared into his chest. It yawned open, revealing a pitch-black gulf, an abyss of eternal darkness that was gobbling her up. Only her head and outstretched arms remained now and they too were quickly being sucked in, fading to a dull ember, and beneath the dying color, a tiny blue glow emanated within the crown of her head.

"Skye!" Madeleine cried. "Remember your faith in God!" With a savageness she didn't know she possessed, Madeleine yanked the cross hanging around her neck, wincing as the chain bit into her skin, snapping the links. She flung it at the gaping hole as Skye completely disappeared, taking it with her.

The black hole was now sealed. Skye had vanished.

Madeleine's hope was crushed. She'd been too late to save her beloved cousin. But it was not too late to right a wrong. She knew she would grieve for Skye all over again. She had lost her twice. But her grief would have to wait. It was time to finish this.

She rose unsteadily to her feet, leaning on Victor for support. He tried to hold her back but she shook off his restraining hand as she stepped forward.

Dead on, she faced the thing that was John Sneed. He was grinning triumphantly, worms dripping from his ghoulish mouth.

She shuddered, but didn't falter.

Sneed expected her to rant and rave at him. He expected her to be consumed with fury and hatred for him. He waited for the onslaught of those hateful, spiteful words to be flung at him out of those perfect, cupid-bow lips. And he welcomed it. Hatred was something he understood. It fed him. But what Madeleine said next thoroughly confused him.

"I'm sorry, Sneed," she said. "I'm sorry for what my grandmother did to you. It was in self-defense but she should have been honest about it. Not covered it up. She shouldn't have buried you in silence. Everyone deserves a proper burial. And I will see to it that you get one."

"No!" he snarled, moving closer to her. And then, he froze in his tracks. He could go no further. A force he could not understand held him in place.

The stench emanating from him was overpowering, but Madeleine held her ground as she faced John Sneed.

A strange look passed over his countenance. A look of shock, and fear. He now had eyes and they were as round and wide-eyed as a terrified horse. The irises were a chocolate brown. He features contorted, as if in pain.

His insides were twisting. What was happening to him? He felt funny, squishy, like a jellyfish. He couldn't hold his form. His tentacle-like arms and legs were dissolving, becoming normal arms and legs, and there was nothing he could do about it. He was losing his strength and his desire to kill. What was she doing to him? Panic seized him in a vise-like grip and wouldn't let him go.

"Stop it!" he cried aloud. "Stop!" He shook with fear, and now stood before Madeleine on ghostly legs, glowing a dull pasty green, no longer black, and they were trembling.

Madeleine stared at the ghost of the man before her. A small part of her still wanted to rip him to shreds for what he had done to her family, but there had been enough violence done at Grace Stone. She wanted to put things right. And to do that, forgiveness had to reign. She now had complete control of her anger and hatred. Compassion and kindness, traits as natural to her as breathing, now ruled her.

Madeleine wept large soggy tears. Unchecked, they dripped off her chin down to the floor, splashing on her cold bare feet. Images of her dying baby flashed behind her eyes, followed by the image of Skye lying in her satin lined coffin. All of this had happened because of the injustice done to one evil man long ago at the hands of her very own grandmother.

The responsibility for her family's home and all that had happened here, now rested upon her shoulders. She was the last of the Fitzgerald women and she had to set things right. She'd felt that way since Skye's death, but she'd run from it.

She had been afraid of it, had buried it in somnambulism and selective amnesia. Not even Dr. Irwin's therapy had made her remember. But returning to Grace Stone did. She remembered every instance of sleepwalking, of Skye whispering to her in her dreams, telling her what to do, what had to be done. Even that night, at seventeen, when she'd frantically dug in the damp, cool earth looking for her grandmother's cross, she remembered. All of it flooded back to her.

She lifted her tear-rimmed eyes and looked at Sneed's face. And then she quietly said, "Please forgive Sarah for the wrong she did to you. I forgive you for killing my daughter." It was the hardest thing she had ever spoken, but in saying it she had released the heaviness that had bogged her heart. The atmosphere in the attic lightened as well, no longer filled with anger and hate. A soft tranquil sigh seemed to flow through Grace Stone Manor, its foundation and walls released from the bonds of its long-held dark secret.

A look of pain and surprise darkened Sneed's craggy features as a tiny hole, bright as gold, formed in his chest. He moaned in fear as it widened. Then his moan turned into a wail.

Within the ring of the gold light, a bright blue-white light was shining out from him, and it steadily grew. He reached for it, to cover it, but it burned his hands. Plumes of gray smoke tapered off the stumps he now had for arms. He groaned in agony and floated backward as if to move away from the burning light but it came with him, came out of him, ever widening, burning out his rib cage.

Within the blue brightness a ghostly arm emerged, followed by a head. To Victor, standing by Madeleine's side, it was as if he were watching a nightmarish birth.

Most of Sneed's torso had vanished as Skye, shining a brilliant blue, floated out of him. Victor covered his ears as the mouth of Sneed contorted and screamed. He was being devoured right before their eyes by that golden rim of fire and blue-white light. Victor could see right through him. Through the ghostly image of Skye emerging from the hole, he could see Bill and Melissa on the other side, staring, dumbstruck, at the unbelievable manifestation taking place in the attic.

Sneed's legs were already gone. He floated in mid air. Only the outline of his torso and his head, glowing a sickly green, were left.

Skye, now fully emerged, turned to face him. A smile brightened her face. The glowing light blue hue surrounded her ghostly body and cascaded down her long hair. And a brighter light within her chest shined outward, enveloping what was left of Sneed.

Her brightness consumed her enemy. The last to go was his head.

His eyes bulged in fear; his mouth fashioned in a silent scream. Skye reached out a ghostly hand and touched the top of his head. A weak moan issued from his floating head, and then it shattered into a thousand fragments. Each piece reflecting with brilliance like a shower of sparks, faded out to nothing before striking the floor.

Beyond the walls of Grace Stone, out in the drenched back garden, the remnant of the fountain exploded, the foundation tearing out of the ground, and uprooting the storm-torn rosebushes. Shards of plaster rained down, littering the soggy earth. A gaping hole of mud was all that was left, exposing rusted out water pipes, a decaying pair of gardening shears, and a worm-infested skeleton.

A shaking dingy skeletal hand grasped one of the pipes, pulled weakly, and then let go. It did not move again.

Skye turned around, encompassing the room, looking at the entourage of shocked faces, but the one she sought out was smiling, coming toward her with outstretched arms.

Skye flew into Madeleine's embrace.

An instant before they touched, she felt herself grow heavy, receiving substance throughout her ghostly body. She didn't float through her cousin as she expected and feared.

She heard a sigh of contentment and joy issue from Madeleine's lips as she felt her cousin's warm body draw her close. She was enveloped in warmth and love. All those years, roaming the house in fear of Sneed had been worth this one glorious moment.

"I've missed you, Sunflower," Skye said, calling her by the nickname Skye's mother, Elise, had given to Madeleine so long ago. She lovingly caressed Madeleine's hair, combing it with her fingers.

"I've missed you, too." Madeleine's voice choked with emotion. She didn't try to hide her tears. They were of joy, not sorrow.

"I have to go now," Skye whispered in her ear. "My oath is fulfilled. I couldn't have done it without you. I won't be haunting your dreams anymore. You'll be okay." She stepped back, holding Madeleine's hands. She looked back over her shoulder at the young couple gaping in awe. "I like Bill and Melissa. They'll make this a good home. Talk them into staying." She gazed into Madeleine's soft blue eyes for a moment. "Sheriff Hopkins said we made a formidable pair."

Madeleine laughed. "That big, sweet fool. He was so right."

"Call him. Let him take care of Sneed's bones. It'll clear up an old case for him. And tell him hello for me."

"I will." Madeleine promised.

Skye hugged her one last time. Stepping back, she took Madeleine's hand and pressed their grandmother's cross into her palm. "You saved me, Mattie. Don't cry when I go. I can't bear it." She wiped Madeleine's cheeks and felt her stiffen at the coolness of her touch. But her cousin didn't flinch away.

"I won't." Madeleine assured her. "This time I get to say good-bye. I love you, Skye. You'll always be in my thoughts and in my heart."

"And I've always loved *you* like a sister. Always will. I want you to know I always enjoyed singing with you. I could never have had a best friend better than you. No one else could measure up to my Mattie. Tell that brat brother of yours that I love him." Skye stepped away from her. A big toothy smile, sans the braces, lit up her brown eyes. "See you on the other side, Cuz." She winked. And just like that, she was gone.

The light in the attic dimmed with her leaving. The two couples stood in silence in the soft glow and dancing shadows made by the lantern, and then quietly began picking their way back to the stairs. No one knew what to say, and wouldn't speak for some time, each lost in their own thoughts.

The stench in the attic was gone, replaced by the rain-washed night air now flowing gently through the broken windows. The storm was over. It was as calm outside as it now was inside.

Chapter 22

May 1, Saturday

The morning dawned, bright and fresh. Sunbeams shone through thin wispy clouds, moving onward toward the east to meet the rising glowing orb. After the deluge of last night's storm, the air was crisp and clean, and filled with the promise of a bright new day, the slate of past wrongs wiped as clean as the morning's breeze.

After trudging out of the attic last night, the battered couples had retired to their rooms; each to be alone with their thoughts and give attention to wounds sustained, mental as well as physical.

Melissa had waited at the Martucci's bedroom door with the dimly glowing lantern while Victor lit candles they'd found on the very top shelf in the linen closet. Maria had missed this stash in her earlier search, but Madeleine had known her Aunt Elise use to store them there. The lantern flickered weakly, exhausting its meager supply of kerosene. Melissa took a few candles with her to the master bedroom.

Melissa had tended to Bill's head wound by the glow of several candles, satisfied he would not need stitches and had no signs of a concussion, wrapping his head turban-style with a fresh, clean bandage. He didn't complain as she helped him bathe, dress him in clean pajamas and robe.

After taking a hot shower, she'd dressed quickly in sweatpants and shirt to warm the chill permeating her bones, threw on socks and tennis shoes, and left Bill to check on Mattie.

Wanting to return to normalcy as soon as possible, knowing it was the best course of action, she took charge. With first-aid kit tucked under her arm and a candle in hand, she'd knocked on the Martucci's door and entered at Victor's bidding.

Mattie and Victor both had showered and changed. Mattie in a soft, flowing housedress and different slippers, she never traveled without several pairs, and Victor, like Bill, had dressed in pajamas and robe of a deep rich burgundy.

Victor sat on the edge of the bed, staring at nothing. In his mind, he was still trying to process what he had witnessed. None of it made sense to him. He didn't believe in ghosts, at least, not until tonight. But he could not deny the horrifying visage of John Sneed. It would never leave him, he was sure. He took a deep breath, shut his eyes, exhaled loudly, and then turned to look at Melissa.

Madeleine was also quiet and subdued at first, understandably so, but allowed Melissa to care for her wounds. In the diffused candlelight, Melissa applied antiseptic and bandages where needed, giving special care to the wound at Madeleine's temple. She was relieved that no stitches were needed.

Victor balked at her administrations when she turned her nursing skills on a puncture wound on the bottom of his foot. Plopping down next to him on the bed, she'd told him to stop being a baby and jerked the said foot across her lap.

Sitting in candle glow at the dressing table, Madeleine caught Melissa by surprise when a soft giggle tinkled from her throat. Melissa winked at her in shared amusement, and took heart in the uplifting sound of Madeleine's voice. It was a hopeful sound in that perhaps the healing had already begun.

Melissa bandaged Victor's foot while telling them she was going downstairs to help Maria fix dinner. She was surprised to hear Victor confess he wasn't very hungry. She joked with him that he would be missing out on a good-n-hearty, body-sustaining, country meal. He'd smiled weakly and thanked her for the offer and said he might reconsider, he'd also offered begrudging thanks for tending to his wound, and then firmly placed his bandaged foot inside his slipper, wincing slightly.

Madeleine, on the other hand, said she would be delighted to try a taste of Melissa's cooking. She'd done very well at trying to be light and convivial considering what she'd just been through. But Melissa had not missed the sadness behind her smile. She admired Madeleine's courage and told her to feel free to pop into the kitchen and chat while she was cooking.

She then left, returning to her room to check on Bill and put her first-aid kit back in the bathroom.

Bill was resting, but not asleep. He was deep in thought, and didn't feel much like talking, but he'd told Melissa to let him know when dinner would be done; his stomach was growling angrily and she'd called to him "poor baby" from the doorway as she was leaving the room. It had been a long time since lunch, almost a lifetime it seemed.

In the meantime, he rested, pondering all the puzzles pieces now that it was all over. It bruised his ego a little that it had been the women, and not he, who had solved the mystery, but he was glad that it was over and done with. Besides, he understood now that even if he had figured it out, he could not have expelled John Sneed. No one but Madeleine could have done that.

Bill plumped his pillows and shut his eyes. The pain at his temple was down to a dull roar and he was feeling sleepy. Did he and Melissa still want the house? At this point, he wasn't sure. He would have to do some thinking about it.

As his breathing slowed and evened out, he drifted off to sleep, vaguely picturing Grace Stone Manor filled with his children and visiting family members. A smile tugged at the corners of his lips as he slept.

Melissa made her way to the kitchen by candlelight to find Maria staring out the large paned window above the sink. The storm had ended and she seemed to be more at ease. On the table, the large candelabra were blazing and the large bowl of potatoes had been whipped creamy smooth. Maria had kept hard at it during the storm. The delicious aroma of warm peaches rose from the pan placed on a cooling rack on the counter.

The radio in the pantry sat in blissful silence.

Donning an apron, Melissa got busy rolling the pork chops in batter. All the while amazed that she could carry on as though nothing had happened. Maria, she knew, was none the wiser, and Melissa kept her mouth shut, deciding it was Madeleine's place to tell her housekeeper anything she deemed necessary.

Madeleine had unexpectedly paid them a visit in the kitchen and received a rib-crushing bear hug from Maria, and then a hot cup of Jasmine tea was placed in her hands.

She looked frail and tired, but yet somehow stronger. There was a clear light shining in her blue eyes and a quiet, understated strength in her tone of voice, a strength that Melissa had not seen since meeting her, but suspected was lying just beneath the surface all along. It's the truth that sets people free. And Madeleine had learned several truths in the last couple of hours, about her family and about herself.

Melissa knew there was an underlying current of sadness lacing Madeline's light demeanor, but above that was a lifting of her shoulders, a straighter rod in her back, as if some heavy burden had been washed away, and gone out with the storm. With all that Madeleine had discovered about her family and about herself came conflicting emotions; a sadness at what happened long ago, and a relief in finally knowing the truth. Melissa figured those waters had to run deep, a well of sadness that Madeleine would have to fill in and eventually release herself from, secure in the knowledge that it was truly, finally over. Melissa had no doubt that Madeleine's courage would see her through it, and she would rise above it.

Dinner was cooked without a hitch, and consumed by candlelight. In silent agreement, no one discussed what had transpired in the attic. They all needed to deal with it their own way and in their own time, but not at the dining table, and not out loud. So, conversation was light and minimal when anyone spoke at all.

Bill ate like a ravenous wolf and even Victor showed up at the table out of respect for the work Melissa had done to prepare them all a meal. After the first few tentative bites, he nodded his head approvingly and dove in heartily, his appetite fully restored. Melissa was very pleased to see that Victor had not lost his desire for food after all.

Maria had hovered near Madeleine until she was satisfied that Madeleine was indeed going to eat. Melissa, not use to housekeepers, nor used to eating a meal while someone else anxiously stood by, so emphatically insisted that Maria join them that Maria, embarrassed, fled the dining room. Whereupon, Melissa marched straight to the kitchen, grabbed a place setting and a protesting Maria, and marched her right back to the dining table.

Melissa informed the Martuccis that for tonight, since she cooked dinner, she was playing hostess and they, including Maria, were her dinner guests. Madeleine's eyes twinkled approvingly in the candlelight as she glanced at Victor, who said nothing but nodded his head in agreement while working over a large steaming ear of corn. Madeleine knew him well; nothing like food to take Victor's mind off unpleasant events. And judging by his intense interest in that ear of corn, he wouldn't care in the least who sat with him at this meal. Propriety was out the window.

Melissa placed Maria on Madeleine's right and was so pleased to see everyone enjoying the meal she'd prepared that her emerald eyes sparkled and between mouthfuls of food she grinned from ear to ear.

By the time everyone had eaten, weariness had seeped into Melissa bones. She was quite sure they all felt the same way, except for Maria, who was still ignorant of what had happened in the attic. Melissa helped clear the table and wash the dishes, then made a hasty retreat to the bedroom to climb in between the sheets and snuggle next to Bill. She slept soundly that night.

Rising early, she dressed quickly in faded jeans and yellow knit top, and went downstairs to help Maria prepare breakfast. Chocolate gravy and biscuits, just as she'd planned. She'd decided last night it was no use anyone starving himself, no matter what the situation, a person could face anything if he wasn't weak from hunger.

She was grinning as she entered the kitchen to help make breakfast. A mouth-watering aroma filled the air. Maria was already frying bacon and chopping ham for omelets and the carafe was filled with dark-roast coffee. Melissa poured a steaming cup of the brew, laced it with milk and sugar, savored her first sip, then set it within easy reach to sip while rolling out biscuit dough.

Bright sunlight lit up the kitchen, gleaming off the polished oak-wood finish. It was hard to imagine the damp, cold darkness of the attic in the light of this fresh new day.

One thing Melissa was glad of was that sometime during the night the power had been restored. She'd awakened with her bedside lamp blazing, and Bill, already showered and dressed, nowhere in sight.

At the kitchen sink, washing the flour off her hands, she spied him through the window, as he entered the mudroom. She waited at the cooking island sipping her coffee, while he washed the dirt off his hands and then entered the kitchen.

"Well, there's some bones out there, all right," he said without preamble. He wore a medium-size bandage on his forehead, a pair of chinos and a long-sleeved flannel shirt. The hems of his pants were slightly muddy leaving brown wet streaks atop his white socks; he'd removed his shoes and left them in the mudroom.

"Yuck!" Melissa made a face of disgust. "You touched them?"

"Just to make sure they were there," he answered, helping himself to a cup of coffee. "I've got Sheriff Hopkins' phone number. I'm gonna give him a call. I believe that's what Mattie wanted anyway. I'll tell her when I see her, or you can." He left the kitchen in his socked-feet, taking his coffee with him.

Maria had not missed this conversation, but didn't comment. She silently crossed herself and began whipping the eggs. She would be told in good time. If not, then it was none of her business. She wasn't sure she wanted to know about buried bones anyway. It was too morbid to bear thinking of, and certainly not before breakfast. *Besides,* she thought hopefully, *he was probably talking about some long-dead animal.*

Bill put his call through to the sheriff on the phone in the library. A young deputy informed Bill that the Sheriff was at home. Hopkins' cell phone number was on the back of the card he'd given Bill. After finding it on the desk, and not reaching him at the station, he punched in the cell number. Bill heard his bass voice answer on the fourth ring.

"Sheriff Hopkins. What can I do for you?" He said, stifling a yawn.

"Ah, Sheriff, this is Bill Hayden. Sorry to call you so early."

"That's quite all right. Been up for a while, most of the night as a matter of fact, what with the storm and all and folks calling up with quite a bit of damage done to their homes." He grunted as if he were trying to sit up. Bill was sure he'd caught the man trying to get some much-needed sleep.

"I think I may have an answer to something you've been wondering about for a long time. That mysterious call you got from Skye Fitzgerald. I believe I know what it was about."

"Oh? And just how would you know that?" he asked doubtfully.

"Well, it's a little complicated. I really think you should come over." Bill paused, then plunged on. No sense keeping the man waiting. "There are some old bones buried in the back garden. That storm we had last night unearthed them. They're definitely human and I believe I know who they belonged to."

"Goodnight! Are you serious?" Sheriff Hopkins said, incredulous and greatly interested.

"Afraid so. I think they're the remains of that missing man your father was looking for back in the forties. His name was John Sneed. And Sheriff, Madeleine Martucci would like to speak with you. It's important."

"I can be there in half in hour. Less." The line went dead in Bill's ear.

He replaced the phone and went back to the kitchen. Melissa was stirring the gravy and it was almost done. The delicious scent of cocoa delighted his senses. He loved chocolate gravy as much as she.

"Mmm-mmm-mmm. Can't wait to delve into that. You might want to set an extra place for the sheriff. He'll be here in about thirty minutes. Probably less."

Seeing Maria busy turning omelets, Bill went to the cabinet. "Can I help?" he asked, reaching for a stack of plates.

"You bet. Thanks." Melissa smiled at him. This morning she felt more like the mistress of the house and knew she'd done the right thing in taking charge last night. It felt right. And it felt good.

She knew they would be staying at Grace Stone, at least for the six months. They had yet to discuss buying the house, but she knew what her answer would be. It was a lovely home, and now she knew its full history. A bit jaded perhaps but it made for an interesting story to be told late at night by the fireside. Her family would get a thrill out of hearing it.

The upturned corners of her lips raised her freckled cheeks; it was going to be nice for her and Bill to make their own history, a good one, she vowed. It would be nice to have a house full of children, maybe three or four. Perhaps they could start on that next year. She loved children. Her smiled deepened.

"Good morning, Melissa." Madeline startled her out of her reverie. "You have such a wonderful glow on your face. That daydream you were having must have been fantastic." She peered closer at Melissa's face. "You've got this creamy texture to your skin. You look wonderful. Sleep well?"

"Yes, I did. And you? How are you this morning?"

"I feel great. I had the most restful night than I've had in a long time. I feel refreshed."

Indeed, Madeleine was telling the truth. She did not look pale and fragile this morning. Her pale pink dress slacks and matching knit top put a rosy color in her soft cheeks and accentuated her blue eyes. She'd pulled her slivery hair back with a matching clasp.

"I know I have things to do today that will probably not be very pleasant, but after last night, I feel like I could take on the world. I'm ready to do whatever needs doing. Including dealing with that." This she said, pointing out the window to the garden beyond.

Just then, Bill returned to gather silverware and glasses. "Good morning, Mattie." He said, flashing her a toothy smile.

"Good morning, Bill."

"Oh, Mattie, I hope you don't mind, but I placed a call to Sheriff Hopkins. He's already on his way here. Was that all right?"

"Yes, thank you. I appreciate that. I wasn't sure exactly what I was going to say to him over the phone. It'll be easier in person." She helped herself to the coffee and sat at the wooden table.

Before going out the door, laden with glasses and silverware, Bill said, "Perhaps you can persuade him to have breakfast with us. I gather he hadn't got much sleep last night and a hot filling breakfast might do him some good."

"I'll try to get him to eat. He used to take meals here often. I think he would like that. Thanks, Bill." He nodded, backing out of the swinging door.

It was easy to see the change in the Haydens and in herself. She was no longer the hostess, but the guest, but it didn't bother her in the least. She was ready now to let go. All that had kept her tied to Grace Stone was now severed. The completion of the task set forth years ago was now done. Skye's oath was fulfilled and Madeleine's task was complete. She was ready now to move on. There remained only one last duty to perform. And she was going to keep her word. She was going to have a funeral for John Sneed.

Forty-five minutes later, Sheriff Hopkins, Bill Hayden, and Victor Martucci were trudging back into the house.

Maria met them at the backdoor with a broom and gave their shoes a good sweeping.

"I just can't believe it." Hopkins expressed what the other men were also feeling. "It gave me the chills seeing those old pruning shears, that's for sure." He rubbed the back of his massive neck and removed his gray, felt cowboy hat. "Still jammed up under his rib cage. Well, I'll have to get a forensics team over here. This is gonna wind up in the papers you know, but I'll try and keep the gossip down and their speculations. But there's nothing I can do about keeping it quiet."

"I understand, Sheriff." Victor said, getting a glass of water. A stiff drink would have been better, but not so early in the morning, and not in front of the sheriff. Victor was still having a hard time believing any of it: The ghosts, the journal, the bones in the back yard, and the fact that his wife had actually been contacted from the other side, and had been for years. It was hard to swallow and so was the water. He still longed for a glass of wine.

They filed into the den, where Madeleine was waiting for them with her grandmother's journal. After greeting Hopkins earlier with a hug and insisting on feeding him breakfast, she'd told him what she'd found and promised to show it to him after his visit to the garden.

She now rose from the loveseat and silently handed him the cracked and faded leather-bound book.

"Will I be getting this back?" she asked quietly.

"Of course, Mattie. We'll make photocopies for our records and return it to you, probably by Monday. I did some quick checking before coming out here. It seems that Sneed grew up in an orphanage down in Louisiana. Raised by Catholic nuns. He was in and out of trouble a lot and ran off before he turned eighteen. God only knows how he turned up here."

He glanced at Bill. "That's why no one came looking for him back in 'forty-two when he'd disappeared. Dad never got that far in his investigation. He didn't have the resources that I've got. There's no way of knowing who his parents were." He sighed. "If you'll excuse me. I'd better get the ball rolling. It's gonna be a long day. I appreciate you feeding me breakfast. I haven't had chocolate gravy in a long time, not since my wife passed away. Thanks." He took his cell phone out of his pocket and went out of the room for privacy, donning his hat.

The sheriff's pronouncement had been correct. It turned out to be a long day, for all of them.

Along with the forensics team came an influx of television and newspaper reporters. They swarmed the house like bees on honey and didn't care how they got the story. Bill came to Maria's aide when she inadvertently opened the door to one obnoxious and persistent newspaper reporter, hauling her backward, and slamming the door in his face. Madeleine wisely stayed away from the windows, but they couldn't stop them from taking pictures of the house. For several hours they were all virtual prisoners, trapped inside Grace Stone Manor.

The discovery of John Sneed's bones made the six o'clock news, and the front page of several Sunday morning newspapers.

Later that evening, right after the news, Bill received a call from Mr. Jensen, his boss, wanting all the details, to which Bill replied that he was not at liberty to discuss it. He promised to tell him what he could later on and hung up. But he was going to wait until it was no longer top news and the excitement had died down. The last thing he wanted was Mr. Jensen talking to reporters, giving them second-hand news for them to distort.

Madeleine had finally explained to Maria about the bones buried in the garden, leaving out a few of the details, and all of what happened in the attic. Maria had crossed herself, offered up a prayer for the man's soul, and then offered up another that God would see them home to Pasadena as soon as possible. She didn't like being this close to death; it gave her chills.

Sunday morning proved to be another beautiful day. Madeleine dressed and left without eating breakfast to attend church. She went alone.

She was grateful the reporters had all gone the night before and sought solace in prayer and in hearing the minister's uplifting sermon. She'd gone to the church her family had attended years ago, but was glad no one there recognized her. She quietly slipped out before the closing prayer had ended, muttering "amen" as she got into the rental car.

Back at Grace Stone, Bill and Melissa braved the clutter of the attic to cover the broken windows with plastic. Victor promised to make a call on Monday and have the glass replaced. By Wednesday the plastic was down, the windows repaired and tightly closed.

Madeleine distanced herself from her family's ruined belongings, not setting foot in the uppermost floor of the house. She decided there was nothing in the attic she wanted to keep and asked Victor to call someone to haul it all away. She didn't want to burden the Haydens with such a difficult and unpleasant chore. The attic was a disaster area and they shouldn't have to clear it out. It was something she felt was her responsibility and Victor didn't argue with her.

Besides getting the new windows on Wednesday the day after Sneed's funeral two men with a large truck arrived early in the morning, cleared out every scrap of paper, wet books, broken pieces of furniture, and tattered clothing from the musty attic. Nothing had been left. Not even the old trunks, the gramophone and records. All that remained was the dirt and cobwebs. Victor paid the movers well above what they had asked, after wincing from the gouge Madeleine placed deep in his ribs.

Melissa was pleased to hear from the mechanic; she could pick up her car on Thursday. Never mind that it cost a hundred and thirty dollars to fix. She would be independent on the road again. She hated being without her own transportation.

Meals were taken in a somewhat jovial mood, although at times Madeleine was very quiet, and Melissa, true to her word, had sampled Maria's Mexican dishes. Although she had enjoyed the food, for some reason it just refused to stay down. Bill eyed her with increasing concern and she silently began to worry if she were having gallbladder trouble. It seemed she was no longer able to digest spicy food.

It never crossed her mind, until the morning of John Sneed's funeral that the problem would be remedied in about eight months, or two more months if she had a normal run of morning sickness and stopped vomiting after the first trimester.

Dressed in a pale pink shirt, gray jacket and skirt, she was rummaging in her disorganized medicine cabinet looking for mascara when a plastic container fell into the sink.

Muttering "crap" under her breath, she picked it up and was about to throw it back on the shelf when her hand froze. That little nagging feeling of having forgotten something important was no longer digging at her sub-conscience. It rose full-bloom to the surface. Staring at her diaphragm, memory slammed her between the eyes.

The last night she and Bill had made love she had forgotten to use a contraceptive!

"Oh, my God," she whispered, and then moaned, "Oh, no!"

She shut her eyes in disbelief, gripping the edge of the sink. *Come on, Melissa, it might not even be that. It could still just be your gallbladder.* But there was only one way to find out for sure. After the funeral she was going straight to the drugstore and get one those home pregnancy tests. And after that, she was making an appointment with her doctor.

The day before Melissa bought the pregnancy test, Madeleine drug Victor to a funeral home to make arrangements for Sneed's remains. She'd kept it simple, the expense down to a minimum. Still, Victor grumbled, pulling out his Visa to pay the dour-faced funeral director. He would have let the county bury the man's bones, but his wife had insisted on giving the skeleton a proper burial. It wasn't that he couldn't afford it, just didn't think it was his place. But one look at Madeline's determined face and he'd laid his credit card on the table. He would do anything she asked, regardless of the price. And he knew, once this was taken care of, they could hop the next plane and head home.

He had then taken Madeleine to an Italian restaurant for lunch. Afterward, he dropped her off at Grace Stone, and then drove back into Tulsa to wind up some business with Mr. Smedley at Pine Ridge.

He had given considerable thought in selling the house and decided to lower the price if the Haydens still wanted to purchase Grace Stone Manor. He wouldn't have done it with any other piece of property but this was a special circumstance. After what everyone had been through, and Bill sustaining a head injury, it was the least he could do. Besides, this was probably his last chance to rid himself of a white elephant. After the publicity the house received he'd never be able to lease it out again, much less sell it. And on top of that, he no longer derided the Haydens for their belief in ghosts. He had come to fully respect Bill and Melissa. He'd even stopped calling them Okies.

Mr. Smedley had been greatly surprised at Victor's generosity but didn't make a comment, just did as he was asked. He drew up the papers; all they needed was Mr. And Mrs. Hayden's signatures. He placed them in his file cabinet for safekeeping.

He pushed his glasses up on the bridge of his large nose, and stared at the door after it closed behind Victor's back. He just couldn't believe that Mr. Martucci was willing to lose a hundred thousand dollars if that couple agreed to the terms. What had gotten into that crazy Californian? Victor Martucci hadn't acted like himself. In the world of business he just wasn't that generous. He pondered the change in the Italian but could not come to any conclusions as to what had caused it. He sighed and shook his head when the telephone rang, moving on to other business.

On Tuesday morning, both couples attended a short funeral service for John Sneed. Maria stayed behind to prepare lunch. Each sat silently, locked within their thoughts. No one heard the funeral director's words; there wasn't much to say about John Sneed.

Bill sat gnawing on a hangnail, wondering how he could write a book about his experiences. He decided it wouldn't be too difficult; make the setting in a different state, in a fictitious town, change their names, add a few made-up details and he would have a book. Yeah. That just might work. And he would get started just as soon as he converted Samuel's office into Bill's office. Melissa had wonderful decorating skills, and had already picked out a large desk and comfortable chair from a catalog; they would be purchasing it on Friday.

He threw a glance in her direction and wondered what was wrong with her. She'd been unusually quiet during the ride here and he didn't like the way her skin had paled in the last couple of hours. He knew she was sick and she just didn't want to admit it. No one vomited as much as she and there not be something wrong. Whether she liked it or not he was taking her to a doctor as soon as possible, even if he had to bodily throw her in the SUV and drive her kicking and screaming. Resolute in his decision, he went back to chewing on the annoying hangnail, silently working out a few details for his book.

Melissa slowly placed a hand on her abdomen; sure that Bill was no longer watching her. Part of her was excited at the prospect of having a baby, but her reasonable side said the timing sucked. She and Bill both came from large families and she guessed it was time to start theirs, but she would really liked to have waited at least one more year. Well, if she were pregnant, she could still work until her last month.

She did a quick calculation, and her heart jerked; the baby would be due just after New Year. She would be as big as a house come Christmas! *Suck it in, Melissa, and deal with it.* Maybe it wouldn't be so bad.

Jeez! What am I thinking? Wouldn't be bad? A Baby! Bill's baby. This was a wonderful blessing. So what about the timing. What about the shopping and the decorating? *Oh, my!* Shopping for a nursery and clothes, for the baby as well as for herself, was going to be fun. Wait till everyone hears. Her parents would shout the rooftop down. Then with a screeching halt, she put on the brakes.

Whoa there, girl! You're not certain that you are pregnant. It's probably just gallstones. Or something else. She felt a little deflated at the thought. Then she patted her tummy. *Cheer up, kiddo. I believe you're in there.* And she would know for sure before this day was over.

She smiled and leaned her head on Bill's shoulder. He looked at her worriedly, and she whispered, "I'm fine."

Bill patted her leg and let his hand rest there, staring at the back of the pew where Victor and Madeleine sat.

Just two more days. Victor patted the three plane tickets safely nestled within his Armani jacket. On Thursday he'd be boarding a plane, and heading home.

He wondered how Jack Pulaski, his apprentice, was getting on running Victor's office all by himself; he would give him a call when he got back to the house.

He smiled, remembering the confidence Jacob Fitzgerald had placed in him each time Victor was promoted in the business. He said a silent of prayer of thanks for his old boss, his deceased and missed father-in-law. He gently squeezed Madeline's hand. Jacob had given him so much more than a start in a profitable business. The man had given him this beautiful woman. His Mattie.

Madeleine turned her palm upward and intertwined her fingers with her husband's. She loved him more than she could say. He had stood by her through the worst times of her life, sustaining her, giving her his strength. He was more understanding than any man she had ever met and was grateful to have him by her side.

Nestled in the pew, Madeleine prayed again for her grandmother, that she would find rest and mercy, and thanked God that everything was now behind her. The last three days she had rested well at night. She'd not had any more nightmares. Skye no longer haunted her dreams, and now, when her head hit the pillow she knew it would remain there till morning, she would not be roaming the dark halls of Grace Stone any more, locked within a mysterious dream.

Soon she would be returning to the bright, sunny skies of California. The thought warmed her soul. She would return to her luncheon dates with her friends, enjoying the work and the fun they shared in raising money for charity, and visiting the children at the shelter. Summer was coming and that meant organizing trips to theme parks with those beautiful children.

But one place she would never return was to the deep leather couch belonging to Dr. Irwin. Her therapy days were over. She would no longer be visiting the past. It truly was behind her. And there it would stay.

After the funeral, Bill and Melissa stopped at the drugstore. She'd told him she wanted to buy some aspirin. She wasn't going to spring the news on him until she was certain and the timing was right. A candle-lit dinner alone with Bill, after the Martuccis had left, would create the right atmosphere.

She slapped her forehead. That was how she'd gotten in this condition in the first place. That is, if she truly were pregnant. Slipping the pregnancy test into her purse, she got back into the car.

At the house, she raced upstairs, headed straight for the bathroom and with shaking hands removed the contents of the box. She carefully followed the instructions. And with nervous agitation waited the allotted time. She then picked up the stick, almost afraid to look, and then let out a loud whoop.

Positive! She was going to have a baby!

Tears sprang to her eyes and she quickly wiped them away, smearing her mascara. She looked at the makeup on the back of her hand. It wouldn't do to have Bill think she'd been crying. He'd pester her until she gave him a satisfactory answer.

She washed her face, hid the pregnancy test box and its contents under some paper towels in the wastebasket and left the bathroom to change clothes.

It was going to be hard keeping the baby a secret but she wanted everything to be perfect when she told Bill. She wiped off the big smile that came unbidden to her lips and went downstairs to eat lunch. She'd be all right as long as she stayed away from spicy food. She patted her tummy. *Little Junior doesn't like spicy food.* She entered the kitchen still trying to keep that huge smile off her telltale face.

She gazed at the cozy kitchen lovingly, caressing the wood cabinets. Home. This was her home now, and this was her kitchen. Last night, she and Bill had decided to purchase the house after all. They just couldn't refuse the generous offer Victor had made. And now they were going to have a family. They would be complete. The Haydens had permanently moved in. There were no Fitzgerald ghosts roaming within the walls of Grace Stone Manor anymore. And from now on this house would be known as The Hayden Residence.

Startled, Melissa gasped and jerked.

Bill stole up behind her, encircling her with his arms, and kissed the back of her neck. She turned and gave him a fierce hug, biting back the tears of happiness that threatened to spill down her creamy cheeks.

"How ya feeling?" he asked.

"I feel wonderful," she answered, nuzzling his neck.

"Hey, there's something I've been meaning to do." He extricated himself from her arms, took her hand and led through the house, going out the front door.

The next thing that happened came as a complete surprise.

Melissa lost her breath when, without warning, Bill swooped her up into his arms and carried her across the threshold.

"Welcome home, Moppet." He gently set her down and kissed her lovingly and long before taking her hand and pulling her up the huge staircase.

Lunch would have to wait.

No graveside service was held for Sneed, but as the men were lowering the coffin, Madeleine bent down, scooped up a handful of dirt and threw it on top.

"May you not rise again until Judgment Day," she whispered.

She then turned, her arm laden with small bouquets of mixed flowers to place on her grandparents' and Aunt and Uncle's graves. This done, she moved to her cousin's headstone.

She stood, dried eyed, staring down at Skye's grave, then knelt to place a single rose upon the freshly mown grass. Sunbeams filtered down through the gently swaying treetops, crowning her silvery-blond hair; birds twittered on the branches. It was a beautiful Spring day.

Madeleine took a deep breath and let it out slowly. It was time to let her go.

"Good-bye, my dearest Skye. See you on the other side."

She rose, taking Victor's arm, turning her back on the past as easily as she'd turned her back on their graves. She felt renewed, alive, and complete. She was whole. She was ready to get on with the rest of her life.

Walking back to the car, she made a decision. Maybe she *should* broaden her horizons a little, and learn to draw from her own inner strength. She'd proved to herself that she was capable. She was strong, confident, and self-assured. Her mind was sound and intact. If her sixty-year-old mother could do it, so could she. Taking a European trip with her mother might be fun. Her mother's cronies seemed to enjoy themselves traipsing around the world, as well as they enjoyed Abby's company. She would check her mother's itinerary and call her as soon as she got home.

Home.

Releasing Victor's arm, she reached up to kiss his warm olive-toned cheek, caressing his face with her fingers. He gave her a tight hug in return and then opened the door for her, ever the gentleman. She settled into the deep leather seat, he closed the door.

Driving out of Tulsa, and finally reaching the paved back road to the house, Madeleine thought, *two more nights at Grace Stone and . . . no*, she corrected herself, *two more nights at the Hayden residence . . . and then home.*

Home.

The word sounded good.

Printed in the United States
36648LVS00005B/121-123

9 781413 771671